I0761605

ANTIHERO

Also by Gregg Hurwitz

THE ORPHAN X NOVELS

Orphan X
The Nowhere Man
Hellbent
Out of the Dark
Into the Fire
Prodigal Son
Dark Horse
The Last Orphan
Lone Wolf
Nemesis

OTHER NOVELS

The Tower
Minutes to Burn
Do No Harm
The Kill Clause
The Program
Troubleshooter
Last Shot
The Crime Writer
Trust No One
They're Watching
You're Next
The Survivor
Tell No Lies
Don't Look Back

YOUNG ADULT NOVELS

The Rains
Last Chance

ANTIHERO

Gregg Hurwitz

MINOTAUR
BOOKS
NEW YORK

This is a work of fiction. All of the characters, organizations, and events portrayed in this novel are either products of the author's imagination or are used fictitiously.

First published in the United States by Minotaur Books, an imprint of St. Martin's Publishing Group

EU Representative: Macmillan Publishers Ireland Ltd, 1st Floor, The Liffey Trust Centre, 117–126 Sheriff Street Upper, Dublin 1, D01 YC43

Printed in the United States of America. For information, address St. Martin's Publishing Group, 120 Broadway, New York, NY 10271.

www.minotaurbooks.com

Library of Congress Cataloging-in-Publication Data

Names: Hurwitz, Gregg author
Title: Antihero / Gregg Hurwitz.
Description: First edition. | New York : Minotaur Books, 2026. | Series: Orphan X ; 11
Identifiers: LCCN 2025041366 | ISBN 9781250871770 hardcover | ISBN 9781250871787 ebook
Subjects: LCGFT: Fiction | Thrillers (Fiction) | Novels
Classification: LCC PS3558.U695 A84 2026
LC record available at https://lccn.loc.gov/2025041366

First Edition: 2026

10 9 8 7 6 5 4 3 2 1

For Jonathan Pageau
As iron sharpens iron

A man who admits no guilt can accept no forgiveness.

—C. S. Lewis

Every man is a variation of yourself.

—William Saroyan

ANTIHERO

1

All Fight. No Flight.

Shiny penny-size blood drops on the white tile floor of the East Los Angeles bodega reflect back the sterile fluorescent lights above. In the immediate wake of the violence, the bodega is deserted, aside from the clerk who clutches his chest with one hand and covers his mouth with the other. His ancient sun-beaten skin is paper thin, and he is frail, bones tenting the fabric of his off-brand polo. He has seen a lot of violence in his day. But nothing like this.

A finger, cleanly sliced off, has landed on the cloudy plastic mat beside the cash register. An arm, severed just below the elbow, rests on the floor a short distance from the checkout counter. The wrist, grotesquely, still wears a retro *Pac-Man* watch. The clerk is incapable of tearing his gaze away.

A display of Hostess desserts is knocked over from the post-ambush struggle, Ho Hos, Twinkies, and Sno Balls strewn across the spattered floor. Ghostly crimson footprints choreograph the struggle where five grown men attacked Lesandro, a fifteen-year-old boy they had mistaken for a rival gang member.

The revelation of Lesandro's mistaken identity came only after half of his limb was cleaved from his body in a single hack. In an instant the boy had been transformed from mistaken target to innocent to witness capable of testifying against his five attackers, his own disfigurement ensuring the hit on him had to proceed. In the momentary confusion, Lesandro had managed—barely—to flee.

A bloody handprint mars the glass of the single automatic door, which bangs open and shut against Lesandro's shed Air Jordan, which lies trapped in the threshold. Night air blows through in sporadic puffs, tasting of car exhaust, oil, carne asada on a distant grill.

If you ease through the oscillating gap into the chill black night, you can follow various footprints for a half block until the red fades away. After that, a convenient trail of dribbled blood continues to mark the way. You might catch up, if not to Lesandro, panting and wild-eyed, then at least to the five men in pursuit of him.

A half block behind him but closing the gap, they wear wifebeaters or white T-shirts with blocks of blue, red, and green. They wear headbands or backward baseball caps with flat brims. They wear expressions of teeth-bared malice and flecks of blood on their cheeks.

You might not believe there is a gang as vicious as MS-13, but that speaks only to the limits of your imagination. The decades-old Trinitarios were birthed in Rikers Island to protect Dominican inmates from the Salvadorans, Latin Kings, Bloods, and other predators feeding inside the lethal prison ecosystem. Their weapons of choice are machetes because, they are fond of saying, a gun runs out of bullets but a blade never does. Torture and murder, home invasions and drug running, they do it all. So vicious are they that the gang itself splinters and those splinters splinter until they are a rageful disintegration of packs turning on themselves, maiming and killing indiscriminately.

An East Coast gang, they have recently spread to make inroads on the left coast, a murderous manifest destiny. These five Trinitarios are at the forefront, franchise openers for East L.A.

Right now they are picking up steam.

All Fight. No Flight.

Lesandro is losing steam. Understandably so.

His sock flops from his shoeless foot. He stumbles and weaves along the sidewalk, occasional passersby darting to safety in doorways or sprinting across the street. His face is pale, lips dry and cracked, flaked with cotton in the corners. Now he can hear the footfall behind him, quickening.

Cupping his stump, he bolts up a narrow and dark side road, the streetlights flickering or shot out overhead. On either side of the potholed stretch of asphalt loom long-abandoned places of business—a graffiti-covered mechanic shop, a shut-down textile-processing plant, a low-income housing unit scorched through with arsonist's fire. Jagged mouths of window openings sip in the night. Discarded furniture rises from dumpsters.

As Lesandro casts a frantic glance over his shoulder, he staggers into a parking meter, which knocks him across the curb and into the street.

A truck bears down.

Not just any truck.

A discreet-armored Ford F-150.

Behind the wheel sits a shadowed form of a man, ordinary of size and bearing.

The truck halts abruptly, veering sharply to barely avoiding finishing what the Trinitarios started in the bodega.

Lesandro slams into the passenger-side door of the truck. Internally lined with bullet-resistant Kevlar, it does not dent. He takes a few wobbly steps up onto the curb and leans against a rough brick wall beside a blown-out window. Breath heaves from him.

His pursuers near, backlit. Their shadows pull high up the dilapidated buildings, a convoy of ghouls. If you squint, you might make out the silhouettes of machetes at their sides, dancing along the wall.

Lesandro is a sweet boy with Gauguin eyes and a broad, pleasing nose. He sags against the brick rise, his face tilted down. He is drooling. At his side, wind sucks through the broken pane, a wail that underscores his own labored breathing.

The men rush forward, closing in on Lesandro.

The truck's passenger door flies open, catching the first in line squarely.

He body-slams into the door, his nose meeting the laminated armor glass of the window. The glass does not crack, but one cheek and two ribs do. The man emits not so much a grunt as an ejection of air, and collapses onto the street. Inside the truck, the dark form in the driver's seat leans over once again, and the door pulls shut above the unconscious body.

The other four men halt in the darkness of the street, weapons dangling at their sides, breath huffing in the February air. Three of the men wield machetes. One holds instead a slender steel pipe. Silence befalls the street.

The driver's door opens.

An Original S.W.A.T. tactical boot sets down onto the street.

The man emerges.

He is known by different names—Orphan X, the Nowhere Man, Evan Smoak.

He removes a rugged-looking phone from his pocket and dials three numbers, gazing calmly at the men. "Yes, hello. Please send ambulances and PD to this location. I'll text decimal coordinates now. There are six injured parties."

The Trinitarios look at him, more perplexed than angry, their heads tilted in comical unison.

"Yes, six," Orphan X continues. "The most acute is a young man with a severed left arm and a finger missing from his right hand. The wound has just been stabilized and I've started fluids. The arm is likely gone but please bring a waterproof bag and ice container for the finger in case it can be located."

"Hey," one of the gangsters says. And then, louder, "Hey!"

Orphan X holds up a just-a-sec finger to him, listening to the question over the phone. "The other injuries? Those have yet to be ascertained."

On the ground by the passenger door, the fallen man releases a moan of pain before falling unconscious again.

"Rapa tu mai," one of his cohorts hisses at Orphan X through irregular gold teeth.

"Depending on how this goes," Orphan X says into the phone, "you may want to send a hearse as well."

He hangs up. Frowns at the screen. Thumbs once. A *bloop* sound effect confirms the conveyance of coordinates to 911.

Casually, he circles the back of his truck, passing within feet of the poleaxed gang members as he walks over to Lesandro. Blood drools from the stump through the thumb and remaining three fingers of the boy's good hand. His teeth chatter.

Orphan X takes the boy gently by the shoulders and slides him down the wall to sit. A breeze whines across the broken glass of the pane to their side. A weathered mural of a young mother and her younger girl remains faded on the brick near them, dates bookending too-short lives, a memorial for the Trinitarios' last innocent bystanders.

Lesandro's teeth chatter some more. "My watch," he says. "I c-can't find my watch."

Crouching over him, Orphan X says, "It's okay. We'll get it soon enough."

"Yo," one of the attackers says, stepping forward. "What the fuck, *mamagüevo*? You know where you are right now?"

The machete tap-tap-taps the outside of his thigh.

Orphan X turns to appraise the man in full. His white T-shirt looks useful.

Orphan X's left hand blurs and a Strider folding knife lifts from his pocket, snapped open by the very gesture. The machete has no chance to lift from the man's side before Orphan X steps forward and punches the knife into the intercostal space between the man's second and third ribs. Air hisses out as the lung collapses.

Orphan X push-kicks him in the hip, spinning him around, grabbing a fistful of shirt at the back collar, and whipping the Strider upward to rake through the fabric.

The man falls out of his own shirt and fetal-curls on the asphalt, lips guppying.

The three remaining men take an inadvertent step away.

Again, Orphan X turns his back on them.

Returns focus to the boy.

He pulls the ribboned shirt taut and starts tying it around the boy's arm, just above the stump. The boy's lost left forearm and hand will be unusable, but the missing finger of the right hand shows a clean amputation line. Given the damage on the other side, it would be beneficial for the boy to retain all five digits of his dominant hand.

One of Lesandro's feet wags back and forth, the dirty sock half pulled off over the toes. His head dips, eyelids fluttering.

"Look at me," Orphan X says. "Look at my eyes. See my nose? We're here together."

Lesandro's gaze comes into brief focus.

"Name. What's your name."

His lips move but the rest of his face stays locked in shock. "L-Lesandro . . . Candella."

"Where is your finger?"

Lesandro jerks his head slightly to the north. "Bodega. Block that way. Where they j-jumped me."

Weak words. Heavily accented English. The rhythm of the accent sounds Dominican.

Orphan X cinches the knot. He proffers the tail of fabric to Lesandro so he can hold it tight. "Fist or mouth?"

Lesandro's right hand clenches weakly. "Mouth."

Orphan X guides the end of the makeshift torniquet to Lesandro's teeth, and the boy clenches down. Orphan X sends a second text to 911. Retrieve severed digit in bodega one block west.

From behind them: "Yo, bitch. We gonna take your head."

Orphan X rises once more, turns to face his recent interlocutor. He's the biggest of the group, a low wide belly stretching a guayabera shirt, slugs of belly fat hanging out the bottom hem on either side.

"How thick is that pipe?" Orphan X asks him.

The fat man's eyes jag briefly to the pipe in his raised fist, time enough for Orphan X to crash forward and lock it up with both hands, slamming it into the man's broad chest. One of the other men swings the machete at Orphan X's head but X skips forward, propelling the fat man with him, and the blade sails past him, embedding in the shoulder of the third man.

An unhuman wail. The injured man falls away, the flesh-buried machete coming with him, his friend staring with dismay.

Orphan X twists the pipe from the fat man's grip and in a single swift motion rotates it up beneath the padded chin, shattering the jaw. Before the man can tumble, Orphan X spins to crack the last man standing on the side of the neck. A debilitating blow that crushes the carotid artery, disrupting blood flow to the brain. It also strikes the vagus nerve, dropping heart rate and blood pressure, and the man himself to the asphalt.

Five men down, drawing rasping breaths or whimpering. The flickering streetlights bathe them in horror-movie lighting.

Orphan X returns to Lesandro. White-faced, the boy holds the end of the tourniquet between his clenched jaws. Orphan X tries to take it back from him, but the boy will not let go.

"Hey. Hey. Look at me. It's okay. You did great. You can let go now."

Lesandro releases his jaws.

Orphan X slips the slender pipe through the knotted fabric and twists it, cinching the tourniquet tighter. After a turn and a half, the boy passes out.

That's good. He could use a break.

Orphan X tucks the pipe beneath the boy's armpit to hold the tension and walks back to his truck.

The man puddled beside the passenger door manages to hoist himself up onto his elbows, blood from his shattered nose streaming over his mouth and chin like a wide-based goatee.

As Orphan X passes, he stoops to strike him in the side of the head, a quick jab that knocks him unconscious once more.

Orphan X hops in the truck and reverses swiftly, tucking the truck into an alley ten meters away. From the locked vaults in the truck bed, he removes a bag of saline, tubing, and duct tape. As he jogs back to the boy, he notices the man with the machete embedded in his shoulder hunched on his side, fingers digging at the leg of his jeans. The denim cuff has hiked up, revealing a revolver in an ankle holster. Orphan X kicks him in the side of the head, knocking him out for good. He removes the revolver, heels it down a sewer grate.

Back to Lesandro. Spiking the saline bag, he slips the catheter into the antecubital vein in the good arm. The boy stirs but does not wake.

Orphan X squeezes the bag to start the saline bolus. Lesandro's eyes flutter open.

Orphan X eases him onto his side, cupping his cheek so it doesn't strike the pavement. "You're safe now," he says. "You can rest some."

At last comes the sound of sirens, perhaps a half mile away.

Orphan X duct-tapes the saline bag to the brick wall above the boy's body, letting gravity do its work.

To his side, the fat man grunts and sits up abruptly and stiffly, a vampire rising from a casket. His lower face is ruinous, a morass of bone and blood, his teeth chipped down to little jagged nubs. The sirens grow louder; Orphan X can even make out the squealing of tires.

As Orphan X walks over, the man raises his hand, fingers splayed against what is coming. He is fortunate to still have both arms to raise.

Orphan X leans over to squeeze his trachea, thumb and fingers expertly seeking out the right arteries, veins, and nerves without crushing the windpipe.

The fat man gurgles and stares up with pleading eyes. When his pupils roll up, Orphan X releases the compression. The man collapses once more, the back of his head knocking the asphalt.

Flashing-light projections come visible on the main street ahead, throwing patterns against the storefronts.

Orphan X returns to Lesandro, checks the saline bag and the infusion. The boy stares up at him, his sclera pronounced. "Wh-what's gonna happen . . . me?"

He looks so scared, so lost.

Orphan X wonders what will happen to this young man. Will he be able to handle what he needs to in order to repair himself? Can he afford the medical interventions necessary to put himself back together? Do Orphan X's responsibilities to Lesandro end once he is out of sight?

These are not the kinds of questions Orphan X has been trained to contend with. Nor are they ones he welcomes.

He crouches over Lesandro once more.

"There will be pain," Orphan X tells him, "and it will be hard. But you will be whole again."

Lesandro nods, tears leaking.

Orphan X rises. The wind tunnel of the narrow street plasters his shirt to his torso. You might make out the outline of his appendix carry holster and the ARES 1911 ghost gun it contains.

All this time he had a pistol. He just never bothered to draw it.

The sirens are close enough now that they sound like a scream. The red-and-blue strobing on the main street grows more intense. Orphan X ducks through the shattered window near Lesandro's curled form, vanishing into the building. As the emergency vehicles sweep around the corner, their approach masks the sound of an F-150 engine turning over and coasting invisibly away.

If you could check Orphan X's vitals, you'd find them normal. Body temperature 98.6°F, heart rate 60, respiratory rate 14, oxygen saturation 99 percent, blood pressure an athletic 105 over 55. He has not broken a sweat.

He is all fight. No flight.

You might wonder if he is real.

You might wonder if anything scares him.

You might wonder if he sleeps and, if he does, what nightmares haunt him.

2

Still He Refused

In the beginning it was dark.

Four concrete walls, concrete ceiling, concrete floor. Windowless.

Evan Smoak had been taken. He didn't know how. The circumstances of his capture hovered back in the haze somewhere before this present flash of consciousness.

It was not entirely unexpected; perhaps it was inevitable. In defiance of the law of man, country, and more, he had killed.

And killed and killed and killed.

He'd been chased from a fugitive's hide into the blinding light of day. Taken hard to the ground, rending the flesh of knees, chest, and chin. Blindfold cinched tight, spit hood over his head, manacles binding hands and feet.

He'd been interrogated. Called to account for every aspect of his sordid past, pressured by fist and fiat to justify his very unsanctioned existence. Each trespass magnified to eclipse whatever humanity he had retained. Each fact decontextualized. Each choice filtered through a prism of worst-imagined intentions, transformed into something worse than a lie, an untruth. Demands were made—to apologize, to affirm what he didn't believe, to bend the knee. To consent to a false story of himself, a hammered-flat narrative far removed from the actual sins he carried in the chinks and fissures of his heart.

But he refused to yield.

He refused to break his code.

He'd been enclosed in this concrete box and questioned with greater enhancement. Fingernails and car batteries. Cattle prod in his side. Waterboarding, sleep deprivation, static blaring through headphones duct-taped to his head, a crown of anguish. Sweat wrung from his pores spattered the concrete, matching spots of a darker hue.

Still he refused to break his code.

His face, released to the media, shot through the veins and arteries of the known universe. Orphan X revealed, exposed. Salacious and damning details propagated through roaring algorithms. War criminal. Terrorist. Fascist. Islamophobe. Killer of Jews. Murderer of Christians. Deep-state operative. Alt-right. Radical left. Anarchist. Instrument of the irredeemably corrupt. Enemy of institutions. Deranged psychopath. Traitor. Committer of high treason. Unraveler of order.

An endless, continuous, exhaustive public accounting of his soul was undertaken. Every act imagined or real was spun and bastardized and toxified. The filth of the world pulsed in quickening waves, a feeding frenzy of escalation, of projection, of insanity itself.

Still he refused to break his code.

He was hauled before a grand jury, ordered to spill details of his secret training, to betray his mentor, to bear outsize responsibility for the transgressions of the system that had broken and remade him in its own image.

Still he refused to break his code.

He was sentenced.

They fetched him from the concrete box. He was marched, chains ghostily clanking, to an antiseptic room with a one-way mirror, sterile lighting, and moppable white tiles. A doctor awaited and a warden and a man of supposed faith. An array of lenses readied to stream his fate to the world.

He was placed upon the cushioned table, ankles bound, arms strapped to the cross's horizontal, spread angel-like. They slid a needle into the femoral vein of his left thigh.

The syringes were lined up, one, two, three, automated so no human hand would have to bear responsibility for the final push.

They asked him for any last words.

Still he refused to break his code.

He turned his head as the first syringe depressed. He watched the blue liquid inch through the clear plastic line and enter his leg.

He felt fire in the meat of his thigh and then radiating through his arteries.

Flayed open, bared to the world, he closed his eyes—

—and awakened.

Floating several feet above the floor of his penthouse condo on the twenty-first story of the Castle Heights Residential Tower. Atop a mattress that was in turn set atop a metal slab that was propelled upward by powerful neodymium rare-earth magnets and tethered by steel cables. A push-pull mirroring the endless battle in his battle-weary heart.

The battle to be the brutal thing of darkness he was.

And to remain human.

For a long time he breathed the dark air of earliest morning, wisps of the dream catching in his mind. That windowless box. A towering bench so high he'd seen only the façade of dark wood and no judge above. The many-eyed stare of the lenses, windows to the world, watching greedily as the syringes sank to push their poison into his blood.

He took it in, all the poison of the world.

He took it.

And then he arose.

3

The Parity of All Thoughts

A mother with children.

That's who you look for first.

The second choice is a couple with kids.

Third: a woman, alone.

You need to pay attention for when it starts to happen.

Rich taste of copper. That's how it begins for me. Then the taste turns into colors and colors into taste, which sounds completely weird but when it happens it makes perfect sense. Dark greens swirl into cobalt and indigo, and then needles sparkle through my brain, a brilliant ticklish pain, and then my thoughts go horizontal, all of them perfectly equal and weightless. The fanged premonition that this will finally be the time I won't come out of it holds the same non-weight in my mind as the gum stuck to the subway seat across from me. The parity of all thoughts is a delirious release.

And right after that? It takes me out.

As the train rolls and rattles me through the intestines of Manhattan, I clutch the laminated oversize index card to my belly. I have it looped around my neck already and I've used yarn for the lanyard instead of string since string almost choked me out once when it caught around my throat. Now I make sure there's plenty of extra yarn for a loose fit.

In my not-terrible handwriting, the first line on the index card reads:

Please help me.

It is all I have to ward off evil—purse snatchers, the fury of my nervous system, the stainless-steel curve of the hand pole three feet from my left temple.

Fourth choice is a man with children.

Fifth—a pack of girls, preferably working-class.

No matter how hard I try to reduce my vulnerability within myself and before the world, it is unavoidable. Reminders are everywhere, in the backup stack of laminated index cards on my office desk in the church basement, in the way I constantly catalog faces of strangers, in how I clutch my backpack in my lap right now, the pillow inside stuffed atop my work files for easy access.

I'm twenty-five but I look no older than nineteen, which I don't say with vanity (because I'm still too young to care to look younger). I say it because a nineteen-year-old-looking girl is at even greater risk when she must trust herself to the charity of the world.

My father named me Anca, which means "merciful grace," because his heart broke wide open at the first sight of me. Imagine how fortunate I am to play this role in our family mythos. Wreathed in smoke from the Pall Mall riding his gesticulations, Tată used to puff himself up big when he told it, full-hearted in his Orthodox Christian chest. How he loved the tiny parentheticals of my knuckles. My impossibly diminutive toes. My light blue eyes.

I'm dark-skinned, which isn't as rare for Romanians as you might think. We are descended from Romans and surrounded by Slavs, so we have all the passion of Italians with Russian defeatism sprinkled atop. Depending on who you ask, we are either optimistic pessimists or pessimistic optimists, though Tată definitely belongs to the latter category. Our family has a hint of Asian somewhere back from all the cross-continent invasions, Genghis Khan and the Ottomans and whatnot. Plus us Southerners are just a stone's throw to East Asia, so who knows who got up to what. In Tată's eyes, I was a great beauty, but I know I am merely pretty-with-some-effort (Tată also taught me to be mindful of humility).

All the more miracle, his love for me, is that I came at the expense of his greatest love. Obstructed labor, the impossible choice—her or me. Together they chose me. In her dying moment, Mamă chose me.

The blessing of that. And the further blessing that my father viewed my creation as a painful miracle he would honor, this immaculate conception of another type—a daughter born from purity.

That gives me something to live up to every day, however imperfectly.

When I was no more than a year old, my father brought us across the world to the affordable Bronx. His great American hopes never materialized, not in the way he hoped, but I never once wanted for food and he held on against the dark spots in his lungs until I graduated high school and finished a year at Mercy College.

He was so strong. That wrenching cough rattling the bathroom walls when he thought I was already asleep. The rust-speckled balls of Kleenex. The coats that hung costume-like on his diminished frame. He stayed for me until three days after my eighteenth birthday. Until I was a legal adult able to get a job and keep our roof over my head. He did that for me, shouldered all that pain for love and duty.

The sixth choice is an elderly man.

Seventh is two females.

Past seven the rankings blur together. At that point, it's up to how much kindness you sense in people's eyes.

The 2 line keeps rocketing north, shaving beneath Central Park. A sketchy stretch, my least favorite. I chose this particular car because it was crowded when I got on in Brooklyn, but by now the passengers have thinned out, my options dwindling. From what

I can see on the snaking turns, the neighboring cars are mostly empty, but I'm not too worried because there's a girl about my age sitting across from me. A micromini skirt shows a whole lot of her body. She has chewed-down nails and wears too much makeup and looks a bit lost but her eyes are soft and soulful and the way she sits with the heels of her hands jammed to the seat at her sides, her elbows locked, and her shoulders jabbed up by her ears makes her seem fragile. I am grateful to have an Option Three.

As always I am dressed modestly, a winter coat over my shirt-dress with long sleeves. The floral pattern sets tiny lilies against a cornflower-blue background. I am coming back from visiting Ioana, an elder from our parish who lives all the way out in Brownsville. It's a bit of a trial for me to get home but it's a broken hip and she cannot get out to the grocery shop and no one else volunteered. I started out after Vespers so it was late to begin with and we all know Ioana needs care and conversation. Despite the complexities that govern my existence, the church has trusted me to be director of social services and that is a responsibility I honor as best as I humanly can.

At the moment it's a bit past midnight. The last-gen subway car is torn up from the crime surge, one of the harvest-orange seats shattered jaggedly into plastic fangs. Across the ceiling ads curves unimaginative graffiti—a giant dick, a floating pair of boobs, and a street tag that resembles bird-shit splatter. With matching black spray paint, the dome casings of the embedded security cameras have been turned opaque, the tang of shellac still heavy in the unvented air. The cabin lights are flickering on and off, too, a quicker strobe than that of the passing stations, and I reassure myself that the lighting change indeed originates from the subway and not inside my head.

We stop at 116th Street. Most everyone else clears off and then it's just me, Option Three, and a passed-out meth-head at the far end. Even over the roar of the train, I can make out raucous laughter in the trailing car. A hyena pack of young men.

A group of young men is always the Last Option.

I look down.

Beneath *Please help me* resides the second line, which serves as a caption.

My Seizure Plan.

My condition urges me to hold perennial humility and for that I am grateful despite how challenging everything else can be.

Don't be scared, the next line pleads.

I get up to two seizures a day.

They last between one and three minutes.

Then I list the basics. *Lay me on my side. Keep me away from sharp objects. Please don't call an ambulance—I can't afford it. I'll be awake soon! Please stay with me until I'm back inside myself.*

I still debate over the sole exclamation mark in case it seems manipulative instead of merely comforting, which is my intent.

Despite all the instructions on the laminated card, my true asks are really prayers: *Please guard over me. Please show me charity. Please have mercy on me.*

The voices from the car behind grow louder. Amused howls mixed with chanting. The mood, were I to guess, is lubricated with alcohol.

Despite Option Three right across from me, I cannot risk being stuck with the Last Option if the young men decide to switch cars. I'm just readying to rise and move on when I taste it.

Copper.

Rich and hot, melted pennies.

An initial flurry of panic claws its way up my throat but I'm practiced enough to soothe it back down. I'm safe in this moment and I have my laminated index card and my pillow in my backpack and an Option Three.

I do, however, need to act fast.

As I gesture to catch the young woman's attention, I'm already tasting colors, but they're still light yellows and golds, so I have a few moments.

"Are you staying on the train?" I try to keep the note of desperation out of my voice.

She sweeps aside blond tresses of blown-out hair to unscrew an AirPod. "Huh?" Her eyes move to the laminated card, which

I'm holding up dumbly like a jail placard. "Wait—seizures? Like, *seizure*-seizures? Okay, okay. Are you having one now?"

"No." I pull my pillow out of my backpack. "Any second."

Option Three swings herself across the aisle of the moving train and plops down next to me, giving her micromini a practiced tuck beneath her thighs. She plucks the laminated index card from my hand, scanning it. Her eyebrows are high. She hums with anxiety.

"It's okay." I rest a calming hand on her forearm. "I'll be okay."

I set my backpack on the floor at my feet. Folding the soft pillow, I rest it on the seat to my right and lie down, nestling my head in its cushion. The dome of the security camera looms sightless overhead, blotted out with spray paint.

The greens come on now but they still taste light—celery and chartreuse.

"Can you . . ." My mind-mouth connection blinks out but then comes back online. ". . . stay with me?"

"How long?" Nervous chattering. "I have to get off to catch the Metro-North. I'm sorry—it's a— There's a helicopter waiting for me in Westchester I can't miss. I have to— Are you sure you're okay?"

"Umm, hang on." I breathe heavily, my head going slurry. "If it gets really bad"—now kelly and sage burst across my palate—"can you roll me onto the floor?" It all seems so ridiculous, the gleaming poles and marigold seats and the terrible lighting that makes my teeth ache. "And if you have to go, would you mind finding someone else"—the taste grows ominously darker, emerald and fern—"who seems kind?"

Somewhere deep inside I'm registering danger but it's just a fact like every other fact. I sort through the sludge of sensation until I zero in on the threat: the chanting from the car behind us. Louder now, accompanied with thumping. The young men are stomping their feet. My thoughts veer zoological—images of baying and hooves, predatory displays and bone-crushing jaws.

All at once the subway brakes screech hellishly. The cabin lights dim and flicker and we are coasting through subterranean semi-darkness and I am trying to say, *Please can you stay with me one more stop,* but my words aren't working anymore and now I'm tasting forest and olive.

Option Three crouches before me. "I'm sorry, sweetie. If it was *literally* any other time I'd wait with you but the helicopter'll leave without me and—and I can't afford to—"

She's clutching my seizure plan and her eyes are wide and I can see beneath the fake lashes and the crust of her mascara how pretty she is even without all that glamming up. But her eyes are party-drug glazed in a way I hadn't noticed before and I can see she isn't thinking clearly and that makes two of us and the brakes are screaming and the boots stomping in the trailing car grow louder.

Her face contorts with regret and for an instant I see straight into her. She is racked with guilt and uncertainty. She is fighting within herself and I pray the right side will win but now the greens are bleeding into blues which means I'm nearly out of time.

Please don't leave me, I don't—can't—say.

She rubs my forehead gently, not knowing that makes the needles in my brain prickle all the more. "I have to go. You'll be okay, sweetie. I promise. Someone'll come. Someone else'll take care of you."

And I feel her shove my laminated index card between my back and the seat so it sticks up. The subway brakes grind away and the pale yellow light of the station ahead beams ever stronger. Lying down, I cannot see the platform but I pray that more people will get on, that even at this late hour the seats around me will fill with families or Good Samaritans.

We shudder into the glaring light and the doors jolt open.

I look at Option Three and form the thought again through the brilliant skewers inside my mind: *Please help me.*

She gets up, hesitates. She is having second thoughts. The doors are still holding open and she hasn't left and my heart readies itself to leap with relief.

She leans forward and kisses me on the temple, feather-soft. Her breath is pot and bubble gum: "I'm sorry. You're good. You'll be okay. Someone else'll watch over you."

Behind me I hear the intercar door bang open on its hinges, lifting the volume on the roar of merriment from the trailing car. As my eyes strain to see what is coming, she says brightly, "See, people are here now."

In a blink, she drifts backward, skimming through the bumpers onto the 125th Street platform. My frozen view stays locked on the doors and her face in the window. As she glances at the men in my blind spot, I see a single note of dismay arrest her face, furling the tiny spot between her eyebrows. She fades away as I lurch forward again and sapphire leaks along the sides of my tongue and I am touched with exquisite pain and the anticipation of release.

Midnight blue spills through my mouth. My brain sparkles. I feel a human presence behind me, the heat and clamor of the pack, and all at once a chilling silence fills the car as I am noticed.

A clank as something drops. And then it rolls into view before my paralyzed face.

A can of black spray paint.

There comes a stir of excitement, yips of delight, and then a voice wrenched high with malice proclaims, "Lookee lookee. What have we here?"

Before the last streaking lights in my head wobble into darkness, I have time for a single last thought.

Please don't let the hyenas get me.

4

Or Else

In the material world, Luke Devine was wetting his beak with Campari and preparing to have sex.

But the material world was not where he was currently located.

Instead he was roving among the countless back burners of his cognition, refining various plans at various stages. Kneecapping a senator from Alabama who was in the pocket of bad influences. Blocking a shipment of Iranian precision-guided missiles en route to Hezbollah via a civilian flight through Beirut–Rafic Hariri International. Obliterating a married Hollywood studio head with a proclivity for undercharging license fees and overpaying for threesomes. There were many more bubbling cauldrons on many more burners as well. He rampaged among them, stoking and stirring, an amphetaminized short-order chef.

Texts and emails, calls and manic scribbled notes—Devine tapped the world to and fro. Lately he'd taken to keeping on his person a garage-door-remote-size gadget with a single button—his personal black box. Between barking orders into it at the army of staff who maintained his Hamptons estate, he sipped his liqueur and small-talked the lady before him. She was a fulsome blonde in a fitted white shirt and a pleated micromini skirt that showed off the bronze musculature of her thighs, which he hoped to soon part.

What? he thought.

Someone had spoken in the present time and space.

"What?" he said aloud.

The young lady twisted a wayward lock around her finger. Her fitted white shirt was now tugged up, exposing her breasts. He had some recollection of being the agent of its migration. He was sitting beside her on a massive curved couch in his expansive master suite. Inside the rectangular cuboid of glass before them twisted a contorted mannequin, trapped in its distress, a coffee table coaxed into artfulness.

Staff buzzed about them through the open space. There were all sorts of other people in the massive master suite, too, and all manner of activity he'd drowned out, his mind bobbing like a cork atop the background commotion.

"I said, I don't think—I can't do this right now. I'm sorry." Her eyes were completely disconnected from the rest of her, and there was nothing sexual in her posture or his. He wondered how they'd arrived at this point and then just halted.

He blinked and then blinked again. What was her name? Alicia? No, that was yesterday's. Or last week's. Time did not exist. It was lost in the wash of his thoughts, an experiential river. He'd been humming at this speed for two days or five, everything a possibility and a reality at the same time, while the rest of the world sludged along in slow motion. He'd run through both hips by the age of forty, requiring double labrum surgery, the metaphor not a hard reach.

When he was at full gallop, he was fearsome.

He was blinding.

He downed the Campari, then palmed a pill into his mouth. Barely—*barely*—he registered the next wave of pharmacological alteration wobbling through his perceptual field. It couldn't slow the engine of his anterior cingulate cortex but it could make him aware of it, how it pulsed and throbbed.

"Okay," he said, to the young woman. "Hold on, just give me a—"

The black box chimed and then spoke: "Putin on the phone from the Residence at Cape Idokopas." Rawlings, Devine's chief of staff, flew into the room, sat phone pressed to his chest, ready for delivery.

Devine waved a hand. "Tell him to try me later."

Rawlings hesitated in disbelief. Then he met the spear of Devine's gaze, blanched, and faded back out of sight, stammering into the phone.

At a desk against the far wall, Underling No. 3 tapped at a laptop. He spoke quietly, as if to himself, but his words came through the black box. "The Leader's whipping votes on the Online Safety Act."

Devine spoke to him and into the black box at the same time. "Give her Missouri Seventh, the fat one with the floofy hair. I caught her being gymnastic with two Tongan rent boys in the pool house last summer."

That was Devine's glimmering magic. The formula was simple. Throw Gatsbyesque bashes at the mansion here on Billionaire's Row. Invite a curated selection of members from the ruling caste. Put every imaginable sin on display. Hide pinhead surveillance cameras in each crack and wrinkle on the premises. Allow the guests to step into their fullest shameful selves. Memorialize them as such, time-stamped and geolocated. Suck their money in squeaky clean through "suggested" investments in his hedge fund. Gobble up their influence, too. Drink it in like blood. And then? Leverage it.

Underling No. 3 rose to show Devine a pleading email on one of three phones he carried. The head of the German opposition party had been caught frequenting a "massage parlor." There were photos. What was he to do?

Devine shuffled through scripts in his head, plucked out the best response, and then spoke through his black box to the invisible team standing by to execute his orders and see to his whims. "He should issue a statement: 'Clearly this is a deepfake. My penis appears too small.'"

Back to the young woman. Something shimmered darkly beneath the surface of her flat eyes, an infectious hesitation that had leapt onto him. She'd experienced some kind of dislocation, a recent trauma no doubt. "I'm sorry," she mumbled again, a touch drunkenly, as she yanked her top roughly down over her torso.

"It's okay," he said, wrenching himself into the present and trying to slow down. Something was wrong within her and, despite his legion wicked impulses, he never took advantage of the afflicted. "What happened?"

She staggered across to tumble onto the bed. ". . . was . . . so awful. This girl . . . she got taken . . ." She burrowed beneath pillows, hiding her head. She swirled in and out of view—wait, no. That was him.

The full glory of his imbibement kicked in, dolly-zooming his perception. He goggled at the scene before him, recalling now the shambolic party spread throughout the master suite. A German tattoo artist perched in a director's chair. A trio of Manhattan socialites swanning around behind Audrey Hepburn sunglasses, leaving perfumed wakes of Shumukh by Nabeel. A high peaty scotch Devine didn't own soaking into the carpet. Two Pekingese dogs prancing about, one of whom had left a tidy arabesque of shit on the shag rug in the corner, the other trapped with the mannequin beneath the coffee table, Devine's role in the matter a hazy recollection. Though he didn't smoke, Luke seemed to be holding a lit cigarette and his mouth burned. In the fireplace, a pyre of logs roared. His unbuttoned linen shirt clung to him like Saran Wrap.

It wasn't that he didn't remember the chain of events that had gotten him here. It was that the chain of logic that had so compellingly brought this moment into existence no longer held.

His stomach pitched with the plummet. He imagined the feathers fluttering down with him, the sting of melting wax. The windows were grayed with dusk—no, cloudy morning. Moments ago—hours ago?—he'd been peering into the inner workings of the universe, his thoughts resonating with each clockwork twirl. Now there was just chaotic rumbling filling his chest, dense enough to blot out clarity.

He tried to say something but the words felt fragmented, puzzle pieces that wouldn't fit together. His stomach churned and roiled. Only now did he realize that the engine block of his brain had come apart, scattered across the floor, whirring and clicking, mechanical parts severed from purpose. The darkness was dizzying, vertiginous, rushing through him, leaving him breathless.

The young woman needed help.

More acutely, *he* needed help.

What had he done?

What *else* had he done?

And worse: What might he do next?

When he set down the black box and reached for the phone, he noticed the tremor in his hand. Dehydration? Meds? Booze?

Fear.

He had lost control. He hated losing control. It was worse, he realized, than death.

Gnawing at the edge of a thumbnail, his knee jacking up and down, he dialed. His breathing came shallow, irregular.

One ring.

Another.

And then that voice, soothing in its equilibrium: "Do you need my help?"

5

Eternal Outsider

Evan sat in his Ford F-150 in a shaded parking spot across the street from the Clark County Firefighters Local 1908 Union Hall. Visible through a water-stained fixed window, the memorial service for his closest friend proceeded. Various folks cycled past the podium and the transmitter he'd hidden beneath the platform lip, offering up their remembrances.

Earpiece screwed in, he streamed the proceedings: *"—when guess who charges outta the barracks in his chonies, waving a locked-and-loaded boomstick? But who's on the roof? Not some muj Santa but the fucking radioman from Operations. Dude screams, almost falls off the roof. Turns out he was up there diddling with the dish when Stojack stormed out and gave him the brown-star cluster."*

Laughter rolled through the earpiece, along with murmured conversations, the clink of bottles, the noise of someone sobbing quietly and receiving comfort. From the other side of the road, Evan noticed the faintest tremble of the windowpane. He could not see the podium from this vantage but he could make out a swath of mourners. Ragged beards on the men, luxuriant hair on the women, a few folks missing limbs. Carrot sticks with dip, cubed orange cheese on Dixie plates, Pabst Blue Ribbon toasts despite the morning hour.

Alone in the truck that Tommy Stojack had built and outfitted for him, Evan listened and observed. The faintest tug at the base of his lumbar on the left side announced itself, a lingering ache from a violent showdown he'd had in a ghost town a couple of months back.

Stretching in the driver's seat, he looked at the military challenge coin leaning against the dashboard's instrument cluster. It read NO GREATER FRIEND. NO WORSE ENEMY.

He'd been given it by a woman he'd once helped. More precisely, he'd been given half of it. The other broken piece she'd gifted to Tommy, who'd been lowered into the dirt of the Southern Nevada Veterans Memorial Cemetery last month.

Before he'd died, Tommy had soldered the halves together for Evan.

"—really loved him. He was a crusty bear. Big ol' softy inside, though. When my . . . When my niece got raped, he took her out twice a week for a year, taught her to shoot. So let's all hoist a glass. Fair winds and following seas, you dear, sweet man."

Tommy was the best armorer and the finest shot Evan had ever known, as well as a procurement and R&D specialist for various three-letter agencies. Dreaded by the bureaucratic class but beloved by spec ops, veterans, and emergency services, he'd been a bridge between Evan and the legitimate world. Now he was gone, leaving behind an armorer's lair stuffed with ordnance, munitions, gear, equipment, and an abyss in a place inside Evan he didn't know he had.

When Evan had deserted the Orphan Program, feared and hunted by those in highest power, he'd had the clothes on his back, brimming bank accounts in nonreporting countries, and not one single relationship. From the age of twelve, he'd been raised apart from anyone else, rotated through grueling training sessions conducted by a blur of subject-matter experts, senseis, and instructors. The only consistent face had been that of his mentor, Jack Johns, who'd overseen his tutelage, teaching him everything but the strange language of intimacy. *The hard part isn't turning you into a killer,* Jack had pounded into his head. *The hard part is keeping you human.*

Staying human while committing unsanctioned assassinations at the behest of orders issuing from the shadowy underbelly of the DoD had proven untenable, even for Orphan X. Evan had finally slipped off the radar, reconstituting himself under another of his operational aliases. As the Nowhere Man, he took on personal missions unsullied by political considerations. That meant helping people who were being terrorized by others, people who had nowhere else to turn.

As the Nowhere Man, he operated as he always had. Alone.

Tommy had become his first anchor to mankind. They'd earned each other's trust, step by step.

They had become friends.

Evan's first.

"—med-boarded out, PTSD bullshit. Man, I was so lost. Still just a kid, twenty-four, wet behind the ears. He catches wind, my phone rings. He says, 'Get to Las Vegas. Worse men than you have crashed on my couch for a spell.' So I do. First morning I go in to hit the rainlocker, thing's full up with—" A chorus of unintelligible shouts. *"That's right. Fucking* moonshine *in the bathtub. Like he's some Prohibition bootlegger."* The slightest crack of the voice. *"Miss you, brother. Broke the mold, that's for sure."*

Evan tried to imagine what would happen when *he* died. No funeral or memorial, no fruit plates and rambling reminiscences—certainly no poster-board prints on easels. He'd never had his picture taken, not since grade-school yearbooks from his foster-home days, and those had been carefully expunged from any public record, along with the other scant traces of his childhood. When he did finally catch a bullet, nothing would change in the world around him. He'd simply remain what he'd always been: the Nowhere Man.

He rested his hands at the ten and two. What the hell was he doing out here eavesdropping on a memorial service? He'd skipped Tommy's funeral. His profession had inured him to rituals that were not his own. He dealt in blood and sweat, not buglers wailing

"Taps" and twenty-one-gun salutes. He had no need for any of it—color guards and flag-folding protocols, higher brass showing off chest candy and unit pins pounded into coffin lids, shovelfuls of dirt and solemn suits with epaulets of closet dust. And now, weepy speeches at a podium, apocryphal tales burnished into legend.

And yet.

Here he was, watching and listening, the eternal outsider looking in.

Behind the window, a grizzled vet hugged a teary young serviceman. A trio of women in tight white jeans marveled at a blown-up photo of younger-days Tommy. A little girl in a bright yellow dress ran through the guests, waving a fairy wand and banging into knees.

Evan would've liked to be in there near the celebration.

He would've liked to say a few words about his friend.

He would've liked to give Tommy a proper good-bye.

But the notion of conveying intimate emotion in a public setting among others raw with grief was unthinkably messy and contaminating, a break from everything he'd been trained to be. It would've required courage that he did not have.

On the passenger seat, the RoamZone gave its distinctive chime. The untraceable encrypted phone was always with him. When he answered as the Nowhere Man, he never knew what new mission would present itself. What he *could* anticipate was that whoever dialed the number was calling from the depths of a hellish personal misery.

Caller ID was blocked.

He answered as he always did.

"Do you need my help?"

"Huh? Wait. Hold on— Do not let the fucking *dog* drink the Charles and Diana Dom Pérignon."

"Devine?"

Evan had come up against the erratic billionaire on a prior mission. They spoke rarely and only on Evan's terms.

This was not on his terms.

"What?" Devine's voice sounded hoarse. "Look—Can you just—Can you just get here?"

"Get where?"

"The Hamptons house."

"Why?"

"I think— I don't know. I don't know why. There's a lot going on and my brain is roaring and I can't— You three! Take your *fucking* purse dogs and get out!—can't seem to find a handle—and—and—there's also a girl here in my bed who saw something bad happen to another girl—kidnapping, maybe?—and I've got all these plates spinning, you see, with great geopolitical import, and I have to make choices and I don't—"

"Stop," Evan said.

Luke stopped.

"You said there's a girl there. In your bed."

"Yes. Yes. A young woman."

Evan took a four count to draw in a breath. He held it.

"Mr. Nowhere? Why are you quiet? That's a—That's a terrifying silence."

"How old is she?"

A rush of an exhale. "Twenty-six. I'm not like *that.*"

"You said she's upset. Why is she upset?"

"I don't know. Hang on." Then, muffled: "Why are you upset?" Another pause. "I don't know. She's still not answering. She's curled up in the bed."

"What happened?"

"Nothing. Nothing happened. I didn't even have sex with her. I couldn't figure it out."

Evan let that pass, stayed on the seam of inquiry. "Does she need medical attention?"

"No."

"Do you?"

"No."

"Drugs?"

"What?"

"Is she on drugs?"

"No, no, no, no, no. At least nothing serious. Champagne. Very fine champagne. In fact, do you know there were only ninety bottles at the royal wedding when—"

"Are *you*?"

"What?"

"Are *you* on drugs?"

"Just the usual."

"Which is?"

"Sixty grams of indica to slow things down. A half liter of booze by now. Maybe two-thirds? Oh—and ketamine."

"Special K?"

"Not club. Prescribed."

"Okay. So: your average Saturday morning."

"Yes! Exactly. Don't go freaking out and getting lethal."

Devine's concern was legitimate. He had greater influence than most nation-states, his power a threat to those in highest power. Evan had been tasked by no less an authority than the president of the United States to execute him, and he nearly had. Ultimately he'd determined that while Devine was a brilliant narcissist and world-class mind-fucker, he was not someone Evan could dispatch in good conscience.

Yet.

"What's the young woman's name?"

"I don't know."

"You don't know the name of the young woman in your bed?"

"I did at some point. There's a lot going on in here."

"Give her the phone."

"Okay. Okay." Sounds of Devine moving.

A new speech was droning on in Evan's other ear: *"—the thing with Stojack was, he was always there, you know? No matter how down-and-out you were. No matter if you'd fucked up six ways from Sunday—pardon, ladies—or were at your worst with your missus or outta yer head with, dunno, shell shock or trauma or whatever they call it nowadays, he didn't judge. He never—"*

Evan unscrewed the earpiece, narrowed his focus.

"She won't take it," Devine said.

"Try again."

"Here. *Here.* Just take the phone. Take it."

A moment later came a feminine voice, hoarse and weak. "Hullo?"

"Hello. What's your name?"

"Monica," she drawled. "Like Santa Monica."

"Are you free to leave?"

"What? Yeah, course."

"Are you safe?"

"Yeah. But you should get here, maybe, if he wants you here. 'Cuz shit's crazy."

"Did he hurt you?"

"What? No. *No.* He's, like, aggressively considerate. Wanting to make sure I don't do anything I don't want to do. But I don't feel like it's about me at all. It's not. It's about him."

"Generally."

"And it's *exhausting.* He won't stop talking. He just won't stop talking."

"You saw something bad happen to a girl?"

"I can't—I don't really know for sure. I don't want to talk about it."

"Why not?"

"Listen, man, I'm not feeling good and I can't really think straight right now with your friend vrooming around—"

"Give me that back. Give it back." Devine sounded winded. "Her perspective isn't the useful one here. It's been two hours and—I can't find the handle. I can't find the handle."

"Devine," Evan said. "Why are you calling me?"

At last Luke Devine paused. His breath whistled across the receiver once, twice, a third time.

When his voice came it was strained and small, an unrecognizable whisper: "I don't . . . I don't know who else to call."

Evan stared across the street at the memorial. A couple of big guys were laughing hard. He could hear their guffaws from the discarded earpiece. A chunky woman sat on a folding chair in the back, tissue pressed to her nose, mascara streaking into black stalactites. In that easel-mounted photo, Tommy looked young and strong, maybe the age Evan was now. His eyes weren't baggy or tired as they'd been since Evan had known him, but they still held the same measure of warmth.

Evan looked down at his hands on the wheel, cursed under his breath. His other adversaries came at him with steel or lead. But Luke Devine flipped reality like a Rubik's Cube, tweaking patterns and perceptions. Within the force field of his influence, he complicated the world, which meant that to contend with him, Evan had to become more complicated himself.

"Are you there?" Devine asked. "Are you still there?"

"I'll be there in twelve hours."

Evan slotted the truck into drive and pulled out from the curb.

6

Kill the Motherfucker

With Tommy gone, the number of allies Evan trusted implicitly had materially diminished. Humming along the I-15 back to Los Angeles, Evan dialed one of the few others.

"Can you clear a flight plan from Van Nuys to East Hampton Airport?" Evan asked.

"Why?"

"Because Luke Devine's out of his mind."

"*No mames!* That *culero* is out of his mind when he's *in* his mind. What is he capable of now? He pulls one wrong lever and he'll touch off World War III."

"That's why I need to get there."

"Why do you not just kill the motherfucker?"

Aragón Urrea was not prone to equivocation.

A self-described "unconventional businessman," Aragón had amassed billions operating outside international law, weaving back and forth across the blurry line between Big Pharma and drug dealing.

Years ago when Aragón had found himself in the grip of a

father's deepest horror, Evan had helped him put his family back together again. To repay the debt, Aragón had vowed to stay on the right side of the law. Mostly. And as a show of gratitude, he'd put his small fleet of private jets at Evan's disposal, which added remarkable efficiency to Evan's Nowhere Man expeditions.

Evan gave the question proper consideration. "Devine's not a nihilist. He's got a code. If someone has a code, I can engage without having to kill them." A brief pause. "Usually."

"Well," Aragón said, disappointed, "at least consider it."

"I do," Evan said. "Then I think about all that horsepower he's got under the hood. And what he could do with it if it's channeled in the right direction."

"If. *If!* When they are that brilliant, they are all devils."

"He's the devil I know."

A sign flew overhead for the toll road to the 10, and Evan clicked on his signal like the law-abiding citizen he was. The Ford F-150, America's most common truck, blended in everywhere, just like Evan. Tommy had outfitted it with a beefed-up suspension, run-flat tires, and a custom push-bumper assembly. Anything put together by Tommy was a pleasure to operate. He made things right.

That's what Evan would've said if he'd had the courage to enter that union hall and stride up to the podium: *That was Tommy. He made things right.*

He thought again of Tommy's off-the-Vegas-Strip lair, its belly stuffed with explosives, its steel doors locked and alarmed, wind-driven sand already starting to layer it back into the surrounding desert dunes. Enough memories to crack Evan into pieces if he reflected on them too long.

A voice text dinged in from Joey, interrupting his thoughts. Though Josephine Morales was merely seventeen years old, an Orphan Program washout, and prodigiously mouthy, she was by a long shot the finest hacker Evan had encountered. When he'd collided with her on a mission years ago, she'd been the last person he wanted to have in his orbit. But they'd slowly worked their way into each other's lives more than Evan cared to admit. Joey now referred to him with faux irritation as her "uncle-person."

He swiped the alert off the screen.

"The devil you know," Aragón said. "Like me."

"No," Evan said. "He's worse than you."

Bink. Bink. Another two voice texts from Joey.

Aragón gave his big booming laugh, the one that resonated in his chest. "So you are going there to help?"

Evan didn't like the answer but he spoke it anyway. "Yes."

"You are strong of mind and pure of heart, *amigo.*"

The affection in Aragón's voice went right into him. It straightened his spine a millimeter or two. Was that why he'd called Aragón instead of texting the pilot directly? To have some—what would it be called? connection?—after saying his remote good-bye to Tommy? To know he wasn't friendless?

Evan reset himself, cleared his throat. "'Strong of mind and pure of heart'? Don't turn into a Mexican sidekick on me, Urrea."

Another grand laugh. "*Vete a la chingada, pinche güero.* I'll have the Lineage jet to Van Nuys in three hours."

"Copy that."

Bink. Bink. Bink. What the hell was going on with Joey?

"I still think you should just kill the motherfucker."

Full circle then.

"Noted. And thank you, my friend." The last phrase slipped out without Evan's thinking.

He was surprised to realize that he'd meant it.

7

Take Me More Seriously

Listen, X, I've been thinking. There are these phases of life, right? Like, turning a page or a new chapter or reboot or whatever. And after the last mission, you've been, dunno, different. *And I have, too. And I realized I don't wanna just be your sidekick like Batgirl who stays back on the computer and does her nails. I have more to offer. I'm more mature, like for sure, since we first*—HEY ASSHEAD, EVER HEARD OF A FUCKING TURN SIGNAL?—*first met and I know you'll say it isn't safe for me to go in the field but that's what I've been trained for. I don't* want *safe. What I'm saying is you should bring me with you next time. I swear I won't screw up. And I know what you're thinking, okay? That I'll be too goofy or all Mexican hood-rat-y and start thwacking bitches with my* chancla *or whatever. But seriously? How much have I kicked ass for you on all these past missions? I mean, I deserve to get a shot. Wait. Wait. Aaarg. I know, I know, you'll get all judgy over "deserve." Hang on. Don't—*

What the fuck! Wait. *I said* don't—

Look. Ignore those first two voice texts. Okay? You weren't supposed to hear them. It was just a tech mishap. I know I'm supposed to say "cancel" instead of don't—

*I waaaaaant it that waaaaay. Tell me—*AIN'T NUTHIN BUT A HEARTACHE—*Wait! Have you— Is this fucking recording right now? Off. Stop! Fuck! Cancel. Stop recording! Fucking* cancel! *No. No, no, no. Please don't. Stop. Stop! I'm not gonna—*

I SAID "SAY IT," *NOT—*

Haha. Okay. Erhm. Right. I get this was all probably amusing to you. Anyways. That's my proposal. Umm. That's it. I just think, uh, I just think it's time you take me more seriously.

In her final voice message, Joey spoke in the voice she used when she thought she was being mature. A touch deeper, throaty.

Evan adored that voice. But showed it no mercy.

He considered for a moment.

A moment longer.

Texted back: kay.

He drove another mile and a half.

Then he grinned.

8

The Good Kind of Bad

The first thing to focus on, Evan knew, was the thrumming ache of the quadratus lumborum muscle stretching across the wing of his left hip. If he was even an inch out of alignment, he could not risk tackling Devine in his full manic-tornado mode.

Which was why he was in bridge position before the freestanding fireplace burning cedar, arched over a foam block anchored like a bridge pile beneath his sacrum. The great room of his penthouse caverned around him, but he kept his focus limited to the periphery of his skin and the sweat beading across his oft-broken collarbones.

He had to get to Southampton quickly, before Devine lost control completely, butterfly-flapping a fleet of nuclear subs into the Taiwan Strait or Jim Jonesing a mass-suicide event. One hour and twenty-seven minutes remained before the Lineage jet taxied to the hangar at Van Nuys.

Evan's skin glistened with the fire, pores popping wide, sweat shoving out of him. Already he'd relaxed through several onion layers of the ache, but a hard little acorn remained, beaded imperviously behind the bone of the iliac crest. He'd torqued the muscle badly in a grappling death match with a *sicario* in a Guaridón surgical suite some time ago, and strained it anew leaping across rooftops fleeing a massive LAPD manhunt with half of an assassin's ear in his cargo pocket. Since he hadn't noticed the reinjury until months after, he'd under-indexed on the immediate repair work, and that had cost him, the tightness roosting into semipermanence.

One hour and twenty-six minutes.

The knot wasn't giving up any ground. He had to set himself in order before submerging himself into the insanity bubbling cauldron-like within Luke Devine's realm. Everything was the same. Fractal. If he didn't work out the strain, it would amoeba outward, conscripting surrounding fiber and ligament, locking him up, limiting his flexibility, how he moved and thought. The knot remained smashed against bone with its arms crossed and its breath held—a blight, a canker, a gremlin's kiss.

Slowly—*slowly*—Evan reached across to the basket set on the hearth and tugged it closer. He did not move his shoulders. Nor head nor eyes. Staring directly up, he groped around until he found the right one.

Blindly he pulled it out and set it up. Then he struck the rim of the 432 Hertz singing bowl with the tiny wooden mallet. Atop its buckwheat-hull-stuffed cushion, the bowl resonated at the pitch he'd selected.

Allowing in more heat, his muscles loosened syrup-like over the block. The knot held on, but he four-square-breathed and let the vibration in through his skin, let it travel through the lax muscles and forge into the snarl itself, losing himself to sensation and memory.

Seventeen-year-old Evan is upstairs in his dormer room in Jack's Virginia farmhouse and there are two women in bed with him. They are in their early twenties and giving him advice and naked.

It is very, very hard to focus.

"Don't ever yank hair," the one called Cassie says. "No one likes that.

And don't slap asses. None of that debasement-porn shit." She smells like Juicy Fruit. Big lips, wide-set eyes, freckles. She trails her nails along his ribs. Horripilation ensues. His flesh makes shapes he didn't know it could make, all of the shapes, all at once.

He focuses to keep his voice from breaking. "Yes, ma'am."

"I mean, unless someone asks *you to," says Morgan. Propped on an elbow, her face hovering over his, she carries the deliciously wicked scent of menthol cigarettes and mouthwash. He feels it imprinting on his brain, pairing with what is happening under the sheets. "I mean, look at these muscles. You'd better be careful how you use them."*

Cassie again: "Anyone ever uses their safe word—"

"What's a safe word?" he blurts.

The young women make eye contact across his chest and crack up a little.

Cassie dips her head, letting her strawberry-blond tresses tickle across his chest. Morgan reaches beneath the covers. The arches of his feet cramp. He feels like he is going to explode or combust and just when he is about to do both she removes her hand, absentmindedly lifts her fingertips to her mouth, and moistens them, dimpling her lower lip. Then she returns her hand.

"Pay attention. To us.*" Morgan's brow furrows in thought, and yet somehow her fingers continue to do what they are doing. "It'll just make it better for you anyways."*

He thinks he might—

—he might die. But he doesn't.

And he keeps doesn't-ing.

Drownproofing, psyops, escrima knife fighting, accents and etiquette, CQB, military history, SERE—of all the training teenage Evan does, this is his favorite.

Also?

The most terrifying.

Like everything else, it started in Jack's study. Mallard-green walls, hardcover tomes, fireplace crackling. Jack ensconced in his armchair, cut-crystal tumbler in hand, the finger of amber already putting a charge into his cheeks. "It's the roar of evolution, of biology, the unbroken line of your ancestors speaking through your DNA. Desire, want, lust. It makes your head swim. But we can't afford for your head to swim. Can we?"

Evan's head was swimming. He sat on the leather couch, hands on his knees, already feeling his blood spike with anticipation. "No," he said. "We can't."

"Any woman you find attractive has the power to undo you. Don't fear that power. Don't let it overtake you. Don't deny it, either, or seek to subjugate it. Look it in the eye."

"That sounds hard." Evan was pressing his knees together. "I'm probably gonna need a lot of practice."

Jack's eyes clicked over to him. Then he did something he rarely, rarely did. He laughed. "All right." Rising with an old-man groan, he exited the study.

Alone, Evan waited, the heat of the fire weighting the air. As his training dictated, he measured his breathing, steadied his pulse, focused on his surroundings.

Jack returned with two young women. "Ms. Cassie, Ms. Morgan, this is Evan."

Evan found his feet. He could not take the women in directly, not yet, instead sensing them, an aura hovering in the doorway, an intoxicating force drawing him in.

Jack said, "Aren't you going to shake hands and introduce yourself?"

Evan did.

"Eye contact," Jack said.

Evan lifted his nervous gaze. His body was honed from more physical disciplines than he could enumerate. Lean yet toned, agile yet strong, powerful yet coordinated. He'd thought that he was secure in it.

Until now.

The women smiled, amused, taking his measure.

"He's young," Jack told the women. "Anyone wants to stop? You stop."

Jack radiated authority. There was nothing lascivious in his tone. He might as well have been recapitulating Confederate battle failures from the Mississippi River Valley.

He turned to Evan, taking both shoulders. From his expression Evan could tell that what was coming was a variation of the speech he'd given Evan outside dojos and sniper ranges, psychology labs and hacker lairs. "You will learn from them. And about yourself. You will show humility and grace. And most important"—Jack drew closer, breathing single-barrel fire, eyes flashing a warning, their foreheads nearly touching—"you will treat them with respect."

Evan nodded.

Upstairs now between the warm flesh of both women, he struggles with many things—insecurity, self-control, embarrassment. But he is not struggling to feel respect for them. That comes naturally enough.

"And also," Cassie is telling him, "don't get all dickish about how you're scoring or about what you're gonna tell other guys. Misogyny is just little-dick cover for fear. But this?" A not-too-firm squeeze makes his blood surge. "It's sacred." She laughs at herself. "Even when it's not, it should be. So act like it."

Evan's breath is irregular but he evens it out. "Yes, ma'am."

"And if you want to get experimental or whatever," Morgan says, her hand tragically retracting, "make sure we're okay with it. We're way *more sensitive. In so many ways. Honor that." She tap-tap-taps on his chest, now motherly, causing confusion to explode delightfully inside his seventeen-year-old chest. "Understand?"*

"Yes, ma'am."

"If you're not sure what to do with a woman, always be more gentle."

An asterisk materializes in Evan's head courtesy of Jack Johnsian mind control: Unless I'm required to kill her.

"Be a gentleman.*" Cassie slaps him, not lightly, across the cheek. He takes the sting without wincing or letting his head snap to the side—no concession to the blow. She stares down at him sternly. "There's never an excuse to not be a gentleman."*

Now her other hand is working. God, her other hand.

She has a cute broad nose and there are light freckles on her eyelids and he feels her breast against his side. Both breasts. Her pink lipstick, once glossy, is flaking slightly, staining a front tooth. That stain is like one panel hanging down on a beautiful billboard, and she looks a touch sad around the eyes, like Tyrell's sister back from Evan's foster-home days. Even so, if he looks past the façade and beholds her in all her fullness, she is glorious. And who ever would have thought the aroma of Juicy Fruit could be an aphrodisiac?

Morgan bites her lip, peers down at him. "And don't pull any jealous shit. Or adolescent ego crap. You want a girl to agree *to go with you, or whatever." She pokes him in the nose with a fingernail, hard enough to smart. "You want her to* want *to do whatever she's doing with you. Never ever get your way just 'cuz you're stronger or can yell louder. Never take power away from a girl just 'cuz you can."*

*Unless I'm required to kill her.

"Be secure,*" Cassie adds, mooshing his cheeks and swinging his face away from Morgan's toward her big hazel eyes. "'Secure' is super sexy."*

This is the point. This is why he is here. To discover parameters in this strange dance between males and females, to learn to first do no harm when it comes to innocents, to ensure that he won't do bad in the service of doing the good kind of bad.

"Mmm. Yeah. Secure." Morgan skims a fingertip along the line of his chin. One of her legs is slung across Evan's lower stomach, the thigh dimpled faintly with a prelude of cellulite. "And, like, quiet. And strong."

He doesn't say, Yes, ma'am.

He is being, like, quiet. And strong.

"He's sort of like that already," Cassie observes, talking to Morgan.

Cassie's lips are plush. She fastens her mouth over his nipple, flicks her tongue absentmindedly, then looks up with a big lazy smile. The remaining lipstick shimmers on her lips, her breath pineapple and orange. His nerves—all of him—stand at attention.

That pink streak on her incisor once more throws static into his system.

The young women are not merely fantasy. They are real.

He is training to become a killer. And yet Jack has tasked him with remaining human. All his other training focuses on the former. This insists on the latter.

For him to become an Orphan worthy of Jack's training, he has to contain all this inside him—how to feel pleasure while not becoming enslaved to it, how to relate interpersonally while maintaining distance, how to protect others in all their idiosyncratic messiness while sustaining operational perfection.

Cassie kisses his sternum and then the top of his stomach and then his internal obliques and Morgan is leaning over his face, lips moving against his mouth, and she is murmuring, "You can handle it. You can handle all this and not lose your mind," and he is trying not to gasp and—

—the singing bowl pitch vibrated through the musculature of his lower back and—there, there—put a wobble into the snarl of muscle fiber, loosening it. At last the knot unstitched against the ridge of hip bone, letting go and sending a sparkler streak of fire down to the pinkie toe of his left foot. His shoulders flattened dead smooth across the mat and his neck twinged and he exhaled and kept exhaling longer than made sense until his back cracked from stem to stern. Rolling off the block, he sagged into the fetal position and lay and breathed and breathed some more.

After a time, awash in endorphins and serotonin, he pulled himself to his feet and stood, swaying slightly, finding his bearings. Shirtless, shoeless, dripping with sweat—he felt feral.

One hour and seventeen minutes to wheels-up.

Walking to his master suite, he felt no twinge in his back. Entering the bathroom, he nudged aside the frosted-glass shower door, which retracted silently into the wall on hidden tracks. He showered in chilly water to dampen inflammation.

Drying off, he moved past his floating bed to the bureau. Each drawer held stacks of identical precision-folded apparel—dark jeans, discreet-tactical cargo pants, gray V-necked T-shirts, black sweatshirts. A dozen tactical shirts with magnetic buttons and machine-vision-thwarting patterns hung in the closet, spaced with precise two-inch gaps.

As he dressed, the recollection of his training with Cassie and Morgan lingered. Though it seemed impossible, he was older now than they were then. Like his other instructors, they had taught him control, discipline, restraint. And—it struck him now—something more. Of all his teachers, they were the only ones who demanded that he see them in their totality.

An hour twelve minutes to departure.

A package resting on the middle shelf in the closet caught his gaze. Wrapped in brown paper and adorned with customs stamps, it had arrived a few days ago from Northampton, England, forwarded through several mailing address. He hadn't opened it yet.

He reached for it, hesitated, hesitated some more, and then took it off the shelf and tore it open. With reverence he lifted the lid off the box inside. A flap of blue polishing cloth bore the coat of arms of the UK's royal warrant. He peeled back the fabric. Nestled toe-to-shin in the cardboard box, they gleamed inside.

A month ago, they'd beckoned to him from the window of Jermyn Street a few blocks off Savile Row. He'd been strolling back to the Savoy after an Alessandro Palazzi free-poured martini at Dukes, the zest of Amalfi lemon lingering on his lips. For a good twenty minutes, he'd stood on the pavement outside the shop, marveling at the camo brogue boots. For as long as he could remember he selected his gear for maximum efficiency and performance. But never had he acquired something simply because it caught his fancy.

He'd gone inside. And ordered a bespoke pair.

And now here they were. The finest Northampton leather, tanned with oak bark from the surrounding countryside and finished with a camouflage design. The generational tradition of excellence that had given rise to them reached back to eight years before Victoria ascended to the throne. Indeed they were functionally perfect—every stitch of the welt, every dot in the brogue pattern, every perforation of the wing tip. Soles bunked, heels buffed, leather hand-burnished to a near-reflective patina.

Each pair of boots had to pass nearly three hundred individual operations and checkpoints before leaving the factory. Base material alchemized into an embodiment of human excellence. Like him, but beautiful.

He peered down into the box, beholding them.

They looked so out of place here in his penthouse with its poured-concrete surfaces and stainless-steel edges. They were decadent, distinctive, noticeable—everything he was not and could never be. Staring at them now he felt— What *did* he feel? Guilt? Pride? Unworthiness?

He closed the lid and put the box away again.

Then he donned his Original S.W.A.T.s, which blended into inconsequentiality beneath the cuffs of his cargo pants. He regarded himself in the mirror on the inside of the closet door.

He looked utterly forgettable. Average size, average build, just a normal guy, not too handsome.

Much better. Now he was ready.

The doorbell rang.

Could that possibly be Joey, uncharacteristically early by a full ten minutes? And ringing the doorbell rather than just breaking in with the duplicate key she'd made behind his back?

He moved to the front door and opened it. He expected the usual—Joey in torn jeans, oversize flannel, muscle undershirt, Big Gulp in hand.

But he scarcely recognized the young woman standing before him in a tailored light gray suit. The contrast-stitched blazer sported notched lapels, and her slim-fit poplin blouse had a stand-up collar, revealing a slender dagger of flesh at the throat. Trousers tight at the waist but flared at the cuffs. Her lush brown-black hair was pulled up out of her face, swept loosely into an elegant topknot as big as a sunflower, her undercut even at both sides and understated. Her usual rucksack had been replaced by a sleek leather portfolio briefcase large enough to accommodate her laptop and the usual half dozen items of hacker hardware she kept on her person at all times.

Evan was relieved to spot a few traces of Recognizable Joey—dimple in her right cheek, Doc Martens with embroidered roses, an emerald nose stud accenting her eyes.

He blinked a few times. "Did you get eaten by a fashion magazine?"

She checked an actual watch that she was wearing on her actual wrist. "We're ten minutes ahead of schedule. I have my truck gassed up and ready downstairs. We can switch vehicles at the Encino safe house. I've already Wazed the route to the airport, no traffic events. I have two sets of spare license plates ready to—"

"Joey. We don't need to do all that. We can just drive to Aragón's private hangar and leave your truck there."

She deflated slightly. "Copy that. I've squared away a professional sitter for Dog so there won't be any disruptions on our mission—"

"This isn't technically a mission."

"—and I left three emergency contacts if anything comes up relating to his care so I won't be distracted from the mission."

Evan had rescued the Rhodesian ridgeback from an underground fighting ring and given him to Joey. At first, in an attempt to avoid growing attached to him, she'd refused to call him anything but Dog. Her ploy had failed disastrously but the generic name had stuck.

"Josephine. It's your dog. You should have your phone on. And what's with the i-banker cosplay?"

"I have to hold focus. The Second Commandment: *How you do anything is how you do everything.*"

"We might need some new Commandments."

At last her young professional façade faltered, old-school Joey excitement shining through. "Really? *Seriously?* New Commandments? Can I choose one?"

"No," Evan said. "And aren't you going to give up and name Dog at some point?"

The scowl came up and all of a sudden she looked like an angry seventeen-year-old again instead of Joey 2.0. "What am I supposed to name him? *Chester?*"

"Yes. Chester. That's the only option."

She stormed past him into the great room, a wisp floating free of the topknot and standing on end from static electricity. "No proper noun can suit him. He's archetypal. He contains multitudes. He's my person. He's *Dog.*"

Evan said, "Right."

"But I *am* relieved I can keep my phone on," she confessed, scratching at her topknot and unleashing a loop of hair that dangled artlessly to her shoulder. "The stupid dog sitter didn't even know how to clean ridgeback ears and we all know the yeasty nightmare that can turn into." She made Gross Yeast Fingers, which so far as Evan could tell had zero relationship to the actual composition of yeast. "So I had to teach her how with the squirt bottle and then Dog did his shaky-shake and got, like, *ear juice* splattered all over me so I had to shower again and this is, like, my backup suit. But you could still be, less, dunno, *discouraging* about my promotion."

After her stiff entrance, jabbering about feelings and fungal dog ears felt bizarrely welcome.

"You're not promoted. There is no promotion. You're just tagging along."

Unfazed, Joey rolled her eyes. "O-*kay.* Whatever you want to call it. But I for one am going to be more professional on this mission—"

"It's not a mission."

"—and I think we could both benefit from taking stuff to, like, the next level. Like: a rebrand." The stray wisp standing out from her head waggled in the air-conditioning like a streamer.

Evan checked his Vertex fob watch. They were no longer running ahead of time. He started for the door but she didn't catch the cue.

"I for one am making some changes. No more Dr Pepper and Red Vines." Joey tapped her portfolio briefcase. "I packed antioxidant trail mix."

"Proud of yourself for that, are you?"

She flushed slightly but kept on. "And you could stand to clean up your act, too. Cut out booze, maybe."

Pausing at the door, he glanced back at her. She looked so earnest. He let himself take her in, all the parts of her, the striving teen and the emerging adult and the little kid beneath it all. Over her right shoulder rose the glass-walled vodka freezer vault, its shelves lined with the purest spirits from six continents.

"I can't quit drinking," he said, unfurling an arm to usher her out. "I've invested too much money in alcohol."

9

The Human Bullshit

Evan stretched out on the luxury jet's queen-size bed, hands folded across his stomach, meditating to the soporific rumble of the engines.

A knock on the flimsy door separating the airborne bedroom from the main cabin.

He opened his eyes. "What?"

Joey stuck her head in. "How about: 'Don't fall in love with Plan A'?"

"Huh?"

She was supposed to be buried in her laptop. He'd asked her to track Lesandro Candella through Epic and Cerner, the prevalent electronic medical-record systems used in California. It was not his habit to keep track of those he helped once they were out of the crosshairs but his habits seemed to be shifting of late without his permission.

"My new Commandment!" Joey said. "The eleventh one or whatever."

"I came up with that."

"No. No. I'm pretty sure you got it from me."

"Joey. I'm meditating."

"We were sitting at the sushi-roll place in Westwood and you were all like, 'I'm not going to your recital,' and I was like, 'Don't fall in love with Plan A.'"

"I'm pretty sure that's not how that happened."

"Whatevs."

She withdrew.

He closed his eyes. Found his breath again.

Another knock.

"What?"

"'Need no praise,'" she said, this time in her movie-trailer voice.

"That's from Jack."

"So what? The other ten were from Jack."

"Josephine. I'm trying to focus. Don't you have some antioxidant trail mix to chew on?"

"Real clever, X. You wait. That's two now. Two for Joey. 'Don't fall in love with Plan A.' And? 'Need no praise.'"

"Neither are—"

But she was gone.

He ground his teeth. Gazed out the window. Took in the cake-frosting layer of stratocumulus clouds floating below the jet. He focused on the softness of the mattress beneath his back, the—

"'There are no arguments to win. Only actions to take.'"

There she was filling out the doorway. Past her he could see the can of Red Bull wedged in the cupholder of her leather seat; evidently her clean-living pledge didn't hold past Kansas.

"That sounds like a motivational poster," Evan said.

Joey screwed up her face, considering, her expression at odds with her suit. "Okay, mebbe. How about—"

"Joey. If you don't get out of here I'm gonna demote you."

"*Demote* me? That means I *did* get a promotion! Can we talk about my new job title?"

"No."

"Like, VP: X Brand Management."

"Joey."

"X-Factor Director at Large."

"Josephine!"

"What?"

"Check if there are emergency parachutes on board."

"Why?"

He raised his head from the pillow, gave her a dead stare.

"Oh," she said. "Okay. I get it. Haha. You want a little space then. You could've just asked professionally."

When the door slid shut this time, he locked it.

Despite the Red Bull, Joey dozed off somewhere over Ohio.

When she woke up, Evan was sitting across from her, perfectly still.

She started. "What? What's wrong?"

She sat forward. Her topknot had come loose, which was a pain since it'd taken her, like, eleventy hours on YouTube to figure it out and now she'd have to deal with it in the executive jet bathroom or whatever it was called.

"Josephine," he said. "I'm glad you're here."

She braced herself. "I'm glad I'm here, too."

"I don't know what we're heading into. Luke Devine is a dangerous man and he has dangerous people around him. He is not a man you allow inside your head. This is not a game. It is not training. All banter, all jokes, the human bullshit between us, that has to stop now. I love you and I'll have your back."

It was the first time he'd ever said it.

No buildup, no context, no depth of emotion in his voice.

Despite that, a giant cry-sob bloomed behind the surface of her face. She could see her reflection in the mirrored band of chrome backing the door to the cockpit. Eyes red and welling, her nose flushed alcoholically. But she did not blink and not a tear fell.

He'd just said it like it was nothing at all and now she had to pretend that it was all cool, that it was just something they both knew already, and said to each other whenever, like, normal people did.

He kept on in that dead-level Orphan voice. "He is not in control and there is a witness there who observed a possible kidnapping. Your job—your only job—is to have *my* back until I can figure out what is going on. That means you're not to speak. That's not open to interpretation."

She regained an iota of her composure and then another. "Okay, you want me to be mute?"

"Not mute."

She risked another glance at her reflection, proud to see that she had her face back under control already, and she thought, *That's right, bitches, I got some Orphan training in me.*

She made sure that when she spoke, she sounded *trés* professional. "So I should be as silent as it's possible to be without impacting the social situation."

He hesitated and she could tell he was turning the Sixth Commandment over in his head: *Question orders.*

He said, "Yes."

"So," she said. "*Some* interpretation."

"Which is now clarified."

"Copy that."

The engines whined, the jet pitched, and the world went weightless. They began their descent into the Hamptons. She'd grabbed for the armrests but Evan hadn't moved at all.

He leaned forward, their knees almost touching, and now his eyes—what color were they? they always changed—had more in them than there was before, and he said, "See you on the other side, J."

"I look forward to it, X."

10

Fuck-Around-and-Find-Out

It was a pocket of heaven.

Devine's was the grandest of the grand estates lining Meadow Lane, a slender spit of sand dunes and hardscaping dropped like God's dock between the Atlantic and Shinnecock Bay. The water was New Englandy slate leavened with tropical aqua, shockingly clear for this splintery stretch of coastline. The breeze held salt and the air held the cries of seagulls and the tremulous bass of the ocean washing itself against rich, powdery sand. The house sign staked in the earth, letters patterned like a kilt, spelled out TARTARUS, named by a Scotsman in the *schmatta* trade with a Miltonian sense of humor. The quartz stone of the circular driveway glinted like crusted diamond. Robins warbled unseen in the poinsettia sway of red maples. In the front gardens bursting through stretches of lush lawn, bees bustled and butterflies docked on moonflowers despite the fact that it was February in New York, which made the invertebrate pageant technically impossible. The front door rose before them like a portcullis made solid just for spite. Devine's mansion alone had no guard shack,

She did have lovely eyelashes. Distinct but not overdone makeup, dark paint around dark eyes, a womanly form constrained by the monkey suit.

Evan said, "That's the hope."

"He did, uh . . ." The guard with a potential gunshot foot in his future scratched at the side of his mustache, his other hand now pointedly farther from his holster. "He did kill the last shift, Kesh."

"The last shift?"

"Of guards. He did, uh, kill them all. Like: *all* of them. Ya know?"

More screaming carried up one of the marble-lined halls upstairs, and a sound like the crash of cymbals.

Kesh wet her lips, which looked suddenly dry. "The Nowhere Man." The corners of her jaw rippled barely, a micro-tensing of the molars. She studied Evan. Then raised her hands, palms out stickup-style. "Boss pays us plenty. Not enough for this."

Evan relaxed his posture and they mirrored him.

"I'm here to help," Evan said. "He called me. How bad is it?"

Kesh set her hands on her hips, blew a wisp of dark-chocolate hair out of her left eye. She wore chunky chestnut highlights. Her uniform was impeccable, and sharp intelligence shined through her expression. "I'll be honest. Pretty out of control, man."

Almost Shattered Ankle said, "We're just trying to hold everything together. It's, uh, it's been a lot."

"Copy that," Evan said. "This is my associate."

In his peripheral, he sensed Joey nod.

There came a slam of a door from somewhere deep in the architecture. A moment later, a spark plug of a man, early thirties, shot across the landing above and then down the staircase, his loafers pitter-pattering over the steps, floating his torso smoothly through the descent. He wore a black suit, sufficiently plain to be forgettable. His bearing and artless crew cut said: marine. Devine favored marines for his inner circle.

A tidy block of a man, he swept a wall of air in front of him. "Hold on, hold on," he said to them all. "Let's just cool heels a minute." He had a hand up to Evan, fingers splayed. His base was set but his posture remained pointedly conciliatory. "We don't need a blasting cap in a powder keg."

Evan said, "Agreed."

"Will Rawlings, chief of staff. I know who you are. Please—just, stay calm."

"I am," Evan said. "Calm."

"Right. Right. This is . . . ?"

"My associate."

Rawlings nodded to Joey and she nodded right back. Shockingly, she made a good mute. Rawlings gave each of his guards a reassuring glance in the eye, and Evan respected him for it. From a thousand mental dossiers, Evan extracted a quick psychological profile for him. Reliable, stalwart, competent. Lots of gym time and creatine and something else to juice it up from time to time. His mother was likely oversexualized, arresting him slightly in adolescent virility. But she was fundamentally good.

Rawlings wore one of those fabric bracelets around his wrist, not as rustic as the usual leather strappy ones, an artistic flourish that tilted him higher on Big Five trait openness. And he had a wedding band, which he actually wore, platinum stamped with the tiny Cartier manhole covers. That meant a wife with her head in the Zeitgeist, exposure to a broader array of outgroups through her friends, increased tolerance for different ideas. That's why Devine would have chosen him—all the conscientiousness of a conservative with a liberal's flexibility. And if pushed, men like Rawlings could show a good amount of fuck-around-and-find-out, without which the other positive attributes were merely hypothetical.

"I don't want to have any violence kick off," Rawlings said. "No trouble. Nothing . . . unpredictable. I know your history here with Mr. Devine."

"He asked me here," Evan said.

"His judgment isn't actually—" Now the sound of something toppling, the wash of spilled gallons of liquid across marble. A string of curses roared out into the cavernous foyer, linked one after another like boxcars, and they went on and on without repeating, a linguistic carnival trick.

The mansion quieted abruptly, the silence even more creepy.

Rawlings cleared his throat, started over. "His judgment isn't in the best place," he said. "I don't know your intentions. But I do know what you're capable of. And he is my responsibility. I hope you can understand that, sir."

Evan considered.

He reached through his shirt, magnetic buttons parting, and drew from his appendix holster. The 1911 spun once in his hand.

The handle stuck out, proffered to Rawlings.

The whole flash of movement happened before anyone else could react.

It took a full two seconds for Rawlings to come off high alert. He'd drawn back, tense on his heels, but he breathed himself back down into his loafers again and took the pistol.

Evan looked past him. Now the staircase was curling up from the west side again—no, south? He stared up at the landing floating way above, a Verona arc of balcony, from which now issued voluminous coughing and sounds of gagging.

Evan reset himself. "Want to show me what's going on?"

11

All of Her All at Once

Anca stirred into hazy consciousness. Her eyes couldn't open. Swelling, a crust of dried blood across her left lid. Her insides ached and her face ached and her parts ached, all of her all at once, a raw throbbing. Acrylic or fiberglass, slick against her bare bottom. The air was damp and liquid sloshed around her, a soupy, fetal immersion. Her nostrils stung. Pain in the side of her neck, the bulge of her shoulder, remembrances of needle punctures.

Bathtub. She was in a bathtub. The water, no more than three inches deep. No, not water. Chemical something. The fumes, they were burning her nose. Pungent, sharp, metallic. Bleach? No, hydrogen peroxide, like she used to scrub stains out of her worn-thin carpet.

Memories rushed her, blips of semi-awakeness. Animal grunts. Malign laughter. Hands on her, all over her, squeezing and grabbing and tweaking. Pressed into a bare mattress, stomach down, limbs spread, fire and more fire inside. Ski masks looming overhead, nonfaces bulging with drugged distortion, dark eyes and smeared wet lips.

All of Her All at Once

Her head lolled forward, an ache clenching her neck and shoulders. She felt presence around her, stirring, a strong masculine scent. Titters, voices. She scrunched her eyes shut hard and tried to pry them open, her right eye yielding a slit.

Moldy grout fingering between cracked white tiles. A jaundiced light slanting through a filthy high-set window. Her knobby knees before her, the soft white flesh of her thigh marred with thumb-wide bruises. The periphery swam into blurry view. Jeans and bare waists and torsos, several forms rimming the bathtub. One of the men had a tattoo of a goat skull covering his left pectoral, phallic ram horns spiraling up, a cyclops eye peering out from its bony forehead. Her insides seized, bringing fresh pain.

"She's up, she's up."

A voice from the other room. "Hit her again."

With terror, she lifted her gaze.

Dark ski masks hovered above, peering down, smooth black-nylon heads. In the dirty light, she cowered, naked, defiled, the object of a bestial séance.

One of the bare-chested men moved, a syringe flashing in his hand.

A prick at her neck, a burn in her blood, and she tumbled back down into darkness.

12
Lion's Den

As Evan and Joey glided up the grand staircase, the dizzying interior of Tartarus seemed to warp and stretch. Joey slid a steadying hand along the banister, a smooth ribbon of African blackwood. Perched high on the wall atop a ledge of Japanese zelkova wood, carvings of the three monkeys peered down at Evan, larger and more menacing than they'd appeared before.

A gurgled shout from above: "*—supposed to bend the knee to 'settled science'?*"

"It's been like this," Rawlings said discreetly and somehow over both shoulders as he led, "for a while."

They reached the landing, the voice growing louder: "*—as if truth is arrived at by some tepid consensus rather than thrusts of genius that punctuate the equilibrium of an age. Curse Copernicus in his slumber, slingshot Darwin out of the firmament! We don't need their disruptive ilk when it comes to—*" A muffled blur, like shouting into a pillow.

At Evan's side, Joey stayed close enough that their elbows brushed.

The hallway to the master suite snaked off to the right. Evan was certain that last time he was here, it darted the other way. There were restroom doors and hidden doors, and then the most important door of all floated into view. Upholstered in plush scarlet fabric, it hid the nerve center of Devine's operation. Fed by illicit database connections and lenses hidden in the nooks and crannies of the vertiginous mansion, the AI data-gathering system matched every face to an identity and that identity to every digital impression it had ever made. It augmented Devine's roaring frontal lobe, cold and preternaturally powered, all-seeing and psychopathically efficient.

Once the system had your biometrics captured, there was no way to stop it chainsawing through your tree rings. Evan's Woolrich button-up and Joey's poplin blouse sported discreet lab-engineered patterns designed to disrupt machine-vision algorithms, rendering them indiscernible to surveillance lenses. This was a formality. At regular intervals, Joey ensured that any digital crumbs they might leave behind proliferated into a hydra head of gnashing dead ends.

"*—no, no, no,*" the voice, now taunting. *"Let's waddle forward together at the pace of eighty-seven-percent agreement, leaving no peer-reviewed Ph.D. behind."*

The double architectural doors at the end of the hall seemed to recede as they approached. A drumroll of tapping dress shoes and then an assistant type shot through and skittered past them, chest heaving, nostril flanges pinked to a pre-cry hue. Ejected from the room after her, an incomprehensible burst of glossolalia heavy on fricatives.

They neared the double doors. Or drew farther away from them.

At last they arrived and stepped through, the heat of a not-yet-visible fire whooshing across their cheeks. The massive master suite telescoped into view—dedicated foyer, condo-size coat closet, en suite office with three easels holding partial Renaissance still lifes, *paintus interruptus.* As they passed a hanging bronze mirror, Evan checked his six from force of habit. Behind him, Joey looked wan but her eyes were focused. Faintest sparkle of sweat at her hairline.

Eyes lowered, two more staff members scampered past, gripping mops and sloshing buckets of water. Evan proceeded, more of the suite drawing into view.

Behind a funeral veil of a wrought-iron screen, a curtain of deep orange wobbled in the massive hearth, throwing sparks and the delicious singed aroma of endangered Brazilian ironwood. Other powerful scents proliferated—cigarette smoke, expensive perfume, dog shit. A tattoo rig lay abandoned, scattered at the edge of a shag rug. Before the fireplace, a cuboid glass table trapped a naked male mannequin twisted in anguish, an art piece Devine enjoyed resting his heels upon. Something crashed into the stone rise above the hearth, and remnants of a crystal glass tinkled down onto the silk splash rug, a sharp-toothed rain.

Next a few desks drew into sight, manned by interchangeable assistants with laptops and briefcases and phones. And then the bed, an Alaskan king with pristine white sheets, across which a half-disrobed young woman sprawled like a low-rent silent-movie starlet.

At last there in the corner, Luke Devine paced, wearing boxers and black socks and an untucked oxford shirt, his hair swirled up around the thinning spot that floated on his crown like a yarmulke or monk's tonsure. He looked like a caught-out paramour in a well-made play or the Little Prince on a bender. Purer-than-baby-blue eyes, frosted like ice, peered out from his doll's face. He was looking right at Evan and Joey and not at them at all.

"—dancing like puppets to algorithms, tearing one another apart, competing to prove they're the very, very *best* at being manipulated." Devine's upper lip snarled up with Rottweilerian derision, a plastic ripple in that smooth, smooth face. "I mean, I get it, you've got to give the monkeys something to do." He washed a delicate hand back and forth above the floor, indicating—Evan assumed—the world of men. "But then you have to rule over monkeys and that gets trying, doesn't it?"

Evan said, "It does."

"Know who's winning? Whoever has the biggest team of lawyers and lobbyists. The Goliaths capable of achieving regulatory capture. It's over."

Evan said, "Till David finds the right stone."

"There are no Davids anymore. Just sheep bleating for a golden calf."

Two steps to Evan's right and one step back, Joey stood poleaxed on her feet and he thought, *You asked for this.*

He tilted his head toward the love seats and the fireplace. "Over there," he told Joey, not ungently.

She hustled out of the line of fire.

Devine approached Evan, his words coming fast, belt-fed rounds. "The only way a law holds down there is because of invisible hands moving up here." He fluttered said hands. "Know what it comes down to? Strong men saying no. And I'm saying fucking *no.* You know how many people comprehend the need for that anymore?"

"Not many," Evan said. "What's that Macallan you drink? Spanish oak casks?"

Devine swayed on his feet, eyes jerking. His brain was on fire, roaring like a coal engine. "The Number Six."

"Get it."

An odd little black box appeared in Devine's hand, a close-up magic trick. He clicked the solitary button and spoke into the box and to the seated assistants at the same time, the word going forth, omnipotent and omnipresent: "Fetch Macallan Number Six."

Evan leaned toward Rawlings and said, quietly, "First aim is to get him settled and keep him alive. I don't give a shit if he winds up with a headache for a month. We've gotta get him down and we've gotta get him hydrated. Fetch lactated Ringer's solution and a line."

Rawlings nodded once and spoke into his wrist: "Hydro kit to lion's den."

Devine had closed his eyes and turned his face to the banks of light streaming through the White House–esque radius windows, basking in the warmth. His eyelids flickered as if in REM, moist pink lips twitching to the side.

"Devine," Evan said. *"Luke."*

"It's you," the woman—Monica—remarked to Evan, rolling languidly in the sheets. She wore a micromini skirt and conspicuous vixen-red panties. The plackets of her unbuttoned blouse balanced in artful opposition along her sumptuously sloped midline, every breath promising a wardrobe malfunction. "It's whatshisname."

She'd nearly been forgotten. Such was the power of Devine's verbal fire hose, sufficient to occlude a vamping damsel poured over a mattress.

Evan said, "Ma'am."

Devine swung to face her, his diminutive form boyish in his socks, his head cocked like a ridgeback's. Pivoting silently, he noticed where she was looking and followed her gaze across the room, tracing a straight line to Evan.

Devine's pupils dilated and then suddenly contracted, fixing on Evan. "Mr. Nowhere Man."

It was as though Devine's brain were running five minutes ahead of reality; he had registered Monica way back then but hadn't caught up to Evan's presence until this moment. Evan imagined the contoured landscapes of Luke's mind, all those pits and crevices to fall into.

"Why are your pants off?" Evan asked.

Devine looked down. "I don't know."

Devine stumbled closer, kicking over a champagne bucket that held, improbably, an upside-down bowling pin.

"Let's slow you down some," Evan said.

Luke blinked five times rapidly. "Whatever for?"

Evan looked past him to Monica.

"You all right?"

"I don't know," she breathed. "A bit drunk and my ears are exhausted and . . . and. . . ."

"No, she's not," Luke said. "She's off behind the eyes and she witnessed something awful. I can't deal with this kind of shit so you have to get her to tell you so *you* can handle—"

"Devine," Evan said. "*Quiet.*"

He returned focus to the young woman on the bed. She gulped in air once, twice. Her eyes looked haunted, pupils dilated from whatever she'd been engaging with.

"You saw something," Evan told her, moving from question to statement. "Something bad."

"They just, like, *set* on her," Monica said, dreamily. "I have a bad feeling about . . ."

"They?" Evan said. "Who?"

"There was a pack, a pack of guys. It was before . . . Oh, Jesus." Covering her mouth, she hurried across the bedroom, her shirt flapping ridiculously, and stumbled through a door that Evan didn't remember being there a moment ago. The clink of a toilet lid thrown up, sounds of fruitful retching.

Devine had locked on to Joey standing over by the fire, noticing her for the first time. "Who are you?"

Evan said, "With me."

"I don't know you." To Evan: "I don't know her. And she's here. Uninvited."

"I assumed you'd be capable of contending with her," Evan said.

Devine nibbled at his inner cheek repetitively. Back to Joey: "If you're going to stay, whoever you are, understand a few things. If you lie or seek to manipulate me one inch, I will dismember your mind. You're what? Seventeen? Eighteen? Your prefrontal cortex isn't even fully myelinated. I know, I know—you're skilled, you're tough, you're nobody's fool. But the way you stand, legs loose, don't know where to put your arms, like you don't have a place in the world. And that perky little suit, trying so, so hard. Dressing for the role. But even though it fits, it still doesn't, not really, am I right?"

Joey looked at Evan, her eyes flared. She sipped in a breath.

He tore his gaze away from her. Leaving her on her own.

"You're a loner," Devine told her. "Difficulty making and holding friends, no parents to speak of, at least any worth anything. Unwanted. An Orphan, just like him."

Evan didn't defend. He didn't protect. She'd said she was ready. Now she had to earn it.

"That diamond around your neck, a little rich for your trailer-park blood, isn't it?" Devine said in a low purr. "A gift? From whom?" His gaze drifted from her to Evan and back once more. "Your shoulders cant toward him submissively. Your eyes search for his help, his approval. You care for him. And him for you. If you fuck with me, here inside my domain, I will use that against you, understand?"

Evan thought, *Don't give anything to him.*

He kept staring at Devine. It took everything he had. He couldn't see Joey's face. He didn't know if her lips were trembling or if her cheeks had colored or if she was about to break. Devine's glare at her was hard, reptilian.

The pause drew out and out. Evan felt his molars grind.

At last Joey's voice sailed over, cool as a jazz riff. "Understood."

A half-second pause. And then Devine exhaled through his teeth, the menace evaporating from his face. He came back into another version of himself, bouncing on his feet, eyes darting for the next distraction to take on.

An assistant flew in, toting a bottle, nearly skidding out on a patch of—dog piss? water? champagne? A crash would have cost thousands of dollars of alcohol.

Devine tossed the flute aside—*smash, tinkle*—and snatched the Macallan out of the young man's hands.

Evan said, "Take a settling sip, and—"

Devine gulped down a fourth of the bottle. Rawlings's hand had raised itself to grind the blond bristles at the flare of his crew cut. He seemed to realize he was literally palm-smacking his forehead and dropped the pose quickly.

Devine leaned closer to Evan, his forehead bulging with terrifying power, his breath fumes. "We have to reverse the Tower of Babel." He was pleading now, eyes bloodshot, cartoonishly bulging. Evan had forgotten how those probing eyes could feel, violating and potent. Devine's loose fist hovered before him, as if he could barely restrain it from snarling into Evan's shirt. "We're all gibbering past each other."

"Devine," Evan said, "if you want my help, you have to cede operational control to me here at the house."

Devine's head retracted on his neck. "Cede control to you? Some street operator?" He spit the words. "You don't have an inkling of what I have to do to keep myself on the rails. And you, all of you, should be grateful I'm willing to do it." Now with menace: "Because you have *no idea* what I'd be like if I didn't."

Evan put twenty-five percent testiness into his voice: "Cede."

"You want to give *me* orders? A control freak with OCD roar-roar-roaring in your brain? Fuck off."

Evan said, "Okay."

He jerked his head at Joey, plucked his gun out of Rawlings's hand, and started out.

Rawlings said, "Let's just hang on," but Evan ignored him.

"That's it, is it?" Luke bellowed after him. "The great Nowhere Man, afraid to speak his real name, scuttling out with his tail tucked?"

Joey hustled to catch up, moving at Evan's side, breathing hard. They walked out of the master suite and down the hall.

"Can't take a little heat?" Devine drifted after them, twenty feet behind, words sharp with disdain. "Scared to play in the chaos, sit at the big-stakes table?"

Unrushed, Evan crossed the landing, started down the grand curve of the staircase. Joey's legs blurred, her carriage stiff, her stare fixed ahead.

"Go on, then! Get out! Back to your squalid little missions, your gutter games, shooting marbles in an alley."

Devine had his hands on the rail of the banister above, screaming down at them over the rush of the waterfall. Below, Keshishian and the guards waited in a loose cluster, a command without a commander.

Evan kept on. Down the stairs. Onto the vast marble plain of the foyer.

Past the waterfall feature, toward the towering front door, Kesh and the guards already parting to make way for his and Joey's egress, pleading in their eyes: *Don't leave us here with him.*

And then Devine shouted, "Wait!"

The word rang off the hard floors, doubled back off the high, high ceiling.

Evan halted. He did not turn around. Joey was two steps ahead now. She pivoted and looked back at him. He could see she was rattled, that she could practically taste the freedom of the porch. The silence drew out, broken only by the white-noise rush of tumbling water.

Devine's words wafted down: "I'm sorry. Okay? I'm sorry."

From the quaver in his voice, Evan knew he meant it.

"Just . . . come back. Come back a moment."

Still Evan faced the door, and Joey's eyes were on him and so were the guards', everyone statue-garden suspended, stunned by Devine's concession.

Evan turned around.

He looked up at Devine floating above, a crazed Juliet. Devine cleared his throat. His mouth bunched and bunched again, as if trying to clear a logjam, the words for once not ejecting with manic dexterity. *"Please."*

Evan's chin gave the slightest dip. Calmly, he started back upstairs.

By the time he and Joey reached the landing, Devine had receded into the master suite.

Evan entered the bedroom, Joey resuming her place by the hearth. At their return, Rawlings heaved a sigh of relief. On the floor at his feet was an old-fashioned black doctor's bag.

Devine was pacing in tight circles, draining what remained of the scotch straight from the bottle. He finally halted, bottle swaying at his side, his torso swaying along with it. For a few seconds he listed on his feet, nearly pitching over. And then he did.

His knees struck the floor and he was vomiting prodigiously, action-painter swaths across the marble, his hands tracing patterns in the finger paint of his bile—Van Gogh's pyrotechnic stars, Byron's cloudless climes, Schumann's Florestanian virtuosity. Tears beaded at the corners of his eyes, springing fully formed as if pushed through the skin itself.

That was good. He needed to purge all the poison.

He groped blindly for his black box, found it, thumbed the button. "Have the maids—bedroom—"

More retching, now unyielding. He looked even more diminutive on the floor, his slender torso, the wreath of soft blond hair around that shiny pate.

Evan crouched before him. "You're not in control, Devine."

Devine laughed. "You think *this* is out of control?" He shoved himself up to sit, wiping his chin, eyes suddenly hard and lucid. "You're like everyone else. You want all the brilliance with none of the mess."

Staff ran in, more mops, more buckets.

"You want me to help the girl," Evan said. "You want me to help you. Then cede."

Devine glared at him, a wild-eyed stare presaging a violent outburst. Evan met it, unblinking. At last a change rippled across Devine's face. He stood up, steady on his feet, abruptly sober. He wiped the bile from his mouth and stared at Evan. "Do. Your. Worst."

Evan walked to the doctor's bag, opened it, and got to work spiking a 1,000 ml bag.

He approached Devine, Ringer's solution and IV needle in hand. He stopped in front of Devine, crowding his space. "Give up the vein."

Devine hesitated. Then he swallowed, cuffed his sleeve twice, and proffered his arm, baring the median antecubital vein.

Evan sank the catheter. Devine didn't flinch. He didn't even blink.

Evan handed the bag to Rawlings. "Take him into the other room."

"Don't you dare," Devine said, "ask my men to lay hands on me."

"Then decree it," Evan said.

"Why?"

"I need space from you and your mouth. So I can fucking think." Evan nodded at the door.

Devine's nostrils quivered. He drew himself up onto his heels, an erect dancer's posture, suddenly elegant, even dignified. "Ten minutes. Ten minutes and we'll resume. Then you'll see. Then you'll fucking see who's in control."

Shoulders pinned back, each movement precise, he glided from the master suite, Rawlings in his wake.

A click as the double doors parted and then swung shut.

A moment of quiet.

Evan exhaled.

The bathroom door opened and Monica stumbled out. Streaks of vomit marred her now-buttoned shirt, untucked to cover the negligible entirety of her micromini skirt. She swayed on bare feet, eyes downcast, her manner confessional.

"There was a girl," she said. "And I left her to them."

13

Who's in Control

Monica sat on the bed, shoulders drooped, picking at an already bleeding cuticle. Her pupils were blown shark-wide, her mind coming in and out from a cocktail of drugs, booze, and trauma. "What if she's dead? If she's dead is it my fault?"

Evan crouched before her but at some distance. He'd trawled a sheet across her lap, covering the flash of red lace between her legs. She'd stammered out a few mosaic pieces, but he was still coaxing the full picture into view.

She lifted a hand, swept up a lock of California Dreamin' blond hair. "But I had to get here. I had to."

"Because you were hired to get here for sex?" Evan asked.

"Uh, *yeah*." She sucked at the nail bed of her thumb, breath hitching. "But I didn't want to. Because— It was so terrible— Was feeling guilty. 'Cuz the girl on the subway."

"Why didn't you just leave here?"

"Dunno." She chewed a puffy lip that was slightly cracked. "I didn't want to miss out."

"On what?"

She looked around. Sprawl of marble floor. French wallpaper on an accent wall. Vaulted ceiling painted heavenly white. "This, I guess."

Across the room behind him, he could hear Joey exhale. She was sitting in the love seat by the hearth, just her and the trapped mannequin before the demonic blaze. Sweat glistened across the bridge of her nose. Along the facing wall, the several mute assistants manning phones and computers at their stations pretended not to exist.

Evan turned back to Monica. "Tell me again about the young woman. You said she was around twenty?"

"They just carried her off. Like a drunk girl at a club. Her leg was like . . ." Monica extended a slender leg from beneath the sheet, let the foot dangle in the air. "It's all I could see of her. They were mobbed all around her, like the whaddayacallits around, like, the president?"

"Bodyguards. How many men?"

"Four. There were four."

"How old?"

"Dunno. Boy-men. Like college, you know? But not— They didn't seem the type."

"Would you recognize them if you saw them again?"

"No. No." She shook her head rapidly, childish. "They had caps on low, like baseball caps? With the flat brims? And it was so fast and I was outside the train and I . . . and I . . ." Her face contorted violently, an ugly-cry twist, and she breathed shallowly, fighting off the memory or a panic attack or both. "I didn't know. I thought they were gonna help her but by the time I *saw*-saw them . . . And I didn't want to yell for help in case . . ."

"In case what?"

She gasped in a breath, steadied herself. "In case they came after me, too. And besides, what if it was nothing? What if it turns out to be . . . ?"

"What time what this?"

"Midnightish. I was running late. I couldn't miss it."

"Couldn't miss what?"

"The helicopter. The one he sent to pick me up."

"What stop was it? Where they carried her off?"

"A Hundred and Twenty-Fifth Street. I had to switch lines, so— Yeah, yeah, definitely One Twenty-Fifth."

Evan shot a look over his shoulder at Joey. She already knew: *Pull surveillance footage.* Her laptop was out on the ledge of her thighs, resting across the light gray wool of her trousers. She sliced her joined fingers back and forth horizontally, mouthed at him: *No signal.*

Monica slumped back, spine curved, head lolling dreamily. "You asked if he hurt me. The guy who lives here. Luke? If he had, what would you've done?"

"Proved that he did," Evan said. "Then killed him."

Her face snapped forward, wearing a grin.

But he wasn't smiling.

Her expression dropped.

Evan said to the interchangeable assistants, "Get Ms. . . . ?"

"Monica," she slurred. "I'm Monica."

"Please get Ms. Monica any medical attention she might need. And a car back to the city."

Rawlings materialized once more at Evan's back. "Mr. Devine is ready to receive you in the drawing room."

14
Break Point

An endless mahogany bar, bookcases, and wainscoting fringed the vast drawing room. Dominating one wall was a huge pencil-and-watercolor portrait of the great Lebanese writer, calligraphed lines of poetry rendered in flowing black: YOUR PAIN IS THE BREAKING OF THE SHELL THAT ENCLOSES YOUR UNDERSTANDING.

Devine stood waiting behind the bar wearing a wrinkleless linen suit, comb marks in his fresh-showered hair, an exemplar of composure. His pallor was fine, his face snake-oil smooth. He didn't look beat-up in the least. He might've just strolled in from a week at the spa.

Evan watched him. Closely.

Devine perched his hands on the bar. "May I offer you something?"

Beside the Kauffman Luxury Vintage, Evan's favorite liquid on the planet, a fluted bottle of Chopin Family Reserve stood proudly on the rise of shelves. The extra-rare young-potato vodka had been rested for two years in half-century-old Polish oak barrels.

Touch of earth, touch of sweetness, and a lingering, warm finish as smooth as a sleight of hand.

Evan pointed. "Neat. Chilled."

From the neighboring barstool, Joey gave him a nervous look. Aside from the three of them, the drawing room was empty.

Evan said, "She'll have an Aperol spritz."

Joey's eyebrows conveyed dismay but she kept her mouth shut. Two cold-air diffusers spun the scent of desert rose through the room. Rawlings caught Evan's eye, gave a tiny nod, and withdrew.

Devine poured two fingers of Chopin into a chilled snifter. Then he fixed Joey's drink in a balloon glass, showcasing the vibrant orange. Equal parts prosecco and Aperol, splash of soda water, large clear ice cubes.

"Aren't you having anything?" Evan asked.

"I am," Devine said, "the picture of temperance." He reached beneath the bar, came up with a gleaming black humidor. The lid lifted, emitting a breath of leather, leaf, and spice. Withdrawing two Romeo y Julietas, he walked a long, long way to the bar's service entrance at the end, exited, and huffed down into one of two facing leather armchairs. Between them sat a low bar cart with a lace metal fringe, laden with smoking accoutrements.

Evan joined him, removing his label, moistening the tip, and opting for a wedge cut. He lit his cigar with a stick of cedar lining from a box which he ignited with a struck match.

Over at the bar, Joey watched breathlessly. She sipped her drink, her face contorting in a microexpression of disgust from the bitterness, and set it carefully back down.

Devine lit up from a triple-jet torch, drew in a puff, and leaned back, crossing his legs to expose a sockless ankle and the sleek tan sole of a size 7 saffiano-leather loafer. "Well?"

"I need to go look into something," Evan said.

"The damsel in distress?"

"Yes."

"The girl the girl saw."

"Yes. But I can't leave you here unsupervised."

"Why not?"

"You know why not. Or you wouldn't have called me."

Devine sipped at his cigar and settled back once more, thin arm dangling at his side, smoke wisping from the down-tilted cherry. "Forgetting your Sun Tzu already? 'Pretend arrogance and encourage inferiority.'" The red-and-gold label glinted. "I've granted *momentary* control to you here at the estate." The faintest wobble modulated his voice, the first indication of internal pressure since his reemergence. "What is it precisely that you are asking for?"

"Why did you call me, Devine?"

Luke sucked the cigar, popped his lips, shot a ring through a ring. "To settle me down. I'm settled. So." A regal tip of his head. "I thank you."

Evan pictured a young woman borne like a coffin off a midnight subway car, engulfed by a pride of predators. His patience was threadbare.

But he couldn't rush. Couldn't risk the damage an unhinged Luke Devine would wreak.

Resetting, he shuffled through dossiers, case files, and profiles in his mind, extracting personality traits, pressure points, angles of leverage. He revisited a sheikh with a propensity for trafficked girls whom he'd sunk beneath the aqua waters of Palm Jumeirah. A Texas heir to an oil fortune whom he'd considered putting a Nowhere Man round into. A beak from Eton with a proclivity for faglets whom he'd dispatched outside Goodhart House.

"The part of you that's blind is running you right now," Evan told him. "And it's gonna run you straight onto infantry pikes. From here? Your options get worse. The fallout gets worse."

The snifter had already warmed against Evan's palm, the subtle aroma dissipated. He swirled the vodka in the wide bowl, gave a sip. Off the broad rim, the Chopin bum-rushed his palate like a 'roided-up forward pack of ruggers.

Devine wore a faint non-smile, a forked vein prominent in his forehead. Pressure building within. "Last chance to grab the deal of deals. Quite the sales pitch."

"Why did you call me, Devine?"

A shit-eating beam. "Can't I just want to see an old friend?"

"Do you even know what a friend is?"

"Sure I do. Someone who can keep up. Someone who can thrust and parry. Someone who knows . . ." The rarest hitch, a hint of emotion lurking deep beneath the surface, a poignant memory flung up.

"Knows what?" Evan pressed.

"Knows precisely what your favorite drink is." His eyes, wistful from some remembered kindness. "And how to serve it."

"That's all cute," Evan said. "But you're compromised like this. You're gonna step on your own dick and start a coup in Africa or release intel on the VP."

"I told you about the VP?"

"Yes," Evan said.

"Hmm. Well, circumspection can be overrated."

"If only there were a memorable adage about valor and discretion."

Devine bobbed forward, tapped the ash from his cigar. "I won't start any fires that don't need to burn."

"There is a young woman out there at risk and the longer I have to deal with you, the more danger she may be in."

"If she's not already dead," Devine said, and Evan resisted the urge to lean forward and snap the slender stalk of his neck.

Receding into the bar, Joey continued to read the room perfectly, listening attentively but not invasively. She smoothed her poplin blouse, crossed her legs high, showing a modest stripe of stockinged ankle. With her elbow on the bar and her crisply elegant bearing, she looked capable of headlining an M&A deal for a Wall Street white-shoe firm. A flash of proudness caught Evan by surprise.

Devine scraped his tongue along his front teeth. "When I'm in this state, I don't miss a thing." He flourished his black box, a nice bit of theater. "Who'd you like to talk to in order to assuage your fears? Prime minister of Germany? President of the Hague's ICC? Newly implanted director of the NIH? I'd offer up the president"—a wicked smirk—"but she and I aren't on the best of terms lately."

Evan held his cigar forked between index and middle fingers, angled upward. He'd taken two puffs and would not require a whole lot more.

Devine's lips twitched. "On occasion I imbibe and let my mind gallop and blow out pressure valves to keep the mental machinery clear." A fissure emerged in his eye, bleeding through the sclera. Evan watched it expand in real time. And yet Devine's mask remained perfectly intact, his serpent's tongue eloquent as ever. "But when it comes to what matters? When I *decide* to be focused? I am perfectly—*perfectly*—in control."

There it was. The break point.

Evan took his last pull on the cigar, let the smoke sheet from the side of his mouth. "In control?"

Devine's pupils jittered and he started to reply but Evan bulldozed over him.

"Your nonverbal tells are all over the place, you're smoking your cigar like a rube—label on, lit with butane, angled downward, tapping the ash like a chain-smoker—and you misquoted Sun Tzu. You've given up two unforced errors"—he allowed the briefest pause so he could watch Devine compute, that mighty brain rewinding and catching the duo of reveals: that he had dirt on the vice president and that he'd installed the new puppet head of the NIH—"you showed me the sole of your foot—try that in a Middle East negotiation—you served me vodka in a snifter—barbaric—and you poured the lady an Aperol spritz without an orange-slice garnish, like some barback on a Caribbean booze cruise." Evan's voice was low, steady, mechanical, unremitting. "You are acting like a slob. Ostentatious, flashy, showing off, misstep after misstep. Manic enough to think you can solve the world."

Evan watched Devine's face change, the muscles loosening of their own volition, those peaked cheeks going slack as the realization roosted inside him. He'd hit Devine hard, stunned him into submissiveness, but his state was fragile and new and would shatter into something else if tapped too hard.

"Why did you call me, Devine?"

The slightest tremor surfaced, wobbling a postage-stamp-size patch of skin beneath Devine's right eye. His lips parted. Nothing came out but a dry rasp of air.

"Why did you call me?"

Devine was on the verge of going either way, steel emerging in the set of his mouth as he regrouped, that big brain tornado-churning, but he hadn't put his mask back together, not fully, not yet. He wet his lips. Hesitated.

"Say it, motherfucker."

Joey's words came low and hard and her voice had not a tremor of anything but precisely the right amount of street.

Devine's head snapped over to her and for an instant, Evan couldn't believe she'd spoken either. She remained poised on her stool, elbow resting on the polished mahogany, legs crossed, giving up not an inch.

Devine looked at his cigar as if it had just appeared in his hand, tilting downward so the burn crept up the interior, scorching the leaf. He came back to Evan, his demeanor off-kilter. He looked punch-stunned, shuddered like a boxer off a hard cross. He dropped the cigar into the ashtray, his gaze creeping past Evan's ridiculous snifter to meet his eyes, and for the first time Evan had seen, he was laid open, vulnerable as a child.

"I . . ." His voice failed. He cleared his throat, began again. "I need your help."

Evan extended his arm, palm out. "Cede."

Devine looked from Evan's hand to the black box at his side. He picked it up, considered it. And then held it across the low bar cart, smoke from the crushed cigar winding around his wrist.

Evan reached to take it but there was a tug, Devine's hand still holding on.

Evan waited.

Devine swallowed once, hard, and relinquished it. "I cede."

Evan held his attention on him, spoke sideways to Joey. "Please pour him two fingers of a low, deep bourbon."

With a single swift motion, Joey vaulted over the bar. She dolloped two fingers of Blanton's Black Label, the Japanese export, into a crosshatch rocks glass. Leaping back over, she strolled across to them and proffered the glass to Devine on a slight tilt. He looked up at her. She looked down. He took it. Contemplated the spirit within.

"I've been swimming in too many different information silos," he confessed quietly. "Western European conservatives. Geoengineers and crypto-anarchists. Pan-African socialists. Evangelical intellectuals. Hellenic philosophers. Talmudic scholars." He fluttered his fingers, as if airing out his thoughts. "And they clash like the gods of old. Fighting it out inside me. So many mythoi, so many systems of meaning. They don't commune with one another. Most of them don't even try. I go through door after door. And come back speaking in tongues."

"So you drink gallons of booze and pop pills."

"'The road of excess leads to the palace of wisdom.'"

"A proverb of Hell."

Devine's pupils dilated nearly imperceptibly as he took in Evan more fully, a pellet of trust conferred for the shared reference. He gazed down into his glass, his face looking suddenly unkempt. Fair eyebrows ruffled, popped blood vessels in his cheeks, ghostly bruises beneath his eyes. The glass of bourbon Joey had poured was still untouched, a good sign that he was indeed coming down.

"How can I know what's enough if I don't know what's too much?" Devine asked. "In order to feed it?"

It, Evan thought. *His mind.*

He said, "Let's get you out of your brain and into your body."

Devine's lips pressed together, amused. "But I can't defend myself there."

"That is," Evan said, "precisely the point."

15
Please Help

The world was out of focus. Anca lay on the warped and splintery exposed plywood of the empty room, drooling, her head drug-thick, stuffed with cotton. Amoeba patches of extant carpet blotted the floor like oil slicks. She was no longer naked, her dress torn and rammed on backward. No underwear. Vague recollections tickled her brain stem—crawling from the tub, finding her dress balled up against the wall like a worn rag, dragging it over her sweat-sticky skin. She stared uncomprehendingly at the ripped cotton fabric splayed out to one side, a crumpled angel wing. The cheery feminine design, tiny lilies against cornflower blue, seemed incomprehensible. No sign of the coat she'd been wearing on the subway, nor the wallet in its pocket, nor her backpack, nor her keys, nor her laminated seizure plan. A stinging scrape at the back of her neck suggested a burn from the yarn lanyard's being ripped off.

She rolled onto her back, pain erupting through her hips and hamstrings from when her legs had been twisted this way and that. Excruciating pressure in her lower abdomen, burning like an infected bladder at the point of bursting. The ache of bruised internal tissue stole her breath. Faceless others had been inside her body when she hadn't even been home inside that body, and the violation of that, the absolute horror, she could not begin to comprehend, let alone contain inside her mortal flesh.

She forced her eyes to focus. Ceiling spots bulged low like udders, and the room smelled appallingly, a barnyard funk. An empty jug of hydrogen peroxide lay toppled on the floor beside her, next to a crumpled pack of Winston cigarettes, an uncapped black Magic Marker, and a ski mask that made her rib cage contract with terror. A ratty pink couch missing a cushion slumped against one wall. Centered in the sparse room was a bare mattress with a ticking stripe pattern on a cheap metal bed frame, horrifying and utilitarian. The smell of the mattress still roosted in her nasal cavities from when her face had been pressed into the polyester. Mold and musk marinated in salt leaked from her tear ducts.

The pain.

Oh, the pain.

Too great to comprehend, too great to mourn, too great even to feel.

She summoned scripture on suffering, James 1: 2–4 and a favorite, Romans 8:18, but they didn't speak to her. They lay flat, words on an imagined page. Eyes clenched, arms hugging her stomach, she reached for the small, still voice instead and it came as it always did.

It's okay, daughter. Be here now. And I will be with you. And we shall bear this together.

On her feet, staggering to the door, scruffy with flakes of red paint, the inset pane security-barred and smudged to opaqueness. It scraped open. Wet stairs rose to the sidewalk—a basement apartment. Smoggy daylight above, late afternoon tilting to dusk. She staggered up from the underworld, the reek of sewage and rotten vegetables pressing in at her. Her tattered dress flapped, caught on the rusted handrail, tugged free. An immense moving truck blotted out the sky. Wind gusted in her face. The city screamed and rattled as it did.

Please Help

Stumbling up the block, her dress slapping at the back of her thigh. Her iPhone, miraculously still in the patch pocket. She reached around to the dress front, lifted the device before her, but her face was so battered the phone didn't recognize her. She couldn't summon the six-digit code. Her legs buckled and she gripped a metal rail.

A construction worker looked up from a jackhammer with a gapped domino smile. "Rough night, honey?"

When he met her wounded human gaze, chagrin rippled his features, transforming him again to a son, a husband, a father. How thin the line was between the sacred and the profane.

"Want me to call someone?" He set down the jackhammer and moved toward her, rough hands swinging on burly arms.

Fear spiked through her. She backed away and hustled off. Burning intensified with each step, hydrogen peroxide against worn-raw flesh, a chemical intrusion atop the others. She tumbled into a Pret a Manger, the door jangling loudly. A long line, folks replenishing for the commute home, tapping at phones, earpieces screwed into their skulls, separate from her, one another, the world.

She bumped into someone. "Sorry, I'm—"

Voices of the displeased and inconvenienced crowded her ears.

"Quit fucking cutting."

"Hello! Hel*lo*! Is there a manager? Can someone handle this please?"

"Jesus Christ, this migrant city's gone Third World."

A kind-faced young woman, maybe Puerto Rican, came around the counter, her skin makeup-commercial dewy. "I'm sorry, ma'am, but you can't be in here. There's a drop-in center on One Twenty-Fifth—"

"I'm . . . not homeless . . ." Anca's voice, so small and meek. "I'm just . . . Will you help me?"

She lost time for a moment. And then her biceps was clenched roughly, a burly dishwasher at her side, and she was moved outside, the doors jangling with her expulsion. She tripped, skinned a knee and the heel of her hand.

She sat on the curb, feet in the gutter. Pedestrians swept behind her, a never-ending current, buzzing with conversations real and virtual. Taxis honked and vendors hawked and overhead a plane made screaming progress across the gray sky.

Fallen, she thought. *We are all so fallen.*

". . . someone please help . . ." Her plea, lost in the wash.

She still couldn't remember her phone code, tapping in familiar patterns and numbers, her shaking hands getting it wrong, wrong, wrong.

Realizing she could use the lock screen shortcut, she brought up her camera, swooped it around. Her left eyelid looked like a cockroach, the flesh of her chin abraded. Scrawled across her cheek in permanent marker, a single word.

WHORE.

Self-pity bloomed in her chest. She felt deeply sorry for herself and what she'd endured, and with that came overpowering sympathy for her broken self.

A bus roared past. Pulling her feet back from the commercial tires, drawing her legs close, she set her shuddering chin atop her knees. ". . . someone . . . please help . . ."

There were people all around.

But no one to hear.

16

The Brain

When Luke rose, he stood unsteadily, as if on new legs. Evan ground out his cigar and moved to his side, not offering his arm but not *not* offering it either. Luke reached over and gripped Evan's biceps to steady himself, the clasp of his fingers almost frail. It might have been the first time they ever touched.

They started out, Joey drawing into place behind them.

Evan spoke into the black box: "Rawlings to drawing room."

Rawlings was waiting at the door already, as if he'd been conjured into existence, and together they all moved up the hall, a procession of the dying king.

Evan said, "I need to get to the city. As quickly as possible."

"I'll have you choppered in." Devine sounded, finally and for once, exhausted.

Rawlings: "I thought you said helicopters aren't allowed in the city anymore."

"Not to pick up a call girl," Devine said. "But this is important. Get Vimal from the Eastern Region Helicopter Council on the phone. And who's that asshole at the FAA, the one with the diaper fetish?"

Rawlings said, "On it."

"You can leave from the helipad on the back lawn." Devine cleared his throat, his fragile grasp tightening on Evan's arm. "We'll put you down on the roof of the fucking UN if we need to."

"Not my style."

A wan grin. "Of course not."

Evan tilted his head to indicate Joey at their heels. "And I need to get her online."

Devine said, "For what?"

"To track the young woman who is in trouble."

"I need access," Joey said. "To the databases."

"Oh, young lady." Devine halted. "You don't understand what access is."

They were standing, Evan realized, before the scarlet door to the inner sanctum, the beehive of servers, sensors, and monitors that gobbled up metrics and trapped them quivering within digital spiderwebs that expanded through the known universe. Every algorithm, every AI neural network, every sniffed data packet or trafficked byte, every information unit parked on every large-scale database and big data warehouse on every encrypted network the wired world over.

Devine's tented fingers dimpled the plush fabric of the door. "You can't imagine the shiny toys I have in there."

"Bet I can," Joey said.

"Meet my most priceless achievement," Devine said. "The Brain." He leaned into his stiff arm and the door swept open.

Josephine gasped.

A few paces across plush maroon carpet waited a Faraday cage the size of a shipping container, its slatted gate invitingly ajar. Within, a keyboard and mouse rested on the blotterless desk before an unbroken image the size of a barn door. Code, recently cracked user accounts, and various camera angles covered the immense image on the screens. The surveillance footage was too much to take in all at once—every corner of Tartarus, various hacked corporate suites on various continents, Tokyo's Shibuya Crossing, and—Was that? Could it possibly be the White House Situation Room? Spare hard drives were shelved above on wall-mounted racks like pizzas awaiting delivery to a battalion or three, all available for a quick hot swap with any failing disks, thanks to RAID 10 fault tolerance and redundancy, along with full racks of preposterously fast SSDs for redundant cache.

They'd eased inside without realizing they had.

The padded door slurped shut behind them, a cushioned bank-vault hatch, Evan's ears popping with the shift in air pressure. Two baroque gilded chaise longues luxuriated on the high-pile carpet, backdropped by flocked scarlet wallpaper stippled with fleurs-de-lis.

Joey's mouth remained open, her face lit with Pre-Raphaelite rapture. The glow of the screen found purchase in her pupils as she stared into the eye of God. Her lips quivered. "Nice setup," she managed.

"The fate of the world can wait." Surprising gentleness touched Devine's voice. "Go find your girl, Mr. Nowhere."

Inside the scarlet room, Rawlings finished acclimating Joey to the system, a speedy process given her hockey-stick learning curve. Devine had retreated for a meal and a rest, handed off in the hallway to a trio of wary staff members who'd arrived and stared stupefied at the black box now residing in Evan's hand.

Joey rubbed her palms together, laced her fingers, twist-and-thrusted them into an eight-knuckle crack. "Hey X, I'm ready to launch here. Whaddaya say you click that black box and order me up some Dr Pepper and Red Vines?"

Evan held the black box out to her.

Joey tilted her head and Rawlings stared at it, confused.

"I don't get it," Joey said.

"You're promoted. You and Rawlings take over once I leave. The only way it'll work is if you're both in charge. Rawlings is smarter and more open than you think. And Rawlings? She's smarter and tougher than you think."

"I can't be in charge," Rawlings said, "of him."

"You can. I'm investing you both with that authority. If there's a problem you answer to me. And I will answer to him."

Evan shook the black box.

At the same time Joey and Rawlings reached for it. At the same time, they withdrew their hands, as if scalded.

Evan repressed a grin, set the black box down on the desk. They could fight over it later. He shot Joey a watch-your-ass look.

And walked out.

17

Fucking Dumb Move

Within channels of concrete, steel, and glass, Devine's helicopter carved through Manhattan. From his lofty perch, Evan surveyed the unearthly panorama through ancient eyes. Piloted on a man-made bird, he felt his bones thrum with the machinery encasing him. As the airborne dreamscape scrolled past at eye level, his gaze took in the denizens laboring within it, pallid faces at science-fiction cubicles, insects tending the hive. It seemed impossible that the crowded island hadn't sunk under the sheer mass of the towering habitats.

Joey's voice memo, routed through his RoamZone, poured into his earpiece, jarring him back into the present.

Hey, hey, that was so badass today, how you read, like, everything *and backed the guards down. And when you told him to get me the Aperol spritz I thought you were being all, "Lemme order for the little lady here." And I was secretly pissed off, I was, but you had a plan after all and that was so cool to watch you operate, like, firsthand. And you totally did it, X. You totally got to Devine.*

He texted: On the bird. Limit comms.

And how 'bout when I stepped in and was all like, "Say it, motherfucker." And that was totally the right timing, right? Like, serious movie moment.

Evan texted: We're in the middle of the mission. Let's not play our favorite hits.

. . .

Okay, but damn. And also? The whole cigar thing—

Evan swiped and tapped.

Notifications silenced.

The rotors beat the air, straining against shoulder bolts and load-bearing screws holding them improbably aloft. He closed his eyes, did several rounds of four-square breathing. Then swiped again.

Notifications allowed.

He texted: Update.

Rawlings is pretty cool, like you said. We're figuring out how to work with each other but the vibe is good, and I'm pretty sure he respects me. And they've given me unfettered access to this beast of an NAS in Devine's secret lair, which is, like, insanely incredible. No one should have this much access and this much power. The Brain can see everything. Which means, right now, I can see everything, so it's like, Orphan J at the helm of the free world. I'm really appreciative you gave me this opp—

Pause.

No, he texted. Update on the young woman who was taken from the subway.

. . .

Oh. Right. Sorry. Thought you wanted color commentary.

Never.

Fine. The surveillance cameras in the subway cars were blacked out. Not a coincidence. And whoever did it—it was spray-painted—knew how to not be seen. The cameras at 125th are glitchy as fuck—thanks, city budget—but I picked up a crew of guys flashing past an ATM camera on Saint Nicholas Avenue. And they're half carrying a girl, her arms over their shoulders, like she's super drunk. And no one really notices. They're just, like, carrying her off in the middle of a crowded city. It's super fucked up, X. Hard to watch.

Facial ID?

Too hard to see her. Visuals are grainy af. And they're, like, mobbed all around her. Smart fuckers, they have baseball caps pulled down low so I can't grab features, nothing. Sending you screen grabs now.

Here they came: *Bink. Bink. Bink.*

He pictured Joey dictating into her phone, fingers fluttering across the keyboard, the massive screen heaving up data at her command.

I tracked them across a kilometer and change via internet-connected cameras, traffic lights, store security, lobby cams, all that, but I lost them on this half block. Hang on, sending map.

Bink.

I'm still scraping the databases looking for cams registered within a five-block radius to see where they reappeared but NYC isn't at full Big Brother London yet so it's spotty going. Maybe the men doubled back with her. Maybe they took a route through a blind spot. Maybe they ducked into one of the buildings along the way or hopped into a car.

Evan clicked on several of the images and zoomed in. The resolution was terrible, as Joey had said. Four military-aged males in hats with flat brims worn low. Jeans, Nikes and Adidas, dark sweatshirts without logos. Because they were stumbling together and handing off the young woman, gait recognition was off the table. The young woman was barely visible, her lolling head a blur. In one freeze-frame, her wrist showed either a bracelet or a band of shadow. Another captured a length of her periwinkle dress. Evan enlarged the smeared face and the wrist and sent Joey the screenshots.

Crisp up pixelation with a digital de-blur tool. Maybe a bracelet? Same for the men's shoes. Let's see if any of the sneakers are collector's items, etc. Can you get a clearer image of the dress pattern, too? And her hair? Zoom in and check for tattoos?

A moment later, Joey's reply voice text came through: Already checked her face—no go. Hair is too blurry. No bracelet as far as I can tell. And the men's sneakers are basic. No visible tats. Here's the dress at higher res.

Bink.

The dress had cleaned up into a decent resolution, showing a pattern of tiny lilies.

Not particularly useful. He scrolled back to the woman being drag-carried off.

The pack-versus-prey image brought him back to the Trinitarios pursuing a young man with a severed arm.

He texted Joey: Update on Lesandro Candella.

. . .

Stable. Transferred from ICU to step-down
unit this am. I'm keeping an eye. Check it.

A link.

Evan clicked.

A security-camera view of Lesandro in a common area in the step-down unit, sitting in one of three aqua-green-vinyl-covered chairs near the nurses' station. He wore a hospital gown and slippers. His left arm terminated in a bulb of bandaging. His right hand was also swathed, the reattached finger held in place by a mechanical-looking splint that no doubt secured the pins. The injured hand was gripping something loosely.

A beige half-arm prosthetic.

It looked cheap and uncomfortable, a lowest-bidder fulfillment for the uninsured.

Lesandro held the detached prosthetic vertically before him, staring at the palm that stared back, the pose reminiscent of Hamlet's if Yorick's skull were replaced with a mannequin arm.

Lesandro looked utterly dejected. It was as if he was looking not at the arm but into the future and finding nothing there worth visiting. He sat so still Evan wondered if the footage was frozen, but a passerby made clear it was not.

After a moment, Lesandro rose and walked out of frame, the prosthetic swinging at his side.

Evan thought about Lesandro's first utterance when he was bleeding on the pavement, words emerging from the depth of life-altering shock: *My watch. I can't find my watch.*

Evan typed: Does he have insurance?

Now Joey switched to text: he works @ gamehut

So that's a no?

y, dum-dum thass no. he applied 4 a financial assistance installment plan from hospital

How much?

so far? 37k 4 arm. 54k 4 finger. w interest @ min payment itll b paid off in . . . hang on . . . 429 months.

Evan rubbed his eyes. With no insurance company to negotiate costs, Lesandro was bearing the full brunt of the not-so-free market.

Cover his expenses anonymously, he texted. Draw from the Luxembourg account, alias Timothy Rackley.

kk

The helicopter banked, lifting Evan's gorge, and he pocketed his RoamZone and tightened his grip on the harness.

They perched not on the roof of the UN but on the crumbling playground asphalt of a fenced-in Title I school, the surrounding streets not unlike the East Baltimore 'hood he'd come of age in. As he climbed out, ducking beneath the rotor wash, he spotted black and brown faces filling the windows of the nearest classroom. The sight brought him back to the Pride House Group Home, foster brothers all around, Evan one of the few white boys in the mix.

He gave a finger flare of a wave and the kids smiled big and waved back, a few jumping up and down on their chairs. A helo setting down on their basketball court might as well have been Santa landing on the roof.

Evan cut back to the subway station and retraced the route the young woman had been carried, skirting the edge of gentrified Art Deco refurbs. Big ugly residential buildings thrust up, interspersed with old-school tenements. Crammed streets, gridlocked traffic, plenty of sidewalk jostling. Check-cashing joints, bodegas, a ubiquitous Pret a Manger. Street vendors hocked busted watches and junk antiques on bedsheets unfurled across the sidewalk. Incense wafted into his face, seasoning the scent of halal-cart kebab. Five-foot-tall South American women sold mango on Popsicle sticks. Basement dry cleaners, cobbler shops, and braiding salons spoke to a vibrant belowground economy. A windowless van screeched up to the curb, and a young African man rolled up a cluster of knock-off Vuitton purses in a blanket like a giant joint and climbed in. The van made another pimp stop twenty feet up the street, vacuuming in another laborer working slave wages.

Evan came to the half block where the young woman and her

pack of kidnappers had evanesced. Slowing down, he examined stoops and balconies, storefronts and foyers. A night laborer with a jackhammer made unsteady progress against a sidewalk rippled by the unruly root of a honey locust. A giant moving van overspilled the bike lane, block letters screaming from the back: HOW'S MY DRIVING? CALL TO REPORT.

Evan cut around it, staying tight to a row of dilapidated brownstones, staring up at the sprawling limestone veined darkly with water infiltration. A drainpipe swung free, rotted through vertically like a slender canoe. The smell of garbage was strong on the air, singeing the back of his tongue.

Irregular movement on a subterranean stairwell drew his eye.

A tatter of fabric fluttering like a sniper's wind sock.

He felt it, an electrical surge at the base of his throat. He moved past the arrowhead fence tops hemming the subterranean level and eased down the slick concrete steps.

Snagged on a lifted splinter of rust from the handrail, the ribbon was no more than six inches long and half as wide. His heart rate ticked up as he reached to pull it free.

Tiny lilies against a blue background.

He stared down the half dozen steps to the barred door below. Set his jaw.

Descended.

Improbably, the door was unlocked. Someone had left in a hurry.

He tugged it open, the loose rubber sweep rasping against the ground.

The smell of mold rushed him, overpowering a chemical reek.

He stepped inside. Crappy subflooring, a few patches of carpet, a tragic pink couch, and a bed positioned in the center of the room like a prop. Or an instrument. In several spots, faint specklings of scarlet varnished the ticking stripes of the mattress.

His heartbeat quickened once more, though it remained shy of ninety.

Beside an empty jug of hydrogen peroxide, an uncapped black Magic Marker, and sundry other trash was a discarded ski mask.

He stared at it.

The missing eyes stared back.

Ominously, the door to the bathroom had been removed. He eased forward another few steps, clearing the sight lines beyond the tub. His boot nudged a splotch of carpet, and he looked down to see a silver-dollar-size impression indenting the stiff fibers, like the peg of a pogo stick. A tool? A weapon? The prong of a floor lamp?

A form cast a shadow across the doorway. "The fuck are you?"

At the threshold stood a ruinous woman, her face a Shar-Pei collapse of folds and smoker's wrinkles. Stained sweatpants, sweatshirt with matching stains, feet shoved into stretched-wide house slippers. Blond hair with startling black roots taken up in a ponytail, flares of wiry gray wisping out at the sides.

She scratched her thigh with the muzzle of a plasticky Kel-Tec 9-mil that looked like it hadn't been cleaned in generations. "This is my place."

"Doesn't look like you sleep here."

"Why do you care where I sleep, perv?" She waved the pistol vaguely in his direction. Her clothes carried the reek of recent cooking, onions and meat. "Comes with the apartment above."

"Yeah?" Evan said. "You rent this out?"

"Why? You lookin'?"

"I suppose I am. Looking."

"You're trespassing's what you are. Don't think I don't deal with tough guys."

"That who you rent to? Tough guys?"

"Not me. Guy who stays here does. Fucking dumb move, that was, me letting him stay here."

"Why's that?"

Easing inside, she tugged at her fatigued elastic waistband, let it snap back into place. "Not like I can report him, can I?"

Evan got it. "You're subletting, too."

"None of your fucking business what I do. I scramble like everyone else to afford to live in this fucking city. You wanna judge me?"

"No," Evan said. "Your guy, he sub-sublets a lot?"

"'Sublet' is a bit grand a term for what he does." She scoffed, her folds shifting, and waved her pistol around some more. "Put it this way. Turn on a black light in here, it'd look like a paintball fight."

"So he doesn't stay here?"

"Rarely. Runs his scams instead. Leaves me to clean up the messes. And there *are* messes." She might've been forty or seventy. What were once pretty sea-green eyes flashed out from the wreckage of her face; in their present context, they looked trapped. "But isn't that what we do? Clean up your messes?"

"I don't know. Is that what you do?"

"Why are you here?"

"Have some business with your subtenant."

"Osman? You gonna beat his ass?"

"Want me to?"

She considered, chewed a chapped lip.

"Where is he?" Evan asked.

"Where's he always." She jerked her chin. "Strip club across the street. Oh, I'm sorry. 'Sports bar.'" Somehow she managed to make air quotes even around the gun frame. "You'll recognize him. He's the smug fuck. Turkish or Armenian."

"Those are," Evan said, "not the same."

"No?"

"So I've been told." He edged toward her. If she did any more baton twirling with the 9-mil he was prepared to break her arm. But he'd prefer not to touch her.

Now she had the pistol pointed at his crotch. His patience was thinning.

"You should be careful," he said. "Any altercation could escalate into a gunfight."

"You're not packing." Clearly, she couldn't make out the ARES hidden in his appendix holster. "So how exactly's that gonna happen here?"

His hand shot out, stripped the crappy pistol from her. He dropped the magazine, caught it between the ring finger and middle finger of his right hand, and jacked the slide to clear the chamber. With his thumb, he flicked the rounds free from the mag one after another so they rained down across her long-suffering house slippers.

"Because," he said, "you brought a gun."

She'd withdrawn against the wall, hands flared in a show of passivity.

He brushed past her and up the stairs.

He stood on the sidewalk, breathing the layered air of the city at nightfall.

He glanced over at the HOW'S MY DRIVING? lettering on the back of the moving truck, ass-coverage for liability. Which likely meant further measures. He checked the rear bumper and around the brake lights to no avail. Circling the truck, he examined the grille next—nothing. Multiple tickets had yellowed beneath the wipers of the bug-splattered windshield; the truck had languished awhile in this spot. No obvious gear was suctioned to the glass. But there on the rearview mirror, forward-facing, was a shiny button dot of a lens, aimed just past where the stairs met the sidewalk. If the thugs and young woman had turned left out of the apartment, he'd be out of luck. But if they'd turned right, the surveillance camera might have captured them.

The moving truck, by definition mobile, wouldn't have shown up in Joey's geofenced search, which zeroed in on fixed cameras. He snapped a shot of the license plate, texted it to her with a brief description of what he needed.

Then he stepped to the edge of the curb and took in the street. A half block away, a Daisy Buchanan–green neon sign beckoned: THE VELVET KITTY.

Behind him, the woman stumbled up the stairs, breathing hard, slotting the reloaded mag back in the gun. She came at him with more bandido-waving. "You think you can just—"

He seized the Kel-Tec out of her flailing hand again, pocketed the mag, and checked the slide. Stepping off the curb, he dropped the pistol and heel-kicked it behind him down a storm drain.

Her screamed expletives accompanied him up the street all the way to the strip club.

18
Bad People

The bouncer looked appropriately menacing for the neighborhood, six foot six, shaved-tight red hair with a touch of curl at the top, sleeve tattoos. A massy torso, firm gut layered over muscle, and ears swollen into pretzels from multiple batterings filled out the stereotype.

His deep-set eyes, black in the dim light of the entry alcove, scanned Evan and didn't seem to like what they saw. "You gonna give us any trouble?"

"Not if no one deserves any."

"Not the right answer," the bouncer said. "The right answer is, 'No, sir.'" He leaned close, which meant leaning down, the scent of icy-menthol breath mints leaking through his teeth. "Because if any trouble gets started by anybody, it gets finished by me. Capiche?"

He looked as white as clotted cream, rendering the "capiche" inadvertently amusing.

Evan nodded. "Live by Velvet Kitty rules, die by Velvet Kitty rules."

A seahorse-shaped cast-iron pull handle nuzzled into the venerable wood of the front door. The bouncer snapped his gum, reached for it, and tugged ceremoniously, as if granting Evan access to a sacred chamber.

Smells assailed him as he entered—sugary perfume ineffectively deployed as deodorant, cigarette smoke borne on clothing, aerosolized glycols from the stage-adjacent haze machines. He stood in the shadows at the periphery to assess the place, note escape routes, identify makeshift weapons. A confusion of club-neon pinks and reds wireframed the stage and various pathways through the dim interior. Mounted flat-screens behind the bar ran NBA highlights and infomercials for walk-in bathtubs. A manager type with slicked-back hair worked over one of the plush booths with a wet vac, a background episode Evan did his best not to linger on. Pool balls clacked on a coin-fed seven-foot table, longneck bottles lining the rails, a boozy parapet. A scattering of regulars commanded what seemed to be their usual spots across barstools, haphazard four-tops, and spectator chairs lining the stage. From the banter he sensed they all knew one another too well, quirks and quotidian failings binding them together in shameful camaraderie.

A smudged whiteboard on an easel declaimed: NOW DANCING: BUBBLES!

Largely ignored by the crepuscular inhabitants, the aforenamed Bubbles chewed gum disconsolately and twerked onstage, her dimpled cheeks fluttering artlessly. Snaking a leg around the pole, she gave a workmanlike spin, her bleached split ends trawling the laminate floor. The haze machine issued a flatulent hiss, misting her like a smoked cocktail. A mindless pop song crackled through shitty speakers: *When ya call my name, 'ts-like a liddle prayer . . .*

Evan thought: *Ambience.*

"Where the fuck's Laeta?" someone at the pool table shouted, waving at the unmanned bar.

The manager powered down the wet vac. "Out back having a smoke. You can grab another bottle and leave cash on the bar but don't touch the hard stuff."

The manager scuttled out of the booth, cutting across the front of the stage. The haze dissipated, revealing Bubbles checking her iPhone. Evan pondered where it had been stored seconds earlier.

"We been over this, Rebecca," the manager snarled as he passed, "stay off your fucking phone onstage."

"I gotta check for the sitter."

"Babysitter," the manager said, gesturing at the sparse onlookers. "Sexy. Just—be a fucking professional." He pointed the wet vac at a stocky guy sitting with a friend at a prime table up front. "I told you, Osman, come eight o'clock, you're outta the VIP seats." He banged through a swinging door into the back, no doubt to decontaminate the wet vac.

Evan followed the aisle lighting to Osman's table, tugged back an empty chair, and sat. From here, a trail of red spots were visible along one of Bubbles-Rebecca's legs. Bedbug bites.

Osman wagged his head at Evan, tapped his knuckles on the wooden surface. "Help you?"

"Yes," Evan said. "Thanks for asking."

The floor-level VIP table was nestled into an alcove, backed by curved brass rails delineating the mezzanine level. Osman's pal sipped at a watery beverage the color of apple juice, maybe a 7 & 7, and the man himself had a Midori sour set before him, garnished with a cherry and a slice of lime. He was a good-looking guy, with powerful shoulders and thick hair, but rot tugged at his eyes and jawline, the lifestyle catching up. Shiny silver Western belt buckle, complementary mall boots, shirtsleeves cuffed to show off muscular, hairy forearms.

"The fuck kind of man cozies up to other men at a strip club?" Osman asked.

"The fuck kind of man drinks a Midori sour in public?"

He bugged his eyes at Evan and then looked at his friend, a theatrical show of disbelief. "Okay. So it's like that, then." He shouted toward the entrance: "Hey, Red Pony!"

But the door was shut, the bouncer outside in the wind. Osman glanced nervously at the rear room into which the manager had vanished. Bubbles was back on her phone. No one else seemed to give a shit.

Osman recalculated, refocused. "Don't fuck around here, pal. First of all, there are two of us."

Evan looked at the friend, who quickly took interest in his drink, using his double stir straws to chase what was left of the ice cubes in circles.

"And second? You don't want to mess with me. I deal with people, bad people, all the time."

"That's what I wanted to talk to you about."

"Yeah?" Osman leaned in. "What makes you think I'll answer?"

"Well," Evan said, "there are two ways we can approach that."

Osman put a perfect smile on display. "If you wanna scare me, you're gonna have to do better than that."

"Noted," Evan said. "You rent out your apartment there"—a flick of his hand in the rough direction—"by the night?"

Osman laughed mirthlessly, cocked his chair back, spread his hands again, looked at his mute friend. "So what?"

"Rent it for what?"

"What do I give a fuck? Whatever they need it for. Affairs. Orgies. Sometimes guys bring girls there, call girls, whatever."

"Girls against their will?"

"No business of mine, man. Someone makes a dumb choice, takes the wrong pill, gets touched in a bad place? I'm gonna wade into that shit? We're in a city of nine million people. I'm gonna, what? Do a full moral inventory of everyone before I conduct business? You do that?"

Evan said, "Yes."

Osman hoisted his drink, offered Evan his first-ever Midori toast. "Well, good on you, pal. Not all of us can be bighearted saviors. I'm just getting by, man, like everyone else."

"What if I told you a young woman was likely raped there last night?"

Osman pooched out his lips in a scowl, shrugged. "My dick's clean so I know *I* didn't do it. I just rent him the room now and then."

"Him," Evan said.

Osman spoke fast, trying to bury the blunder. "You gonna go after the company made the bed she was raped on, too? The guy sold the mattress?"

"No."

"So why you bustin' *my* balls?"

"Because," Evan said. "You can tell me who rented your place last night."

"No. I can't. It's, like, *anonymous*. And even if it wasn't, I'm a businessman. I make business arrangements. So a client lucked into an amenable situation last night. I'm gonna stick my neck out for some broad got herself into something she woke up the next morning and regretted? Why'm I gonna borrow trouble?"

"A young woman was hurt," Evan said. "There's a code."

"A code. A code?" Osman brayed laughter, jerked this thumb at his friend, who maintained steadfast scientific interest in his cocktail. "There is no fucking higher code. Not for me, not for you, and certainly not for some split tail who got what she—"

Evan's muscles moved so fast he nearly forgot that he'd commanded them to do so. By the time he caught up to them, he'd already kicked the chair out from under Osman and palmed the back of his head to hasten the slamming of his face into the table. Stripping the ridiculous belt from the loops of Osman's jeans, Evan nosed it through the buckle, fastened the noose over his neck, swept the free length of leather over a brass rail, and ratcheted him against the balustrade.

Osman spun in a kind of squat, heels poking at the floor, fingers scrabbling at the strip of leather throttling his windpipe. Gripping the end of the belt to maintain tension, Evan sat back down, the movement wrenching Osman up another few inches.

Evan turned coolly to face Osman's mute sidekick, who sat with his drink suspended halfway to his mouth, lips still ajar in anticipation of receiving the stir straws.

Evan said, "Go on."

The friend dropped his drink, shoved back from the table, and bolted. The rest of the place had stilled to take notice, but there was no dramatic record skip or adrenalized rubbernecking. These walls had seen a lot.

Blood clogged Osman's shattered nose, his eyes streaming, future bruising already stirring beneath the skin of his neck.

Evan leaned close. "You want me to act like I've got a code?" he said, in a low, calm voice. "Or act like I don't have one? Because I can do either."

"Code," Osman sputtered. "Code."

Evan let the man's weight pulley the belt an inch or two around the brass rail, allowing more weight to his legs. "Name," he said.

". . . Don't have . . . name. I . . . swear . . ."

Evan took back the slack he'd allowed. "How's he pay you?"

". . . tell you . . . anything . . . Just . . ." Osman's bulging eyes flicked over Evan's shoulder and he smiled, blood leaking into his mouth, outlining his incisors.

But Evan had already noted the heavy footsteps. The flight of the associate had alerted the bouncer. Red Pony conveyed his massive frame along the lit runway of the aisle, seemingly unrushed.

Bubbles used the interlude to sit on the stage and scroll through her phone. No sign of the manager; he was likely still unclogging the wet vac.

Comfortably sitting on his chair and racking Osman against the balustrade, Evan waited for the bouncer to arrive. No sneak attack, no sucker punch, just an overly confident sidling up with those Popeye arms crossed.

"Okay, chief. We talked about this, 'member?"

"I remember."

"There are two ways we can approach this."

"Hey," Evan said, "that's my line."

Osman sputtered and spun, spine corkscrewed, head crimped between the rails, soles shoved into the floor.

"Do you want to be happy?" the bouncer said. "Or you want to be right?"

"Right," Evan said. "I want to be right."

The bouncer leaned forward, cinched a lobster-claw hand around Evan's shoulder.

Maintaining his grip on the end of the belt, Evan drove the sole of his boot back, hammering the bouncer's shin, knocking his legs out from under him. The bouncer's shoes slipped on the slick laminate, his top-heavy form penduluming down, chest and chin cracking the floor simultaneously. Evan lifted his chair, spun it around, and set it down with the front rail across the back of the bouncer's neck, pinning his head to the floor. He'd miscalculated the height of the chair's crossbar by an eighth of an inch, so it dimpled the sausage roll of fat at the base of the guy's skull more aggressively than he'd intended.

Against the bar rails, Osman twisted, his neck grooved with fingernail scrapes.

Evan gave him back a few inches again. "How's he pay you?"

". . . through . . . VenSend . . . Show you . . . Just let me . . ." His hand fumbled at his trousers.

Evan reached instead and ripped the iPhone out, tearing the pocket. Beneath his chair, the bouncer drew wheezy breath. Resettling his weight on the chair, Evan nudged the phone to life, turned it to capture face ID, and shoved the screen in Osman's face. "Where?"

Panting, chest quivering, Osman punched at the screen, bringing up VenSend, a Solventry app complete with the omnipresent logo, that inane smiley-face daisy atop a stem. His thumb tapped at the screen until it showed a recent payment of $199 from YngTl69.

". . . him . . ." The word sandpapered through Osman's constricted throat, making Evan realize he'd unwittingly tightened his grip. ". . . all I know . . . swear . . . I . . ."

Evan released the belt. Osman toppled forward, banged off the table, and slid to the floor, gasping. Crawling away on elbows and knees, glistening strands of snot dangling from his face, he made meager progress.

Evan rose, lifting the crossbar of his chair from the back of the bouncer's neck. The crew around the pool table watched him silently, holding their cue sticks before them with the butts resting between their feet.

Evan nodded at them. They nodded back.

Bubbles-Rebecca looked up from her phone.

Evan said, "Ma'am."

She grinned. "Sir."

The rear door swung open, the manager launching through. He froze, taking in the tableau.

Evan nodded at Osman. "Wouldn't relinquish the VIP table."

The manager cleared his throat but no words came out.

Evan peeled a hundred from his money clip, set it on the edge of the stage before Rebecca. "For the sitter," he said, in a stage whisper.

She smiled again, twirled a lock of dehydrated hair around a finger.

The song had ended. The other patrons stayed motionless in their spots. Osman breathed wetly as he scraped his way across the floor. Evan stepped over him on his way out.

19

The Bronx Kill

Using a fake account under the name Jake Van Dorn, Evan rode an Uber Black north along Malcolm X Boulevard.

While he'd been busy playing tetherball with Osman's head, Joey had pwned the moving truck's surveillance camera. While the assailants had not shown up on the recordings, a few frames of footage had captured an injured young woman stumbling off the sidewalk a few paces to the right of the basement stairs. Flower-patterned dress in tatters, contusions everywhere, gaze hollow with shock. In Joey's capable hands, Devine's powerful facial-identification software had done its job.

Anca Dumitrescu, twenty-five years of age, no criminal record. Her place of employment, a Romanian Orthodox Church called Sfânta Maria, was in the Bronx, as well as her residential address, toward which Evan was currently beelining.

In Joey's adrenalized voice over the RoamZone, he could hear how shaken she was at the sight of the battered young woman. "I called the church, said I was a friend worried about her since she'd gone missing. And they were, like, really sweet and concerned. She shows up there every day, like, religiously—ha—but she didn't come this morning, didn't call in sick, nothing, and they couldn't reach her on the phone or at her place and they said that wasn't like her at all, that she's really professional and responsible and a really caring person. And, I mean, did you see her, X? She looks so broken. It's like some scene from a war or something. You have to find her. You have to get to her."

"I will."

The Escalade banked onto the Macombs Dam Bridge, its Gothic Revival abutments, latticework gates, and stone-end piers a perfect Early Republic collaboration of old-world beauty and new-world engineering.

"You jailbroke Osman's phone?" he asked.

Joey had texted a link to the purloined phone that Evan had opened, allowing her remote access. "Yep. Have everything downloaded here in Devine's creepy Orwell room. I'll turn that thing inside out."

Evan rolled down the window and flipped Osman's phone out onto the roadway.

"Cracking the VenSend database is gonna take some time," Joey continued. "We know about Solventry's encryptions and they've kept up with the race even after Allman's, uh, departure. But I left a few backdoors in the system so I'm already leapfrogging through their VPNs and proxies with various credentials. I'll pin down a physical address for YngTl69 within twenty-four hours at most."

"I need a vehicle," Evan said. "For base camp, mobile office—something comfortable. Can you have one meet me at Ms. Dumitrescu's address?"

"Okay, okay. Hang on." Muffled phone, then Joey saying: "What? He wants a car."

A voice replying in the background.

She came back to Evan: "Rawlings is asking if you want diplomatic plates."

Down below, the slate-green chop of the Harlem River surged south toward the narrow strait of the Bronx Kill.

Evan said, "Why the hell not."

Wanting to leave no trail even under an assumed name, Evan asked to be dropped off a half mile from Anca's apartment. It was hard to draw a full breath in the Bronx. Few public spaces, heavy concentrations of projects and run-down mid-rises, dark red brick buildings rising block after block, uniform as Legos. But the night streets burst with vibrancy and anything-goes possibility that made Evan feel at home. Food stalls flaunted gourmet opulence that could outclass any trendy SoHo brasserie—jerk chicken and Jamaican patties, rice and beans, empanadas and arepas. Body shops and coin laundries, bucket drumming and three-card monte, the pleasing duet of Puerto Rican Spanish harmonizing with Dominican patois.

A worn but stately walnut front door served as the exhausted gatekeeper for the five stories of crumbling brick that composed Anca Dumitrescu's building. The lock guard had been jimmied and remounted so many times that a half-inch gap exposed the dead bolt. Evan could have gotten through with a flathead screwdriver, but there was no need. He punched a random button on the call box, announced himself as a Solventry delivery man, and was buzzed through without a query.

The dusty transom leaked streetlight amber across the chipped tile foyer. Rickety doors guarded a tiny elevator that looked retro-fitted to the building, a taped sign reading CIRCUIT BREAKER OUT. WILL FIX IN A.M. To the right, a blocky wooden staircase rose through L turns and square landings, the banister polished by a century of hands. Evan made his way up, blading his body at intervals to let residents pass—a babushka with a kerchief framing her wizened face, a storm of boys with baseball gloves, a woman in an electric-blue bodycon latex dress hauling a folded shopping cart.

Reaching the third floor, he moved down the dim hall. A few of the apartments had doormats; others displayed plastic plants.

Number 33 had a simple wooden cross mounted above the peephole.

He knocked.

No answer.

Setting his ear to the door, he listened for signs of life within. Not even a vibration.

In his cargo pocket, the RoamZone gave its distinctive chime, caller ID showing Joey.

He answered: "Go."

"Okay, there's an incoming request for Devine and you put me and Rawlings in charge, so we're calling you."

"What is it?"

"Some plan afoot to short-sell the rial."

"Why are you bothering me with this?"

"Because supposedly it's a big deal. Something about undercutting Tehran? Looks like"—a rustle of paper—"the State Department is involved without being, like, *involved*-involved. And a bunch of Polish oligarchs want Devine to back it."

"What's Rawlings say?"

"Doesn't know. And we don't want to ask Devine obviously since he needs to, like, chillax and get his brain back online so he doesn't destroy the known universe."

"Then no."

"But it's supposed to counterbalance terrorism in the—"

"Joey. I'm busy. Let's not worry about the rial. Let's worry about Ms. Dumitrescu."

Movement at the far end of the hall drew his attention. Hanging up, he flattened to the door, an instinct to diminish profile.

Backlighting threw a stooped shadow forward from the landing, a distorted form stretching across the worn carpet of the corridor.

And then she stepped into view.

Anca Dumitrescu stumbled off the top step and leaned against a wall, clutching her lower stomach. She was missing one shoe, the exposed foot swollen, her shredded dress haphazardly shifted around her torso, barely covering her. One shoulder was bare, her elbow pinning the fabric to hide her breast. Left eye swollen nearly shut, scrapes and bruises marring her legs and arms, hazel-brown hair a matted tangle.

Had she *walked* here from Harlem?

Shouldering into the wall for support, she staggered up the corridor toward Evan, not seeming to note his presence. As she drew nearer, he could make out a word penned in Magic Marker across the abraded skin of her cheek.

WHORE.

Stepping away from the door, he faced her, showing his hands out in front of him, the least threatening posture he knew how to assume. Only the moment before she reached him did she register his presence.

Her head tilted back to take him in, cracked lips parting but making no sound.

She collapsed and he caught her as she fell, striking the door with his shoulder, the cross falling off its mount and coming apart on the floor.

20
Just the World

A blip of unconsciousness and then Anca's good eye opened, the other parting a slit. Evan sat on the floor cradling her awkwardly in his lap and she did a double take at his face and then shoved herself up and away from him. He stood back, giving her a five-foot standoff as she clawed her way up the wall to her feet.

The stained dress parted and he saw blood between her legs, dried on her inner thighs. The Ninth Commandment, *Always play offense,* spun into his mind and he grabbed for it to anchor himself. A murderous instinct seized him—to respond on her behalf, to act, to avenge—but he fought it down, entrapped it in a box with the broken Commandment, buried the box deep. No emotion was constructive right now except hers.

She drew herself erect, squared herself with heartbreaking dignity. "You were . . . waiting?"

"Yes."

"For me?"

"Yes."

She shivered against the cold. "Who are you?"

"I'm here to help."

"I didn't ask for your help." No accent, but she spoke with a formality that implied English as a second language.

"No," Evan said. "You didn't."

"So how . . ." Her trembling hand circled the air, drawing the words she couldn't form. She'd fallen out of time.

"What do you need?" Evan asked gently. "Right now."

She blinked at him. Soft, full face, broad nose, strong eyebrows topped with blunt bangs. In any other context, she would have looked youthful, but her eyes were ancient from what they'd seen.

She rested a palm against the door. ". . . to go inside."

"Okay."

"To be alone."

"Okay."

"And I need to not move. Just to—not move."

"Okay. Do you have a key?"

She patted at her thighs, one bare, the other curtained with a ragged fringe of fabric. She shook her head. "I don't have anything."

"May I pick the lock for you?"

She swayed on her feet, hugging herself around her midsection. "Please."

He extracted a triangle pick and tension wrench from his lower left cargo pocket, inserted them, and opened the door as easily as if he had a key.

She stared past the violated lock and across the threshold. "I'm that unsafe," she observed, nodding, agreeing with the words as she spoke them. "I've always been that unsafe."

"Right now you are safe," Evan said.

"I don't feel safe."

"I know." He held the door for her. "Where would you like me to be?"

Her gaze moved to him. It was as though she'd forgotten he was there. "Outside."

"I will wait," he said. "Right here."

She moved into the apartment, closed the door. The dead bolt clicked, and then came the rattle of the security chain.

He heard her collapse—the slap of her palm against the floor, the soft thump of her body.

Silence.

More silence.

And then a deep wail, a pained gasp, a brief paralyzed silence. And then keening.

Evan squatted outside the door.

He'd heard so much across his operational years, but he'd never heard sounds like the sounds she was making. His stomach twisted. Measuring his breaths, he rubbed his palm across the top of his head, realized he was doing it, stopped.

He summoned the Fourth Commandment: *Never make it personal.* Useless. He discarded it, too.

The sobs kept on.

Quietly, he lowered himself down and sat with his back to the door. The hall smelled damp, wet boots and soggy carpet.

He waited. Waited some more.

She quieted. He could hear her wet breathing. Her fingernails scraping lightly across the floor. Then silence.

More waiting.

"Are you still there?" Her voice—hoarse but steadier.

"I am."

"The cross fell. From my door. I would like the pieces."

"Okay."

A moment later, there was a jangling of the chain. The door opened a gap. Her hand squirmed through. He passed her the two wooden pieces.

The door closed. Relocked.

A gentle thunk. Her forehead leaning against the far side of the door? Once again he could make out her breathing.

"What . . ." A screeching intake of air interrupted her, an echo of a sob. When she spoke again, she'd gathered herself. ". . . do I do now?"

"Maybe a sip of water?"

"Yes," she said. "Yes."

Footsteps trailed away.

A full two minutes passed.

Footsteps trailed back.

Again her voice came through the door. "Now . . . now what?"

"Medical attention would be helpful."

"*No,*" she said. "I don't want anyone looking at me."

"Okay." For a time he breathed along with her. "Are you cold?"

"Yes. I am cold. So very cold."

"Maybe find some other clothes to warm up. Put the dress and your shoe in a bag."

"A bag?"

"Like a grocery bag."

This time she was gone for longer.

And then: "I have on a sweater. And a wool skirt. And my trench coat. And boots."

"Are you still cold?"

"Yes. So cold. I need . . . I need to shower."

"You might . . . You might consider not doing that right now."

"Why not?"

"In case you decide to do a rape kit." The harshness of the term landed bruisingly, even on his own ears. "Forensics, I mean."

"For what?"

He pictured that entry in Osman's phone, YngTl69, who'd sublet the basement apartment in which she'd been raped. "To help catch those who did this to you."

"This is the world," she said. "Sin and separation. This is just the world."

"I'm not sure I understand."

"I don't need a kit. I don't need to catch anyone. Those who did this to me, they will answer."

He was confused. "How?"

"In the only way that matters."

He chewed his lower lip and sat with that a moment. "Either way you might reconsider going to the hospital. You can decide there what you want to do. And what you don't want to do."

Silence.

"I can call an ambulance."

"No ambulance," she said. "I can't afford an ambulance."

"I can pay for it."

"No," she said. "Thank you. But no."

"A taxi."

Sudden impatience: "Who are you?"

"Evan. My name is Evan."

"That's not what I'm asking. Why are you . . . ? How did you find me?"

"A young woman from the subway saw what happened to you."

Long pause. "Miniskirt. Gentle eyes."

"Yes. She told a . . . someone and they told me. An associate tracked you through surveillance cameras. And I followed the trail."

"Why?"

"Because I help people."

The door pulled open, snapping the security chain taut, showing a sliver of face. Intense light blue eyes, sweat-tangled bangs, permanent-markered expletive scrawled on her cheek. "Why do you help people?"

"It's just what I do."

Her eyes flicked down. "There is blood. On your shirt."

He followed her gaze. Sure enough, a thin trailing pattern of crimson drops marred the side of his shirt, elongated downward in the direction it had erupted from Osman's nose.

"Yes," Evan said. "Sorry."

She studied him. "Can I trust you?"

"I don't know," he said. "*Can* you trust me?"

Her stare picked across his face. "My condition forces me to have radical trust at inconvenient times. But I've never experienced a time this inconvenient."

He wondered at her condition but now was not the moment to ask. He shuffled through acceptable responses, but his repertoire had nothing for this. He considered the little speech he sometimes gave, found it just as useless. It came apart like the last two Commandments, but he reassembled it, turned it on its head.

"Ms. Dumitrescu," he said, softly. "I'd like you to look at me. Look at me closely. And ask yourself: Do I look dangerous?"

"Yes," she breathed.

"Dangerous to *you*?"

She didn't speak but he felt the sharp intelligence of her gaze as it X-rayed him. She was looking straight through the mask of his features right into him. She searched. Searched some more.

The door closed firmly in his face.

The chain unhooked.

It opened.

Anca stepped forth.

21
Disembodied

Taz Kinley seemed like a quiet kid but no one understood that he wasn't quiet at all, not on the inside. They had all sorts of names for what went on in his head—ADHD, oppositional-defiant disorder, conduct disorder, Asperger's.

He had his own term for it, too: MDB.

Modern Dude Brain.

His favorite diagnosis that they'd saddled him with was NOS. *Not Otherwise Specified.* Which meant, of course, that *they*—the schools, the social workers, the court-appointed shrinks, the parole officers—couldn't figure out what the fuck he was.

The thing was, all these creaking old people and institutions and IRL meat puppets were sawdust and rot. They were long past their expiration date and didn't even know it. What was real was what was happening in cyberspace right now beneath his thumbs.

His favorite porn site had been using AI lately to play with eye width and lash length of the skanks to maximize that hentai look, getting it just right so middle-aged normies wouldn't be sure whether they should fuck them or protect them and man, if only you could do both. His favorite underground MMA fighter had bitten off the nose of a Bulgarian challenger in an unregulated match broadcast on an onion link on Tor, unleashing a world of meme-ery: THE NOSE KNOWS! OH NOSE! VALDEMMART! Taz hadn't seen original footage yet, was still chasing it around behind the content regulators but, in a way, if you've seen the memes you've seen the real thing.

He was hungry, wanted Chipotle, the most chow for the cheapest price. Money was running low again—it always did—which is why he'd assembled the posse.

Finn-Finn stuck his phone under Taz's nose and snickered, breath like baloney. "Check it, man." He tittered. "Check it, check it."

They were on a street, dodging pedestrians and shooting through scaffolding sheds on the sidewalks because Manhattan was forever under construction, tearing itself apart and putting itself back together.

Huddled between his phone and Taz, Finn-Finn banged into one of the uprights with his shoulder, spun around, bulled through a baby stroller, found himself on the receiving end of a stream of mama-bear invective in Korean. Cost of doing business in the big bad city.

"Hang on, hang on." Finn-Finn said everything twice. Thus his name.

The fucking MMA fight wasn't loading on the onion site Taz had found on the /r/mma subreddit, the linked site buffering forever, and he figured it'd come up *Content Removed, Copyright Infringed,* or *Blocked Due to Community Standards.* An alert pinged in—his Adderall dealer sharing a link to the red room of a surgeon in Estonia with unusual proclivities but Taz was pretty sure it was a scam since you had to pay to watch it.

They were crossing a street.

Finally Finn-Finn's shit had loaded, a radical prank site, some hammered college kid in Dublin squatting over his sleeping roommate's head, and Taz shoved him away, said, "Seen it."

"What? What is it?" Big Dumb Mikey, always one step behind, tugged at Finn-Finn's elbow. Mikey had the backpack filled with research supplies, an ironic seafoam-green JanSport, not one of the trendy Herschels the private-school turds flaunted.

B-Roll glided next to them like a shark. B-Roll had been through some fucked-up shit with his single mom's boyfriends growing up, so you never messed with him. He didn't remember anything before the age of eight. Paranoid, too, used burner cell phones and shit, stayed off the radar.

B-Roll's face was severe, skin stretched tight over bone, intense eyes, and he was wiry as fuck, all muscle. His schlong curved to the right like a banana, thus Banana-Man to B-Man to B-Roll 'cuz B-Roll was more derogatory, like what you'd leave on the cutting-room floor. He worked food-service gigs here and there, had told Taz once that all you need to have as many pretty girls as you want is a server apron and access to roofies and once you got good, you didn't even need roofies no more. He could go forever, B-Roll, especially when he was snorting star-spangled powder.

Taz was at the pickup counter now and some porker in a Hermione tie was staring at him and he thought about her in a position from a video he'd seen last week and it was sorta gross and sorta not and he said, "Huhn?"

"I said"—she checked the receipt stapled to the bag again, all bitchy—"'Taz Kinley.'"

"Yeup."

She handed him his order, a weighty fucking bag. That was Chipotle, didn't jew you on the burrito size. Swinging away, face to phone, he checked RedLite. RedLite had his algo down from his viewing history, the best, best shit, and they were sending him alerts of girls with *Big Naturals and Big Butts* and corsets pinching their waists in between the bulges down to nothing.

He had guac on his cheek—weird—and no napkins. His burrito was mostly done and he was way full and it looked like he'd eaten a ton of chips, too. Finn-Finn and Mikey were laughing at something on TikTok and B-Roll was glaring all psycho at the tools waiting in line, his jaw clenched like a steroidal pit bull.

The juicy corset parade was interrupted by a commercial for some new first-person-shooter game from Solventry, *Karnage* something, a total *CoD* rip-off they'd been shoving at him through the pre-rolls 24/7. *Skip Ads in 3 . . . 2 . . . 1.* He cleared it and then on the other screen the MMA fight loaded—finally!—not the whole thing but the clip where his boy leaned over the pinned Bulgarian and ripped his fucking nose off, not just the cap, the whole fucking thing, like a Viking savage, and spit it at the crowd.

Taz felt the sidewalk beneath his sneaks now, Finn-Finn at his side, and he vaguely sensed Mikey and B-Roll behind him but if not they had location services on and they'd figure it out if they got separated. He'd forgotten where they were going and he stopped, people streaming around him at the crosswalk.

Finn-Finn said, "Mikey's place, Mikey's place," and pointed.

Taz said, "'N'kay."

A woman walked past them and she had a flowy skirt under her coat and long blond hair that caught in the wind and she was dressed all classy, a hostess at a nice restaurant or a sales chick at one of the fancy boutiques on Madison maybe, and he thought about what it might be like to be with a real woman like her with smart eyeglasses and a career. Taz was only nineteen, the youngest of the posse by a full six months, but the possibility of a woman like her had been exhausted before he even had a chance. It had been bled out of the world he'd been raised in. Everything was fake, wasn't it? Makeup and filters and outrage and spin-spin-spin. Aside from when they went hunting, circling up prey, he barely knew where he was in space anymore—what city block, what his body was doing, where he was on the sliding scale between the inside of his mind and the world outside it. The singularity was already here, man. He was disembodied. And more powerful for it.

People pretended to get all judgy about how things were. It was so funny. For as long as Taz could remember he'd never felt like a kid. The world didn't treat them like kids, never had. There weren't children, not in this era. They were a future voting bloc, a key consumer base, drivers of content and culture. It was so funny, how the gray suits ceded all the power to them, politicians citing favorite rappers, corps scrambling to pump out shows and commercials using last week's slang, teachers fighting to stay relevant and "connect." And none of it worked. They were already dinosaur bones, never even saw the comet coming.

When the walls came tumbling down, they'd be the ones who'd rule the rubble, him and Finn-Finn, Mikey and B-Roll. No rules and no laws suited them just fine. They knew how to play the game the way everyone else in the world was playing it, the way it had always been played with lesser tools and shorter reach. Taz was happy to let the i-bankers and social justice warriors fight and fret over the bullshit while his posse picked over the battlefield, stripping Rolexes and NFT drop mints from the dead bodies.

"Didja see this? Didja?" Mikey now showing him some argument on Twitter or X or whatever it was now, drone footage of a tank getting blown up somewhere and a heat signature stumbling out and giving the drone the finger an instant before white phosphorous ammo lit his ass up. And what was so funny was that they blurred out the guy's hand flipping the bird but still showed his body getting demolished.

"Kewl," Taz said. "'S like that new Solventry game, whatzit-called?"

B-Roll said, *"Kings of Karnage."*

Finn-Finn said, *"KoK. WoW. CoD.* Nothing's new. Nothing's ever new."

An email alert sailed in from Taz's stupid HVAC tech vocational-training class. He'd enrolled to get reduced sentencing for another public-intoxication charge, but they didn't always check if you finished. All of a sudden they were at Mikey's place.

Mikey's mom was gone—she was always working or servicing some booty call—and there was shit for food but Mikey found a half sleeve of stale mini-doughnuts and they scarfed them down except for B-Roll who was following some low-sugar podcaster diet this month.

Taz waved at Mikey's backpack. "'S do it."

Mikey dumped out the contents. A bunch of big blocky high-school yearbooks, old-fashioned ones they could thumb through and mark up like catalogs. Mikey worked as a school janitor now and then, shit work that moved him around from high school to high school. But it gave him access and he could lift new yearbooks from the school libraries. They passed them around, leafed through the pages.

They were shopping. Shopping for the hunt. They needed new product to pound and they couldn't count on stumbling upon some half-conscious chick on the 2 line again.

There were so many hot girls. It was endless, just like online. The posse could slide into their DMs, sweet-talk them into a meetup. Most of them were willing if B-Roll threw a little bad-boy charm. They were starved for attention. A shocking number would do whatever for money. Taz paid them with dummy Amazon or Solventry gift cards they stole from the Starbucks rack and wrote *$500* on in Magic Marker.

Mikey was scritching at his scraggly beard over that gross dried-out port-wine stain and marking pages like a maniac. He had a low bar, so they had to veto him all the time. They had to maintain standards.

B-Roll said, "I'm sick of these high-school girls. Let's get some real talent." He preferred adult services on Craigslist and places like that.

"Nn-nn," Taz said. "You can tell professionals. Need freshies."

Professionals scared Taz. They scared all of them except for B-Roll since B-Roll was B-Roll. Women who actually *chose* to do this shit could be intimidating. They didn't give a fuck. He'd tried a few times with them, couldn't get it up.

He grabbed the next yearbook. There was a pretty Latina girl at Forest Hills but who the fuck wanted to go to Queens. Still, she might be worth it. She'd played Belle in *Beauty and the Beast,* her costume dress showing a decent amount of tit.

What was weird though was his stare kept going to her face. Reminded him of a girl he went to elementary school with. Early playdates. He'd line up his toy soldiers across shoeboxes and building blocks and they'd lie on their stomachs like snipers and shoot them down with rubber bands. Blanca. That was her name. Blanca. She'd kissed him on the cheek once and he'd run into the bathroom and hid until her mom picked her up. And this girl? Belle from *Beauty and the Beast*? Her name was Blanca, too!

A pulse of confusion seized his chest. He didn't like the sensation. What the posse did was what everyone had always done. He'd read the stuff plenty, ancient Romans and Ottoman concubines and

Persian harems. Nordic mofos used to rape and pillage. Explorers went to foreign lands, shot the men, humped native women. Morality was just a trend. Like years from now if the burning-planet-methane-reductionist-animal-rights whackadoodles had their way maybe no one would eat meat. And everyone would have to care about microaggressions against chickens.

He laughed out loud. He was a modern philosopher, Taz was. No one had ever thought about the world the way he had.

With a Magic Marker he circled Blanca's picture but then he had, like, a horror-movie brain glitch, a strobe memory of Other Blanca and him side by side on his carpet, pinging the toy soldiers, high-fiving when a rubber band clipped one of the little plastic men. Her eyes used to smile, too, when she did, tiny crinkles at the edges. She wore pink hair ties, had a spout ponytail high on her head like Ariana Grande. They'd been for-real friends, even after she kissed him on the cheek that one time.

Now he felt sick. Had he eaten? That burrito. He'd eaten a burrito. Maybe his meds were making him nauseated. Light-headed, too. He'd forgotten the afternoon dose. Withdrawal? He was sick of sitting here on the futon with potato-chip crumbs and these yearbooks scattered everywhere.

That's what he'd do then. He'd palm one of Mikey's mom's clonidines from her medicine cabinet.

He was standing over the toilet now, taking a leak.

His face in the mirror looked dead blank, like the Michael Myers mask from *Halloween*. He barely recognized himself anymore when he wasn't in a selfie pose. He stuck out his tongue, tried to make his eyes look less shallow. His eyebrows, the color of wet sand, were as thick as Band-Aids. They sagged around the outer edges of his eyes, making him look soft, forever apologetic. He pulled up his shirt, snuck a peek at the cartoon Tasmanian Devil tat Mikey had started on his chest with his cousin Dirty Pete's iron. Mikey's goat skull was great, detail work like a Tony Hawk, so he'd claimed he knew what he was doing, learned from Dirty Pete who'd learned in the pen, but they'd been rolling on molly that night so the Tasmanian Devil outline looked more like an elephant footprint. He said his cousin would fix it for three hundred but who the fuck had three hundo for Dirty Pete to turn an elephant footprint into a Tasmanian Devil?

By the time he came out, Mikey had downloaded the new *Karnage* game, the boys splayed across the futon and floor, shooting motherfuckers up like the guy from the tank who'd flipped off the drone.

A dozen or so yearbook pages had been torn out, the ones with the circled school pictures stacked on the coffee table. Some promising options. They'd start outreach in the morning. Blanca from Forest Hills was right on top.

Another wave of light-headedness swept through Taz. Had he taken the clonidine or not? Did it matter if he took another or would that cross bad with the Seroquel and Adderall?

That picture of Blanca stared up at him. He didn't like how it made him feel. Not at all.

The vape pen in his pocket loaded with indica might make things right for him. He took a hit. He might as well rest up and chill.

They had to go hunting in the morning.

22
Lucky

In the Uber, Anca stared out the window, one hand curled around her seat belt. Sitting beside her, Evan could make out part of her face in the window's reflection. Stone expression, lips a grim line, hair a tangled mess.

The driver wore a backward snap cap with PLAYAH embroidered on the front panel, shocks of Irish red hair curling out over his ears like wings. His head bopped to softly played rap.

Anca squirmed, pressing her legs together, and hunched forward. She glanced over at him, winced, said quietly, "Itches."

Evan said, "Almost there."

Her face spasmed in grief but she fought it down. "I'm not married." Her voice was hoarse, so quiet he could barely hear her. "I have not been with a man."

Her hands gripped her thighs, squeezing, her knuckles bloodless.

He understood. There weren't words for something like this. There just weren't.

He said, "I'm very sorry."

"I want to shower. I can't stand this another second."

"Would you like to turn back?"

She stared out the window. "Will they poke and prod me?"

"They won't do anything you don't allow."

"That is not," she said, "the question I asked."

"They will want to examine you," Evan said. "And treat you."

Her nod came like a quiver. "Will they make me . . . describe what happened?"

"Yes. They will ask. And if you decide to do a kit—"

"I can't put it into words. It was impossible, what happened to me." She turned away again. Passing lights strobed across her reflection. "But of course, everything is possible."

The driver was in a world of his own, softly mouthing lyrics from the next track, something about putting Molly all in her champagne.

Evan said, "Maybe you can describe it from outside yourself."

Her head snapped over. "Outside myself?"

"Like a scene. Like something that happened to someone else."

"Do you think you have any right, in any way," and here she clenched her teeth with Eastern European ire, "any right to tell me *anything* right now?"

"No," Evan said.

"What then? More instructions that you're going to explain to me about what I need to do next?"

"No," Evan said.

"Good. Okay, then. I don't want to hear your advice." She turned back to her window, her fist shoved to her mouth.

The Uber accelerated and then braked hard, a horn blaring at them for five full seconds. Their driver cut hard around a corner, and then they skimmed beneath streetlights, bars of shadow flurrying across them.

Anca squeezed her legs together again, curled into herself.

To give her some privacy, Evan focused on the back of the driver's seat, the bopping PLAYAH cap. *Took her home, 'n' I enjoyed that, she ain't even know it.*

Anca's gaze remained fixed out the window. When she spoke, her cracked voice surprised him: "She sat on the subway. And clutched the laminated seizure plan to her belly."

Evan waited. Gave her room.

She swallowed dryly. Reset herself.

"A mother with children. That's who she looked for first. The second choice was a couple with kids. Third: a woman, alone." At last she turned her bruised face to him. "She needed to pay attention for when it started to happen."

Anca sat on the crinkly paper of the ER exam-room table. A face peered back from the mirror across, blanched and haggard in the harsh fluorescent lighting. They'd taken photos of her bruises already and the word written across her face. The gap in her hospital gown revealed the dick drawn in Magic Marker across her shoulder blade, a match for the image tagging the subway car she'd been kidnapped out of. She'd required a hand mirror to see it. The sexual-assault nurse examiner had helped her try to wash it off, along with the *WHORE* on her cheek; though faded, stains still stood out against the reddened skin.

She could scrub all she wanted but it would always be there on that spot, an echo of her violation, a reminder that her own skin could be claimed by someone else.

They were talking now, the nurse, police officer, social worker, a resident, and the attending. It was crowded, little space, no privacy. The examination and treatment had been excruciating, though as compassionate as possible. Out in the hall, the statue of Saint Bernadette Soubirous kneeling with a rosary laced across her praying hands had given Anca some comfort. Thank goodness for Catholic hospitals.

They'd started her on antibiotics to protect against . . . diseases. She'd be HIV-tested in seventy-two hours. She had needed stitches. Significant signs of tearing and—and—

Her thoughts left her.

Aches and burns. Aside from that, only numbness. Flesh deadened from local anesthetics, mind deadened from Ativan, her body an empty warehouse. She wondered if she would ever feel again, feel any sensation not inflicted by *them*, something, anything to let her know she was alive—the burn of an oven-hot pan against her palm, a glob of peanut butter trudging down her throat, the ache in her hip flexors from standing during the Paschal Vigil.

I will never be the same again, she told herself.

It was something she needed to hear. She gave herself permission to be here in this anguish in this moment, to let it have as much of her as it demanded.

The police officer jotted more notes for her report, the physician more notes for his chart. Proficiency on display. They'd done this plenty. Words from the discussion flew in at her.

She'd been soaked in hydrogen peroxide to remove traces of DNA. The officer said, not quite sufficiently under her breath, "What kind of fucking brain do you have to have to do that to someone." A bite mark on Anca's shoulder was not sufficiently defined to make a dental impression from. Opiates had shown up on the urine tox screen. While the doctor couldn't say for sure, she'd seen this before and guessed it was something like four to five hundred micrograms of fentanyl. The officer said they'd been seeing lots of overdoses and Anca was lucky it hadn't been more.

Lucky.

They couldn't risk stepping on the fentanyl with morphine, so they'd injected her with ketorolac for the pain. Her body, punctured again and again, shot through with things that did not belong inside her. Plus the hours lost to trauma meant she'd missed two doses of meds. Along with stress and sleep deprivation that meant she had an uptick of seizures to look forward to. She crossed herself, wound up with her hands hugging opposite shoulders, hunched. She did not want to be inside her body. It was not safe in here.

"Please excuse me. I need a moment." Anca slid off the exam table gingerly and walked up the hall. Entering the bathroom, she gathered two hand towels, lowered the toilet seat, and sat. Burying her face in the wad of paper, she wept silently.

Five minutes passed. Perhaps ten.

There came a banging at the door. "C'mon, lady! Hurry up in there!"

She lifted her face. The paper towels were soaked through. Her throat clutched and her mouth gasp-gasp-gasped, still in sobbing rhythm. It took a moment longer but she found her voice: "Yes, yes. I'm sorry. Just a moment."

"You're not the only one has to take a shit."

"I'm sorry," she said. "I'm sorry."

The orange plastic chair in the waiting room seemed designed for maximum discomfort. Evan wasn't sure whether Anca would want his help or not after her examination but wanted to be here in the event that she did.

Aside from being maximally gentle, he was unsure how to interact with her.

This was always the hardest part for him, understanding the cryptic give-and-take of human engagement, the strange language of intimacy. For the first time in a while, he thought of Mia Hall, the district attorney who lived downstairs from him at Castle Heights. She always seemed to know what to do in situations like these. A devoted single mother to her ten-year-old boy, Peter, she was warm and tough, maternal and strong, and had an unerring sense of how to provide care and comfort. Evan wasn't great at care and comfort. He was much better at inflicting retribution.

Through the big window behind the intake desks, he'd seen Anca limp to the bathroom. She'd looked on the verge of crumbling. If she broke down in front of him, was he supposed to hug her? Ask if she wanted to be hugged? Or not intrude on her personal space no matter what? Mia would've just gone over and done whatever the right Mia thing was to do. Last month he'd discovered that she'd been temporarily assigned to the San Francisco DA's office to help them dig out from a heavy workload. Between that and her extended trip back East with Peter, he hadn't seen her in months. He wished she were here as a resource for Anca.

But.

As great as Mia was, she couldn't do what Candy McClure could do.

Barring Evan, Candy—aka Orphan V—was the deadliest graduate of the Program. Soon enough, he would go on the hunt for

YngTl69 and his associates. When he did, he had to ensure that Anca was protected.

Candy McClure knew how to break any of the 206 bones in the human body. Knew how to dissolve them, too, in concentrated sulfuric acid. She'd once attempted to liquefy Evan, back when he'd first escaped the Orphan Program and she'd been tasked with neutralizing him. Instead she'd fallen atop her plastic jugs herself in the course of a fight between them, turning her back into a topography of scar tissue. Aside from the mottled skin she kept hidden beneath high-backed dresses, she was a flawless physical specimen, able to render men paralyzed through soft power or hard.

He dialed, waiting through several rings.

And then she answered: "X."

Wind whipped across the receiver. She was driving with her windows rolled down. Or galloping on a horse. Or perhaps riding a precision-guided missile. With Candy, one never quite knew.

"I'm in the Bronx," Evan said. "I need you here to help watch a woman."

"Why the hell," Candy said, "do *I* have to watch her?"

Evan told her.

"Be there tomorrow," Candy said.

Bundled in a too-big sweater and a coat, damp hair finger-combed into place, Anca stood before Evan, her arms crossed low over her midsection. The staff had shown her to a care room with a shower, a merciful bit of privacy after all she'd been through. She'd taken nearly a half hour to clean herself.

He'd waited dutifully in the hall.

As he'd advised, she'd requested her ER medical report, and handed it to him wordlessly on her way into the care room. He'd reviewed it, her degradation spelled out in antiseptic clinical phrasing. He'd read plenty of forensic files and after-action reports, seen bodily wreckage reduced to unavoidable data points. These words were particularly difficult to apply to Anca, her delicate body, her gentle, dignified nature.

He offered the report back now and she folded it into a pocket.

The swelling on her eye had come down considerably. She looked like a different person. Faint lettering persisted on her cheek. Her hand floated by it. "It won't come off. And my back . . ."

"Rubbing alcohol," Evan said.

She smelled sharply clean, antibacterial soap and tea-tree shampoo. "You have experience with this?"

"Camo paint," Evan told her. "Sniper black."

"I see," she said.

She was short, around five foot three. Slender wrists poked from the cuffed-back sleeves of her sweater, the pisiform bone at the outer edge of her wrist no bigger than a pea.

Despite his average size, Evan felt large and rough before her.

"My seizure plan, I am . . . I am naked without it. I had an extra in my backpack but it is lost. The backups are in my office at the church." A flash of irises, the color of clear sky, met him. She started to talk, stopped, bit her lower lip.

"I can stay with you," Evan said. "If you'd like."

She nodded.

"Would you like me to call a car?"

Her lips firmed. She blinked several times rapidly, getting up her nerve. "The subway," she said. "I will take the subway."

At first Evan didn't understand.

And then he did.

Wind whipped Anca's hair. She'd halted about twenty feet from the mouth of the subway entrance. Hot air rushed upward across their cheeks, smelling of grease, peanuts, industrial heat.

"I don't think . . . I'm not sure I can."

Evan said, "Okay."

He didn't move. She didn't either.

She took a wobbling step forward. Another.

He followed her.

People bumped up against him from behind, the pedestrian current spilling around them, but he made sure to block for her, a boulder in the stream. A few grumbles and passive-aggressive sighs.

Moving even more hesitantly, Anca drew closer to the top step.

She stopped at the verge, peering down. A sense of depth was suddenly apparent, stairs tunneling sharply into the underworld. And yet, she faced it. She set a trembling hand on the metal rail, cringing at the bustle drifting past them, and the screech and rumble of trains moving invisibly below.

"Move it, buddy, wouldja?"

Anca didn't seem to hear. Evan kept his back squared, shielding the lane behind her. In front of him, her shoulders rose and fell, rose and fell.

Tentatively she started down.

He followed.

23

A Man Who Answers to No One

The subway train rocketed beneath the metric gigatons of the city. Across from Evan, Anca flinched at every noise. Brakes squealed. Fasteners and joints rattled. Ventilation whooshed. They clattered through darkness and light, darkness and light.

One of her diminutive hands gripped the other, a timid clasp on her lap. Seeming to notice, she unclenched her fingers and sat taller.

They'd moved through three cars before she'd chosen her spot. A few weary souls swayed at the far end, dangling from grab bars or pinning down blue molded seats of easily disinfected plastic. The sparseness of riders and the cacophonous rush of gray noise offered them privacy. As the tracks banked, the train slammed into an abrupt snake-wind, the trailing cars vanishing through the intercarriage windows and then slotting back into realignment like a magic trick.

At the jostling, Anca winced, the ketorolac wearing off. Over the course of Evan's missions, he might've met a tougher person than her. But he could not be sure.

He tipped his chin down, a nonverbal inquiry: *Are you okay?* The question had to be asked but the words were too stupid to speak.

"It's all different." She looked around tentatively. "Everything is different. I don't recognize where I am but of course I know where I am. I don't understand what I am paying attention to now. What I'm . . . What I'm seeing."

"There were five men at the station," Evan said. "Four on the platform and one sitting on the stairs. Three in the first car, seven in the second, two in here not including me."

Her mouth held slightly ajar. "Yes," she breathed. "Yes." Again he felt that X-ray stare, the sense of her taking a deeper inventory. "How . . . ?"

"It's how I see, too."

Her youthful face looked weary, and in that weariness he could see premonitions of the older woman she'd one day become. "Camo paint," she said. "Sniper black. Is that who you are?"

"It is part of who I was."

"Evan," she said, trying on his name. "Who are you now?"

"That. And more."

"Who do you answer to?"

"No one."

Her mouth set, lips pursed. "A man who answers to no one is very dangerous."

"Yes," he said.

"Is that why you came to find me? To go after . . . those who did this?"

"To help you. I didn't know where you were. If you were still being held. All I had was the description of what happened given by the young woman who abandoned you."

"Abandoned me?" Anca blinked at him as if he were inane. "Bless her. If she hadn't remembered me, I wouldn't have had your help. If your associate hadn't tracked me down. If your friend hadn't provided the helicopter to fly you here. So many people heeding the call. I wasn't abandoned. I was *found*."

Someone coughed and her head snapped over, the cord of the sternocleidomastoid muscle pronounced at the side of her neck. It took a moment for her shoulders to relax once more.

"You were found," Evan said. "And now they must be found."

"Whatever happens to them, it must be legitimate. It can't come from a man who answers to no one."

These were men who believed it their right to carry off an impaired woman, to drug her, to gratify themselves with her unconscious body, to bite and bruise and mark her skin, to bathe her violated flesh in chemicals to remove forensic traces. Who'd left her discarded with blood between her legs in an underground apartment with no money, no ID, mere shreds of clothing, and an eye nearly swollen shut. That had to be answered for in this life. It just had to.

Anca's case and the inconclusive forensics would get plopped down on the bureaucratic conveyor belt with scant chance of progressing through a sluggish crime lab to an overtaxed detective bureau to an overburdened DA's office.

"What is," he asked, "the legitimate way to handle what happened to you?"

"That's not for me to say. They will be judged before Someone Else."

"They need to be judged here."

"Vengeance is not mine to have. I refuse to give my heart to it."

"I don't understand."

"You don't need to," she said.

"What they did to you—"

"What is it, your vengeance? Who's it for? For you?"

"No."

"For me? Protective of me, are you? Is that what this is about?"

"In part. Yes."

"So protective that you can't see them for who they are?"

"Who are they?"

"Humans. Fallen, wretched humans in need of saving. More than I am. They are already in hell. Right now, as we speak." She scrutinized his reaction. "*What?*"

"I tend to give religion a wide berth, along with politics."

"Why's that?"

"The hypocrisy chafes me."

Her gaze narrowed. "I will make this right with God and then He will let me understand and then maybe someday I might even find forgiveness. But I am not my damage. I will not harden and hate. What happened to me is not for you. It is not your wound to heal. And it is not the flag you'll wave into war. I don't allow it. I won't allow it."

The criteria for Saint Augustine's just-war theory appeared in Evan's head, and he ticked off the boxes, one after another, though two and nine admittedly proved shaky.

"Men like this don't stop," he said. "We have a responsibility to the other girls and women they will hurt next."

"How dare you," she said. "How *dare* you talk to me about my responsibility right now."

"There's a place where forgiveness ends and duty begins."

The sides of her nose reddened with fury, her eyes hard as basalt. "And there's a place where your justice ends because it's *your* justice. Because you're only one man."

It was incredible to see a face so delicate snarl like that.

They rode in silence until her stop.

Unsteady from pain and meds, Anca clutched Evan's biceps as they glided upward on the escalator. The circle of the world above irised ever larger until they stepped into the night air.

She shuddered against him and again he felt her birdlike delicateness. She gestured faintly. "A few blocks this way."

He kept his arm on offer and she kept her grasp. At his side, she coasted forward, light on her feet, as if something were carrying her. They threaded through foot traffic, the night quieter than made sense for the Bronx.

The church was more austere than he'd anticipated, a humble white-stucco building fringed with black mold at the gutter lines. Barred windows, weather-beaten mosaics, several metal crosses rising from the roof sat alongside dishes and vent pipes. Security lights and snarled wires cluttered the eaves. The sole note of grandeur was a hexagonal cupola, its peak topped with a Latin cross featuring a lower beam of a footrest.

They stepped between a row of scraggly trees with whitewashed trunks thrusting crookedly from the pavement and crossed the street. A broad set of newly poured concrete steps led to a brief plaza and the plain wooden front door.

Anca slowed as they neared, her grip tightening on Evan's arm.

"Wait," she said. "Hold on, please."

She stooped, hands on her knees.

"Would you like to sit down?"

Her mouth pulsed, as if tasting something bitter. "Need to . . . get horizontal."

She slumped and he caught her, easing them down on the front steps of the church. Her head lolled and then came back. "Please . . . help."

"I will."

"Can you stay?"

"Yes."

"You're gonna need to—"

"I understand the protocols. It's okay. I got you."

"I don't have . . ."—her eyes rolled up to white, fluttered back momentarily—"pillow." The words came slurred: *doan have plillow.*

Evan cradled her, nestled her head in his lap, her temple on the meat of his thigh.

She gazed up at him.

"I have you, okay? Look at me. I have you."

"Don't leave me here alone." *Doane lee me hee lone.*

"I'll be with you until you're back."

A few shuddering breaths. Her hand clawed at his shirt, made a fist in the fabric.

"It's okay," he said. "I won't leave you."

Her hand went limp.

Her eyes, shut and fluttering, lost to a dark kind of rapture.

She seized. Legs kicking, hip rattling on the step, her free elbow flailing until he pinned it gently down. Rolling her partially onto her side, he kept her head tilted, horseshoe-gripping her chin and cheeks, popping the mouth open to make sure her tongue was clear.

Passersby kept passing by, an oblivious parade of pant legs and loafers, Air Jordans and high heels.

"Dude, get a room. Your girlfriend's freakin' out."

Evan glanced up at the cruel smirk of a young man in a hoodie, automatically calculating the strike point at the hinge of his jaw to knock the lower mandible clear off the temporomandibular joint. But he focused back on the young woman convulsing in his arms. He brushed the hair from her face, guarded her elbows and knees, kept her safe.

On the steps of the church, he held her. Her parted lips were full and pink, her eyelids fluttering beatifically. She was lost to an aura, her features alight with a preternatural luster.

The seizure lasted nearly three minutes.

But felt a lot longer.

At last, she quieted, stirring gently in his arms.

"I remember now," she said, her voice little more than a rasp. "I saw it." Her eyes blinked unseeingly. "A goat-skull tattoo on one of their chests. Devil horns."

Lifting a tremulous hand, she felt her cheeks with her palm, as if checking that her face was still there, and then wiped the tears watering from the sides of her eyes. Pushing up out of his lap, she groaned. She leaned forward and let a few breaths shudder through her.

Rising under her own power, she continued up the steps to the church.

The homely outside of the church cracked open to reveal an interior befitting a Fabergé egg. Gold and bronze iconography everywhere—bejeweled crucifixes and ornately carved newel-posts, countless vigil lights guttering in an immense candlestand, display tables overburdened with art. A massive box with carved fringes resembled an abandoned palanquin. A half-dome painting beneath an empty rear balcony depicted the Last Supper, nimbusless Judas looking shifty. Imagery abounded, relics crowding every surface, pictures tucked into the frames of larger paintings. A marble baptismal font, mosaics, a throne befitting a Middle-earth king. Beside the ceiling plate of an elaborate chandelier, Christ peered down from a gold-wreathed spot of heavenly blue. A glow suffused the church, bleeding through stained-glass saints to blanket the pews and idols and living souls with a many-colored raiment.

The simple wooden pews of the tiny church were crowded, everyone standing. A priest in elaborate vestments of iridescent bottle-fly green prayed in Romanian. He was bookended by life-size standing icons of Christ and Mary, and backdropped by a vast decorative partition wallpapered with icon panels, each as detailed as the next. Among the shimmering imagery, he seemed a part of the church itself, which of course he was. Between his incantations, a small choir lifted their voices in four-part harmony, transforming the service into a continuous song. The acoustics were shockingly good, the hymns seeming to emanate from the carved and painted faces all around.

Evan and Anca stood unnoticed where the door let in at the side of the nave, Anca seemingly as surprised as he was to find a service in full swing. The heavy door clicked shut at their backs. The priest's attention moved to them, his pale, concave face filling with joy. He halted in midsentence, breath catching, and then the focus of the congregation found them.

Utter silence.

The priest took an unsure step off the pulpit toward Anca and then another, broad sleeves hanging like bat wings from his spread arms. Beneath his robes, he floated toward her, staring as if unsure that she was real. Her eyes filled with tears to match his. Nearing, he lifted a bejeweled blessing cross from around his neck, and she closed her eyes and kissed it. As he set it upon her head, whooping and cries broke loose, Evan jostled to the fringe as the congregation surrounded Anca. Confusion pulsed in his chest, to have allowed himself to be pushed to the periphery, to lose someone he was protecting to a mob. But of course it was not a mob, it was a community, and he felt a sense of loss that his muscle memory had never been taught to distinguish between the two.

There were Slavic three-cheek kisses, nose bumping, the worshippers crossing themselves in threes right to left, thumbs and first two fingers pinched together. Double bowing and more kissing—kissing the icons, the edge of the priest's sleeves, the crosses around their necks. And Anca in the center, held in an immense embrace.

"Father," a woman cried in accented English, "should we finish the Akathist service?"

"Why keep praying," he said, "when our prayers have been answered?"

24

Utter Fucking Helplessness

Anca remained statue-frozen outside her apartment door, her hand pinched around the backup key she'd inserted into the lock, her head lowered. She'd been motionless for maybe ten seconds. It was like someone had hit pause. Evan stood behind her, waiting.

"Will you . . . ?" Her voice trailed off.

He waited.

"Will you please go inside and check the closets, beneath the bed?"

He said, "Yes."

He knew no one was inside but that wasn't the point.

She glanced nervously over a shoulder up the hall. "I'll come in with you and wait just inside the door."

She stepped aside and he entered.

Her sparse apartment was scrupulously kept. Couch and love seat protected by plastic covers, dark wood furniture without a speck, counters wiped clean. Inexpensive furnishings and decor were proudly displayed. Frayed kilim rug, chipped bowl atop tattered tablecloth, profoundly mediocre floral still life, sun-faded and framed in shiny black plastic, everything maintained with the temperance of someone who'd inherited the rigors of communist scarcity. A rickety secretary desk held candles and pictures of family—dour antecedents posing stiffly, a vibrant young woman Evan took to be Anca's mother, and a host of shots of Anca at various ages with her father, a robust man with a beard, a warm smile, and a scattering of stubble rounding out his balding pate. Young Anca on his knee, atop his shoulders, at his side holding a fishing pole. He was a bear of a man, Anca his cub.

Resting atop a window AC unit were a postcard-size image of Jesus and a photographic portrait of a saint or priest with a soft beard and piercing blue eyes. In the kitchenette nook, an ancient refrigerator hummed and clanked, its door clad with various magnets—a U.S. flag, Michael Jackson, the Statue of Liberty. There were no intruders in the cabinets or dishwasher.

Reversing course, Evan passed Anca by the front door. She was shouldered into a coatrack, face wan, eyes wide with concern. He flashed her an all-clear sign and then moved to safe her bedroom. IKEA bed, battered nightstand, pastel comforter. A decal of flowering ivy stretched along one wall and around a prison-small window, the street view impaired by a skein of telephone wires. A floating shelf held a few tiny succulents, a stuffed-animal penguin from the Bronx Zoo, and a row of novels—Russian, twentieth-century American lit, and some obligatory Mihai Eminescu. A normal young woman's room. What had he expected, velvet Jesus paintings and bloody crucifixes?

His RoamZone dinged, a text from Joey: yr car out frnt, mercedes, keys on lft rear tire.

Leaning closer to the window, he peered down. Shiny and out of place at the curb, a 450 EQS+ in silver metallic.

He could live with that.

Another ping: still finding a beachhead for vensend systems. gimme til manana + ill have something on yngtl69.

Copy, he texted back. And check databases for goat skull tatt on left pec.

Next he safed the bathroom, raking back the shower curtain. All clear.

The second bedroom was impeccably preserved, the bed made up bounce-a-quarter tight, a wool blanket folded lengthwise across the foot. On a side table rested a plastic bowl filled with painted eggs, each one strikingly unique. A dried sponge on the windowsill acted as a reverse floral frog for Romanian and U.S. toothpick flags, fanned up in a peacock display of patriotism. A wall poster showed peasants in embroidered clothes linked arm in arm in a hora circle dance. The white lettering beneath read, I LOVE AMERICA, THE COUNTRY OF MY FREE ADOPTION. IT EMBODIES ALL THE FREEDOMS. The grateful immigrant, he thought, lifeblood of American democracy.

Evan checked the closet and under the bed and then turned to leave. Beside the door, a weathered cowboy hat hung on a hook over a well-loved jean jacket. Beneath it on the floor rested a pair of worn slippers, stretched in the shape of her father's feet.

He took a moment with that one.

Anca was where he'd left her, waiting nervously just inside the front door. "No one here," he said. "You're safe."

"They have my keys," she said.

"My associate arranged for a locksmith to be here in the morning," Evan said. "I figured you might want the locks changed and a security system put in."

"I cannot afford a security system."

"It's been covered."

"No," she said. "Just the locks. I can pay for new dead bolts."

She eased a few steps into the living room, peering around. "I wasn't scared to be in here when I first came back. But I'm scared now. That doesn't make any sense."

"Nothing has to make sense right now."

"They have my keys," she said, again.

"I can sleep in my car," Evan said. "Where you can see me from the window. Cell phone on. Would that be helpful?"

She nodded several times. Her face was blank. She swayed on her feet.

"Can I get you something to eat or drink?"

She blinked slowly, refocusing on him. "What?"

"Something to eat or drink?"

"Tea," she said.

He held his arm wide, cueing her to move to the kitchen. After a slight tape delay, she followed. She sat at the tiny table for two with its place setting for one, folded her hands on the cheap vinyl place mat, and stared at nothing.

He rummaged through the cabinets. Jars of pickled cauliflower, turnips, and red peppers proliferated. Stacked ceramic plates showed dazzling earth-tone patterns or crude images of fish and trees. He found a mug along with an infuser and box of loose tea labeled CEAI NEGRU. He boiled water, steeped the tea for three and a half minutes. Quarter teaspoon of honey from a jar on the counter, a sprig of mint from the refrigerator. He set the mug down before her along with a paper towel from the roll, just one skinny strip so as not to waste.

The Second Commandment, *How you do anything is how you do everything.*

"Would you like me to sit with you or leave you alone?"

"Sit."

He sat.

She cupped her hands around the mug, lifted it to her face, closed her eyes, and breathed in the steam. Though the swelling around her eye had come down, the bruise was spreading unevenly along her temple, purple yielding to yellow.

A question had been eating at him. "You walked home," he said. "All the way from Harlem."

"Yes."

"Why?"

"They took my wallet. I had no money for a cab, no subway card. No one would help." Through the steam, her eyes held steady. "You saw what I looked like."

She'd looked terrible. Homeless, mentally ill, drug ravaged. Human wreckage beyond salvation, another inconvenient face like those from war zones or Third World disasters. In her three-hour walk from Harlem to the Bronx, she'd passed thousands of people. No one had stepped forward. Not a single person.

His jaw had tightened. He noted her noting it. Despite coming in and out of a trauma daze, she was still attuned to those around her.

"I'm not going to hand my suffering over to you," she said. "To a force of violence who answers to no one and nothing. Because where does that lead?"

"To less brutality."

"You use brutality to eliminate brutality?"

"I've found strongly worded letters to be ineffective."

She made a noise of exasperation. "You are trying to fix, what?"

"The bigger picture."

"There is no bigger picture. *This.* This is everything. Right here, now. Heaven and hell. This is all there is. You think you see clearly, Evan of the Immaculate Perception, but you're looking too high." With her knuckles, she knocked the table and then her chest. "This? This is real." She lifted the hem of her skirt, rubbed the frayed edge with her thumb. "This is real." Her fingertips lifted to her bruised cheek. "This is real." Her hands went back to the tea, mist spooling up around her face. "The retribution you seek is not yours to have. You will not kill them. Not on my behalf. Promise me. Promise me you will not kill anyone."

Evan felt the hardness of the chair against his back, cold air on his face. He did not answer.

"Are you the one who was brutalized?" she asked.

"No."

"Then you are not the one who will decide. *Promise me.*"

He couldn't make the words come out. Her gaze was unremitting. She was an extraordinarily patient woman.

"I won't kill them," Evan said. "But I will hurt them."

"You want them to what? Suffer?"

He considered. "I wouldn't mind it."

"And you want to be the perpetrator of that suffering?"

"I'm willing to."

"Willing? Or wanting?"

"I want to ensure they cannot do this again. That means they must suffer. I don't mind that they suffer at my hands. I want them to know why. I want them to see the evil inside them for what it is and know that they are being punished for it."

She'd received the words but he had no read on how she might respond.

"They *are* suffering," she said finally. "They *are* being punished. And there is much more to come."

"Why are you concerned for them?"

"I'm not concerned for them," she said. "I'm concerned for *you*."

She made no sense. No sense at all. But that was okay. He'd just told her that nothing had to make sense right now. He would honor his pledge to her. He would not kill them.

But he would make them answer.

She sipped her tea, closed her eyes, head nodding as she dozed off. Evan reached across the table and gently took the mug from her hands so it wouldn't spill and burn her.

"Maybe you'd like to lie down?"

"Yes. Yes." She stood. "You will be outside? Where I can see you?"

"Yes."

She trudged behind him to the front door.

He paused at the threshold. "Until we get the locks changed, you can slide a chair beneath the doorknob."

"I thought you'd be watching."

"I will be. It's not necessary. Just if it makes you feel better."

"It would."

He stepped outside, eased the door shut. He'd gotten a few steps down the hall when the door opened behind him.

"Evan."

He turned.

She looked small there in the narrow slice of open doorway. "What would happen if you lived your life as if all your choices were sacred?"

He said, "What makes you think I don't?"

Her brow furrowed; she was pondering. "Maybe we have different definitions of what constitutes sacred."

"Of that," Evan said, "I'm sure."

It was nearly eleven o'clock by the time he took up his post in the Mercedes outside Anca's apartment. The leather-upholstered driver's seat with its adjustable lumbar and bolsters, heater, and ten variations of massage beat his usual lookout posts and sniper hides on tree branches, attics, and heaps of rubble.

A silhouette drifted into view up at Anca's window. She lifted a hand in a plaintive wave.

He waved back.

The bedroom light clicked off.

He reclined the seat. The wave massage vibrated his lower back. The plush pillow fronting the headrest cradled his neck. Through the windshield he had a perfect vantage to the entrance of Anca's building across the street. Settling back, he let himself drift into a state of low-alertness that nearly qualified as dozing.

Shortly after two in the morning, he came alert at a form beelining across the road at him. Anca, wrapped to the neck in a bathrobe, feet stomped into boots, her cheeks flushed with barely restrained anger. She rapped hard on the window, though he was already reaching to lower it.

"*Hypocrisy*," she said. "You said you dismiss religion because of hypocrisy. The hypocrisy isn't in religion. It's in being human!" She was standing on the sidewalk, shouting at him, wind whipping her bathrobe around her calves. "Just because someone tries to follow His way doesn't mean that they can act perfectly. That's like saying that having laws is hypocritical because there are criminals who break them."

Her hair was shoved to one side from sleep, her hands clenched, and she canted forward on her toes as if barely holding herself back from getting angrier. Her glare held tangible rage, pain, and utter fucking helplessness.

Evan said, "Amen."

She stood a moment longer, her face pale in the night wind. A strand of hair had blown across her eyes and she trapped it with cupped fingers and fixed it behind an ear. She blinked a few times, disoriented, as if suddenly finding herself back in her body. All the heat had washed out of her.

She moved backward a few steps, then turned, scurried across the street, and disappeared once again into her building.

Evan surfaced from the hinterland between sleep and waking at Anca's form once more moving toward his car, this time less aggressively and in the gray light of morning. She was dressed in jeans and a bulky cable sweater, a knit hat pushing a jagged fray of bangs across her forehead.

He got the window down before she had an opportunity for more vehement knocking, though she seemed in a civil mood.

She ducked down to peek at him. "Devoted," she observed.

He gave a reassuring shrug, if shrugs could be reassuring.

"You have behaved honorably."

He wasn't sure what to say, and another communicative shrug would have been overkill, so he said nothing.

Anca jerked her head toward the backseat. "Who's that?"

Evan turned.

Candy was sitting behind him, fresh faced and beaming, one elbow slung across the armrest, the other hooked on the windowsill.

She smiled that wide smile. "His better half," she said.

25

Crazy Beasts

These days you didn't even need a tracking device or anything. They posted their fucking locations for you. Blanca from *Beauty and the Beast* had checked in at a Joe & the Juice in SoHo. Bridge-and-tunnel girl movin' on up!

They'd split up in twos 'cuz that made for better hunting, and Taz was with B-Roll, a way stronger team than Finn-Finn and Big Mikey. B-Roll had the look, the swagger, and the sweet rap.

By the time they got to SoHo, Blanca was gone but they just waited and watched her Insta story and sure enough she pinged a manicure selfie from a nail place around the corner: Rhinestone flowers, y'all!

Taz and B-Roll chilled outside till Blanca and her friend rolled out of the place, did a wide-arm singy hug thing, and split in opposite directions. Blanca was super cute IRL, high cheekbones, them big dark eyes, wearing a crop top even in cold-ass February with baggy pants rolled twice at the waistband, showing off that tan flat belly. *Dayum.*

B-Roll lit up a pre-roll from the stash Mikey's cousin had boosted last month in a home invasion, toked deep, and started over to Blanca. Taz gave him the usual lead, a ten-foot standoff, holding back to see how the sitch developed.

B-Roll sidled up next to her, joint dangling in the corner of his mouth the way he could do, like it was stapled to his bottom lip. "Hey, li'l girl."

Her mouth got all pert and she looked up through curled lashes. "Who's little?"

B-Roll shrugged at her. He was five years older, which was a lot older, and he was built, had that bad-boy lined-jaw beard the chicks dug. So, yeah, she was little. That was one of his moves, give 'em a smackdown and wait for them to crawl back.

"Look at you, just smokin' a joint in the full light of day," she said.

"You smoke, li'l girl?"

A lips-pooched smirk, tilt of the head. "Sometimes maybe I been known to."

They walked side by side up the crowded sidewalk.

Taz held back but he could smell her perfume, something sugary, and her top eyelids and throat sparkled with that glittery lotion stuff. But then his brain tweaked like before and he was back as a kid playing with Other Blanca. She was so sweet and he—he was pretty sweet back then, too. He remembered when he split his pinkie toe on the doorjamb and cried a little, how she put a Band-Aid on for him and didn't even make fun, and—

"Hold up," B-Roll said to Blanca up ahead. "Check this." He crimped his tongue around the still-lit joint, popped it into his mouth, closed his lips, then Jack-in-the-Boxed that fucker back out. Long draw, dragon-smoke through his nose, no hands all the way.

B-Roll being B-Roll.

Blanca laughed. "Impressive."

"Really?"

She shook her head. "Not really. Not impressive at all."

"Hey," B-Roll said. "Ain't I seen you?"

"Can't you do better than that?"

"No, no, I mean it. Wait!" He snapped his fingers, the epiphany hitting. "I saw you in *Beauty and the Beast*. Forest Hills, yeah?"

Even from a few steps behind, Taz could see her get all glowy. Tipping her head, that perky little chin jutting out at him, touching her hair, all that shit. "Really? You saw *that*?" Dismissive hand wave. "That was stoopid."

She seemed so nice. Funny, too.

Taz's stomach felt all knotted and the weirdest fantasy swept through him—that he should dart forward and grab her hand and run her away from B-Roll and it would just be the two of them and they could just laugh and joke and she'd talk with Taz and he could tell her stuff, thoughts and feelings and shit, and she could do the same and they'd actually, like, *connect* with each other and it could feel like it once felt when he was a little kid with Other Blanca. WTF was even going on with him?

A big guy stepped out of a souvenir shop and Taz made to pivot with the joystick, thumb twitching on the D-pad, L2 shoulder button for full-auto fire, but then he remembered he wasn't playing *Kings of Karnage* but was outside in the real world and he thought, *Dayum*. Life was surreal.

"You were good for real," B-Roll was telling her. "My kid sister wanted to go. I take care of her."

"Aw, you do? How old?"

"She's ten. Mom's second marriage, you know how that goes."

"Yeah, yeah, I do for sure. I got a little sister, too. Six. They can be a pain."

"She's a cutie, though. Luce. Know what she's big-time into? Polly Pockets."

"I remember those!"

"Right?" B-Roll said. "I just got her the koala purse playset."

"No way! *I* had that."

"I bet you had that. You look like a koala purse playset girl."

"Do I, now? A koala purse playset *little* girl?"

"Well," B-Roll said, and had her hanging on his every word. "Maybe not a *little* little girl."

He held the joint out at his side, not looking over.

She took it, did a nervous little hit with her head ducked like anyone cared, gave a cough and a giggle. Another two delicate tiny coughs like hiccups. "Harsh, man. That shit is harsh."

"Seriously, right?" B-Roll said. "It's cool, though." He pinched the joint, took a deep-ass drag, held it as he flicked the joint into the gutter, where it tumbled and sparked. "I know," he said, in that drawn-in-breath-toke voice, "I'm a beast." He blew out hard into the face of a passing gray suit, who scowled but kept walking, tail tucked. "Wait," B-Roll said, leaning in at her, "if I'm Beast, what's that make you?"

"Awright," she laughed. "Awright. I see what you're doing there."

Lurking a few steps behind them, jostled by shoppers, Taz watched. He had no idea how B-Roll could do it, man. All that give-and-take. The words just came out like music. Taz had plenty of words, just could never get them outta his head in any kind of decent order. Again he thought about sweeping Blanca off somewhere but he could never get away with that with B-Roll around.

B-Roll grabbed Blanca's arm, ducking them into an alcove at the Sephora store, the crowd sweeping past. Taz took a post across from them by the door, turned mostly away, pretending to check his phone. Blanca didn't notice shit.

"What's your name?" B-Roll asked.

"Blanca. You?"

"B-Roll."

"B-Roll. B-Roll?" That giggle, man. Straight white teeth. "What kind of name's B-Roll?"

"That's my DJ name."

"You're a DJ?"

"Nah. Just messin'. It's just my name. My boys, ya know? They're crazy."

"Crazy beasts like you?"

"Crazy beasts like me." B-Roll gave that smile. He knew how to stand with his shoulders back, made his chest look even bigger than it was.

Taz had a sunken chest and no matter how much he lifted he couldn't get pecs. His shoulders slumped, too. But still, he could work on standing better like B-Roll did.

B-Roll was about to make the move. After dozens of hunting

expeditions, Taz could read it. He had Manny's number on speed dial on his phone. One text and Manny would ping them an address they could use nearby, had crash pads all over the city for super-short-term rental. Like a human Airbnb, Manny was. Once Taz Snapped Finn-Finn and Big Mikey the location they'd all meet up and party.

Taz just wished it didn't have to be with Blanca.

"Wanna hang some?" B-Roll said.

"When?"

"When? *When?* Dunno. You know what they say. No time like the present."

Blanca blushed. It was real fucking cute, reminded Taz of when Other Blanca'd get all demure when she shot a toy soldier off its perch. Her hair always smelled like green apples. Taz's stomach hurt even more now. He didn't know why. He couldn't remember if he'd taken his meds or if he'd eaten. Didn't know what day it was either. Couldn't remember much of anything.

Blanca blushed. "Now?"

"When else? When better? Carpe muthafuckin' diem."

She ground the toe of her sneaker into the sidewalk. "Wish I could. But I gotta go."

For the first time, Taz's stomach unclenched. B-Roll caught him staring, gave him a hard glare, and Taz split focus back to his phone. The text to Manny was ready to send, his thumb hovering.

"I got homework," Blanca said.

"Homework," B-Roll said, in a lame voice. "*Home*work."

"Yeah, well." She brushed bangs out of her face. They wisped back across her big eyes.

B-Roll reached for her face, fixed them bangs for her, and she looked up at him like she was waiting to receive the communion wafer. "Maybe I could see you some other time."

Taz lowered the phone. They needed cash and content so he was supposed to be pissed off that Blanca had pushed off the hookup. But he was feeling something instead. Relief. Relief? Why that?

"I don't know," Blanca said. "My parents are pretty strict."

"I don't blame them," B-Roll said. "'F I had a daughter like you."

She blushed. "They got marriage therapy Friday nights."

"Marriage therapy, huh?"

Blanca rolled her eyes. "You know."

"Yeah, yeah, I know. Friday night? I have Luce, gotta babysit. Hey, maybe we could watch a Disney movie together. Like, *The Little Mermaid*?"

"I *love* that movie. I wanted to be Ariel."

"Wanna know a secret?" B-Roll said. "I *still* wanna be Ariel."

A big laugh.

B-Roll took out his phone, swung it over to her. "I'll hit you up."

She shook her head like she couldn't believe she was about to do something crazy, then took the phone and pecked in her digits.

She handed it back, all flirty. "See ya, Beast."

B-Roll let his gaze linger on her and she let him let it. "See ya," he said, "Beauty."

"Stoopid." She gave a little headshake but blushed deep and then she was gone.

B-Roll spun around to Taz.

They bumped fists.

They walked for a while, B-Roll whistling through his teeth.

Taz's throat was dry. "Maybe . . ." He had to clear his throat. "Don't you think maybe she's wrong for us?" He gave a shrug he hoped was casual. "Too, dunno, wholesome and shit."

"Wholesome's what we're looking for," B-Roll said. "Wholesome sells."

Taz flushed with—what? Embarrassment? Fear? Dread? He looked away quickly to hide his face. "You sure as shit know how to get 'em."

B-Roll spit once on the sidewalk. "Fish in a barrel," he said.

26

Hissy Fit

"X, I nailed the fucker! I had to hack, like, three different services at Solventry but I finally got to a linked bank account with a physical address. Texting now."

The RoamZone dinged with a downtown address, along with an abbreviated dossier Joey had put together. YngTl69 proved to be Manny Llorente, a former human resources IT manager. No record of working or paying taxes for the past three years. He'd fallen off the radar entirely, odd for a guy with a B.A. from Stony Brook, zero priors, and no known criminal associates.

"And I haveta tell you, Devine's setup here? The Brain? It is literally *sick*."

Literally, Evan thought.

He'd stepped out of Anca's living room to take the call, easing into her father's preserved bedroom for privacy. He peeked out through the cracked door to check on Candy.

Given the nature of the mission, she'd gone to great lengths to present plainly in order to smother her magnetism. Sweater and black jeans, touch of smoke at the eyes, blond hair held in a simple ponytail. She still looked far from unalluring, but this was the closest to unalluring Candy McClure could manage. When unimpeded, her sensuality was an electromagnetic force field, acting on everything it came into contact with.

At the moment, she was sitting cross-legged on the couch, listening intently to Anca. Her lips were pursed, head slightly cocked to match Anca's, a loose corkscrew of hair edging one cheek. Evan had seen her focused plenty of times but never with so much connection in her gaze.

Emerging from the foster-care system and the Orphan Program unscathed was impossible. As hard as it had been for Evan, he hadn't had to run either gauntlet as a female. Candy had endured both, and each had left its claw marks.

That's what he'd picked up on, a resonance between the women.

They sat close and spoke softly, and for a moment Evan saw their faces as mirror images. He blinked and the illusion was gone.

Joey's voice pierced his distraction: "He's got all kinds of miners and massive GPU farms training various LLMs."

"Any headway identifying the men?" Evan asked. "The goat-skull tattoo?"

"Those are a dime a dozen in the demo. Which speaks to the demo, you ask me."

Easing back from the door, Evan swiped through the dossier, finding Manny Llorente's driver's-license photograph. Beige lined polo shirt, generic side part, visible bifocal line on his eyeglasses—a paragon of the banality of evil.

"Alsos," Joey continued, for some reason choosing the plural, "Rawlings and I caught another incoming request for Devine we want to run by you since he's still on, like, time-out from being a global mastermind."

Evan released a breath as calmly as he could manage. "What?"

"I guess there's a sitch brewing in North Korea—"

"Josephine, we are *not* dealing with North Korea right now," he said, and hung up.

He double-checked Manny Llorente's Tribeca address and the magazine in his ARES 1911 before emerging from the bedroom.

"Everything okay?" Anca asked.

In Candy's presence, Anca seemed more at ease. She'd draped a retro boho fringed shawl across her shoulders, dark green patterned with roses.

Evan said, "I have to run an errand."

"An errand." Crisp phrasing.

"Yes. Candy will cover your six while I'm gone. Locksmith should be here within the hour."

"What happens if those men come before then?"

Candy said, "Then I will strip their faces off their skulls with my French-manicure gels and nail them over your mantel as decorative art."

Anca's head swiveled from her to Evan and then back to Candy. "Who *are* you people?"

"We're like angels," Candy said. "But the ones from the Old Testament."

"Well, no one's to die on your 'errand,'" Anca said to Evan. "That I've made clear."

Candy leaned back and stretched her arms across the couch back, her mouth twisting slyly as she looked up at Evan. "I'm sure you can improvise."

"How long do you think the locksmith will need?" Anca asked, phone in hand with her calendar open. "The Divine Liturgy's at eleven thirty."

"Can't you skip it this week?" Candy asked.

"No. I cannot."

Evan said, "Candy will accompany you."

"Sure I won't ignite when I cross the threshold?" Candy said.

Anca said, "If so we'll douse you with holy water."

"Is that a joke, Ms. Dumitrescu?" Evan said.

"Don't tell anyone. I'm not ready to be funny yet."

Evan started out.

"Did I go out to your car in the middle of the night?" Anca asked.

He halted. "Yes."

"What did I say?" The damage was still evident on her face. And behind it. "Everything's . . . hazy."

"It's not important."

"Was I rude?"

"No."

Anca studied him. Her forehead crinkled. "Sorry."

"You don't have to be."

"And . . . thank you. I haven't said thank you."

"You don't have to say that, either."

"Yes," Anca said. "I do."

Candy watched the exchange, mouth tensed with quiet amusement.

Anca was staring at Evan expectantly.

He wondered why it was hard to say.

He dropped eye contact, cleared his throat. "You're welcome."

27
Just the Middleman

Tribeca was ideal for ordering forty-five-dollar seared scallops, spotting celebrities swathed in sunglasses and flipped-up hoodies, and marveling at the brick and cast-iron industrial aesthetic of converted historic warehouses.

And fire escapes.

Evan loved fire escapes.

They were like escalators designed for breaking and entering.

He pattered up three flights, the soles of his Original S.W.A.T.s finding easy traction on the mesh latticework of the steel-grated steps. The final rise delivered him to a brief balcony softened with artificial grass and backed by a massive window shedding bleary late-morning light into a soaring architectural loft. A sleek translucent blind the color of aged bamboo dimmed the lazy sun for the man working inside. Facing away, he slouched on a low modern couch aimed at a massive wall flickering with light from a projector, shoulders rippling as he presumably typed on a cordless keyboard in his lap. One foot was propped atop the hardware tower of a high-powered rig as he clacked away at the computer desktop cast upon the giant screen of white paint.

A door of dark-tinted glass, unlocked here seventy feet above the bustling sidewalk, let into the loft. When Evan turned the chunky handle to enter, he could hear screaming music barely muffled by the giant padded headphones clamped around Manny Llorente's head. Aggressive guitar licks, piercing sync, raw vocals with voiceless uvular fricatives and harsh consonant clusters signaled Neue Deutsche Härte. Evan had heard plenty of the German heavy-metal offshoot when he'd tracked a cell of National Socialist Underground nail-bomb engineers through Eastern European clubs, leaving them garroted in cocaine-dusted toilet stalls.

He swung the door behind him, a moderate slam that went unnoticed. Manny stayed hunched forward over his keyboard, head bopping. Even from behind, it was clear that he'd put on some weight since his driver's-license picture, his body softened from luxury. His hair had thinned, not enough to turn the side part into a comb-over yet, but it would get there soon enough.

Scattered haphazardly among expensive, soulless furnishings were bizarre props. A latex-lined coffin. Wooden pillories, the holes for head and hands burnished with use. A flattened space-saver vacuum storage bag the width of an upright piano. A black lacquer credenza supported mounds of papers, a cluster of Solventry overnight envelopes, and a metal tray with a jumble of flash drives. Next to it stretched a lineup of industrial-size paper and multimedia shredders. The walls held weighty framed art-ish photographs of orgasmic females, red lips parted wantonly to receive, black-and-white bellies contoured like landscapes, detached torsos buttoned with tight nipples.

The daylight, even muted, turned the wall-high projected desktop into a mirror of golden light. But when Evan eased forward, the glow shifted into clarity, images coming visible.

His breath kept on steady as ever. Instead, he felt the hitch in his heart.

The wall was tiled with living windows, dozens upon dozens arrayed in a video grid, each square writhing and pulsing. His vision glazed to take it in as a unified blob, a squirming bed of sucking and pumping and throbbing and spitting, a barnyard muddle. There was nothing coy or erotic or even sexual about it, just humans burrowed down into debasement, reduced to their barest existential function, base hedonism expressed to the surface and lit with unforgiving brightness. Every imaginable version was on display and some unimaginable ones as well, siblings and stepmoms, frenzied mobs pounding around the nucleus of a nearly obscured form, suffocating girls vacuum-sealed inside storage bags, writhing like gaffed fish. The anatomy was distorted, impossibly swollen and cinched, contorted and defiled, reduced to digital squares and sent roaring algorithmically into the wild.

Evan's pupils contracted, the vision made horrifyingly specific. For an instant he felt as if he were standing upside down on the ceiling of another world, the shafted projection an inversion of the stained-glass glow of Anca's church, the mosaicked likenesses a perversion of the icon panels of the ecclesiastical partition.

A horror-image swam into his mind, that pogo-stick depression in the extant patch of carpet in that dingy subterranean fuck pad—one foot of a tripod.

A tripod to hold a video camera.

They had recorded it.

Her.

They had recorded her.

And propagated her debasement to the world.

Bile clawed up his throat. He could practically feel the give of Manny's soft neck within his clenched hands, the crackling yield of the trachea's cartilage rings. Before it was done Evan would tilt the head back and stare down into the fading light of Manny's eyes so he would fear judgment in his dying breath.

And yet. A promise had been extracted from Evan.

His fingers had tensed in anticipation, tendons aching with flexed restraint. He'd floated forward to stand just behind Manny. Those plush headphones disgorged the tinny scream of metal rock, an orchestral swell beneath the fiendish riot of the forever footage.

Each video had a logo watermark, a zesty font proclaiming: Young Tail Productionz!

Username YngTl69 coaxed to prurient elongation.

Manny shifted abruptly on the couch and slung his headphones down around his neck. He toggled a button on the keyboard and snapped a headset on, mic floating by his mouth. "You got the Manny Man."

A pause.

"Wut?" Another pause as he listened to the caller. "She got chlamydia *and* gonorrhea?" A snort. Then: "Yeah, I suppose I *do* think it's funny. Lookit, these girls know they get whatever's coming when they submit to the pony. Which shoot was it?" Beat. "*Those* guys? They claim they test every month, but it's a high-risk biz. Shit happens on high-risk gigs. Just ask offshore welders and elevator mechanics." He listened briefly. "Well, that's what the triple cocktail's for, right? No one likes to see condoms, bro. It's a turn-off. Plus, I mean, you wanna live or you wanna live scared?" He drummed his fingertips atop his head. "I'm not getting involved. She's a grown-up. Tell her to act like one."

Manny disconnected the call, flung the headset onto the couch beside him. He nudged up the volume on the computer, myriad audio tracks playing over one another, a cacophony of tongues: *Once you go white, baby, it's all right. It's as big as my arm. Put it across your face. Now take it. You want more? Yeah baby, gimme more.* Moans of pain. Slapping. Sounds of feigned pleasure giving way to gagging.

Manny's fingertips fluttered across the keyboard, bringing one video to the fore. Using an editing tool, he blurred out the man's face but kept the woman's. In one of the background clips Evan spotted the pink couch from the ratty subterranean apartment, bowed under the weight of a half dozen undulating forms.

His rage simmered, reached boiling point.

He said, "Excuse me."

Manny started as if cattle-prodded, jerking around on the couch and nearly toppling off. "What the hell? Who are you? How'd you get in here?"

Evan said, "Mute the videos."

Manny grabbed the keyboard, dropped it, picked it up again, punched at it panickily. The loft went blissfully silent.

"Bro, look, whatever you want, you can have. I got plenty of everything and hookups for everything else." Manny's voice quavered, the tone entirely different from the one he'd used on the call. "Just . . . chill, okay? Let's keep it cool." His forearm twitched.

"Two days ago you rented an apartment for a pack of young men to rape a woman and record it for you."

"What? *Rape?* I don't do rape. I mean, not *real* rape."

"And yet that is what happened. So you could post it as entertainment. And make money."

"Money? You want money? You can have whatever I made from it. Or whatever else."

Evan held unremitting eye contact until Manny wilted on the couch. "What then?" he said in a little-boy voice. "Why are you here?"

"For answers."

"But I don't know anything. I mean, it's just a business model. It's just a—"

Evan lifted his hand slightly and Manny froze.

"This instant is a dividing line," Evan said. "Between life as you know it. And what is to come."

Manny's mouth stretched wide, clown-like. He tried to talk but his voice came hoarse. Cleared his throat. "I'm not sure what answers you want but I'm just the middleman. I'm the money guy, bro, a producer, a little editing. I just clean up what's already happened, give people what they want. I don't do any of this"—his hand swept to indicate the muted projections—"I just monetize it. That's all I am. A middleman."

Evan's gaze lifted. The visuals flew at him, a woodchipper spout into his eyes. He imagined this man sitting here taking this in around the clock for weeks, months, years. He imagined it barging into the heads of countless people of all generations, setting their expectations, morphing their brains. Millions of participants, some even willing. Legion more consumers.

He took in Manny once more. His mouth held that perverse widened shape of terror, verging on a sob. The lower lip had curled over, dimpling the chin. Evan heard an echo of the tough-guy dialogue Manny had tried on over the phone: *These girls know they get whatever's coming.*

"It's so hard," Evan said, "acting like you're a man. Hoping no one else will see."

Manny's mouth pulsed. The word came out half formed. "What?"

"What happens when your bluff gets called."

His face broke. Silent cries, mouth gaping, eyes pinched. "Don't hurt me, man. I'm just a middleman."

"There is no such thing," Evan said, "as 'just.'"

"What do you want? Who are you?"

"The Nowhere Man."

"God. Oh God." Manny curled over, clutching his stomach. "If I tell you everything you want, will you let me go?"

"No." Slowly Evan walked around the couch, cutting the light of the projector so it threw his dark form a story high, blotting out the images. He turned to face Manny. "But you might live."

"Okay, okay." Manny drew in a screeching breath, collected himself. "What do you want to know?"

"The operation. How's it work?"

Manny shuddered off another sob, straightened up. "I'm just a producer."

"Which means what?"

"Content provider. I rent out props for the talent if they need it."

"The talent."

"Ya know, fetish stuff, S&M, toys, whatever. I have crash pads I rent around the city when they need a set. But a lot of the vids come in from around the world and I help place 'em for a cut."

Evan half turned, the light seaming his face, half of it in blazing light, the other taking in the wall of abasement. A Japanese adolescent in a schoolgirl uniform flopped inside a sealed vacuum bag, folded legs zippered against her bare buttocks. She stilled. The clip ended.

Evan pointed, his arm a massive beam, a wing span of the *Cristo Redentor* embracing Guanabara Bay. "That young woman. Does she die?"

"What? What? No. No, no, no. Of course not. He lets them out once they pass out. We don't make snuff films." Manny grabbed the keyboard, pulled up excised footage of a bored-looking bearded man freeing the girl's still form from the suctioned vacuum bag. She jerked in a few breaths, reviving, and then sobbed uncontrollably against the floor. The man stepped across her, sat in a chair in the background, lit up a cigarette. "That's illegal and not, like, our jam. Not *at all.* I'd never participate in anything like—"

"Why do you make it look like a snuff film?"

"Just—I don't know—people have preferences, bro. You know that. It's just what gets them off. I mean, most violent porn is watched by women. Didja know that? Know why?"

Evan stared at him.

"It's a way for them to explore their sexuality without having to own their desire. Like, they can say it's not their fault. It was forced on them. But really, that's what they want. Get it?"

Evan reached in his pocket and Manny squealed. But he only withdrew his RoamZone. Calling up a picture of Anca, he faced it at Manny. "Do you recognize this woman?"

"Uh-uh, bro." Manny coughed out a noise of overwhelmedness, fanned a hand at the countless projected tiles of the video grid. "So many girls. So much product."

Staring at Manny Llorente's sweaty face, Evan realized that Manny didn't think about the women he exploited any more than most people think of a living cow when they eat a burger.

"Chest tattoo," Evan said. "Goat skull, devil horns."

"Oh," Manny said. "Right, right, right. Yeah, I can give you that. That's one of the guys from the White On Posse."

"White On Posse?"

"White On White, White On Black, White On Brown, White On Yellow, ya know. They're a low-rent operation, four dicks and a camcorder." He seemed relieved to have information to impart but he gave a double take at Evan's expression and blanched. "Look, bro. Like I said, I'm just the middleman."

"Say it again." Evan stepped forward, loomed over him. "Say you're just the middleman one more time."

Manny's Adam's apple throbbed, a tiny fist. His mouth clamped so hard his lips turned white.

"How do I find them?" Evan said. "The White On Posse?"

"No idea."

Evan's shoulders tensed and Manny threw up his arms. "Wait, I swear! I swear it! They use burner phones for our comms. They email the footage or—or courier a thumb drive or whatever if the file's too big. I prep the vids, upload, place it with the platform, and zero-pass wipe my local files twice. It's an anonymous business. We keep it clean, bro. We keep it clean."

"Why do you keep it clean," Evan said. Not a question. *"Middleman."*

Manny's mouth elongated once more, wet lips stretching.

"Answer."

"'Cuz who knows what's what?" Manny said, with a sudden burst of defiance. "If there's a raid. Maybe someone's underage. Maybe someone has regrets, claimed they were forced. I don't know. I don't care. I'm just a . . . just a . . ." Shallow jerked inhalations, a hysterical fit shaping up.

Evan slapped him, snapping his head to one side. "Catch your breath. Neither of us has time for a panic attack."

The imprint of Evan's hand bloomed on Manny's cheek.

"Find the latest White On Posse video."

"I don't have 'em anymore," Manny said. "I zeroed out the files."

"Friday," Evan said. "The assault was Friday. That's two days ago."

"Two days is a lifetime, bro," Manny said. "So much product to keep up with. They shoot long, bro, marathon sessions, which means massive video files"—Evan's stomach wrenched—"so they would've messengered it Saturday, which means I dealt with it yesterday. Compressed it, sent it off, and wiped the files."

The guy truly didn't remember. He'd edited the video and didn't even remember Anca's face.

"Zipped it off where?" Evan said. "What's the platform?"

"RedLite. They're the biggest. There's so much on there. Everyone's doing this, bro. It's the whole world." Manny's eyes toggled nervously over to the black-lacquered credenza.

Evan traced his gaze. Strode across. That tangle of flash drives waited in the metal tray at the edge by the row of industrial shredders, their next stop on the assembly line.

The drives were all shapes and colors, many of them labeled with a date and description. He poked through them. One said, *2/6, Subway chick, WoW.*

Subway chick. White On White.

Evan lifted it, let it dangle in the light. Saliva leaked along his lower molars, a premonition of nausea. In psyops training and in the field, he'd endured footage. War crimes, hostage videos, Hamas and ISIS, experiments from Nazi camps, cartel leaders feeding naked men to their dogs. But he'd not watched the torture of someone he knew personally.

He'd faded away inside his dread but snapped back into present awareness. Behind him, Manny was weeping quietly on the couch.

His fist clenched around the flash drive. In his palm pressed around the unyielding metal, he could feel the pulse of his heartbeat. With effort, he unclenched his jaw.

And turned around.

The time for talking was over.

28
Olive Branch

The soft whirring in the background was distracting. Almost as much as Manny Llorente's muffled pleas. *"God, please. Please, just wait. Hang on—hang on!"* A choked scream.

But sitting on Manny's sleek modern couch, Evan wasn't paying attention to him. He was focused on talking to Joey over the RoamZone.

"I need you to locate Deputy Assistant Director in Charge Naomi Templeton," he said. "Right now in real time."

"Templeton?" Joey sounded breathless, a rare occurrence.

Evan's and Templeton's paths had crossed many times over the years. She was a top-notch agent, ordained for the Secret Service as if for the priesthood. Her father had run the "big show," Presidential Protective Detail, and she'd earned her way up the chain with an impeccable work ethic and unimpeachable principles. She had hunted Evan through the years, seeking to bring him down for his vigilantism. But they spoke each other's language and their respective codes had found resonance, flip sides of the same coin.

They were enemies. She was devoted to his capture. And yet he trusted her.

Years ago, he'd managed to steal the encryption keys to her Boeing Black smartphone and had kept a back door open to it. This would be useful for pinning down her location. With Devine's resources and Joey's brain, everything else could be speedily arranged from there.

"Yes," Evan said. And told Joey what he needed.

He'd shut off the projector to enjoy the relative quiet of the loft. But the background whirring kept on, reaching a different pitch as it neared its goal.

"*—please please just—don't. I told you everything. I ta-ta—*" The rest was smothered.

Joey said, "Even with Devine's resources, that'll take some doing."

"*—bro, just one second, I ca-ca-can't—*"

"That's okay." Evan leaned back on the low couch, relaxing into the lumbar bolster. "I'm not in a rush."

Naomi Templeton ran her hand across her father's grave marker, reading the etched markings with her fingertips like braille. Two dates, a name, beloved husband and father. No mention of his legendary status within the Service. *In the end that's all there is,* she thought. *A brief span of time and what we are to those we loved.*

She already had the first date, of course. She had the name, too, prominent in D.C. As for the third slot, what would they carve on her tombstone? Daughter? Sister? Though in her early thirties, she was perennially single. Men seemed balky around her, unsure of her broad shoulders, her bluntly cut straw-blond hair, her hard, pretty features unenhanced by makeup. Mascara made her eyes water, screwed up her target acquisition. When it came to work, she was as confident as she was competent, could field-strip a SIG Sauer blindfolded and choke out a suspect nine different ways. They could read it in her, today's boy-men, and that rarely primed them for the demure banter over cocktails they seemed to prefer.

Her rise through the Service had been meteoric. Her early professional years had brought predictable grumblings about nepotism, but at this point no one could deny her accomplishments and exemplary service. Given her usual closeness with the president, Naomi had found herself elevated into a new role. Technically her new title was deputy assistant director of strategic intelligence, though she had significant overlap with the Office of Professional Responsibility as well, guiding policies around compliance, integrity, and accountability. She was a beneficiary of an anomaly allowed at the highest reaches of government to those who showed great talent: her pay grade remained firmly set but her responsibilities ranged freely. One of her key purviews was quarterbacking investigations that drew the president's personal interest and contending with all matters pertaining to Orphan X, who continued to draw more resources than any individual deserved.

She was trusted. And rightly so.

Rising, she drew in the cold February air. D.C. was stark in winter, the trees forked and bare, charcoal trunks against banks of melting snow. Breath clouding, she walked out of the cemetery. Her new Jeep Wrangler waited at the curb, hardtop on, snow dusted across the amusingly named Sting Gray clear coat.

As she neared the driver's door, a bike messenger pedaled at her, wheels improbably holding on the icy sidewalk. She watched his eyes lock on her, mentally charted the draw from her hip holster, position of cover across the hood, angle to his critical mass. But as he skidded to a stop on the sidewalk, he addressed her nonthreateningly, his voice cracking adolescently: "Ms. Templeton?"

"Deputy Assistant Director Templeton," she said, because he'd put her on alert and she was feeling bitchy.

She stayed tense as he reached into his bag, withdrew a heart-shaped box of chocolates.

He proffered it across the Jeep's hood, wisely keeping some distance. "You have a Valentine's admirer."

She said, flatly, "It's only the eighth."

"Looks like he's planning ahead." The young man's cheeks were flushed from the cold. He hesitated, taking in her squared position behind the Wrangler. "Or she."

"It would be a 'he,'" she said. "Not all straight women look like Bambi."

He licked his chapped lips nervously. "Sorry. Didn't mean to imply . . . Everyone's just touchy these days, so, you know."

He shook the box in his gloved hand.

Embossed on the arterial-red cover was a naked woman with flowing hair astride a horse, Lady Godiva riding her stallion through town to bring justice to the overtaxed masses.

A pulse quickened low in Naomi's stomach, one part alarm, one part excitement.

She took the box, popped the cover. Nestled in among the chocolates, a flat, featureless phone sans logo. Her gaze lifted but already the messenger was biking off, dodging parking meters.

Paranoia nibbled at her brain stem. Though she knew it was pointless, she couldn't resist turning a slow three-sixty there by her Jeep, eyes picking across windows and rooftops.

The phone shrilled, startling her, and she dropped the box, chocolates bouncing out and scattering across the hood. She pried out the phone, lifted it to her face.

"X."

"Templeton."

Her breath misted and misted again.

"I'm texting you an address," he said. In her hand, the phone hummed. "You'll find all sorts of illegal shit here."

"What do you expect me to do?"

"Conduct a federal raid."

"This may come as a surprise, but I don't work for you."

"No. But we could work together."

"'Work together'? If I ever catch you, I'm putting your ass away."

"Obviously," Evan said. "But in the meantime . . ."

"I'd have to be fully transparent, clear anything like this with the director, deputy director, and chief counsel, not to mention half the fucking Office of Professional Responsibility, which I happen to—"

"Naomi."

He almost never used her first name.

"This is an olive branch," he said. "You can strangle it with red tape, bury it beneath subcommittees and oversight panels, have legal hack it up into kindling. And we'll be right back where we started."

"Which is?"

"Where you represent the law in all its indispensability, righteousness, and necessity. And I represent those the law fails."

One of the dark chocolates wagged in the breeze. She thought, *Fuck it,* picked it up, took a bite. Cherry filling. Gross. She spit it out. Bit another. Ganache. Score.

"Or?" she mumbled around the chocolate.

"Or you can figure out which of your colleagues are more than bureaucrats, which of them are actually willing to discharge their duties cleanly in investigative, prosecutorial, and judicial channels at the federal level. Clear a lane of sanctioned competence. And I'll hand you a case to drive through that lane lawfully."

"Lawfully? You? Doth mine ears deceive me?"

"Figure it out and fast. I won't wait for the usual excuses."

"Is that a threat?"

"It is a statement of fact."

"What are you, Batman?"

"Impatient. That's what I am."

The wind blew hard, flecks of almost-snow pinpricking her cheeks. She popped the second half of the truffle in her mouth, chewed while she contemplated the impossible. "If you want to do anything like this, you have to be reachable in some way. I'd be out over my skis. Far."

"You can contact me at 1–855–2-NOWHERE."

"That's real?" She sucked in another icy breath. "Of course it's real."

"Don't bother," he said. "You'll never trace it."

"Regardless, I'm giving the number to technical security. It covers my ass, keeps me legitimate the way you're asking me to be."

"If you'd like to waste resources," Evan said, "be my guest."

She turned around, set her rear end against the Wrangler, let her eyes pick once more across parked vehicles and surrounding buildings. "Why deliver a burner? You could've just called on my work phone."

"Because," Evan said, "this is a courtship."

The line severed.

She forwarded herself the links from the burner and then stared at it. Thought about all the dead ends it would lead to, all the digital threads spinning off into nothingness. It felt like something, a concrete piece of Orphan X. But she knew that was an illusion. Wasted resources, indeed. How odd that she trusted that to be true. She actually trusted Orphan X.

Snapping the phone in half, she dropped it down a storm drain. Plucking another chocolate off the hood, she climbed in the Wrangler and roared off to the Joint Operations Center, the taste of sea salt caramel leaking deliciously along the side of her tongue.

Rising from the couch, Evan set his hands on his lower back and arched, stretching his spine and taking in the soaring ceiling of the architectural loft. Behind him, Manny's complaints grew both more frantic and more muffled.

"—begging you, bro, don't leave me—mmfff—mfff—"

The whir of the vacuum reached a high whine.

Evan strode around the couch.

Manny lay on the floor trapped inside the massive storage bag, the seal nearly airtight. The vacuum sucked free the last remaining air, the clear polyethylene-nylon suctioning to his body. Every wrinkle in his clothes smashed to his flesh, the sidewalls of his nose pinched tight, glasses cracked but holding shape, denting the flesh around his eyes and temples. His face was frozen in a silent scream, the plastic concave inside his mouth, tight enough to outline the seam of every tooth.

He looked like a vacuum-sealed sausage.

Having reached its limit, the device shut off.

Manny's eyes were open, unable to blink given the plastic layer crushed against his lids. But his eyes twitched as Evan looked down at him.

He flopped epileptically. *"Mmmff! Mmffndtd!"*

His head cracked the reclaimed-wood floorboards. He jolted around like the young women in the almost-snuff films he commissioned. Spasms rattled through him. He arched stiffly.

And then stilled.

The silence was refreshing.

Evan stepped one leg across his paralyzed form. Straddling him, he flicked up his Strider knife and bent down.

Manny was almost out, but his pupils tightened with terror.

Evan lowered the tip of the blade to Manny's face.

The suctioned cup plastering the inside of Manny's mouth dimpled under the point. Then popped.

The tiny hole allowed the faintest hiss.

Manny gagged, sucking desperately at the trickle of air. The storage bag had loosened barely across his face. He'd be able to maintain a flow of oxygen sufficient to stay conscious and fend off brain damage.

Barely.

His sobs were stifled. Gulping against the pinhead incision, he gagged, eyes watering. A full-blown panic attack that would know no end.

Rustling weakly against the floor, he sucked and huffed, sucked and huffed.

Evan leaned down.

Manny's pupils contracted even more.

"I have called the authorities to come find you."

As much as was possible, which was not much, Manny's features went lax with relief.

"In D.C.," Evan added. "I'd guess it will take at least an hour for them to coordinate a response here."

Fresh terror bloomed beneath the skin of Manny's face. He lost air, passed out, came back online. Broken blood vessels squiggled through his cheeks, across his nose.

"For that hour, I want you to know that the only reason you are alive is because a woman you helped rape decreed it so. Every sip of breath you take, you think about the grace she has shown you."

Manny's tear ducts leaked, the moisture held in place against the clear plastic, his eye sockets turned to submarine portholes.

As Evan headed back toward the fire escape, Manny tried to scream. But not much sound could escape.

Halfway onto the balcony, Evan hesitated. Lowered his head and cursed.

The soles of his boots knocked against the reclaimed wood as he reapproached with intent, knife in hand. Manny squirmed and bucked.

Evan pinned him to the floor with a knee in his chest, bent down over him, leading with the knife. A jab at his face.

The Strider had opened up the hole over Manny's mouth.

Manny sucked oxygen, legs doing a mermaid flop. "Th-thank you," he stuttered between gasps. "Th-th—"

Evan leaned close, their noses almost touching. "You don't deserve this much air."

He tore himself off Manny before his darker instincts could prevail.

The sound of Manny's unmuffled sobbing followed him across the loft and out onto the fire escape. Even halfway down, he could still hear the wails.

29

The Help That Is Coming

On Evan's drive back to the Bronx, the flash drive in his cargo pocket refused to recede into the background of his attention. The metal rectangle dimpled the skin of his thigh, a loaded pistol with the safety off.

He dreaded having to watch what was on it.

But he needed to see if he could identify Anca's captors, and that meant having to observe what they'd done to her.

For privacy, he booked a room a few blocks from Anca's apartment. The hotel was a converted turn-of-the-century opera house, Italian Renaissance Revival with rusticated stone and tall arched windows. The room was cheap, clean, utilitarian.

Sitting on a maroon bed runner festooned with beige flowers, he stared at the laptop he'd picked up at a Best Buy, set up on the facing dresser. Firming his jaw, he withdrew the thumb drive from his pocket, inserted it, and called up the MP4 video.

The cursor floated above the PLAY arrow.

His mouth was dry. His hands gripped his knees.

The Fourth Commandment: *Never make it personal.*

He took a breath. Locked himself down.

And clicked.

He observed forensically.

A Hieronymus Bosch tableau.

Four assailants. Black ski masks. Stark lighting interspersed with shadow.

A horned-goat-skull tattoo glistened on the sweaty pectoral of the biggest man. One of the others had a sunken chest and a tat as well, low-quality work that looked like a blue blob. The third man was wolfish and muscular, a triangle of manscaped chest hair, eight-pack definition suggesting steroids or heavy supplements. He was the definitive leader, silently directing movements and setting the tone in all its hideous variance. The last guy cackled like a jester, repeating himself frequently: "My turn! My turn!"

Evan modulated his breathing, his heart rate. He took in data, noted details, assessed what might be useful. But then he felt it skittering at the edges of his thoughts, biting at his perception, tugging it out of shape.

Emotion.

Body temperature rising. Sweat prickling his eyes. He armed his forehead, refocusing, but it just came on stronger, hurling itself against the door, thudding to get in.

Don't let it, he told himself. *Do not let it in.*

He looked for distinctive marks and scars, listened for spoken clues, noted cadences of speech, read posture and body language.

Goat-Skull Tattoo made only vowel sounds, unbridled id unrestrained by the alphabet.

Don't let it in.

Eight-Pack grabbed a piece of Anca's anatomy, made it bulge for the camera.

Evan hit PAUSE, took a moment to catch his breath. He needed Joey on digital forensics ASAP but could he subject her to this? She'd asked. She'd asked to come along. He emailed her the file, hesitated, and then sent it to Naomi Templeton as well. The progress bar showed he was only fourteen minutes into the recording. There was another hour and fifty-seven minutes. It felt intolerable to watch any longer. And yet Anca had actually endured it.

He resumed.

The men shifted her sluggish body around on the bed, adjusting her as they pleased, feeding on her, off her, shaking her in the fangs of their depravity. There was nothing she could say or do or be to make it stop. She floated through the dimmed twilight between cognizance and oblivion, between life and death, suspended in a drugged purgatory.

Don't let it in.

A compulsion nearly overtook him, to erupt to his feet and hammer his fist through the wall. But there would be damage. He would break a finger or dislocate a knuckle and healing time would be costly in the execution of his mission.

Don't let it in.

The level of psychopathic detachment in the assailants was not unfamiliar to him. He had encountered it plenty and even embodied it himself when a situation demanded reprisal of the become-a-monster-to-hunt-monsters variety. Manny Llorente had learned as much. But right now, even as his eyes registered what was happening on the screen, his ability to observe it objectively began to slip. Fighting to hold emotion at bay, to keep himself in check, to hold everything out except what he needed to note operationally, he'd—

—slid forward off the bed, taking the comforter with him. Crouching, gangster low to the carpet, coiled like a snake. The mattress was against his shoulders and the video kept on unimpeded and it didn't show merely a victim and her assailants, it showed Anca Dumitrescu, the woman he'd come to know and admire, a woman who kept a stuffed-animal penguin from the Bronx Zoo and made jokes about holy water and clasped her tiny hands when she was distressed. Without knowing it, his guard had lowered, and he had to take her in as her full self. And now he was watching the violation happening to her specifically, to Anca, experiencing what she had experienced as a whole person with dreams and pain and fears and choices, not as an object being ravished or a victim to be analyzed or an ideal to be avenged, but a human subjected to the ultimate degradation and brutality, and he felt, he *felt* her.

His RoamZone was out and he had dialed Joey and she'd already answered and when he could find words, he said, "The video of Anca, it was uploaded to RedLite."

Joey's breath left her as if she'd been struck in the gut. "RedLite? They're the parent company for, like, a kabillion porn sites."

"I need you to find it, Joey. Do you understand?"

"You want me to—"

"Search it out there and everywhere it has been reposted online."

"You want me to—deep-dive into that—see them, her like that? That'll be awful."

His cheeks were wet. "You are the help. Right now, for this, you are the help that is coming."

"I understand," Joey said. "I will. I will do it."

"Erase every trace, take it down, hit it with a DDOS attack, anything and everything. I want this shit expunged. Period. Every IP address of everyone who watches it, downloads it, I want their device shredded. A worm or virus that infects any computer that touches this piece of content. A digital fucking STD."

"Got it. I'll—"

"Devine will have whatever RE or exploit tools you need. He's got plenty of green-badged friends at the agencies. Wipe that footage from every corner of the web. Every viewing is another violation. There can't be a single trace of what she went through out there. For more miscreants to watch and . . . and . . ."

"You okay, X?"

"Identify those four animals. Gait biometrics, voice recognition, every single angle. They're still out there. They're out there and they will do this again. This is what they do."

"X. You okay?"

"Yes."

"You sure?"

"Just get it done."

"X. I will."

A pause.
"X?"
A longer pause.
"X?"
"Thank you, J."
Click.

"Can you . . . Will you help me?"

Candy glanced over from her post at the living-room window. In the wake of Anca's attack, her view of humanity had dimmed ever further. She'd been surveilling the street, hoping for somebody to do something terrible in clear view so she'd have a reason to beat them senseless.

Anca stood in the slim crack of the bathroom door, towel wrapped tightly around her midsection, steam rolling over her shoulders. An awkward, self-conscious slump, wisp of hair curled across her throat, Venus on that big-ass shell.

Candy said, "Yes."

She walked over. Anca hesitated before stepping back and allowing the door gap to widen. The bathroom was small, close quarters, choked with steam.

Candy cleared her throat. "What do you need?"

Anca's chin dipped, eyes lowered. She turned timidly and let the towel slide a few inches off her shoulder blade, showing the obscene drawing. The skin around it had been scrubbed red, the black marker faded but still clearly visible.

Candy wondered at the amount of work it had taken Anca to clear the matching filth from her cheek. In the mirror, Candy saw Anca's features contort briefly into a sob. She fought her face back into control and Candy pretended not to have noticed.

Anca reached for a bottle on the lip of the sink beside a nearly depleted bag of cotton balls. She handed the rubbing alcohol to Candy. "I can't reach it well enough."

Candy set the bottle back down. "Olive oil works, too," she said. "Gentler on the skin."

"It'll take longer."

"It's okay," Candy said. "I have time."

Anca's cheeks were flushed from the heat of the shower or maybe from something else. Her eyes brimmed.

She nodded with gratitude.

It was either day or night, Devine decided, before realizing that was not exactly a Kantian bit of reasoning. He lay in Egyptian-cotton sheets with a four-figure thread count, too tired to sleep, fragmented notions piercing his spinning mind, stuck through the white matter like shards. He did not feel at home inside himself. And there was nowhere else to go.

Even so, he could not give up. A verse from *Pirkei Avot* fell like rainwater through the hollowness at his core: *It is not incumbent upon you to complete the work, but neither are you at liberty to desist from it.* God, he loved the channelers of the first Book, those who'd leapt to touch the numinous unknown and pair it with the light inside every human.

Rolling onto his side, he used the meat of his biceps as a pillow, curling fetally. Shade-muted light fell in melon slices from the radius windows to lie across him. A moment of peace.

Then there came a tapping of footsteps. Two sets.

Rawlings cleared his throat. "Sorry to bother you, sir."

"I need to go full cyberwarfare," the girl said. "And there's a next-level boot-and-nuke secure-eraser malware I need to access."

Devine did not stir. Only his lips moved. "For what?"

"To wipe uploaded footage of a gang rape off the internet."

The girl had put toughness into her voice to showcase resilience, but Devine could hear what it was covering. Horror.

They were fallen.

They were all so fallen.

When Devine blinked, he was surprised to see a wet spot on the pillowcase beneath his face.

"It's behind about a dozen firewalls at NSA's Tailored Access Operations," the girl—Josephine?—said. "I can hack it but it'll take time. I don't have time. I need a shortcut. I need your help."

A coldness fell upon Devine. An exhalation shuddered out of him like a shiver.

"I have an acquaintance at SIGINT at NSA," Devine said. "A major general who visited here last fall and couldn't help but bite a shiny, shiny apple."

Rawlings said, "I know the one. May I call him under your authority?"

"You may indeed," Devine said. "What time is it?"

"Time to rest," the girl said.

Devine laughed. His whole body ached with the movement.

"That is," he said, "one superpower I wish I had."

30

Last Man Standing

Anca was wiping the surfaces of her apartment with an obsessive energy that Evan knew all too well. She'd barely paused at his entrance, flurrying from coffee table to secretary desk, her spray bottle and worn rag sparing no speck or streak.

Candy sat on the plastic-covered sofa watching with an expression that took Evan a full five seconds to name, since he'd never seen it on her face: helplessness. Catching his eye, she arched her perfect brows, held her hands wide, palms flared upward.

"Anca," Evan said, "I have to talk to you."

"That's fine." Anca lifted the family pictures, wiping down the frames and thunking them back into place. "And I have to talk to both of you. You've been incredibly helpful and the dead bolts are changed now and I need to be strong. I have to be strong again, and independent."

Evan eased farther inside. "I understand."

Her laminated seizure plan rested on the couch beside Candy, its lanyard of yellow yarn puddled atop it. Candy tracked his gaze, mouthed: *Two seizures today.*

Evan said, again, "There's something I have to tell you."

"Which means," Anca continued, her voice rising over his, "that I'll need to learn how to stay alone in the apartment again. I start work again tomorrow—"

"Work?" Candy said. "Can't you take some time off?"

"I've already used my vacation days."

"How about sick days?"

"Them as well. Last summer I took a pilgrimage to see the frescoes at the Monastery of Suceviţa."

Candy said, "I'm sure the church can give you a bit more—"

"My suffering does not earn me special favor." Anca wiped down the top of the AC unit, showing tender attention to the Jesus postcard. Snapping the rag, she headed into the kitchen, her gait still strained from the damage inside her. "Besides," she said, as Evan and Candy followed her in, "I can't afford not to work. There's rent and now a mess of medical bills and I still have my student loan to pay off from my year of college, twenty-seven thousand dollars compounding at five-point-five percent."

"I can pay off your student loan," Evan said.

Anca turned crisply on her heel, twisting a wadded-up dish towel inside a coffee mug. "I filled out the forms. I signed my name. I took the courses. It's my responsibility to pay it off. Why would you? Because I was violated?"

Evan said, dumbly, "Yes."

She shook the coffee mug at him. "You need to think through your principles."

Women are impossible, he thought. *At least the good ones.*

"It's not a sin to take care of yourself," he said.

"Oh. That's it then." Tilting into a fight, her voice tremulous with outrage. "You think I'm holier than thou. 'Saint Anca.'"

"I didn't say that."

"I didn't say you *said* it."

Evan looked to Candy for backup, but she gave him elevated eyebrows once more with a you're-on-your-own head tilt and sank into the chair at the tiny table set for one.

"Anca," he tried again, "there's something I need to tell you."

"You have an infuriating way of not answering questions." She slammed the mug into the cupboard, looked around frantically for something else to clean or dry. "'Pain insists upon being attended to,'" she said, in a cadence implying a quotation. "That's what I am doing. Attending to my suffering. And attempting to face the worst with my best."

"Brave," Evan ventured. "But—"

"No." Anca shook her head. "It's not courage. No matter how humbled we think we are, we can always be humbled further."

"What, then? Fear?"

"No. Not fear. Not exactly." Anca scratched at her hairline. "Awe."

"I don't put much stock in awe."

"How cute," Anca said, breezing past him, "that you think it's up to you."

He reached after her to catch her by the arm, but Candy flared her fingers at him, the motion abrupt and surreptitious at the same time: *Don't touch her right now.*

He got it, nodded his thanks.

Candy rose and went into the living room at Evan's side. Now Anca was fussing in a coat closet, wrestling out a vacuum cleaner. The floor was spotless. She turned it on, began sliding it back and forth with manic abandon.

"Anca," Evan said. *"Anca."*

Candy moved over to her. Anca struck Candy's foot with the vacuum. She looked up, blinking, her chest heaving.

She shut off the vacuum. Her lips trembled. One arm straight, the other reaching across her midsection to grip the locked elbow. "What?"

"There were cameras," Evan said. "They had cameras." He hated the words coming out of his mouth, hated himself for being the instrument to deliver them.

"Cameras? *Cameras?* What? Why?"

"They recorded you," he said quietly. "And released it."

She looked as though he'd struck her, and in a sense he had. She dropped the handle of the vacuum. It clattered on the floor.

Hovering a half step off his ribs, Candy exhaled a long, slow breath through clenched teeth.

Anca's hand fluttered behind her, feeling for the wall. She caught it. Leaned. Her knees buckled but she didn't go down. Inch by inch she drew herself erect.

"I believe . . ." She faded out. Came back in. "I need to lie down. Just, please . . ." She waved a hand at them and then turned and walked unsteadily into her bedroom. The door closed softly behind her.

Evan looked down at the floor. Beside him, he could hear Candy's breathing. It sounded ragged. For a time they just stood there.

"Know what was included in my training?" she asked.

She was not looking at him. She stared straight ahead and he stared ahead along with her. He waited.

"If I was fully overpowered, getting raped, how to relax my muscles to minimize physical damage. They didn't make us practice. Not *fully.*" She punched the last word hard, a bit of fury leaking through. "But there were . . . simulations." She made a kind of snicker that was drained of amusement. "Were you ever trained for anything like that?"

Evan said, "No."

In his peripheral vision, he sensed Candy nod and then nod some more. "In the foster homes, it wasn't a simulation. When I turned . . . when I turned thirteen, I became immensely palatable to men." Her hands cupped her narrow waist, shoved resentfully down over the bulge of her hips as if sloughing off an outer skin. "My curves." Her upper lip peeled back in a snarl, and the snarl was in her voice, too. "They 'couldn't help themselves.' The first time, I was paralyzed, numb, terrified. I couldn't talk, could barely move. I felt . . . I felt like I was six years old."

Evan didn't know where to look. Didn't know what to say.

"My first year in the Program, a female instructor took my trauma history. Bitter old bitch with coffee breath and crumbly makeup. Know what she told me?"

Evan did not.

"'You had power. To flirt or rebuff or draw lines. To not be undone by their wiles, their projections of power. You had the power to speak up. To say *no.* To scream and fight. But you didn't. You stayed silent. Stuck in obedience. In compliance. Never relinquish control again.'" Candy breathed a bit more. "I was in a chair in an interrogation room. She was standing over me. She had a ballpoint pen in her shirt pocket. I wanted to rip it free and stab it through her fucking eye socket." She wet her lips, swallowed, pulled her head back. "But I didn't."

"What *did* you do?"

"Took the lesson," Candy said. "That's what I fucking did."

The distinctive ring of the RoamZone rescued him.

Caller ID showed Naomi Templeton.

Candy waved her hand: *Take it.*

Stepping into the hall, he answered. "Go."

"We found Manny Llorente," Templeton said. "He was in bad shape."

"He should be thankful for the shape he was left in."

Templeton muttered a few choice words away from the phone. She came back to the receiver. "He's in custody. We're processing what we found. There's plenty. The primary porn operation is legal but there's a lot of shit around the edges that looks to be illicit. Underage, kidnapping, assault."

"Burn it to the ground."

A text dinged in from Joey: ive got boot n nuke malware chewing thru the interwebs. itll be wiped everywhere by days end.

"A lot of the videos and victims will be hard to source," Templeton said. "I assume the video file you sent us was your point of entry into the mission?"

"Yes."

"The woman's name?"

"I need to talk to her before I escalate the case."

"Do."

Templeton was interrupted again by Joey: redlite will still have it on their servers, tho. ull need 2 go there + do a physical wipe on site.

Evan texted her back: Where's RedLite HQ?

"We need a victim testimony," Templeton continued.

Evan said, "I'm not sure if that's possible."

its in our home town, uv course, porn capital of the world.

Templeton: "With an official statement, we can open another lane of investigation and start pulling warrants."

Evan paced in the hallway. "She doesn't need to go through that."

"Yes. She does. You asked to do this legitimately. This is how it works. We don't get to pursue a case and make arrests without evidence. Obviously. You know this."

Joey again: ill get u malware loaded on 2 flash drives. meet u dwntwn 4 dinner 2nite 4 handoff. will txt u address.

Evan gave Joey a thumbs-up, not the emoji but the little one that rode the top of the text bubble. Joey's incessant teasing had motivated him to step up his pictogram-usage game.

Back to Templeton, he said, "She already filed charges for the assault with NYPD."

Joey: ran tattoos thru FBI + NIST databases no hits will keep digging 4 IDs.

He texted back: Find them.

"With kidnapping, we're hooking the case federal," Templeton said. "That's the point. That's why you called me. We can use the first report but we need her to give a full statement to an assistant U.S. attorney. It's not open for negotiation if you want us to prosecute on her behalf."

Evan stopped outside Anca's door. The simple wooden cross had been repaired and set back in place. For some reason, the sight irked him. He pressed the ledge of his knuckles to the jamb, shoved until he felt the pinch of bone into flesh.

Evan said, "If I can convince her, you be there, then. You personally. I don't trust anyone else."

"Fine."

"I'll be there, too. With her."

In the pause, he heard a breeze blow across the phone.

"How do you know I won't arrest you?" Templeton asked.

"Give me your word you won't."

"That's all you want? My word?"

"Yes."

Templeton heaved a sigh. "Okay. You have my word."

"She's in a fragile state."

"I watched the video." That was all she needed to say.

"I'll find an opening to discuss this with her. You figure out an off-the-radar place and manner where we can meet if I can convince her."

He hung up, drew a breath, and then went back inside. Candy sat in the armchair leaning forward, blond hair arcing to frame her face on both sides. Her hands were clasped, her feet set solidly on the floor.

Evan started for Anca's bedroom.

Candy said, "No."

"No?"

"Leave her alone."

"I have to meet Joey to pick up some malware. I'll head to L.A. tomorrow, pay RedLite a visit. In the meantime, Templeton agreed to pursue a federal investigation. Anca has to make a statement."

"Don't ask her now. She isn't ready for anything right now. Except rest."

"Those pieces of shit are still out there," Evan said. "Among a city filled with young women."

"So find them. And kill them. You don't need a statement from her to do that."

"I swore to her that I wouldn't kill them."

"So find them. And maim them."

"Okay."

"Castration isn't murder." Candy's knuckles were bloodless. Still her gaze did not lift. "Just an observation," she said.

31

No, Please

If there was one thing Evan was profoundly not in the mood for, it was the speakeasy-lounge vibe of the place Joey had selected. There were peated shishito peppers and whipped French feta and a thousand kinds of whiskey but nary a proper vodka. The crowded, narrow bowling-alley space hummed with stock tips and pickup lines, rat-a-tatting cocktail shakers, the clatter of designer flatware. Scarlet lighting infused high rows of glass cabinets lining the walls. At the far end of the restaurant before a curtain of red velvet, a Betty Boop singer in a sequined dress swayed on a cramped stage, mouthing baby-girl oohs and aahs with sultry aplomb. She had the demure-sex-bomb look down, round-faced with neotenous big eyes, a flapper coiffure, and a bright cherry garter that flashed alluringly beneath the high-cut hem of her dress.

Sunk in a plush maroon booth with button tufting, Joey looked more adult than made sense, glowing with a fresh confidence likely derived from her promotion. She wore a one-shoulder black dress and dark eyeliner, her hair in an expensive-looking sweep no doubt fashioned by a team of stylists Devine kept stored in one of the pantries. Shimmer makeup at her temple added a lustrous shine to her smooth bronze skin and her lips were painted an uncharacteristically bright shade of ruby.

He didn't like any of it.

He wondered when he'd become such a fucking prude. He suspected that two hours and eleven minutes of video footage had something to do with it.

He sipped at his martini, an unimaginative but proficient vodka that he'd ordered dry because who the hell wanted aromatized wine sullying five-times-distilled Picardy soft winter wheat and limestone-rich water hauled a hundred and fifty meters up from a Gensac aquifer. Joey slurped at a gin-and-elderflower abomination rife with juniper, mint, blueberry, blackberry, rosemary, and lemon. He took a European view of her underage drinking; the offense was not that she was drinking but that she was drinking something that smelled like hippie bath oil.

In the gutter-wide alley between their booth and a neighboring table, a finance type with a booze-blotched pasty face tried to get jiggy with a hot young thing, his hands waving overhead as she twerked into him. Laughing drunkenly, he threw high fives to his seated associates.

Joey's voice lasered in at him: "X, you okay?"

The "top shelf" vodka was warm, insufficiently shaken. "Yes."

Her hand dipped into her clutch purse—when the hell had she acquired a clutch purse?—and slid a handful of flash drives across the table at him. They looked official-issue, each featuring the RedLite logo. "These are locked and loaded with all kinds of malicious shit," she said. "Buffer overflows, boot-sector viruses, network share infectors. I made sure you have backups. Once one is plugged into a computer logged into the closed network, the worm'll replicate itself through the system."

"It'll wipe any trace of Anca from the servers?"

Joey said, "It'll do a helluva lot more than that."

When Evan blinked, a strobe image flashed behind his lids: *Goat Skull thrusts and grunts, his bare torso greased with sweat.*

"Collateral damage?" Evan asked.

"Vast."

"Good."

"I should be able to hit some of their browser histories and bank accounts too, gut their profits, clean the money, donate it to, dunno, places like Children of the Night to help child prostitutes or something."

Joey adjusted her hair and he tracked the tilt of her shoulders, caught her angling toward a young man with artfully curated stubble elbowed into the bar. She noticed Evan watching her, jerked her hand away from her face. "What?"

Something smoldered in his chest, a burning heap of refuse. He shook his head.

"What's going on, X? You've been all weird since you got here."

Eight-Pack grabs at Anca, squeezing and mugging for the camera, rocker tongue stuck through the ski-mask hole.

"Why are you dressed up, J?"

"What? Dressed *up*? We're, like, out in a restaurant in New York. What do you want me to wear? A gunnysack?"

The man dancing by their booth lost his balance, setting a palm down next to Joey's bread plate to avoid toppling. He brayed laughter, his external jugular vein visible at the side of his neck. Evan's three-tined fork was an inch and change off his right hand. The angle was good.

My turn! My turn!

"You are on a mission, Joey. You shouldn't be making eyes at random men in a bar."

"I'm hardly ma—"

His voice stayed dead calm. "This is a mission. Not happy hour."

A waiter heaved forth from the crowd, swinging down at Joey. Evan's hand twitched. A quick snatch to grab the shirt collar, slam his head to the table, and ready the table knife over his ear.

The waiter leaned toward Joey and Evan let him. Mouth at her ear above her bared neck. "The gentleman at the bar sent this over."

Yellow-looking syrup in a coupe glass with a fucking dandelion floating in it.

Joey's cheeks colored. As the waiter withdrew, she looked down at the drink, not touching it. Her voice, quiet: "Men always send Candy drinks."

Black wool faces, naked bodies feasting.

The dandelion was imperfect, one side dimpled from the bartender's thumb, the thrown-off symmetry like a stitching needle through Evan's frontal lobe. A crack in the cushion pressed unevenly into his right hamstring. There were two wet drops on the tabletop and a smudge of something that looked sticky, and a stray hair glistened atop the booth nine inches to the left of Joey's shoulder, wagging in the vented air. The egress routes intensified in his mind, blueprint routes through the throbbing crowd looping in his mind with compulsive intensity. The filter had snapped into high, his obsessive attention going hard now, raining hell down on everything like a fire hose he couldn't control.

"Candy could murder every single person in this lounge with escargot tongs." Evan's tone was quiet, steady, observational. "Do not compare yourself to Candy. You haven't earned what she has. You are operational. Right now. Your job is to remain unnoticed, inconspicuous. Not to present ostentatiously and elicit shitty cocktails from men at the bar. You want more responsibility. *Earn it.*"

A different means of handling the conflict flickered into awareness, a scantily lit corridor in his mind. But then another image arrested him: *Anca's limp leg shoved aside, the ankle handed off.* He slammed the door, doubled down: "You can be the focus of the room," he told Joey, words as steady and unvaried as a computer printout, "or focus on the room. You can't do both."

The color in her cheeks clarified into twinning circles. "Look, I'm sorry, okay. I haven't been to New York, ever. It's like a dream. Not all of us got to swan around like a less charming James Bond for half our lives."

A stab of chagrin registered across the divide, in the other side of himself. He'd missed it. He'd missed the whole lane of her experience. The First Commandment: *Assume nothing.*

But this was not the time or place for chagrin.

"Do not use any tone or body language that is noteworthy," he said. "Check your mood. Mind your emotion. Watch your vitals. Sip the drink."

She was sucking air shallowly. He watched her slowly wind her way back into control. He blinked and saw that she looked—through another lens—like a beautiful young woman.

The scruffled guy was cutting through the crowd, coming for them. Watch on right wrist made him a lefty. Jacket too sleek to hide a holster unless it was a high-ride. Expensive loafers would have slick leather soles, no traction.

The guy smiled too broadly as he approached, smug, working himself up. "Hello. I'm so sorry to intrude. I assume this is your daughter?"

Joey's face had gone numb, lifeless. She did not look up at the man; she kept her stare evenly on Evan, her words as dead as sand: "Not interested."

The guy lingered, unsurely. His crotch was a foot and a half off Evan's left elbow. A hammer punch would render him in need of hospitalization. Evan's hand had already made a loose fist.

Evan stared into Joey's emerald eyes and she stared into his. Nothing else existed.

The guy made a dismissive chortle and withdrew.

Joey lifted her napkin and wiped the bright red from her lips. Reaching up, she pulled free a clasp from the back of her hair, and her black-brown locks tumbled forward, hiding her face. She wriggled a too-large coat up from the booth behind her and across her shoulders, covering her bare skin.

Now she looked like not much.

"RedLite's in Century City, probably visible from your penthouse," she said. "I arranged a private jet for you out of Teterboro tomorrow morning. Devine's fleet, untraceable tail number, both ends covered to ensure no FAA ramp check. You're a blogger with a giant sex-positive Substack following. Melinda's anchoring the legend, backstopping your bona fides."

Melinda Truong, his brilliant forger, could counterfeit embossments, holograms, U.S. passport paper, NFTs, and virtually anything else. Standing up a fake Substack account and generating a backlog of AI articles would be child's play for her.

"You'll get thirty minutes with the chief content officer Tuesday at noon," Joey said. "That gives you tomorrow to case the operation. In the meantime Candy holds protection around Anca and I'll identify the offenders."

Lowball glasses clinked drunkenly at the neighboring table, the sound of smacked glass redolent of a sniper round piercing a window. One of the men tilted back abruptly in his chair—*pressed into the bare mattress, stomach down*—nearing Joey and—*unconscious form flipped like a living doll*—Evan almost kicked out the wooden rear legs and brought him tumbling onto his back where—*hands clutching and grasping, red grip marks across pale flesh*—he could drop a kneecap onto the throat to shatter the trachea.

The pack of drunken men was within touching distance of Joey. One of the guys pawed at the woman he'd been dancing with and she let his fat hand slide across her belly.

Evan's heartbeat had quickened, the pulse tangible at the side of his neck. If he didn't want to draw in a close-quarters space crowded with no-shoots, he had his Strider, the table knife, fork, the jagged peg of a torn-off chair leg. A clean strike at the bread plate could break it into shards, a double-wrap of the cloth napkin protecting his palm on the grip. Joey's coupe glass could be ground into an eye socket, extra points for the blinding sting of alcohol.

If he eliminated them all now there would no longer be a threat to Joey.

But there wasn't.

There wasn't a threat to Joey.

"I have to go," he said. "I'm not safe to be around right now."

Joey wilted.

He threw cash on the table and sliced through the throng, adhering strictly to the third of his five pre-charted routes to the front exit.

Driving through Midtown toward the Bronx, Evan was completely locked in. High visual alertness, a mental map of surrounding blocks continuously unfolding around him as he forged north, heart rate resting around 60 bpm.

And yet.

He could not let go of the way Joey had wilted when he left, hidden beneath her hair and an oversize coat.

Guilt wrestled with righteous annoyance.

The delta between the training he'd undergone and the operations he'd conducted and Joey's abbreviated time in the Orphan Program was substantial. It was also worrisome. He didn't know if she'd been stress-tested sufficiently to be field-operational. He couldn't even be sure if she could handle a basic waterboarding.

He avoided the FDR, driving through interior city streets to maximize alternative routes. A light rain fell, making the asphalt shimmer. Coasting up First Avenue, he found himself dialing Aragón.

"Hola, amigo."

Evan said, "I think I screwed up."

"Screwed up how?"

Three greens in a row, street signs for Sixty-Third, Sixty-Fourth, Sixty-Fifth whipping by overhead. Evan cleared his throat. "Handling a situation with Joey."

"Explain to me."

Evan did.

Aragón said, "Zoom me."

"Why?"

"So I can see you."

"Why?"

"To understand better, yes? To see."

"I don't Zoom."

"So call with whatever *pinche* encrypted shit you use."

The median strip hemmed Evan in on the left, giving him two

decently flowing northbound lanes to work with. Parked cars clogged the third. Skyscrapers towered on either side. Even in the fancy Mercedes, it felt claustrophobic, like burrowing through a maze.

"I'm driving."

"Then pull over."

"I'm in Manhattan. I can't find a space."

Aragón laughed at him. Not a kind laugh. "Cabrón de Ningún Lado, world-class assassin, can wipe out an entire cartel with a fountain pen. But he cannot find parking. This is so sad, no?" He'd infused more Mexican street into his already robust accent, so Evan knew he had to trust what was coming at him.

He said, "Fine."

Cutting the line, he revved the gas and then punched the brake, wrenching the steering wheel. All four tires flew across the slick pavement, the car arcing into a controlled 270-degree skid. Still rotating, he floated across the neighboring lane behind a garbage truck and skipped between two parked cars and up across a curb ramp to tuck neatly into the side of a loading bay, nose pointed out, passenger door inches from the concrete embankment, bumper a foot and a half from the rolled-down dock door. He cut the engine, lights muting, disappearing as surely as a hawk swooping into a hidden roost. The entire maneuver had taken less than two seconds.

Beyond the windshield, the city kept on in all its gyroscopic wonder without him.

Cloaked in darkness, he redialed through his *pinche* encrypted shit.

Aragón's face loomed large. He was ensconced in his *patrón* armchair in the living room, that row of antique books behind him like he was a lawyer on a TV commercial. "You're all shadowy. How do you say? The noir."

"Yes. The noir."

"I am glad you are done whining like a *maricón* about parking," Aragón said. "And you know I support *maricones* so don't be sensitive. You know what I am saying. Now as for Josephine, she showed up looking, what? Visible?"

"Ostentatious."

"I don't know that word. But whatever. She is a woman. Women are amazing. They are so deep and twisty and, eh, *intuitiva*. How they think? It is so different. And the feelings! It's hard to believe they are the same species let alone that we are supposed to mate with them."

"Joey's not a woman. Not entirely. And no one's mating with her anytime soon."

"Fine. Females, then. Who knows what they have to negotiate in any setting? So you thought she was— What's your word?"

"Ostentatious."

"Too visible. Have *you* ever been to a club as a woman?"

Rhetorical questions annoyed Evan. He refused to answer.

Aragón was undeterred. "Then how do you know what she must do to figure her way and—*cómo se dice?*—ah, read the room? And this mission, it has you not so steady, eh? It has brought up fear in you. So you are seeing only Josephine's blind spots, not the possibilities or advantages of her approach. Maybe what she sees covers *your* blind spots."

"I don't have blind spots. Not operationally."

"Okay. So is that what you want for her? To be just like you?"

Evan started to answer, stopped, bit down on the inside of his lower lip. Aragón waited knowingly. A woman walked by with a little yappy dog. The light cycled from yellow to red to green. Across the street, a guy in a pickup tried to parallel park, missed the angle, got in on the second try.

Evan said, "No."

"If you demand perfection, you will break her. Or create someone who is perfect in one way and one way only. Allow her more leeway."

Evan said, "Fine."

"But on the other hand?" Aragón shrugged. "Screw her feelings. She wants to operate? She has to learn."

"Helpful," Evan said.

Someone shouted, *"A la mesa!"*

"Coming!" Aragón rose from his armchair with a groan. "Keep open," he told Evan. "Get rid of this black-and-white Nowhere

Man thinking. And you will see what to do with Josephine. It is like with this woman you are helping. Sometimes we learn the most from people we most disagree with."

"Five minutes ago, you wanted me to execute Luke Devine."

"That *hijo de su chingada madre* isn't 'people,'" he said, and hung up.

32

The Parable of Anca Dumitrescu

Even reclining on Anca's couch, Candy looked coiled. That's how she was, an embodiment of latent energy. Until she went kinetic.

At the moment, her eyes were ice blue. Evan couldn't remember if that was their real color. They changed depending on what she was wearing and she also had a variety of contact lenses that aided her chameleonlike propensity. It wasn't merely about disguise, this ability, it was an alteration of her carriage and bearing, energy and posture. She could ignite your attention and then recede right before your eyes.

At the moment she seemed fully in the version he recognized as most like herself. But he could never be sure.

Flicking aside the magazine she'd been reading, she drew herself upright on the couch, a tigress-like undulation of her spine. "How'd it go with Joey?"

Evan looked at her.

Candy said, "That well?"

Evan said, "Anca?"

"Sleeping like a baby. I checked on her a few times. She's out cold. Hasn't moved an inch."

"She needs to sleep for a month," Evan said.

Candy gave a nod, her eyes distant.

Despite Anca's best efforts, the apartment smelled of dust. Motes spun in the yellowed glow filtered through the lampshade. A touch of moisture in the air, a harbinger of mold, the smell of wet brick. Cold Bronx night leaked through a draft in the window with a moan. The paint along the sill had flaked elegantly into a mosaic of cracked mud.

Candy said, "You fly back tomorrow to deal with RedLite?"

"Yes."

"I booked a room at your hotel," Candy said. "She wants to sleep here alone tonight."

"I'm not sure that's a good idea."

"It's not up to us," Candy said. "Is it?"

Before Evan could reply, screaming ripped through the living room. A high-pitched undulated wail.

He knew the sound. Night terrors morphing into a panic attack.

Candy was halfway to the closed bedroom door already, having levitated directly onto her feet. "Got it, I got it—"

She blew inside, the door sweeping shut behind her. The screaming kept on. And on. Deep screeching breaths, wails guttering into sobs.

The sound—unadulterated anguish—was nearly unbearable. Evan paced around the living room, fingers shoved through his hair.

The keening kept on undiminished. Unintelligible words pushed through a constricted throat and a grief-spasmed diaphragm. One lamentation came audible—"*Why, why, why—*"

Between wails, he could make out Candy's murmuring, low and cooing, the softest he'd ever heard her voice.

Just when the sobbing seemed to quiet down, the screams resumed, throttling back up, strident peaks interspersed with breathless weeping.

Evan paced some more.

Sweat matted his shirt, made his cargo pants cling to his legs. A dozen times he debated entering the bedroom and a dozen times he resisted the urge.

Fifteen excruciating minutes passed. And then another fifteen.

Anca's moans grew hoarse and finally gave out.

The silence was even more awful.

Evan checked his Vertex fob watch. Forty-seven minutes had passed. He'd never known anyone to cry for that long. He didn't know anyone could.

He was over at the window leaning on the sill, dried paint razoring his palms, the draft lifting his hair, cooling the sweat on his forehead. What was this darkness he felt roosting in his own chest, a shadow of anguish caught like an infection?

The bedroom door clicked and he spun around.

Candy emerged. A flush touched her cheekbones and she looked uncharacteristically rumpled, wrinkles wadding her shirt in whorls, wet splotches darkening her chest, her shoulder.

She returned to her spot on the couch and sat, elbows on knees, staring at the union of her hands. She breathed evenly, steadily.

Evan walked over to her, stood a moment in silence. "Does she need medical?"

Candy shook her head, the curved points of her long bangs brushing her chin.

"What did you do?" he asked.

"I held her."

"You." His voice was flat with a not unkind disbelief. "Held her."

"Yes. I'm not a fucking animal." Her eyes flicked up and she must have seen the words knife into him because her face softened. "Oh," she said. "You're in mission mode. If you weren't, you would've known to do it, too."

No, he thought. *I wouldn't have.*

Instead, he said, "You good?"

"No," Candy said. "I want to be held and comforted."

"Really?"

Her lips twitched. "No."

A squeak of hinges. Anca filled the doorway, her face pallid, lips and eyelids raw and rouged pink. She wore a sweater and a winter coat and a pair of boots with thick laces.

"I need . . ." Her voice cracked. She reset herself. "I need to go to the store."

"I'll go with you," Evan said.

"No," she said. "Thank you. I must start to be in the world myself. I want to go alone."

She started for the door, hesitated with her hand on the knob. Then she turned.

"I saw hell," she said. "I was there." A quick intake of air jerked her chest, the aftermath of sobbing. "Tată used to say that hell is locked from the inside. And we all have the key. You two? Helped me find the key."

She dipped her head, a demure gesture of gratitude. And then she left.

Candy and Evan did not look at each other. They had no idea what to say.

He started for the door.

"Don't," Candy said. "She asked you not to."

He hesitated.

And then continued out.

At the end of the hall, the elevator door had just closed behind Anca.

He jogged to the stairs and took them down in great bounds, not young-man parkouring but six steps a leap, landing squarely a boot at a time. He felt no twinge in his back, no complaint of the quadratus lumborum he'd wisely worked out before the mission.

Blowing through the lobby, he shot out through the spitting rain and across four lanes of sparse traffic, joining a current of pedestrians on the sidewalk. Umbrellas were in abundance, a surveillance advantage. A mustached vendor stood outside a newsstand, hocking his wares like a carnival barker: "Ponchos, 'brellas, coffee!"

Without breaking stride, Evan dipped his shoulder and liberated a cheap umbrella from the bouquet blooming from a wooden merch bucket. Telescoping, it *foomp*ed open, shielding his face as Anca emerged from her building.

Sliding along the opposite sidewalk, he tracked her, one bobbing umbrella among many.

She walked briskly, body language tight and scared, a hand fisting the throat of her jacket shut, the other shoved in a pocket. Shoulders elevated, head ducked submissively, eyes low to the ground. She gave passersby a wide berth, moving skittishly.

She looked terrified.

He eased past a streetlight, across an alley, through a cluster of men smoking sickly sweet cigarillos. When Anca entered a bodega, he loitered at the crosswalk. Taking a twenty-dollar bill from his pocket, he folded it into a stiff rectangle and tucked it into the top of his pocket for easy reach. Then he pretended to study his phone.

Big glass windows protected with accordion security shutters provided a diamond-split vantage into the bodega.

He watched Anca shop.

Hesitating in the first aisle, she plucked a blocky green package from the shelf.

Adult diapers.

To manage the damage to her.

Something sharp-edged turned in his chest. Even beneath the umbrella, flecks of rain pelted his cheeks. He had forgotten to breathe.

As Anca moved to the counter to pay, she held her shoulders back and her posture upright, a bulwark against shame. The clerk started to bag her purchase in a translucent plastic bag and she pointed behind the counter, had him switch to discreet paper.

Curling the top against the rain, she stepped back outside and started back, package tucked beneath her arm.

Across the street, Evan stalked her.

She looked jittery, eyes darting up alleys. Someone behind her popped an umbrella open and she started, her expression wild. She moved faster, feet blurring in a trot.

Halfway up the next block, a clamor erupted before her—bus hissing to a stop, two homeless men squabbling schizophrenically at the bench. Just beyond, a grizzled beggar lay propped like a pile of rags against the side of a stoop, cardboard sign tilted against her hip, dirt-blackened hand loose around a Big Gulp cup that had spilled a slick of pennies onto the sidewalk. She was passed out, head tilted severely back against the rugged stone, face glazed from one substance or another, mouth stretched open, a drugged retreat. Her daughter, no older than five, lingered at her side in a daze, mouth moving silently. Grime formed crescents beneath her nails, her cheeks marred with Dickensian smudges. She'd plucked a dandelion from a weed that had sprouted in a sidewalk crack and spun it between thumb and forefinger, marveling down at the yellow bloom as if it were a kaleidoscope.

Jerking away from the bus stop racket, Anca curled into herself, ducking her head, shoulders hunched protectively. The little girl locked on her.

Over the rain and traffic and the bus-stop quarrel, Evan couldn't make out the girl's words, but he could read lips.

For you, she said, raising the dandelion as Anca passed. *Lookit my flower for you.*

Anca kept her gaze lowered, shuttered up within herself. At her back, the deranged argument at the bus stop continued.

For you, the girl said again, twisting the yellow bud.

Anca stepped around her and the beggar's outstretched legs, her nose wrinkling at the odor.

A few steps past, Anca halted. Splotches turned the bag under her arm a darker brown. Rain peppered her cheeks, pasted her hair along her forehead and cheeks. She was breathing hard; even from across the street, Evan could see the rise and fall of her chest.

She gathered herself up. And then turned to crouch by the girl, grimacing through pain.

Taking the proffered flower, Anca looked into the girl's eyes. *Thank you,* her mouth said.

The girl's smile was delirious and yet genuine joy shined through. Mouth ajar in a childlike grin, peg teeth showing. She held Anca's gaze as Anca rose, tucking the flower behind her ear.

Anca continued on.

Evan shadowed her. Passing the newsstand from which he'd appropriated the umbrella, he bumped into the vendor, sliding the twenty-dollar bill into his back pocket. "'Scuse me."

Anca entered her building.

She stood a moment in the lobby, facing away, rainwater dripping off her, shuddering. Her shoulders canted. One arm dipped low. Her head sagged. The package dropped.

And then she slumped to the floor.

Dumping the umbrella, Evan sprinted across the street, horns blaring.

Banging into the lobby, he slid to her on his knees.

She was convulsing, irises half-moons beneath her upper lids, cheek jittering against the worn tile. He slid a hand beneath her face, tugged her into his lap, rolled her onto her side, checked her airway. Snaggles of hair tangled across her forehead, curtaining her eyes. He smoothed it back. Her boots kicked and squeaked against the floor, her fingernails clattering. Her back arched and arched again.

He held her.

She was unconscious, so it felt safe for him to do so.

At last she stilled.

Her head lolled. Long, long blinks.

And then she gazed up at him. Awareness came into her slowly but palpably.

"I'm sorry," Evan said. "I was following you."

Her words came out fuzzy. "I know."

"No, you didn't."

"You're right." The faintest smile. "I didn't."

She pushed herself up to a sitting position on the floor, and he helped her.

"I saw you," he said. "With the girl."

Propped on one arm, Anca breathed a few times, steadying herself. "It takes so much meanness to keep good out."

"Yes," Evan said, "and to protect it sometimes."

She gave a slight nod, more reassuring than affirming.

The dandelion had fallen from her hair. She picked it up from the tiles. It was slightly crushed, like the one floating in Joey's cocktail.

Anca rose and stood once more on wobbling legs, gripping Evan's arm until she found her balance. With a quavering hand, she slid the dandelion back behind her ear.

"Onward," she said, and turned to summon the elevator.

There it is, he thought. *The Parable of Anca Dumitrescu.*

33

This Is Me

The walls of the Opera House Hotel were clad with framed newspaper clippings featuring Barrymore and Houdini and more dazzling erstwhile performers. Evan and Candy walked shoulder to shoulder down the hall, separate room keys in hand.

After settling Anca in, they'd taken their leave, Candy promising to check in on her in the morning and to broach the topic, when appropriate, of her giving a statement to Deputy Assistant Director Naomi Templeton. Evan could grab about six hours of shut-eye before leaving for his flight. Six hours were sufficient to sustain him with no deterioration of reflexes or mental acuity. A mattress would be nice.

He could smell Candy's perfume—no, not perfume, but something softer. Lotion, perhaps. Plumeria. As they moved down the corridor, the backs of their hands brushed and they drew apart. Candy pulled slightly ahead and the light caught the side of her neck, pooling in the faint indentation of the supraclavicular fossa just above the sleek stroke of her clavicle. Her pale pink fitted raincoat was jogged back on her shoulders, showing a half-moon at the back of her collar just above the wreckage of the scar tissue. Her trapezius was smoothly defined, strong and feminine. The rain had left a sheen across her cheek. It glistened. The spot beneath her ear looked soft.

Distracting.

Reaching his room, he peeled left, and she drifted ahead, honeying the air with the slightest trace of that lotion—tropical, floral, not too sweet. Her hips swayed but not theatrically. That was just how Candy McClure moved.

She reached a doorway midway up the corridor.

His electronic key card was pressed to the reader. A flickering green dot accompanied the click of the yielding lock. Her key card was in her hands. Her manicured nails drummed against the plastic. She looked down the hall at him.

He looked back at her.

The diffuse overhead light shone through her eyes. They were still blindingly blue.

"This is me," Evan said.

"And this," Candy said, "is me."

Neither of them moved. The overheads hummed. Somewhere outside, a horn blared and someone laughed caustically and a street performer improvised not half badly on a saxophone.

"I like how you are with her," Candy said.

Evan said, "Same."

Her mouth was rose-colored and full, though he was unsure if she was wearing lipstick. Her coat was unbuttoned, showing a knife of flesh at her throat, the collar dark with leaked rainwater. Her gaze scanned him. He felt it like heat.

"Come here," she said.

He came.

His heart thundered. The training spun through his mind, to regulate his vitals, take down his blood pressure, suppress nonverbal tells. But her long lashes blinked, those eyes flashing up through them, and he thought: *Fuck it.*

Her mouth was parted and she was breathing hard.

He was breathing hard, too.

He stopped in front of her.

They looked at each other.

With a swing of her pocketed hand, she let her raincoat part. Her blouse was damp, the outline of her bra discernible. She was wearing a skirt, not short but not *not* short either, and her visible leg was bare and long and finely toned. She lifted it ballerina-slow and wrapped it around him, around the back of one of his thighs, gathering him in slower than seemed possible with not a tremor in her weight-bearing leg.

She brought his lips to her waiting mouth.

She was impossibly plush and tasted vaguely sweet. Her hand was at the side of his neck, thumb and forefinger splayed up his jaw, holding him. They broke apart, foreheads touching, and breathed into each other.

"Would you like to come in?"

He said, "Yes."

She traced her fingertips across his cheek, his lips, hooked them into his mouth and tugged at his lower lip. "I know what you're expecting. I am Candy McClure. But let me tell you something: I am not here to match your expectations."

Evan said, "Understood."

"I am not an object."

"Understood."

"I will be with you as you will be with me."

"Understood."

Her leg uncoiled, liberating him, and set down without the slightest vibration of the rest of her body. Her palm moved unseen to the card reader and the lock submitted to her touch. She evanesced into the room. With a slight pivot of his boot, Evan halted the door an inch before it shut behind her.

He could still smell her, her lotion, taste her mouth.

He pulled himself into courage rung by rung, and entered.

34

Intimate

It was gentle and intimate and lovely.

It was not the fantasy.

It was better.

It is not polite to inquire further.

35

White Horse

An enormous painting across from the tousled bed featured an exceedingly feminine flower, pillowy petals of pinks and peaches, as if Mapplethorpe had tumbled into a Georgia O'Keeffe.

Candy rested her cheek, hot with exertion, against Evan's chest. They stared at the art.

"Subtle," she remarked.

"Quite," he said.

The ball of his shoulder tingled. Moments ago she'd had her mouth fastened to it, sucking greedily, as he moved above her. The radio was on, a full-rasp country tenor singing with more soul than made human sense: *This love is gettin' kinda dane-ja-rus.*

She traced her nails across the top of his stomach. He felt it in his spinal cord.

"She's so wholesome. Like she was designed by Disney in 1937."

"I know."

"And she's actually good," Candy said. "A good person."

"I know," Evan said.

"It's so annoying."

"I know."

"I wonder what that would be like."

"Me, too."

More rasp from the radio, dangerous love feeling like a loaded gun.

"I almost can't believe what they did to her. But of course I can."

"I know."

"You have to"—her hand tightened against his chest—"put them in the ground."

"I can't. I swore an oath."

"She's not your liege."

"No," Evan said.

"What then? Why do you owe them anything because of her?"

"It's her pain. Hers to carry. And if I react more than she wants me to, I'm taking it from her."

Candy nuzzled into his neck. "I know," she said. "But I really, really want you to."

He smiled, ran his fingers through her hair, kissed her forehead.

The tenderness of the impulse surprised him. It seemed to surprise her, too.

It brought him back to the times he'd spent with Mia. They'd had a closeness as well beyond the physicality that had felt as unsettling as it did intoxicating.

Candy tipped her head up at him. Her eyes scrutinized him. Now they looked sea-green, picking up hints from the bedspread, coiled around her hips like the bustled train of a dress. She lay on her side, tilted toward him. She pinched her lip between her teeth, pensive.

"Do you want to see my back?" she asked.

They'd faced each other the whole time.

He swallowed dryly. "Yes."

She scooted over, still on her side. And then rolled flat onto her belly.

The contrast was breathtaking. The front of her was glorious and smooth. The back of her, seamed almost perfectly like one half of a mold, was mottled and uneven. Her nape and the backs of her arms had been spared as well as the dip of her lumbar curve, her shoulders and mid-back bearing the damage. Over the course of dozens of skin grafts, it had healed into a swirling landscape.

He was breathless.

She propped her chin atop her stacked forearms and studied him studying her.

"You can touch it," she said.

He reached out and stroked the uneven flesh with his palm. It was smooth and rough at once. She didn't wince.

He had done this. He had done this to her.

"It doesn't weep anymore," she said. "There's barely any pain and not much itching. Mostly numb now. Pins and needles if I take a bath."

He felt his focus loosen, his vision gone glassy.

She cocked her head. "What?"

"What am I supposed to say about this if we are . . ."

"If we are what?"

"*Real* to each other?"

She let the question settle. The song kept on, no cowboy, no white horse, no sunset, not there yet.

"I was trying to kill you. You were outnumbered eight to one. I fired at your face from close range. I'd brought the jugs of sulfuric acid myself, to dissolve your body after we killed you. I was in a different mode. Operational. And you were, too. So maybe? We don't have anything to settle. Maybe more complicated isn't more right. Maybe this"—a gesture to the room, the two of them, the rain-tapped windowpane—"is just as real, too."

He brushed her bangs out of her face. She smiled and flipped over in a single quick motion, tucking into his side. The back of her head rested on the meat of his biceps and he looked down at her and she looked up at him.

She nipped his nose. Not too hard but hard enough to let him know she could do it harder.

"What's your name?" she asked.

"Evan."

"Evan." When she giggled, she looked twenty-three years old. "I'm Candy."

36

Scary Fucking Friend

Manny Llorente was terrified. And profoundly sore.

His tendons hurt and his cartilage hurt and his fucking fascia hurt. His skin was marbled with purple blotches from popped blood vessels, which was evidently what happened when you got yourself vacuum-sealed like a chicken breast. The handcuffs hadn't helped either, or the hard plastic backseat of the fed car, or the harder bench he'd slept on in holding.

Metropolitan Detention Center in Brooklyn was as bad as his worst nightmares, but the booking officer told him he was lucky the even-worse MCC had closed, said it had been nicknamed the Guantánamo of New York. Petrified, Manny watched a cockroach scuttle across the concrete seam where floor met wall.

After he'd been processed, he'd been deloused, given prison blues in which to await arraignment, and handed a tidy square of belongings—sheet, pillow, slip-on shoes, toothbrush, bar of soap. His disposable thin-as-paper underwear chafed the insides of his thighs. He could not believe this was real. He could not believe any of this was actually happening to him.

A scrawny meth-head roommate and an overflowing toilet welcomed him to his jail cell. The power was out, the cell like a walk-in freezer, and the sheet on the stained mattress was threadbare and scratchy.

"What're you in for?" the cellmate asked.

"I'm not," Manny said. Even to his own ears, his voice was high-pitched, warbling with denial. "I'll be out any second. My lawyer's coming to get me. I'm not supposed to be here."

The air was thick and stifling, reeked of sewage, and—and—

He was hyperventilating, choking on his own breath.

A correctional officer was banging on the bars. Manny hadn't passed out, not exactly, but he felt distant from himself, segregated from the terror crawling through his veins.

"You asked for a call," the CO said, unlocking the door.

Manny's legs shook as he marched down the corridor. Arms stuck through bars, whistles, the repetitious grunts of someone jacking off.

The phone bank was crowded, the narrow room reeking of BO.

Manny was given a phone card with limited minutes. He called his brother again.

"Did you talk to a lawyer?"

"Yeah, man. Told you. He's on it."

"When can he get here?"

"It's Sunday, man."

"You don't get it, Richie. I can't be here. Do you hear me? I cannot be here. This is a place for animals. I'm not gonna make it. I'm not cut out for this. I can't be in here. Not a second longer. I have money, so much fucking money, you have to make this happen for me. You have to—"

"Manny, I told you. I did what you asked. I got an expensive lawyer. I handled it for you."

Behind Manny, a big Mexican dude with a goatee circled his finger: *Hurry it up.* His slicked-back hair and robust mustache glistened with sweat. A sumo-wide beer gut stretched his inmate shirt low, sagging down past his crotch. His pants, bizarrely, had neat creases from an iron.

Manny came back to the call, gripping the old-fashioned black receiver, whisper-shouting into the phone. "This isn't fucking *handled*, Richie."

"I gotta go. Maddie has softball practice."

"I can't be in here, man. I cannot be in here."

A long pause. In the background, Manny could hear voices, a door shutting, his niece laughing. Sounds of life, of ordinary life in an ordinary house. His heart ached for it, for anything like it. To be out of here.

"I told you, Manny. Your *job*"—Richie said the word the way he felt about it—"it's not a good job. I told you it was bad fucking news, Manny. That it would come to this."

"What are you saying, Richie? You saying I *deserve* this? You saying I got what was coming?"

Scratching noises, then a muffled shout, "Be there in a second, sweet girl." Richie came back to the line. "Know what, Manny? Maybe you do."

He cut the line.

Manny stood there until the dial tone bleated in his ear. Outside, he had so much power. But in here?

Bile welled up in him, scouring his throat, resentment and rage and marrow-deep terror. He didn't know what to do, where to vent everything boiling inside him.

He had a number.

They did use burners, the White On Posse, but that scrawny douche ringleader—what'd he call himself? Taz?—sometimes texted from his real phone. Manny got on him about that, couldn't take the risk, and every time the dumb little shit pinged him, the digits scorched his memory.

He punched them now.

One ring. Two. Three.

"Yuh?"

The kid could barely talk. His brain, rotting inside the skull.

"You stupid motherfucker," Manny hissed. "You fucked me."

"Wha? Wud happened?" Taz didn't sound particularly concerned. In fact, he sounded stoned.

"I'm in fucking MDC is what you did. 'Cuz of that dumb bitch you grabbed off the subway. She has a scary fucking friend."

Bobbling sounds as the phone was handed over.

A different voice. Harder. "Dude, relax, relax."

"It'll blow over," a third voice said.

He was on speaker.

Someone else: "Like when we dealt with that one crazy pastor."

"This is no fucking pastor," Manny said. "Far from it. And you guys are next."

"No way he finds us. We're fine."

"You're not fine. My whole operation is *burned*."

Stuttering laughter, slow and medicated. "We're fine. We can do this ourselves. We got the cameras. We got the dicks."

More stoned sniggering.

The connection broke. A lobster-claw hand had hooked over the cradle switch. Meat swayed beneath the forearm, thick as a thigh. From behind, a yielding wall of flesh shoved into Manny, a stink like mildew wafting over his shoulder. A wash of cold shuddered through him, his sphincter tightening. He was afraid to turn around.

"I tol' you to hang up, *ese*."

Manny stepped away, eyes lowered. "Sorry, I'm sorry."

The fat man faced him, head cocked back, looking down his nose, breathing noisily through his nostrils. Manny felt the breeze of the exhalation. On the side of the man's neck, *13* was inked in a Roman font. Three dots at the corner of his eye. *M*s on his chin, both cheeks.

Mexican Mafia.

"Word is you a chomo."

"Chomo?"

"A skinner, bitch. Diaper sniper. Kiddie fiddler."

"No." Manny backed away, glancing around for a correctional officer. "No, no, no. I was just a middleman. The money guy—an editor, bro. Like: film editing. Coding. A producer. That's it. That's all. Just a middleman."

"So you *make* kiddie porn?"

"No, no, no. I didn't. I don't. None of the girls were underage, man."

The fat man wet his lips. "*Girls*," he said.

Manny was crying. He couldn't help it. He'd shriveled up right there against the wall. "No, not like that."

The fat man grabbed the saggy hem of his shirt and tugged it high, leaning back and wheezing with the effort.

Across his heart was an elaborate tat of a Mexican girl in what looked like a confirmation dress, a lace veil pulled back from her face. In flowing script beneath: *Celeste Garcia* and two dates showing a twelve-year lifespan.

He let go of his shirt but it stayed high, riding the bulge of his gut.

"My angel," the man said. "She was my angel."

I'm just the middleman, Manny thought, but he couldn't push the words out of his head.

"See ya on the unit," the fat man said. "Chomo."

37

No One Stops Dirty Pete

Dirty Pete's pre-rolls wuz scattered across the coffee table with the yearbooks, and Big Mikey's mom was out, so everyone was smoking and they were so, so stoned. They'd cracked a window in the kitchen but there was no way the house wouldn't reek like skunk weed by the time she got home but who gave a fuck, they'd be too high to care, and what was she gonna do anyways, get all high and moral when she was always out giving up ass?

Taz spun his phone nervously on his knee. They'd just hung up with Manny and man did Manny have his panties in a knot.

"'We got the cameras,'" Finn-Finn said. "'We got the dicks.'" He slapped B-Roll's leg. "That's some funny shit, man. Funny shit."

Finn-Finn'd bought, like, *all* the Corn Nuts for a taste test, so the bags were lined up next to the pre-rolls. They were drinking triple sec 'cuz it's all Mikey's mom had in the cabinet and it tasted like the love child of an apricot and an orange. Gross as fuck, especially outta paper Dixie cups, but it's what they had except for NyQuil Cold & Flu and that shit supercharged Taz's clonidine in a way that was seriously *no bueno.*

"Barbecue, man." Mikey was chewing with his mouth open, had bits of Corn Nuts in his beard. "No question."

"Barbecue tastes like BO smells," B-Roll said. "Jalapeño Cheddar all the way."

Mikey said, "We can go straight to RedLite with our content." *Content.* He liked acting all professional. "Set up our own account and shit. Can't we, Taz Devil Man?"

Taz had looked into it. It'd be a pain to take over from Manny but he knew how. Set up vendor account and reg, route identity verifications through disposable emails, deal with commission fees and integration capabilities. He'd cut the vids in Adobe Premiere Pro, could cycle thirty-day free trials through anonymous Simon Mall gift cards to dodge having to pay for it. Technical specs for the upload would be easy AF 'cuz no one gave a shit if porn was shot on a potato or filmed in 8K. Payments could go through VenSend and they'd split up the cash. All they had to do was keep the content flowing.

But the thing was? He didn't want to. Didn't want to go through with it. Not since Blanca and B-Roll. He didn't know what was happening to him. In this world? Getting soft was not an option.

He said, "Yuh."

They had the stack of torn-out yearbook pages with the product circled, Blanca from Forest Hills peering out from the top. It was like she was looking right at Taz. B-Roll had her lined up for Friday night still. She was so pretty in her school picture with that sweet smile and Taz's brain glitched to—

—Other Blanca, Third-Grade Blanca lying next to him on her stomach, rubber band at full draw, ready to snap some army men off their shoeboxes, and she smiles at him and he smiles at her, and she leans over and kisses his cheek, and they're kids really, just kids, and he feels—

—he felt . . . He doesn't know what he—

"We worried?" Finn-Finn said. "We worried 'bout this Manny shit?"

"Nah," B-Roll said. He was playing *Kings of Karnage* with the volume low and he was shooting up motherfuckers and they did that blood-splat-on-the-camera-lens thing, which was cool. "Bring it, bitches."

"The scary fucking friend, though. What about him? What about him?"

Mikey snorted. "Scary to *Manny.* Manny's a pussy. Like, one step from a gray suit."

Taz's phone lit up with notifications—*bink bink bink*—all the shiny little apps tallying and tallying, 27,238 unread emails, three hundred something texts, and the socials all blinking and chiming, numbers hanging off every icon like Christmas ornaments. But he couldn't focus. Not with Blanca looking up at him.

She had a six-year-old sister she looked after. Fucked-up parents with marriage therapy on Friday nights. She did homework and shit.

"I think we should pass on this Blanca chick. Not worth it." Taz was shocked that he'd spoken. The words were out there now, floating in the air like in a cartoon.

"The fuck, Taz? The fuck?" Finn-Finn said. "She's perfect."

"I'm starting to think you like this little bitch," B-Roll said. "Starting to think we gotta worry about you, little man."

"Nah, nah. Fuck that." Taz was shaking his head too hard, like a little kid. "Just thinking business plan. We got plenty of White On Brown already and—"

Mikey tossed another handful into his mouth. "Ranch. Ranch is solid, too. Sometimes you gotta stick to the classics."

"Mexican Street Corn," Finn-Finn said. "Duh."

Now a *Kings of Karnage* commercial was rolling on Taz's phone and it was weird seeing it here while B-Roll played it out there, like worlds colliding and shit, which is how it felt inside Taz's chest with the Blancas.

"Mexican Street Corn's outta bounds," Mikey said. "We're going with the classic suite. You can have Chile Picante con Limón"—he brought a shitty accent hard, which cracked them up—"but Mexican Street Corn's, like, a specialty flavor."

"Yeah, fag," B-Roll said. "No specialty flavors."

Taz needed to get outta his head, away from Blanca. He needed to get numb. He toked deep, held the smoke in his lungs. His vision was getting wobbly at the edges and he couldn't remember if he'd not taken Adderall or taken it twice but he figured the former so he blew out the smoke, popped another, washed it down with triple sec syrup.

"Wha'oud we do anyhow?" His words were slurry. "'Bout th' Manny thing."

B-Roll fired and fired, fingers jamming on the remote, grenades flying, jaw clenched, eyes all don't-fuck-with-me intense like they got. "Hunt the hunter."

"How would we find him?" Finn-Finn said. "How?"

"Through the bitch."

"How'da we track her down? We don't even know who she is. We don't even know."

"I got her DNA sample right here," Mikey said, and everyone cracked up at his gesture.

"Gross. Gross. You're fucking gross."

"I *am* Dirty Pete's cousin," Mikey said, smiling big, and Taz could see the pride beneath because Taz always noticed shit like that. He got it, though. Dirty Pete was next level.

Taz was higher than the Empire State. His stomach was boiling with acid, weird, so he did another shot to settle it down, took another hit since pot helped with nausea and shit. His phone was up again in front of his face and he was swiping through TikTok—*flick flick flick*—trying to distract himself from—from what? It didn't matter. It wasn't working.

"Original flavor, man. It's where it's at. I keep coming back to it." Mikey emptied a bag into his mouth, Corn Nuts spilling everywhere. B-Roll passed Taz a pre-roll over his shoulder called Green-Eyed Wombat—sativa? hybrid?—and he took a long-ass hit and everything got swimmy.

"Wait! Wait! I got it! I got it!" Finn-Finn stood up and fell over but no one even laughed, they were too far gone except for B-Roll, who kept smoking NPCs in *Karnage* like it was nuthin', and Finn-Finn stumbled off somewhere, lost in his own high.

Taz's phone slipped through his fingers, bounced on the dirty-ass carpet. It took a lotta focus to lean forward on the couch and pick it back up.

Then Finn-Finn was standing there, swaying, holding something, something blurry.

Taz said, “Huh?”

“Her wallet, man. We have her wallet.”

And Taz squinted and saw it was a girl’s wallet, one of the longer ones to hold all their tampons or whatever. And Finn-Finn turned it inside out and a bunch of shit rained down on the Corn Nuts and the pre-rolls and the torn-out yearbook pages.

Taz picked something up outta the mess. A state ID.

He squinted at it. It was the chick from the subway.

Anca Dumitrescu.

There was an address, too.

He had another weird impulse—that he should hide the license, make it go away. Make it all go away.

But before he could do anything B-Roll grabbed the ID outta his hands and looked at it and then passed it around.

“The fuck kinda name’s Dumatreshka?” Big Mikey said.

Finn-Finn grabbed it next, pecked in the last name on his phone. “Romanian, man. It’s Romanian.”

They laughed at that ’cuz what were the odds.

“We could do White On Romanian,” Mikey said.

B-Roll said, “Romanians are *white*, you dumb motherfucker.”

Taz’s coordination was wobbly. What if he barfed right here, barfed all over the yearbook pages, and then they’d haveta throw them out and—

Finn-Finn was talking to him.

Taz said, “Huh?”

“I said, ‘What d’we do?’”

B-Roll had his back to them, working the remote with both hands. “We could snuff her.”

“Huh,” Taz said. “Nhnn.”

“Kill her,” Finn-Finn said. “Like *kill* kill her?”

“Why not?” B-Roll said, shoot-shoot-shooting on the game. He accidently smoked an innocent, a mom pushing a stroller on a crosswalk, and the screen flashed red, but who cared, there were more bad guys pouring out of an Escalade behind her and he lit those mofos up like Christmas.

“Dunno.” Finn-Finn shrugged. “Dunno.”

B-Roll said, “I mean, just if we have to.”

"No." Big Mikey held up a Corn Nut and stared at it with one eye scrunched up like he was a jeweler or some shit. "Nope. I'm *definitely* changing my vote back to barbecue."

"We don't really *kill* people, though, ya know," Finn-Finn said. "I mean, ya know?"

Big Mikey popped the Corn Nut into his mouth. "Let's deal with the scary fucking friend first. He's the threat."

"How do we find him?" Finn-Finn said. "How?"

B-Roll said, "Track her to get to him."

Taz's phone alerted and it was some fucking *viral news* text alert that people somewhere were doing genocide but he remembered another text alert from earlier that'd said the *other* side was doing genocide. The words were blurry. He stared at the screen, trying to make sense of anything.

"Then what?" Finn-Finn said. "We take him out?"

"I could call Dirty Pete," Mikey said.

That brought a hush. Dirty Pete was a big deal and you didn't take his name in vain.

"He's dirty," Finn-Finn said. "He's so dirty."

"Dirty Pete," Mikey said proudly, "is *so* dirty."

"Could Dirty Pete take him is the question," B-Roll said.

"You seen Dirty Pete," Mikey said. "He could take anyone, man. I mean, he killed this big black motherfucker in the joint. Like the head of a gang or something. Took him right out in the pen. No one stops Dirty Pete."

"Mex Street Corn," Finn-Finn said, chewing and squinting, like he was some wine guy at a restaurant swishing around a mouthful of whatever. "It's where it's at."

"The thing is . . ." Big Mikey trailed off.

Finn-Finn said, "What? What?"

"Once you hand it over to Dirty Pete, it's his game." He puffed on the pre-roll some more. "It's his game, awright."

"We wanna risk that?" Finn-Finn asked.

"Fine by me," B-Roll said. "Let him clean it all up. Taz?"

Taz was so wasted that it felt like he was walking along the edge of a skyscraper and he couldn't look down 'cuz if he looked down he'd see where he was and he didn't want that, didn't want to know where he was. The only thing to do was not look and keep going so he nodded and then nodded again. "Right on." Came out *ride on.*

"Wonder if we could even get him," Mikey said. "I mean, this is small-league shit for Dirty Pete."

"Thought you said he needs money bad since he got out," B-Roll said. "Don't he have a kid he's gotta support?"

"Eleven years old."

"Well, then." B-Roll finished the game, started a new one, hit the Green Wombat, tilted his head back. "We could pay him."

Finn-Finn: "How much? How much?"

B-Roll shrugged. "Five hundo?"

"For what? For what *zactly*?"

"To handle the scary fucking friend. And the girl, too, if he has to."

"Handle them how?"

"You got fucking ears, Finn-Finn?" Big Mikey said. "However he needs to. That's the deal with Dirty Pete."

B-Roll looked at Taz again. Taz was having trouble keeping his head online. His eyelids felt like concrete. He shrugged.

"I'll call him," Mikey said. "Should I call him?"

Taz realized everyone was looking at him, B-Roll with suspicion in his eyes. Maybe Taz was pot paranoid but it seemed like everyone was looking right inside him at his thoughts, and he felt wobbly like he was gonna fall right off the skyscraper.

He shrugged again. "Fuggit."

Mikey scraped beneath his nails nervously with his front teeth, like he was scooping out dirt. "Okay. Green light. That's the green light, then." He dialed. Scratched the back of his head, the hair standing up. "Yo, Pete. Whaddup Cuz?"

Pause.

"Awright. Thass cool. All good. Listen, we might have a job for you."

Pause.

"Yeah," Mikey said. "A real job. Guy causing trouble. Need him, ya know, handled."

Pause.

"Yeah, we could pay. We was thinkin' . . ." Mikey looked at them wide-eyed, a bit panicked. "Six hundo."

They could hear Dirty Pete's raised voice through the line even though the phone was shoved to Mikey's cheek.

"Okay. Sure, man. Two grand. I get it." B-Roll and Finn-Finn groaned but Mikey waved at them violently to shut up, said into the phone, "Didn't mean no disrespect, Cuz. We don't play this shit like you do, ya know? Still learning."

He listened for a while, then put the phone to his barrel chest and whispered, "He said he only takes sure things since the kid. He can't go back to the pen, can't risk a firearm offense neither. Gotta be clean and easy. This guy he's gotta handle—the job. Is this a sure thing?"

"Yeah," B-Roll said. "Tell him we've looked into it. He's just an ordinary dude. It's fine."

Mikey scraped the phone back up along his scraggly beard. "It's fine."

B-Roll leaned forward and poked at Anca's shit on the table.

"Okay," Mikey said into the phone. "Got it. No worries. We'll do our legwork, Cuz, get back to you when we got more info." A pause. "And the cash. Right. The cash."

B-Roll turned Anca's wallet inside out and a slip of folded paper wagged out from an inner pocket. He plucked it out, unfolded it. A Joker smile split his face and he shoved the little paper in front of Taz. A buncha words and numbers swam in and out of focus.

Usernames and passwords.

Email, text, iCal, location services, all that shit.

"Game changer right here," B-Roll said, holding up the paper triumphantly to show the others.

They could get into her stuff. They could get in and see everything and Dirty Pete would know just how to track her. Which meant he could figure out how to track the scary fucking friend, too, prob'ly. Which meant everything was going to another level and there was nothing Taz could do to slow things down or get off the ride.

There was whooping and high-fives all around, and then Finn-Finn said, "Mexican Street Corn counts. I Googled that shit and it's just as old as Ranch," and B-Roll threw the remote aside, said, "*Kings of Karnage* sucks ass anyways," and Mikey still looked nervous, chewing at the side of his thumbnail, and Taz thought maybe it was time to just give up, swerve off the edge of the skyscraper and tumble into a forever fall. But now his face was in the couch and there were Funyuns bits in the crack between the cushions, like, a lot, and they were all gross and fuzzed with dust and shit and then he saw his saliva drooling into the crack and he thought about Other Blanca and whatever tha hell they'd just agreed to with Dirty Pete and when oblivion came he welcomed it.

38

Four-Month Orgasm

Behind the wheel of his F-150, Evan felt more comfortable than he had since he'd last been on the West Coast. The seat cushioning had settled in the shape of his body, the steering wheel smooth beneath his palms. Tommy had given him this version of home, a hermit-crab shell to armor him when he forged out onto the streets of Los Angeles.

The drive from Van Nuys Airport had been shockingly trafficless, L.A. granting Evan one of her small, surprising mercies.

As he coasted through the porte cochere of Castle Heights, the valet leapt excitedly from his director's chair. With a dimpled chin and surfer locks, he was stuck in Angeleno purgatory, too handsome to be a valet but not distinctively handsome enough to be a TV star. Since Evan never allowed him behind the wheel of his three-ton pickup, he was stuck parking foreign cars with boringly smooth transitions and electric hums.

Evan debated how far he should take what Joey had referred to as his rebranding. Maybe give the kid a shot. Approaching, he slowed, saw the kid's *Endless Summer* eyes light up.

At the last minute, Evan's instincts kicked in and he vroomed past and down the ramp, Lucy with the football, leaving the valet gazing forlornly after him.

He parked between the two concrete pillars, mounted the steps to the lobby, and took his customary pause to reset himself inside his alias: boring resident and neighbor, importer of industrial cleaning supplies.

Steeling himself for the onslaught of neighborly concerns that often awaited him on the other side of the door, he closed his eyes, took a few deep breaths. The smell of Candy lingered on him, sugar and plumeria, bringing him back to the hotel-room sheets and the warmth of her flesh as that country song rasped from the radio.

He pushed through the door, moved swiftly past the mail slots, and ran directly into Mia Hall.

Mia was wearing a sundress.

Another of L.A.'s small, surprising mercies: sundresses in February.

It wasn't too short but it was just short enough to show the groove of the vastus lateralis muscle at the outside of her thigh. Her chestnut hair spun in loose curls along her cheeks, a heap of it taken up in the back in a messy bun. Auburn highlights turned up the volume on the rust-colored flecks in her eyes. A birthmark kissed her temple.

Also? She was wearing a sundress.

Her ten-year-old boy, Peter, stood behind her, holding a Lego school project on a cardboard platter, his eyes lowered with uncharacteristic shyness. He'd grown some, his limbs not quite matching his body anymore, as if they'd elongated at a separate rate from the rest of him. He made no move for Evan, neither the habitual "Evan Smoak" battle cry, nor the smash-hug, nor the gymnastic leap into Evan's arms like a golden retriever in a dog-food commercial. Instead he looked at the floor and twisted the tip of his sneaker into the marble like Joey used to.

The boy was growing up.

Mia blinked a few times and Evan tried to think of something to say.

They hadn't seen each other in months.

And Evan thought to tell the boy, *Look up at me. Look at my eyes. That's how people will know to trust you.* But he couldn't edify him as Jack had once edified Evan. It would've been an intrusion. And he thought that's what community was for. While Evan was lucky to have a few scattered relationships to count after Tommy died, he would never live in a community formed of friendship. And within such a community would be the only context where he'd be able to do that, to tell a boy he should look up at you for his own good.

Instead, Evan said, "Hello H."

Peter's forehead furrowed. His croaky voice, a hint deeper: "Why 'H'?"

"Because, Hall, if I made you Code Name *P* then I'd have to call you 'pee.'"

Peter's eyes twitched once and then they shot up when the joke landed and he looked Evan in the face and brayed laughter and he was recognizable again, still the child Evan knew.

"Okay, E."

"E, huh?"

"Yeah. Evil E. Agent E. Like that."

"Clever," Evan said. "But who could ever take an alias like that seriously?"

"Who says you should be taken seriously?" Mia said.

He noticed once more: She was wearing a sundress.

Evan nodded in greeting. "Counselor."

"Mr. Danger." The old jest about the middle name she'd jokingly assigned him. She had a vague sense of the lethal work he undertook, had even glimpsed an instance or two firsthand, but they'd dodged ever truly clarifying who he was. As a DA, if she ever gained higher resolution about Evan, she'd be compelled to arrest him.

"How was your stint with the San Francisco DA?" he asked.

"You know, fighting crime, cape and tights and whatnot."

"*Tactical* tights?"

"Lululemon leggings."

Peter peered over the top of his Lego diorama, his charcoal eyes moving from his mom's face to Evan's.

"What's that?" Evan asked, just to have something to ask.

Peter hoisted the project proudly. "School project for Mr. Cobbledick."

At the name, Evan felt his eyebrows lift, and his gaze found Mia. Her crow's-feet had tightened slightly to prevent laughter, but her eyes said, *Just don't.*

Fortunately, Peter kept on: "I installed magnets under them to show attraction and repulsion."

Mia's mouth twitched playfully. "Mr. Danger could certainly stand to learn about the laws of attraction."

Evan shifted, a trace of Candy's plumeria wafting from his shirt.

"If you think about it," Peter said, "magnets are just wireless Legos on an atomic level."

"How about if I don't think about it?" Evan said.

"Then," Peter said, grinning, "they still are."

At the pause in the banter, they stood for a moment awkwardly. Behind the security desk, Joaquin politely pretended not to notice them. Through the glass doors to the swimming pool, Evan could make out some of the older residents doing water aerobics. They looked slow and ridiculous, bloated from age and neglect, but the rigor of their movement, their synchrony, elevated the spectacle into something approximating beauty.

"Well," Evan said, "I should head up."

"Oh, I didn't mention?" Mia said, checking her watch. "We have to stop by the HOA for a vote."

Heat rushed to Evan's cheeks, an embarrassing display. "You're kidding."

"Yes," Mia said. "I'm kidding."

"I'm not, Mr. Smoak." The dreaded voice lofted from behind Evan. "We have a vote tonight at eight P.M. regarding grass length for the landscaping borders."

Hugh Walters, 20C, long-reigning Homeowners Association president and world-class busybody, oversaw Castle Heights regulations with Stalinist rigor. Absent his usual black-rimmed fifties-engineer eyeglasses, he was wheeling a shopping cart brimming with flowers, a genocide of peonies. At his side was his newish girlfriend and newish HOA copresident, Lorilee Smithson, 3F, with Boba, her cousin's oft-borrowed purse dog, stuffed in a capacious Louis Vuitton.

"Ev!" Lorilee shrieked, crushing Evan in a claustrophobic embrace, her fake breasts inorganically rigid against his chest. "It's been fore-evah!"

He extricated himself. To hide her amusement, Mia pretended to scratch her nose.

"Do we really require a vote," Evan said flatly, "on grass length?"

"Every reg alteration requires a supermajority, Mr. Smoak." Hugh was sporting two days' growth, which on him looked like cosplay. "In addition to the Grass Length Initiative, we also have to vote on barbecue-grill restrictions for the balconies. Some of the new residents have been using a, let's just say, *liberal* interpretation of our fire-hazard parameters."

"Mom, I'm heading up," Peter said. "I haveta do state capitals."

"Okay, honey." Mia's mouth was pursed. There were few things she enjoyed more than watching Evan in social distress. "I think I'll stay and . . . visit."

"I should go, too," Evan said.

But when he started off, Mia wove her arm through his, trapping him at her side. Over the plumeria, he caught a whiff of lemongrass, the smell of Mia, his olfactory cortex exploding in delightful confusion.

"How have you two been?" Mia asked, holding Evan firm.

"Our relationship has been a-maze-ing!" Lorilee said. "Who knew it was supposed to be this easy! It's been like . . . like a four-month orgasm."

Bile tickled the back of Evan's throat.

"We've been moving into pure positivity," Hugh said.

"Everything bad we take in just as *information*," Lorilee said. "Devoid of emotional content. I mean, the other day I dropped a coffee mug in the kitchen and I just stared at it. Normally I'd be upset, a busted mug, shards and mess, oh no. But instead, I thought about how my normal reactions were about material attachment and I just don't have to have any. I don't have to have any at all."

"Wow, Lorilee," Mia said, squeezing Evan's biceps. "That's wonderful."

The scent of the peonies was overpowering. Evan wondered if Hugh was going to blanket the duvet with them, Vegas-style.

"We've shed our 'yeah, *but*' selves," Hugh volunteered. "And become 'yes, *and*' people."

"Yes, *and*" people annoyed the shit out of Evan, but he elected not to say as much.

"We have, haven't we, baby?" Lorilee's gold glitter nail extensions picked at Hugh's hair attentively, the manner vaguely simian.

"Where are your glasses, Hugh?" Mia asked.

"I got contacts." Hugh beamed, squeezing Lorilee's hand. "Her idea."

"Isn't he ruggedly handsome?" Lorilee squealed.

Hugh was many things, ruggedly handsome not among them.

Evan said, "I need to leave now."

"We can ride up together!" Hugh said.

"The cart," Evan said. "I don't think we'll all fit."

"We can squeeze in," Mia said.

"I don't want to inconvenience them," Evan said, rotating his hand at Joaquin to call the elevator.

Mia, practically bubbling with glee: "I'm sure it's no trouble."

"It really isn't, Ev."

The car came and Evan helped wheel the cart inside and then stood back in the lobby, enduring Hugh and Lorilee's protestations as the doors closed.

Mia cracked up.

From the security desk, Joaquin said, "Damn, Ms. Hall. You cold."

Evan said, "She is an evil woman."

"Us prosecutors," Mia said. "We're accustomed to putting suspects under pressure."

"What am I suspected of?"

"What *aren't* you suspected of, Mr. Danger?"

The elevator returned and they got on.

As it whined upward, Mia tucked her hands behind her, leaned against the grab rail, and stared at him. "'It's been like a four-month orgasm,'" she repeated.

"Sounds exhausting."

"I threw up in my mouth a little."

"I hope they hydrated."

"Electrolytes."

"Deep stretching."

"Tantric breathing."

"IV Red Bull."

Mia laughed her big laugh. Tugging at her bun, she let her hair cascade down around her shoulders, a beautiful mess. "You seem different, Evan."

"Different how?"

"I don't know." She squinted at him, the light freckles across the bridge of her nose bunching. "I'm not sure."

They reached her floor, the twelfth, and she smacked the button to hold the car. An alarm shrilled, not too loud but designed to irritate, no doubt another Hugh-driven safety initiative.

"The break gave me some perspective," she said. "On us. Whatever we are. Whatever we aren't."

Evan was unsure what he was feeling. But it was something.

He said, "And?"

"It's a lot less confusing. Being apart."

He waited. The alarm kept blaring. He realized she was anticipating a reply.

"What makes it confusing?"

"It just seems like . . ." She cocked her head, studied him. Her eyes were deep, soulful, a shimmering brown. "I live in the real world, Evan. And you don't seem . . ."

"Real?"

She shrugged. "Not in a mean way. But you know what I mean."

"If you prick me," he said, "do I not bleed?"

Her eyes twinkled. It was a cheap word for it but that's what they did.

"If I tickle you, do you not laugh?" quoth Mia. "If I poison you, do you not die? And if I wrong you—" She caught herself.

He said, "Shall I not revenge?"

"Okay," she said. "But seriously. No. You're in your own world. Not the one where the rest of us live."

"What's that mean?"

"Like . . ." Finger to her chin, contemplating. "You'd never make it through a real date, for instance."

"You don't think I could handle a date?"

She gave a charming one-shoulder shrug. "You can try."

Neither of them looked away.

"When might I try?"

"Tonight at eight."

"Where are you going?"

"To see a Beatles tribute band."

He swallowed. She tried to cover her amusement with her hand, but her smile was too big for that.

She slapped the button once more, stepping out as the doors slid shut. "It's either that or the HOA meeting."

"See ya at eight," he said.

39

The Shortest Fucking Nowhere Man Mission Ever

Extra Small Petite Teen! 579k views.

The videos on rotation on RedLite's home page were stomach churning.

For the better part of the day, Evan had been set up in a café booth off the lobby of the high-rise housing the corp's Century City headquarters. With a laptop, the Aircrack-ng and bettercap software suite, and an external Wi-Fi card with a long-range antenna, he'd found the hidden SSID, cracked its encrypted credentials, and joined the RedLite network. For such a big operation, their digital security was surprisingly middling. It took only a few deauthentication requests before he cracked a four-way handshake and was watching their internal surveillance webcam feeds.

Joey could have handled it remotely in half the time, but he'd done it himself to ensure his digital-intrusion skills didn't atrophy. At least, that's what he told himself. Though somewhere he knew it was less about staying in practice and more about maintaining distance from Joey. He couldn't believe he'd involved her in a mission this execrable. Having her in the middle of this depravity, seventeen years young and prepossessing, loosened his emotional dial too much.

He could not afford that, not mid-mission, not sitting here spying on the building he planned to infiltrate in less than twenty-four hours.

The inner life of RedLite was generic to the point of parody. The operation, rendered across two dozen live feeds, could have been anything—escrow service, insurance company, real estate agency. Workers beetled about in their cubicles, typed robotically, or Keuriged coffee pods into mugs with logos matching those on Joey's flash drives. The workers looked to be about forty percent female, which surprised him initially and then did not. The conference rooms were industrial-modern-by-way-of-IKEA in design, and there was a dearth of primary colors. It was like watching a video game of an ant farm.

This morning in the Vault, Evan's digital command center hidden behind a trick door in his penthouse, he'd done a deep dive on RedLite's financials. Or at least as deep a dive as could be done on a corporation stunningly expert at legal evasion. Registered in the tax haven of Luxembourg, RedLite had literally dozens of phantom corporations that spawned dozens more. Even if he successfully executed the takedown he'd planned with Joey, it would take resources and expertise well beyond his own to make sure the consortium stayed down for the count. Beyond RedLite's main website, they had hundreds of others, a massive interlinked ecosystem driving consumers from site to site, page to page. They were a major mover, if not *the* major mover, of internet traffic, their sites drawing eight billion visits a month.

All of which made their not-more-than-adequate network security so puzzling.

On a resized window, another video listing flicked by:

She Can't Breathe! 87k views.

The physical security inside RedLite's three floors was relatively professional. Metal detector at reception, RFID badges, access cards, departmental segregation. Guest movement inside would be severely restricted and surveilled. One security guard floated around reception. He was built like a minotaur and looked peak dipshit-young.

Boys With Braces! 720k views.

Unsurprisingly there were no surveillance cams inside the office of the chief content officer, Anton DeGrado, whom Evan was to meet in twenty-four hours' time. DeGrado's online presence was scarce, but he popped up here and there tagged on news-adjacent social-media posts. He was early thirties posing as early twenties. Boyish frame, hands stuffed in the pockets of a designer hoodie, expensively vivid sneakers. In posed photos he went for a rakish stray-dog look, over-under with the eyes, forehead furled disarmingly, shoulders hoisted in a whatever shrug.

Evan despised him.

He despised this whole vaguely sanctioned business.

They Destroy Her! 1.1M views.

The screen grab attached to this one showed a pigtailed girl who only maybe was eighteen assaulted from all sides, wincing in pleasure-pain or just pain depending on which way you looked at it.

Evan's heart rate had risen three to five beats per minute.

The RoamZone rang, jarring him out of his low simmer. The area code showed 818, the city listing Van Nuys, CA.

His thumb hesitated over the virtual green button, tapped.

"Do you need my help?"

Wet, shaky breathing. The back end of a good cry. That happened sometimes up front.

He waited.

Then: "H-hello?"

"Do you need my help?"

"I think so."

"Where did you get this number?"

"I, uh, I'm a high-school volunteer in Querida Alonso's third-grade classroom?" That odd uptalk pattern iGen used, where every sentence ended as a question. "And her mom? Neva? She said you helped when Querida was taken?"

Evan had indeed.

He checked his Vertex fob watch. It was a touch past three o'clock. School had just gotten out.

"She saw I was . . . I guess I was crying? After the school play? And she asked what was wrong?"

"What *is* wrong?"

She Gets What She Wants! 3.1M views.

"I, um . . ." A hushed voice. "It's too embarrassing to say."

"It's okay," he said. "I can wait."

She took him up on the offer.

In the ensuing silence, he checked the phone to make sure the connection hadn't dropped. After another spell, he checked again.

Finally, she pushed out the words: "There's a guy? Like, a few years older? And we hung out a little. And I sent him, like, a . . . like a picture? And now, um . . ."

Evan waited.

And waited.

And waited some more.

"He says I have to do . . . more? Or he's gonna send the picture of me to everyone I know. Like, to my whole school? And I found out . . . He's actually done it. Before, I mean. To girls? And I don't know what to do. I don't know . . ."

Quiet, desperate cries.

It Won't Fit! 223k views.

"And he keeps calling me. And calling me. And telling me what he's gonna do and I'm not sleeping, not anymore, and I just . . ." The next words came out hoarse, almost without sound: "I just wanna die."

"What's your name?"

"Kenzie."

"Kenzie. It's gonna be okay now. What's his name?"

"Tyler. Tyler Russell."

"I will handle Tyler Russell. Where's he live?"

"I don't know. I only saw him at the mall."

"You just need to—"

A spirited ringtone erupted over the line. "God!" The sound of her phone clattering to the floor. Shuffling noises. Then Kenzie came back on, voice thin with panic: "It's him. He's FaceTiming, like, *right now*!"

"Hold on," Evan said, swiping his screen to find the right app. "I'm gonna text you a remote-access link to your phone. So I can watch the call and he won't know I'm there."

"But I have to answer! I have to answer or else—"

"It's coming right now, Kenzie."

He generated the link, pinged it over.

"I missed it! Oh my God, I missed the call." She was sobbing. "He told me I couldn't. He told me if I did—"

"Kenzie, he'll call back. Do you see the link?"

"Yes."

"If you agree to let me into your phone, I can track him down."

Another shriek. "He's calling! He's calling back right now!"

"It's okay. Just click the link."

"Okay! Shit, okay."

Her screen came up, filling the RoamZone's visual field. Evan pressed to record the feed. "Answer."

"What do I tell him?"

His eyes swept the laptop screen—

Stepdad Surprises Her! 559 views.

—and he felt a sharp edge of hostility slice through his operational calm.

"Tell him you'll get him pictures tonight. When you're alone."

"Okay. Shit, shit, shit." Kenzie's face was there in the corner, half in shadow, her selfie view. A sweet-looking kid, should be babysitting or lying in a heap of friends watching a movie. Automatically, she peered into the camera and fixed her hair, sweeping her bangs to one side. Her instinct to look good, to please, even under these circumstances, was hard to watch.

She wiped her nose and answered, her face a flushed mess.

"Kenzie, Kenzie, Kenzie." Tyler Russell was walking outdoors, phone jostling along at his side, angled up to capture his face and a swath of blue sky. He barely bothered to look down at her. As the lens careened around, Evan caught glimpses of him between strobes of sun glare. High-school junior or senior, shock of blond hair, strong jaw, sports tank top putting gym-enhanced biceps on display. "I told you what'ud happen if you didn't pick up when I called."

"I'm sorry. When you called? I was in the bathroom. I'm sorry, okay?"

"Now we all know girls take their phones into the bathroom, don't we, Kenzie?" Tyler looked down now, shadowed eyes peering out beneath a baseball cap, nasty little grin dimpling both cheeks.

"I forgot it. On the couch."

Tyler's lens swung around some more, showing a small backyard with wooden fencing, a trampoline, a chicken coop, and an aluminum-framed aboveground pool centered on a square of grass. In front of him, a golden retriever wriggled and barked. "I still don't have those pictures I asked for, Kenzie. I really want them. I really like you. I feel like you're stalling me."

"I can't just take them wherever."

Tyler leaned down, his phone leaning with him as he picked up a tennis ball. He threw it into a stand of bushes in the corner of the yard, and the dog shot off, tail wagging. A voice shouted in the background, "Tyler Joseph, you're gonna get Cooper covered in burs again!"

"Mom! Shut *up*! I'm on a call!" Tyler focused again on the FaceTime, adolescent outburst forgotten, that tight little grin resuming. "You got a bathroom, Kenzie. That's privacy."

"I just haven't been . . . able to . . ." She was hyperventilating, jerking in tiny breaths.

Is She Sleeping? 994k views.

Heat had crept across the back of Evan's neck. His grip had tightened on the RoamZone. Easing the laptop lid shut, he gathered his things into a rucksack.

The conversation continued: "So now I think I'll have to ask for something more. Something . . . *better.*" Tyler struck a theatrical pose, gripping his chin in his palm, one finger elongated to tap his cheek pensively. "Maybe I don't want *pictures* anymore." A sadistic pause. "Maybe I need you to send me vids."

"Videos?"

Across decades of operations, Evan had seen countless faces of cruelty. But casual brutality seemed to be growing more widespread every day, quickening algorithmically.

"Just for me," Tyler said. "Me and you. Or?" He paused by a rusty tricycle in the weeds, his dog returning the ball and waiting pantingly. "I have your school's official Insta all teed up. I friended it yesterday. So I could just start posting your JPEG in the comments . . ."

Evan was outside now, walking briskly. His truck waited at a well-fed meter up the block.

"Please don't? Just—please, please, please? I'll do it, okay? I'll do it tonight. I promise."

"But Kenzie, I haven't even told you what I *want* yet."

What He Wanted! Evan thought. Tyler Russell's personalized caption, waiting to gather views.

As Tyler explained his desires in elaborate terms, Evan slid into his driver's seat, reopened the laptop, emailed himself a chunk of the current footage, rewound to when Tyler had leaned down to pick up the tennis ball. At one point, the front panel of his baseball cap caught the light and Evan froze the screen. The logo was a bulldog head, baseball bats crossed behind it like swords on a family crest. Evan dragged it into *image search* and Google spat out *Burbank High School baseball team.* In the DMV databases, *Tyler Joseph Russell, Burbank CA* yielded precisely two profiles, the first featuring a bearded guy with a Class B commercial driver's license.

The second had the right face and an address on North Lincoln.

"I don't know . . ." Kenzie's words sputtered off.

"You don't know what?"

Her face twitched. With the pressure at full blast, she'd forgotten to play along. "If I can do that."

"Which?"

A horrified whisper: "Any of it."

"You can do it for me. Just for me and you. Tell you what, Kenzie. I'll give you until midnight."

The FaceTime call disconnected.

Evan called Kenzie back.

She snatched up the phone on a half ring, answering in a near shriek: "What?"

"It's me."

"I can't. I can't do any of that. I can't, I can't, I can't." She'd moved into a fall of light now, and Evan could make out her palatial bedroom, a fireplace in the background.

"You won't have to."

His voice was utterly emotionless. The Fourth Commandment. He couldn't let anything personal bubble to the surface. Not Joey at the club with drunken men spinning around her. Not Osman, Manny Llorente, Goat-Skull Tattoo, or Anton DeGrado with his screaming video captions and millions of views. Something had been building inside him since the moment Anca had collapsed in his arms in her hallway and he'd had nowhere to direct it.

A wobble: "Wh-why not?"

"Because I am heading to Tyler Russell right now," Evan said.

He hung up, punched the address into nav, selected a twenty-three-minute route, and started off.

This was going to be the shortest fucking Nowhere Man mission ever.

40

Do I Look Scared?

The fourth home on the east side of the street was much like its neighbors, interwar single-story houses on postage-stamp lots, tended with pride. A working-class community with great working-class character, one of the few in Los Angeles that had neither genericized with gentrification nor degenerated into poverty.

Front walk of concrete pavers, wicker chairs on a narrow porch, screen door and open windows compensating for no central AC. A few dead potted plants, a scattering of shoes by the doormat, a metal baseball bat propped by the jamb.

Evan's hostility toward Tyler Russell had quickened with proximity.

I told you what would happen if you didn't pick up when I called.

Kenzie's mission had high emotional stakes and low operational risk. Despite the latter, he upheld the Third Commandment—*Master your surroundings*—taking several drive-bys, assessing the house from the rear alley, and acquainting himself with the surrounding network of streets.

He parked the Ford F-150 across the street and one house up, the built-to-spec push-bumper assembly pointed for Victory Boulevard. For his escape route he could head to the 1–5 and down to the tangle of the 134. If things got sporty, as Tommy used to say, he could jog northwest and lose himself in airport traffic.

Before he could get out, the RoamZone chimed.

Joey: y r u ignoring me?

Even from across the street, he spotted shadows moving beyond the screen door. The golden retriever barked and barked some more.

He swiped Joey's text off the screen and called Candy.

"How is she?" he asked.

"We're back at the hospital."

"What happened?"

"She had a seizure at work. The convulsions, they tore some of her, um, stitches. She's having them redone."

Evan shut his eyes, breathed.

But Kenzie, I haven't even told you what I want *yet.*

"X? You there?"

"Yeah. Jesus."

"Right."

"Is she okay?"

"She doesn't complain."

"No," Evan said. "She doesn't."

"But you can bet it's retraumatizing as fuck for her in there."

"Right."

"Those guys, those fucking animals. Do you think they have any idea?"

"Of what?"

"The pain. That she's even real?"

Tell you what, Kenzie. I'll give you until midnight.

Evan said, "No," and hung up.

He got out of the truck. The door slammed shut behind him harder than he'd intended.

He took the pavers swiftly. Felt that storm brewing, the cutting edge of hostility razoring his insides.

He banged on the screen-door frame.

His fist didn't loosen when he lowered it.

Tyler Joseph Russell came into shaded view. "Who are you?"

Evan said, "Friend of Kenzie's."

His voice was dead flat, devoid of affect, psychopathic. It was completely under control. The rest of him, less so.

Tyler's head reared back. "You can't come here, man." He unclipped the hook for the screen, stepped outside, hand in Evan's chest, pushing him back a few steps. He was a big kid, six feet, around 210 pounds.

From the shadowy glimpse Evan had caught of Kenzie, she'd looked petite. Slender neck, thin arms. Next to a kid this size, what chance would she have?

Evan looked down at the hand on his shirt. Tyler removed it.

"You her dad?"

"No."

"Look, dude," Tyler said, "I don't know what creepy shit you're up to with her. But what's between me and her? Is none of your business."

Evan looked at him.

"I'm not fucking around, man." Tyler reached behind him, picked up the metal baseball bat.

Evan looked at him some more.

Tyler lunged forward, shoved Evan back another step with his free hand.

Evan let him.

Tyler drew the bat back.

Evan let him.

Tyler feinted with the bat.

Evan let him.

He felt heat shifting inside him, magma brewing, working toward eruption.

"Young man." Evan's voice was low, so calm it scared him. "You're hopping around, waving that bat, sounding off. But I want to you look at me. Look at me closely. And ask yourself: Do I look scared?"

Tyler's lips compressed and his nostrils flared, head tilting back.

Evan noted the arrangement of his features, his limbs—what tensed, what did not.

The muscles in Tyler's chest shifted. An extreme lower jaw jut indicated an adrenaline surge. Evan watched it build.

Tyler swung the bat.

At Evan's head. A death blow.

Evan ducked it, popped up, delivered a shotokan front kick to Tyler Russell's chest. His base had been set, the delivery perfect, the ball of his foot driving straight into the solar plexus.

Tyler left his feet.

He flew through the screen door, the mesh going with him, the frame barely rattling. He hit the floorboards, wind knocked out. Flopping around, mouth gaping, he fought off the netting.

Evan was on him.

He hauled him up, slammed his cheek down onto an entryway table lined with family photos, and dragged his face through the frames. Crashes and shattered glass.

Evan ran Tyler into the family room and threw him into an empty La-Z-Boy, which upended, dumping him by the open sliding glass door to the backyard. Evan kicked him across the threshold, then onto the back porch, and then off the back porch. Then he picked him up and threw him, bouncing him off the railing. Tyler clipped the chicken coop as he fell, the frail wooden frame exploding, chickens bursting out in an eruption of feathers. The dog—Cooper—sprinted in circles, barking furiously.

Tyler's face was cut up, arm raised. "Wait, man, I won't—"

The rectangular outline of his phone showed in the front pocket of his sweats. Leaning down, Evan ripped it straight through the fabric. He paused only to drop the phone—and the extorted image of Kenzie it contained—into a cargo pocket before he grabbed Tyler by the collar, hauled him up, and rammed him into the side of the aboveground pool. The aluminum siding gave off a sound like a cymbal crash.

Evan jammed Tyler's head in the water until he took in a gulp of water, and then hauled him out. Tyler spat and blubbered. The dog was at Evan's heels, going crazy but too afraid to bite. Tyler shook his head, eyes shut in fear.

"Look at me," Evan said. "Look at me. *Look at me.*"

Tyler managed.

"If you ever contact or harass Kenzie again—or any other young woman—I will come back for you. And I will drown you where we stand."

He dunked Tyler again, shoved his head and shoulders in deep.

A wail from behind: "Stop! *Stop!*"

Evan turned.

Tyler's mother stood on the back porch, hand over her mouth, crying. At her side a shell-shocked little girl around six, her features blank, eyes wide and brimming. Behind them, the father. He wore a bright blue polo shirt and a telemarketer headset, the boom microphone wand shoved up by his temple. Much slighter than his son, he looked terrified.

"Please don't hurt him any more," the father said. "Please don't hurt our boy."

Evan let go of Tyler. The kid slid backward off the rim of the pool and fell onto the thinning lawn, vomiting water. The dog whimpered and tucked himself behind the mother's legs.

Evan's arms were wet to the shoulders. His hip flexor tingled from the exertion of the front kick. His breathing had barely quickened.

The Fourth Commandment had gone up in smoke, embers and ash floating away, clearing the view of what he had done. Tyler squirmed and retched on the lawn, bits of grass stuck to his face. His younger sister ran to him and knelt at his side, petting his arm. Tentatively, the mother followed, giving Evan wide berth.

He was not a monster. But that part of him had come out. It had come out and taken over.

Evan walked back toward the house, mounting the few steps to the porch.

The father remained in place, trembling.

Evan halted at his side. They faced in opposite directions. Body odor came off the man, the stink of panic fear.

"He's abusing and harassing young women," Evan said. "Sexually."

The father's nod looked like a tremor. "When? How?"

"He coerces them into sending him pictures."

"So just online?" A shaky exhalation of relief. "Not in real life?"

Slowly, Evan turned his head. "Would you like me to start terrorizing you? *Just* online?"

The father didn't shake his head so much as let it shudder.

Evan looked at the wartime tableau he'd created—military-aged male injured on the ground, mother and sister weeping over him. The mother lifted her face, flushed with fear, anger creeping in. On his side, Tyler curled into her, head in her lap, knees drawn in to his chest. She put her arm around her daughter's shoulders and hugged her in tightly.

Evan exited through the house, retracing the trail of wreckage he'd made with her son's body.

41

Can't Handle This

Once Evan reached Beverly Hills, he pulled over at a meter to make the call from the side of the road. Kenzie wept silently, not fully believing that the threat was over.

"How do I know for sure?"

"I took his phone," Evan said.

"What if he uploaded it?"

"As soon as I get home, I'll hack into his system and wipe all his photos from the cloud. Obliterate his entire digital identity."

"What if he has it somewhere else?"

"Kenzie," Evan said softly, "he's too scared to ever bother you again."

"What did you do?"

"Nothing he didn't deserve."

A stunned silence. A motorcycle whipped by, the sound rising to a high-pitched roar and then fading.

"You didn't . . ." Her voice, hushed with horror. He realized that she was terrified. "You didn't kill him, did you?"

"No. He's fine. No permanent injuries."

She wept some more. It sounded like relief. It was confusing. Females were often confusing to him.

When she caught her breath, she said, "Thank God. Thank you. I don't know . . . I don't know what to say."

"I have one thing to ask of you. One thing only. That you find someone else who needs help. Someone in a terrible situation, like you were. Someone being terrorized with nowhere else to turn."

"Why do you want *me* to do it?"

"Because you'll see what I can't see. You'll notice what I don't notice."

And, he thought, *because it will help you to help someone else.*

"Okay," she said. "And I give them your number?"

"Yes."

"1–855–2-NOWHERE?"

"Yes."

"And you'll help them like you helped me?"

"Yes."

"And you won't kill anyone?"

He did not respond.

"I don't want to pass on, like, an assassin phone number or something. I don't want to be responsible for that. I'm just a kid."

He did not respond.

"Hello?"

"I will not kill anyone," he said, "unless it's life or death for the person I am helping."

"I can't," she said. "I can't do that."

Traffic whirred by on Wilshire, and his thoughts whirred along with it.

"I can't handle this. I'm sorry. Thank you but I'm sorry. I'm sorry. I just—I can't handle this."

She hung up.

After a time, the call cut off. He'd forgotten to disconnect the line.

The city blasted by around him, oblivious, six lanes of drivers in their own separate bubbles, going their own separate ways.

He wondered what the hell held it together.

Joey had texted again.

Just four words, but they had hit Evan in the heart or whatever the correct metaphor was for such matters.

Back in the penthouse, he banged away his frustration on the speed bag.

He tried not to think of the look on Tyler Russell's sister's face or his mother's wails.

He tried not to think of Anca in the hospital getting re-sutured.

He tried not to think about the aggressive protectiveness that had roared up inside him, scalding Joey at the club.

He didn't have the words to explain any of this to himself, let alone to Joey. Rage and fear, guilt and vigilance, the strange responsibilities he had to her at various levels, responsibilities that crashed into one another with exquisite confusion. He hadn't learned to name complexities of emotion like this, to shape them and push them out of himself in a manner discernible to others. It was the opposite of everything he'd been built to be. And no matter how hard he struggled to learn this different language, it eluded him.

His attack on Tyler had been a ruse.

Painful to admit.

It had not been a properly conducted mission. Evan had done his bullshit drive-bys and recon but he'd known there was no legitimate physical threat. That's why he hadn't bothered to clear the house for no-shoots.

He'd charged over there looking for an excuse. He'd baited the kid into taking a swing at him so he could smash up the furniture with his face.

He'd beaten Tyler Joseph Russell with the might of the world just to knock some sense into him through the cracks.

What was he supposed to do instead? Leave Kenzie to the legal process? Trust the courts and the lawyers, the politicians and media, the educators and corporations to protect her? To stop places like RedLite from spewing bile and brutality into the face of reprobates like Tyler Russell 24/7?

All the while, the pack of predators who'd fed on Anca were out there still, prowling the streets of New York, looking for their next victim.

How was he supposed to trust Kenzie to this world? Trust Anca to it?

Trust Joey?

But he had to. Or else people could go storming into houses playing battering-ram with asshole kids' faces whenever they wanted.

So they'd better clean up the institutions. Root out corruption and capture. They'd better get to it and fast.

But also?

Perhaps Evan had a responsibility to be part of the cleanup.

He did not like that idea. It was not his skill set.

Arms burning, he walked over to the couch where he'd left the RoamZone. With a sweaty finger, he tapped the screen, once more bringing up Joey's text.

> what'd i do wrong?

How pathetic that four words had rendered him incapable of responding. Rolling his wrists, he let his boxing wraps unwind, spiraling free to puddle on the training mat.

He hit the heavy bag.

He hit the heavy bag.

He hit the heavy bag until his knuckles bled.

After a shower, Evan iced his hands and then dressed to see Mia. The usual boots and gray V-necked T-shirt. Black jeans in place of cargo pants, his concession to date night.

The RoamZone rang. A 631 Southampton area code, likely Joey calling from Devine's estate.

Good. If it was her, they'd keep it to business.

He answered. "Do you need my help?"

Rawlings said, "Yes."

Evan took a second to reset. The words almost left his mouth: *Is Joey okay?* But he caught them.

Devine's chief of staff continued: "We have it from credible sources that the Islamic Republic is back-channeling with Russia through OPEC Plus to cinch off oil supply before the U.S. Consumer Price Index quarterly."

That was it, then. Joey had stepped back to let Rawlings take point with Evan.

It stung. But he refused to admit it stung.

Evan said, "They're trying to tank the president's numbers?"

"Yes. The party in general. Getting a head start on the midterms. We've had outreach for Mr. Devine to support increased domestic production as a counterweight. It'll take some regulatory changes and tax incentives, which requires him making calls to key members of Congress and some leaders in the private sector. Mr. Devine has been resting."

"Luke? Resting?"

"I know. It's fucking weird, sir, if you'll pardon my language. But he's actually listening to the instructions you laid out. And we don't know whether to pull him into this."

Evan went to the closet and extracted the royal shoebox. He sat on the floating bed, rested it across his knees like a Christmas present in a movie. "How's his mood?"

"Seems like he's coming down."

"But he's not in his right head? Whatever the hell that is?"

"Not fully, no."

"Is President Donahue-Carr taking countermeasures? Against the oil price-gouging?"

"We have signals that indeed she is."

Evan raised the lid and stared at those pristine camo brogue boots, yin-yang nestled beneath the flap of blue polishing cloth. "What are they?"

"She's backchanneled to the Fed to raise interest rates, adjust reserve requirements for banks, and sell bonds on the open market. It'll be announced at a press conference tomorrow."

"So the bullshit on either side should cancel itself out," Evan said. "Before the quarterly CPI."

"I suppose that's one way of looking at it."

He lifted the boot. It smelled of prime Northampton leather. "Don't get involved. If Devine's resting, let him rest."

"There's also this matter in North Korea."

"He is no condition to deal with North Korea at the moment," Evan said. "Nor are we."

"Yes, sir."

How's Joey?

He caught that question, too. Hung up.

Now both boots were out of the box, in his hands.

Did he dare try them on?

He removed his Original S.W.A.T.s and slid his feet into the new boots. They felt as perfect as an ARES 1911 seated in his palm.

He laced them up.

He stood.

He couldn't remember the last time he'd worn something so elegant. He felt ridiculous, indulgent, and gratified in a manner he could scarcely understand.

Leaving the bedroom, he walked up the brief hall into the great room and took a big lap around the penthouse, past the kitchen with its island, living wall of herbs, and freezer vault filled with the world's finest vodkas, past the wall of ceiling-to-floor glass facing downtown, past the weight stations and training mats and the water-heavy bag marred with powdered chalk from his fists. As he strolled, he stared down at the boots. He could scarcely believe they belonged to him.

Did he dare wear them in public?

Would they make him stand out as he'd berated Joey for standing out?

And yet, this was a date.

He checked his Vertex fob watch.

It was time to pick up Mia.

He stood facing the front door, unsure what to do.

42
Orphan Standards

Candy followed Anca through the grocery store. Anca sniffed heads of lettuce and pressure-tested pears, tomatoes, avocados, holding each food up to an unerring ideal. She didn't seem to be checking merely for freshness or plumpness but for some intangible that was particular to each item, a maximum ripeness for the respective flavor profile. It was a different kind of perfectionism from Candy's; different from Evan's, too, which sometimes lapsed into OCD.

Like X, Candy had been trained to choose her food primarily for purity, a discipline useful in Third World areas of operation with questionable quality standards. Orphan standards resulted in a consistent flavor, too, she supposed, a cleanness on the palate, but they were more about maximizing vigor and minimizing maladies than they were about culinary delight. Minerals and earthiness drawn out of salmon, basil, spring water—or, for X, vodka. Rigor and excellence joined in one true thing.

Anca was deliberating mightily over a box of cremini mushrooms. Something shifted in her affect. Eyes darting around, breath coming harder, hand hooking over the edge of the produce display.

Candy said, "You okay?"

"I think so. Light-headed." Her mouth pulsed as if tasting something. "Waiting to see if the colors start coming." She sloughed off her new backpack, removed her seizure plan, and slipped it around her neck.

Candy nodded at the laminated card. "You don't need that. I'm here."

When Anca looked up at her, her face was washed pale with distress. "What if you leave?"

The question resonated in the hollow of Candy's chest.

She said, "I will not."

Anca drew in a deep breath, blew it out. Around them shopping carts clattered. Hidden speakers played a relaxed instrumental version of "Hotel California," sacrilegious in its laxative smoothness. Nothing happened.

And then more nothing happened.

Finally Anca's hand unclenched from the rail of the mushroom bin. "Just a panic attack. From being out. Out here."

"It's okay. You're safe."

"How do you know?"

The grocery store had five aisles of which one remained in clear sight now, the others out of view or partially visible given the convex security mirrors in the ceilings. Candy had tallied seven people in the first row, four in the second, five in the third, none in the fourth, and two in the fifth. Of the eighteen, six were men. Two were with spouses, confirmed by wedding rings and affect. One was elderly, a non-threat. Another homeless, broken flip-flops connoting he was not undercover. A military-aged man in Condiments and Spices wore running shorts and a T-shirt insufficient to hide a gun; an Apple Watch on his right wrist profiled him as left-handed in case she needed to fight him. The zit-faced teenager in a hoodie browsing Pet Supplies was sufficiently skinny that she could snap him like kindling should the need arise. Three checkout ladies in the front, a butcher, and two stockers working the floor, all uniformed and wearing clip-on IDs with proper photos. There were two sets of automated doors in the front, one bathroom unoccupied and fed by token coins, a door behind the butcher counter leading to storage, and a side door letting out into an alley with a cargo bay. They had a subway stop a block and half east, another one a half mile to the north, and multiple streets, stores, and lobbies in which to lose themselves. If she had to hijack a vehicle, they were less than a mile from Interstate 87, 1.2 from the Bronx River Parkway, and 3.5 miles northeast of the Willis Avenue Bridge in case they needed to bolt for greater population density and Manhattan police presence.

Candy said, "Because I do."

"There are a lot of men in here."

"Six," Candy said.

Anca nodded. "It feels like I'm being watched. Everywhere I go." She assessed another box of mushrooms, found them wanting, put them back. "Will that ever go away?"

"It'll decrease with time. And it'll help once the men who did this to you are . . . dealt with."

"Is that where Evan is now? Dealing with them?"

"No. He's dealing with the company that profits from videos like the ones they make."

Candy heard the front doors part, watched another man enter in the surveillance mirror. Distorted form ambling in, glancing around, big, burly, bearded. The elderly man and one of the married couples had left. Down to five.

"I overheard you and Evan disagreeing last night. About whether I should talk to a law-enforcement woman. Give a statement. About the men who . . . did this to me."

Candy said, "Yes."

"There are many others?" Anca asked. "That they have done this to?"

Candy took Anca's arm, moving them toward checkout. "Yes."

As Anca unloaded her basket onto the conveyor, Candy backed up, peering up an aisle, trying to spot the newest man to enter. She caught a glimpse of him cutting the corner, heading to Paper Products. Young guy, scraggly beard, what looked like a port-wine-stain birthmark on his cheek.

She heeled back to Anca, helped gather up the bags.

They stepped outside into the cold, Candy surveying pedestrians, parked cars, passing vehicles.

A half block behind them, the grocery doors dinged open. Candy glanced back.

The young man with the beard and the birthmark emerged. He wore a thick canvas jacket, hands stuffed inside. Weight back on his heels, he stared after them.

Was he checking Candy out? It happened plenty.

She swung around, walking backward, eye-fucking him.

He stared back. Unmoving.

The air tasted of rain. A wet breeze pulled at her hair, tugged at her sleeves, but there was a stillness between her and the young man, an unseen crackling of menace. She felt electricity between them and up her spine, a tightening of her skin at the back of her neck.

She could drop the grocery bags and run him down. But that would leave Anca here unguarded. And besides, he could be any rando city freak eyeing her.

His teeth came visible in that scraggly beard. He flicked his chin back in acknowledgment, wheeled into a turn, and disappeared around the corner.

Anca had pivoted as well, staring at the blank spot on the sidewalk where the man had stood.

"Was that"—Anca's voice quavered—"one of them?"

Candy shook her head. "Don't know."

"That's the problem. Could be anyone. Could be everyone."

They kept on toward Anca's apartment.

Anca plodded at Candy's side, bags swinging, head lowered. "They are still out there."

Not a question so much as an observation that she was still getting her head around.

Candy said, "Yes."

"They will do this to others."

Candy said, "Yes."

"Okay," Anca said. "Yes, then."

"Yes, what?"

"I will do it. I will talk to her. The law-enforcement lady."

They reached Anca's building and she shouldered through the door into the lobby. Candy gave another sweeping glance around behind them, the sidewalks dark, the asphalt gleaming with humidity, the pedestrians with faces shadowed by hats and umbrellas. That electricity pulsed once more, tingling up her spine. Paranoia took hold, feeding on itself as it always did.

She stepped inside, drawing the door shut against rain and darkness.

Could be anyone.

Could be everyone.

43

All the Lonely People

The Twist 'n' Shouters!

A one-night event at a club in the deep Valley.

That's where they were headed in Mia's venerable Acura.

On the drive over, she updated Evan on Peter (big into science, crush on a girl named Lola, heartbreakingly graduated from superhero-themed school supplies) and her stint in San Francisco (under-resourced, rampant property crime, balancing incarceration and rehabilitation).

"And what's been going on with you?"

"Not much," Evan said.

Mia scratched at her hairline and stared through the windshield.

Evan's dread mounted as they neared the venue. Parking was plentiful. The air tasted of a distant forest fire. He came around to open the driver's door for Mia and offer his hand.

She wore a fitted royal-blue cocktail dress that hit just above the knee, a slight flare at the skirt accentuating her curves. A small strap purse with a subtle metallic sheen picked up her dangling silver earrings. She was in pointed toe-pumps with medium heels, so he proffered his arm and she took it. A high ponytail strictly bound her hair, a new look for her, all that curly wildness wrangled into sleekness, her fine features on stark display.

A sparse line had formed at the venue.

The bouncer checked IDs with his head cocked back and an aura of constrained I-might-have-to-beat-your-ass-later threat. The prison-ink cross at his temple sometimes stood for white supremacy but sometimes didn't. Evan watched him engage with a black couple ahead of them in line but noted no variation in his behavior.

He checked Evan's fake but real driver's license, a perfect artifact from the unimprovable Melinda Truong, and then Evan and Mia were inside. Folks milled around a bar to the right, and booths and tables were scattered across two levels framing a dance floor and stage. A DJ warmed up the room, a few people dancing. The place was maybe half full, but given the size of the building, it looked more empty than not. Evan noted emergency exits, perches in the lighting rig, faces and body language, compiling and filing, contingency planning.

"Would you like a drink?" Mia asked.

He scanned the offerings. They had Absolut, Smirnoff, and SKYY Blood Orange. Alas. The pours were heavy. Thick plastic cups, no doubt a security measure. Since he wasn't eight years old, he refused to drink from a plastic cup.

"No, thank you."

Mia got a Bombay Sapphire and tonic and they sat at a cocktail table at the fringe. He felt rudderless. It struck him that he was unaccustomed to being anywhere without purpose.

The crowd was variegated. Hair crimped and curled, a half dozen college girls in bright dresses bounce-bopped with one another, glimmering like tropical fish and shining with youth. A stylish guy picked at the edge of their dance circle with half-decent freestyle moves, waiting for an opening. A young married couple were locked in their own *fête à deux,* the wife staring at her man with a look of devoted longing that would've put Elizabeth Barrett Browning to shame. A white dude wearing a kerchief do-rag and a wifebeater spun in a crazy whirling solo dance, veins popping in his arms. At a front table, an ancient biker king with a troll face sat proudly, dense of beard and shiny of head, his ladies up and dancing by their chairs. A dude with a scowl and a grunge 'stache hustled along the dance floor's perimeter, displaying on his arm the girl with the best, best hair, a glowing golden blonde—the alpha couple supreme. An entourage followed them like Lorenz ducklings, the future bridal party.

Every interaction a negotiation, every face a story.

So many combinations—a buck leading a herd of does, a doe holding flirty court with a herd of bucks. A gentlemanly seventy-year-old with a face like a brown paper bag helped keep a nervously laughing twentysomething on beat, teaching her dance steps with respectful care. She was cute as hell, wide hips and a huge beaming smile that stirred something in Evan's cells, the beat of a deep-buried genetic drum. A confusion of instincts—attraction versus a need to protect. She was only a few years older than Joey. He turned down the volume on the drumbeat.

"Would you like to dance?" Mia asked.

He looked across the table at her. In comparison to the girl on the dance floor, she was a woman: vastly more powerful and attractive for it.

Evan didn't dance.

He said, "No, thank you."

Mia slurped at her gin and tonic. The straw was robust, designed for rapid imbibing. "So," she said, "how 'bout them Dodgers?"

He looked at her blankly.

"Remember when I told you that you wouldn't make it through a single real date with me?"

"I'm not very good at this, am I?"

"No," she said, and brushed a wisp of hair off his forehead. "You're *atrocious* at it."

"Fair," he said. "Let's start over."

"Okay. What's new with you, Evan?"

Her smart-ass intonation made him smirk. Still, no natural response came to him. He thought about Devine vomiting in the master suite, the foursome of rapists roaming New York, the high-school extortionist he'd nearly drowned in an aboveground pool a few hours ago.

"I got new boots," he said.

"I noticed about the boots," she said, amused. "And was going to ask about said boots."

He stuck his foot out from the table and waggled it.

"They are excellent," Mia said.

That was precisely what they were.

"What else?" Mia asked.

"I've been going by a new code name."

"What's that?"

"Mr. Cobbledick."

She guffawed, covered her mouth. "I mean, can you even imagine? I could barely get through the parent-teacher meeting with a straight face."

A feedback whine cut off their conversation, and then the band was announced to distracted applause and a few lonely whoops. The curtain came up and there they were: the imitation Beatles. The mop-top wigs were terrible, heads flopping back and forth as they opened with a stunningly prosaic rendition of "Love Me Do." The music was mercifully loud, nearly sufficient to eclipse the out-of-tune vocals.

George, the oldest, was the clear leader of the band. During the chorus, he roamed the stage, frowning and signaling to his bandmates and the sound guys, calling for adjustments that had no discernible effect. Softening into middle age, John was a middling talent who'd probably had the third-best voice from his high school back in the day, no doubt drove the girls crazy playing proms. His Lennon glasses were lensless. Paul looked five years past his prime, rouged cheeks highlighting his round face to young him up. He was mustering his residual talent as best he could, but his voice was mostly shot, the strain lending it a decidedly non–Fab Four rasp. Ringo looked to be two steps out of music college, Berklee or USC's Thornton perhaps, and it seemed to be dawning on him in real time that this was what an entertainer's life looked like. The most skilled, he played with a barely suppressed fuck-my-life depressive rage, eyes knifing off into the middle distance as his hands flicked the drumsticks robotically.

As the band rolled into the next set, the prix fixe dinner arrived, all courses in rapid succession—wilted salad, stringy asparagus, potatoes with grainy innards, chicken slimed in fatty skin. Evan poked and nibbled and then opted for strategic rearrangement on the plate.

"Let's hear it for Ringo!" George said, clapping overhead. "C'mon, that's all you got for Ringo?"

The food, the drink, the music, the dancing—there was nothing outstanding anywhere in sight. And yet everyone seemed to be having fun. They were drinking and drinking and drinking their well booze from thick outdoor cups, nodding along glassy-eyed or dancing out of step. Evan did not understand. Speaker static crackled at intervals throughout "Please Please Me," and he was starting to feel ill and was not sure what he was doing here or how to remain here. Out of the corner of his eye, he noticed Mia glance over at him, concerned.

"We have T-shirts and CDs for sale at the booth," George said. "They make wonderful Christmas gifts."

"Christmas!" John shticked. "It's February!"

"*Late* Christmas gifts."

A sole lady in the audience laughed, a dry cackle.

"We're gonna take a quick break—but we'll be back soon for a . . . *Magical Mystery Tour*!" John airplaned his arms at a tilt, wiggled his fingers, and flew himself off the stage. The others followed, except for Paul, who hopped arthritically off the platform and approached.

Mia rose to receive him, and he kissed her on both cheeks. "Hello, honey. And thank you for coming to see us." His affect, completely different offstage.

"How's Phil?"

"Been home three weeks. Doing better. Still drinking through a straw so it's smoothies, smoothies, smoothies. But thank you. You are our legal goddess." He looked askance at Evan. "Who's Mr. Man here?"

"A friend."

"Friend?" Paul shook his head. "Foolish, foolish man."

He swept off rather grandly, disappearing backstage.

"His husband," Mia said. "Beaten with a tire jack leaving a club."

"Why?"

"Why do you think?" she said. "I prosecuted the offender. He's serving seven years. And they won a fifty-thousand-dollar settlement in civil."

"Seven years? Fifty K? That's it?"

"That's all we could get. And all the defendant had." Mia fanned a hand around the room. "This is the world I live in. Where I have to make decisions about the law. Where I negotiate small victories for people like Phil and Sam. In the everyday grind."

Evan tried to imagine a legal action against RedLite with their Luxembourg holding company, endless phantom corps, and legion lawyers. Building a case, pulling warrants, motions and filings, summonses and court delays. It would take forever. And during that forever, Anca Dumitrescu would be uploaded anew, raped again and again over the course of perennial viewings.

"You think that works?" Evan said. "For people without money, resources, connections—you see them having a fair shot?"

"I don't see the fair shot, Evan. I make it. I *am* it." Mia's pique showed in the flush coming up in her cheeks, muting those faint freckles. "In fact, that's the *only* way it works. Anything else? Is a threat to that system."

Her reaction seemed pointed, aimed directly at him.

"I offended you," he observed.

"No," she said, though he knew he had. "I just don't have the luxury of ignoring all the rules. Like some people."

"Allegedly," he said.

Her nostrils flared. "Allegedly," she conceded.

The band reemerged to scattered applause, their wigs now shaggy. John shaded his eyes, surveyed the spotty attendance with a hammy squint. "Glad to be back out among all you fine . . . *dozens* of people. From the looks of it, we're already on a first-name basis with everyone here."

Evan leaned in, spoke softly to Mia. "The rules," he said, "sometimes take too long."

"We can't have people bombing around outside the law. Above all this."

"Maybe the people who—theoretically—do that, maybe they can work with you."

"What?" Mia cocked her head, trying to hear him over the *nah nah nah nahs* from "Hey Jude." Leaning closer, she shouted into his ear. "Work with me? What are you talking about?"

"Bring certain situations to a head. Drag deviants out from the shadows. And leave them in the light."

"I'm a sworn officer of the State of California." She was yelling now over the music but also just yelling. "I took an oath to faithfully perform my duties and uphold the Constitution and the laws of this state. I will neither engage with illicit activities nor coordinate with criminals."

"A similar arrangement might have been struck already with someone," Evan said. "She's federal."

"Are you sleeping with *her*?" A flare of jealousy made Mia suddenly look much younger. Her eyes blazed, dark brown flecked with gold. There was so much to her, depth and fire.

He said, "No."

"Don't. Whatever you're playing at is complicated enough."

He eased back into his chair. The meaty scent wafting from the mass-produced lemon caper chicken was making him nauseated. One table over, a blond girl had dandruff flakes shot through her cornrows. The band was up there mustering their damndest, pushing everything they had through a foggy haze of mediocrity. The biker king had grabbed the arm of one of his women, yanking her down to scold her. The stylish kid with the tricky moves had made it into the dance circle of young women but they broke apart and re-formed, expelling him once more to the periphery. The wash light caught him in the face, highlighting pitted acne scars along his jawline. No one was dancing with the older gentleman anymore; he sat alone at a cocktail table gazing disconsolately toward the stage, pulling on a longneck bottle and tapping a cowboy boot.

It was all . . . What was it? It was sad. So real and so sad. Painful even, the kind of pain Evan couldn't source, the kind of pain that suffused his body and his thoughts, soaking right into him.

"What?" Mia was slanting toward him, shoulders offset. He'd zoned out.

The band wailed off-key about all the lonely people. The asparagus leaked a faint smell of sewage. Dry mouth. He swallowed.

"I can't"—his throat gummed up; he cleared it—"manage this. You're right. I don't know how . . . I can't . . ."

Where doooo they all belong?

The guy with the do-rag pulled at a vape pen, the pouches around his eyes pronounced. Ringo rat-a-tat-tatted, hands disconnected from the rest of him, head wagging along with the beat, the life force draining out of him. George tried to catch his drummer's eye and give him a scowl of a rebuke. The young married couple were back at their table, having an argument. She was crying and shaking her phone at him and he had his hands out wide, shoulders hoisted in an enduring shrug. Evan looked away, down, the boiled potatoes on his plate cracked like eggs. His gorge lifted.

Forcing the words out: ". . . *feel* all this."

Mia's stare was unremitting. "I can. I do. This is where I have to exist. I can't just fly above it, twisting arms and breaking legs and deciding that I'm better than this. There's such *arrogance* in that."

Evan felt the shields rise, the portcullis drop. He mentally ran the charted routes to the exits. Checked the stage platforms above for the glint of a scope, the billowing curtain at stage left for a protruding suppressor. "Yes, ma'am."

Mia pulled her head back as if slapped. "'*Yes, ma'am*'?"

She'd taken him here, out of his element, to prove a point. And she'd proven it. She wasn't interested in anything else from him. He had only one mode left: respond respectfully and exfil. So: *Yes, ma'am.*

He stood and started out. Three steps away, he halted. His body temperature, up two to three degrees. Emotion tumbled in his chest. He steadied his breathing, walked back to Mia.

Her eyebrows were lifted in surprise, her expression deciding between dismay and indignation.

He leaned close so his voice could be heard over the music. "Arrogant, maybe," he said. "Also? I rappelled down nine stories, swung through your window, and took down two men intent on harming you and your son. And when Peter was taken I delivered him back into your arms. And you walked across the dead bodies I left so you could get to him."

His gaze was level, dead-calm, and not one ounce aggressive.

Her eyes stabbed him. Her face was enflamed, lit like a great cat, her high cheekbones seemingly higher.

She opened her mouth to retort.

Closed it.

Nodded once, crisply.

She said, "I understand."

He walked out.

44
Impossible Balance

Overcooked asparagus and rubber chicken roiled in Evan's gut. He moved into the parking lot, cut behind the row of stores and restaurants to the west, and barfed in front of a dumpster.

Hand in front of his mouth like an idiot, spewing everywhere, like he'd never cleared bad food from his system before. Splattering his shirt, his arm, his stupid fancy boots, everything a mess. It was thundering in his ears, sensation and knowing—how profoundly he didn't fit here, anywhere, how lacking he was to encounter the world on its actual terms. He'd been designed wrong, sharpened and tempered like a sword, sent into the worst of humanity as a thing of destruction, and there was no coming back from that, no reentry into the embrace of community.

Ripping his shirt off, he wiped himself down, blew acidic chunks from his nose, cleared his throat, and spit and spit again. Despite the night chill, he was hot, steam rising off his bare shoulders, his mind a roaring furnace of his countless shortcomings.

Melodramatic urges surged up in him—punch the side of the dumpster, throw a rock through the back window of the gelato shop, scream and rip his hair out from the roots.

Instead he blew his nose again into his shirt, tossed it into the dumpster, and started walking for home. It was almost precisely the distance of a marathon, an easy walk if the cold didn't catch up to him, and worst case he could summon an Uber if the driver would stop for a shirtless guy who smelled like puke.

He started off along the weedy shoulder of a frontage road. Behind a ridge of scraggly bushes and a guardrail to his left, the 101 raced by, red and white streaks of high beams and brake lights.

He sensed the crackle of car tires behind him and prayed it was a crew of assholes looking to rough someone up. Blading his body, profile glance over his shoulder.

An Acura.

Fuck.

Mia crept level with him. He kept walking, didn't look over.

The frontage road was dark and empty, just the two of them crawling along.

"Evan."

He ignored her. The cold bit at him now, skin pulling taut across his ribs. He tried not to shudder. Lost in the weakness of emotion, he felt like he was thirteen years old.

"Evan. Get in."

He kept walking. Shame burned his face. He had no skills for this, no contingency plan, no idea what to say.

"You're shirtless behind a Denny's," Mia said. "Get in. Don't be a snowflake."

He could not concede any of the stated facts. He was in fact shirtless behind a Denny's. And the fact that the babe-just-get-in-the-car situation had gender-flipped wasn't lost on him.

The Acura matched his pace.

"Evan," she said again.

"I got you," she said. "I got you, okay?"

"Get in," she said.

"Evan," she said.

"Evan," she said.

"Nowhere Man."

He halted.

At first he wasn't certain he'd heard her right. A trick of the wind, a whisper from his subconscious, a murmur escaping the bewilderment swirling inside him. It was impossible that she knew this, that she knew him.

All of a sudden everything was crisp. The whine of passing vehicles, the bob of the pollution-coated branches, the shine of diffuse light off the hood of her car.

"What did you say?"

She looked at him through the rolled-down passenger window. "You heard me. I got you. Get in."

They drove in silence all the way to the 405 and up over the Sepulveda Pass. Evan wore a too-small Columbia Law School sweatshirt Mia had in the trunk that choked him at the collar. She glanced over at him and glanced over again. "What?"

"It's tight on me."

"Of course it is." She smirked, not unkindly. "Sorry. Just enjoying the symbolism."

He reached up, tore the collar down vertically a few inches at the throat, a boxer's cut. She did not object.

They passed the Getty, a white palace up high on the right, then dropped down into the Los Angeles Basin.

"Is that . . . ?" He stopped.

"What?"

"All there is?"

"What do you mean?" Mia asked.

"That's what I'm protecting? For other people? It's for that? That's what they do?"

"That's not all we do. But yes. People spend a lot of time in quiet comforts, getting by, fighting off loneliness."

Sunset Boulevard flew past and then Moraga. Wilshire Boulevard came up, their exit.

"I always thought it was so much more," he said.

Evan walked Mia to her condo and cleaned up in the bathroom while she paid the babysitter. Peter was sleeping.

When he came back out, she was sitting on the couch, hugging a shaggy lavender throw pillow to her stomach. Jangly brass streamed from digital speakers, Thelonious Monk's "'Round Midnight." The place smelled of one of those plug-in air diffusers, a wintry flavor, apple and cinnamon. Textbooks were piled on the coffee table, thick like religious tomes. A dozen mostly dead lilies drooped in a cobalt-blue vase, adding a sickly sweet aroma to the diffuser. A laundry basket sat heaped high in the hall, a lavish sundae, ready to be moved to the next station. In the kitchen, a pizza box sat atop the burners, lid open, chewed crusts piled like bones.

Her condo was messy and welcoming, abundant with signs of life.

He pictured what he was going home to, sharp edges and wiped surfaces, concrete, glass, stainless steel. There was such comfort in it. Discomfort, too, but of a known variety. There he could function. There he knew who he was.

"When we were seeing each other," Mia said, "I thought I could, dunno . . ." She looked to the ceiling for her next words. "Go with the flow. Be a free woman."

He tugged at the ripped collar. "Aren't you a free woman?"

"Of course. Free to have responsibilities."

"I understand."

"But I can't. Just go with the flow. It's like . . . like being on perennial vacation. Nothing to build on. So nothing builds."

That feeling was back, soaking into him, flesh, bone, and marrow. A contamination of sentiment. He said, "I understand."

"Do you?"

He stared at his scabby knuckles. "I can't live with one foot in each world either. Just turn it on and turn it off."

"I can imagine, given your training."

"How long have you known . . . ?" He couldn't finish the sentence. He'd never spoken that phrase out loud. Not once.

"I am," she said, with levity in her voice, "a trained professional." She tapped the cushion next to her and he sat and together they breathed apple and cinnamon and looked at each other. "I've seen you do the impossible too many times to not put it together."

"You gonna try'n arrest me?"

That smile. Man, that smile. She loosed her hair and shook it out so it fell gloriously around her neck. "Not tonight. I'd need more evidence. Build a case. Those things take time. Sometimes too much time."

He actually laughed.

"I love you, you know, Evan. More than just . . . whatever we are. Like we're family. But not in a gross way given we, you know. But I can't keep doing this." Her finger toggled from him to her to him to her, the back-and-forth of the dance they did around their attraction, the impossibility of acting on it, the impossibility of ignoring it, the impossibility of them. "Not with Peter. He needs something solid if he's to learn to be solid for someone else someday."

Evan stared at the laundry, the browning lilies. "Right," he said.

"Okay," she said.

"But also? If he's away at a sleepover . . ." Evan broke. He felt a big dumb smile bloom across his face.

"What?" She was trying not to crack up now. "What are you possibly smiling at?"

"I was gonna say a joke. But it's so bad."

"Let's hear it. Come on."

"I can't."

"I believe in you."

He recovered. "If he's away at a sleepover," he said, "don't forget my middle name."

Silence. Her face did not move for maybe three full seconds, a very long time with a terrible joke hanging in the air.

And then she laughed, a graceless, beautiful bark of a laugh.

"Mr. Danger, I can promise you this. I will *never* be your booty call."

"'Booty call,'" he said. "Verbal escalation. Asymmetrical tactical response."

She flopped her hand down on the cushion next to him, palm up. He took it. They held hands like third-graders. Her skin was warm, soft. He caught the faint scent of lemongrass, knew it was coming off her skin, tried not to look at the gentle slope at the side of her throat where that rich chestnut hair fell.

"This is solid, too," she said, squeezing his hand. "But for Peter, what I want for him, it's a different kind of solid."

"Like what?"

She considered for a long time. "My friends, my *people,* I have access to them differently. In the messy uncertainty. I can be there for them and them for me. And that strength to receive help, and to give it, to trust when you don't know what else to do? That's intimacy."

I don't know how to do that, he thought.

She watched him closely. "It doesn't make my way any better than yours. But that's a point of connection I need. To feel, hmm, to feel *not alone.* And if you can provide that, great. And if you can't, I understand. But I know what I need. I've tried it your way. It doesn't work for me."

"I understand."

He released his grip. A moment later she loosened her hand, too, letting him go. He looked at her softly, with affection, rose, and started out.

With his hand on the doorknob, he halted.

He contemplated one thing he could offer to her, not as an olive branch or a gift, but as a point of connection they both needed. It took awhile but he was patient, standing there, thinking, his usual freedom just beyond the door. She was patient, too.

He turned around. He walked back over. She remained sitting on the couch.

"If I do that," he said, "if I include you in the . . . uncertainty, then you cannot prosecute me."

"No." Her eyes were shining, those rust flecks pronounced in the deep, wise brown. "When it comes to my people, I must recuse myself."

"Okay."

"Okay, what?"

Deep breath. Exhale. He said, "Joey."

And then he told her. He told her about the confusion of allowing Joey in the field, the necessity of letting her flounder and fail so she could strengthen herself, the overwhelming urge to control her so she'd be safe. The impossible balance of holding her close and letting her go into the horrors that lurked everywhere.

When he finished, Mia was silent. The diffuser hissed out a mist and then another.

Finally Mia said, "To care about someone properly, it's sacrificial. You have to surrender them to the world. Or else you'll devour them."

No one had ever taught Evan that. He'd never had to know it. In fact, the whole point of his training and solitary existence was to never have to know it.

"She wants that world," Mia continued. "She's an adult."

"Not for two hundred and sixty-six days," he said.

"If you're gonna put her into a mission, you goddamned better make sure you prepare her for it. But. Don't allow an inch of your own untherapized bullshit in there. Not one inch. Everything—*everything*—must be about what is best for her. If she wants you to have that responsibility and you take it on, you hold yourself to the highest standard. It's a sacred oath to raise someone. A sacred oath to let them grow properly. Even if that means losing them."

He nodded. Nodded again. "I can still bop her in the snout though?"

"Once in a while."

At the door, Mia kissed him good-bye on the side of the mouth. It was with warmth but not that kind of warmth. She set her hand on his cheek. "I'll be waiting in the light. For whatever you drag out of the darkness."

He said, "Copy that."

"Good-bye, Nowhere Man."

"Good-bye, District Attorney Hall."

Walking away, he felt the warmth of her palm fading from his cheek.

45

Half Naked and Flapping in the Breeze

Wearing nothing but boxer briefs, Evan sat cross-legged on his floating bed. Spine erect, hair damp from the shower, Mia's sweat-shirt tumbling in the dryer, the rest of today's clothes smoldering in the fireplace in the great room.

It was time to call Joey.

And yet.

A splotch of bird shit marred the bedroom window near the top.

How could he talk to Joey with a distraction *that* pronounced smack in his visual field?

He tried to ignore it.

His efforts didn't last long.

He fetched a paper towel from the kitchen, folded it into quarters, and dampened the edge. Back in the master suite, he cranked the window open, stood on the sill twenty-one stories up, and leaned around the outswung bullet-resistant polycarbonate-thermoplastic-resin pane.

Couldn't reach.

It was an architectural window, significantly taller than he was.

The white amoeba was crusted on, floating just out of reach, a tactically positioned bombing.

He came back inside, shuddering, to regroup.

There was no way he'd be able to sleep, not with that stain blemishing the polished glass. Into the bathroom, nudging the shower door back on its carbon-steel barn-door wheels. It vanished soundlessly into its recessed slot in the wall. He gripped the hot-water lever, waited for the hum of embedded sensors to read the vein patterns of his palm, then turned it the wrong way. A concealed door parted from the tile pattern, opening into the irregular four hundred square feet of the Vault. OLED screens covered three of the walls, horseshoeing an L-shaped sheet-metal desk stacked with hardware. Windows populated the screens, countless law-enforcement databases that had been hacked into with methods and means that could be elaborately detailed in book chapters' worth of exposition.

Reaching the row of weapon lockers in the back, he withdrew a length of military fastrope and snapped it once between his fists, its aramid fibers five times stronger than steel at the same weight.

Back to the bedroom, grown chilly with the night breeze. He tied the rope to one of the steel cables anchoring his bed. The other end he wrapped around his arm. He got a yoga block from the back of the closet and set it on the windowsill. Hopping up, he balanced on the block, using the rope to hold steady, and leaned all the way out and around the angled pane.

Now he could reach the bird shit. Straining, he swiped with the moist paper towel, then flipped it to clear the smudge marks with the dry side because no one needed water stains.

The yoga block buckled and almost popped free but he tensed his ankle and the arch of his foot and brought it back to solidity. The thrice-wrapped fastrope cut into his forearm, holding tight. It was bracingly cold up here in the wind current given his damp hair and boxer briefs. As he swung himself back inside, he spotted an elderly lady in an apartment window across Wilshire staring at him, her mouth slightly ajar.

He pivoted back into the bedroom, jumped down, and cranked the window shut once more. The woman was still staring at him, holding the collar of her housecoat tight at her throat. How ridiculous he must have looked half naked and flapping in the breeze.

He waved.

She did not wave back.

The pane was now clear.

He lowered the innocuous-looking periwinkle sunscreen that was in fact woven of a titanium composite sufficient to halt a sniper round. He didn't want the sullied paper towel dirtying his trash can, so he tore it up into small sections and flushed them. Then he washed his hands in water hot enough to turn his skin red, using three applications of soap to scour off any residual guano.

Back to bed.

He found his Zen seated posture once more.

Now for the hard part.

His eyes picked around the room for other imperfections to set right. Realizing he was seeking distraction, he tightened the vise on his OCD, picked up the RoamZone.

Her latest text peered out at him: what'd i do wrong?

He dialed.

"X?" She sounded nervous.

He cleared his throat. "You didn't do anything wrong."

He kept his back straight, his breathing steady.

"Feels like I did."

"You didn't."

"Then what went down?"

"Let's talk in person. After the mission."

"Why not now?"

"Finding these fucking guys, Joey? And getting them off the street? It's all that matters."

"Fine."

Silence.

Then: "I hate when you're disappointed in me."

So bare. So simple. So pure. He had to remind himself to breathe.

"It's okay," she said quickly. "We don't have to talk about it now."

Good, he almost said.

"Oh, X?"

"What?"

"Can you go see Dog?"

"Why?"

"He needs human contact. P.S.: So do you. Plus I need you to send me a picture."

"Why?"

"'Cuz I want to see him."

He tried to process. "You already know what he looks like."

"God. *Really?*"

"Yes."

"Because it makes me feel good. To see him. It's, dunno. Like a hormone release. Or brain stuff."

"Brain stuff," he repeated flatly.

"Fine! Dopamine release in the nucleus accumbens, serotonin triggered in the raphe nuclei, endorphin flood from positive imagery. Or in human language: It makes me happy."

"Can't you have the dog sitter text a picture?"

"No."

"Why not?"

"Because the dog sitter is not you. And I want you to see Dog."

"Why?"

"Gawd! Are you seriously for real? Because he likes you! And he'll be happy to see you. And I'll be happy to know he saw you. And then you can send me a picture of that happy moment and it will make me happy because unlike someone I am a human person."

"Oh," he said.

"You are," she said, "tha worst."

"You, too," he said, and severed the call with great relief.

46

The Scrotum Was Fair Game

"Hey, brother, glad you made it!"

Anton DeGrado swung his head and torso around the doorframe into the RedLite lobby, where Evan had been waiting for twenty minutes under the affable watch of a comely redheaded receptionist. When she'd checked Evan's ID, logged him into the system, and assigned him a visitor access card, she'd done some light flirting, flashing unlikely violet eyes. He'd also received a somber nod of kinship from the gym-swollen security guard standing sentry by the water cooler, a Taser gun on his belt.

"Jake Van Dorn, yeah? Jake the Rake! I read some of your pieces. Good stuff, good stuff." DeGrado swooped toward Evan, winding up for an amphetaminized handshake. Firm grip, sawing motion, aggressive gregariousness.

As always, Melinda Truong's backstop for Evan's alias had held up—Substack articles, bits and pieces across various AI-generated blogs, a LinkedIn profile.

Evan said, "Thanks for finding the time, Mr. DeGrado."

"Mr. DeGrado! *Psssht!* Anton, Anton." Now he launched an

elaborate handshake ritual with thumb clasps and knuckle bumps, less street than playground. "We're informal here, kind of like a big family, aren't we, Gracie?"

The redhead flashed a professional smile and shot them what seemed an obligatory wink.

DeGrado wore lime-green designer sneakers, a fashion utility kilt, and a beige guayabera with hibiscus appliqués that looked like a woman's blouse. "C'mon, let's get back to my office."

He gestured for Evan to scan his card at the wall sensor, and then Evan followed him up a stark white corridor. The kilt was ridiculous, with nail pockets, folds, and steampunk chains. It was easy to imagine the sales clerk in a Beverly Hills boutique making the sale, telling DeGrado this was the new look, that he'd be on fashion's cutting edge.

A dome security camera gleamed on the ceiling, but Evan wasn't concerned, given the facial-recognition-thwarting hidden pattern of his long-sleeved button-up.

"Want anything? Water, tea, Red Bull, kombucha, espresso? We got one of those machines makes lattes, all that, even the matcha stuff with all the antioxidants."

"Tea would be great, thank you," Evan said.

"Detour thisaway." DeGrado rested a guiding hand on Evan's shoulder, steered him into a self-serve kitchenette. A tic twitched his left eye. He had a slight overbite he compensated for musculoskeletally with a self-conscious jutting of his lower jaw. "Help yourself."

Evan busied himself over the tea boxes, pretending to peruse the offerings as he freed a threaded catch inside his shirt cuff.

"How's the Substack game? You figure out how to monetize your blog okay?"

"Yes," Evan said, letting one of Joey's RedLite flash drives slide from his sleeve onto the countertop beside the coffee stir sticks. "Positive sexuality is good business."

"You know, I'm *so happy* you said that." DeGrado came over to Evan, leaning on the counter. His pinkie was an inch from the discarded flash drive with its shiny RedLite logo. "People don't always get what folks like you and me do. That it's about *freedom*."

Evan dropped a green-tea sachet into his mug and turned for the trash can, drawing DeGrado's attention with him. "People who are scared of sexuality," Evan said, "want to control it."

"Ex-zactly! That's *exactly* right."

Evan dunked the tea bag a few times, standing over the trash can. He scratched his knee through the fabric of his blogger slacks, loosing another flash drive from the tiny pocket he'd sewn in next to his patella. The drive slithered down the front of his leg, easing into view atop the toe of his boot. As he flicked it off, he dropped the tea bag through the swing lid of the trash can, the noise covering the faint clattering of the flash drive onto the tile floor.

He spun around, blocking the drive with his heel, and gestured for the door.

DeGrado led the way out, checking a watch with a face like a hockey puck, inanely large and crowded with subdials. "I'm sorry but I only have about twenty minutes. Frankie's jet already landed—"

"Frankie?"

"Our CEO. So we have to make sure, you know, everything's locked down and squared away."

Two middle-aged women in frumpy dresses passed, offering the boss a nervous grin. They were followed by an older man with a three-piece suit, a dense trimmed beard, and slicked-back hair dyed an unlikely mahogany. DeGrado aimed a finger gun at him: "Need those content-clearance docs for Asia by EOD, buddy. Don't let me down!"

The man offered a rakish two-finger yes-sir tap of his forehead. DeGrado and Evan kept on. They passed a bathroom door with classic male and female symbols and also a pictogram of a male bending the female over. A rare aberration in the antiseptic corporate design. DeGrado followed Evan's stare and chuckled. "If you can't have a sense of humor at work, why bother working?"

"Agree," Evan said. "Mind if I duck in a sec?"

"Of course. But a warning, brother. No glory holes in the stalls!" He offered a fist bump in parting.

Evan went inside, set down his mug of tea by the sink, and then dug in his pocket for a few more flash drives. One he left on the counter by the soap dispenser. Another on the floor. A third on the toilet tank lid in the handicap stall.

He washed his hands thoroughly, dumped out the tea—because who ingested anything after it had entered a public bathroom—and exited.

DeGrado grinned big. "All set?"

"All set."

He ushered Evan around a corner toward his office. "Are you gonna run photographs? With the piece?"

"No."

"Okay." DeGrado paused outside his door. "Because if you decide to I can have my press girl get you some headshots. If it's helpful, ya know, to put a face to the name."

"I'll keep that in mind."

DeGrado swung inside. The door was hefty, likely soundproofed for midday assignations, no doubt one of many job perks. In contrast to the generic office world they'd left, his suite was a stately pleasure dome. Brass-studded leather armchairs, a curved walnut desk on a raised platform, modern canvases with artless action-painting splashes.

DeGrado fell into a massive Bond-villain swivel chair behind the desk, swung around, and propped his ridiculous lime-green sneakers on the desktop. A hot-pink neon sign behind him glowed #PROUDSLUT.

"Please," he said. "Sit."

The armchair opposite was significantly lower, so Evan had to look up at DeGrado. Mercifully the knee-length kilt had gathered to swathe his thighs.

DeGrado splayed his hands and then tented his fingers over his solar plexus. He looked like he was posing for the cover of a finance magazine from 1986. "Ask me anything," he said grandly.

"Some people might be concerned that some of the content you run is illicit—"

"Look, we all have haters," he cut in. "Everyone who accomplishes anything in life does. Guys like me and you, right? Tall poppy syndrome, they call it. It's, like, an Australian term."

He had sad-sack eyes, top and bottom pouches like slider buns, and when he spoke his hands flopped outward apologetically. *This is just how it is,* those hands said. *How it's always been.* The eye tic, the try-hard jaw jut, the way his lazy tongue softened his "r"s, residual from a childhood speech impediment—it all spoke to a guy who'd spent his life scrambling as hard as he could to stay king of the shitheap.

"Of course there are complaints out there," he went on. "But what we ask in here is: What's our 'why'? And it's this: A judgment-free environment. Free choice, free speech, free sex, pro-women, pro-desire, pro-play, pro dignity of sex work, pro-safety, pro paying workers, pro giving people what they secretly want. And we do our best. We do our best. We verify all vendors who post, which helps us get around CSAM and IBSA laws—oh, sorry, Child Sexual Abuse Material, Image Based Sexual Abuse. So it's on them. It's on them if they post something illegal. We do our part but we're like the post office. Someone wants to mail something illegal, it's not like we can search inside every envelope, can we?"

"So some of your content is illegal?"

"I mean, we host two hundred terabytes of video. At peak hours we serve ten thousand pages per second. We're talking billions and billions of views. You know how much a billion is, brother? That's, like, *everyone*. Everyone's watching. And the Christian right or feminazis or whoever can always claim that maybe one or two of them are blackmail tapes, nonconsensual, trafficking, underage, posted under fake user verifications, whatever. But this is the world we live in. And here in the real world? Good enough is great."

"Well, I'm sure you have procedures in place for legit complaints," Evan said.

"Of course we get file-takedown requests, people asking us to block IP addresses, all that. And of course we take every reasonable measure, dialogue internally, roll takedown requests through legal, comply with court orders." A conspiratorial flicker came across DeGrado's face, a bid for comradery. "But—off the record now—it's not like we can investigate every time some holy roller files a complaint. There are so many fake requests. I'm sure you can imagine. Some activist gets a wild hair, boom-boom-boom, they just file a bunch. We can't be expected to take down work product every time someone's got bunched panties or we'd spend all our time and manpower investigating instead of, you know, doing our job. And we have mouths to feed, right?" A wink. "And to fill. I mean, we create so much revenue for people. Not just the subscriptions, but ad revenue, too, helping grow small businesses. Propecia, dildos, sports cars, power drinks, concert tickets, steaks, hair-growth pills, whatever. Our vendors get a piece of all that. We make them stakeholders. It's very democratic."

Evan thought of the money flowing into the VenSend accounts of Anca's rapists, paid to them because they had raped her.

"Injustice" wasn't a strong enough word. It was grotesque. Commercialized monstrosity.

"Plus?" DeGrado loved to talk. And Evan was happy to let him. "Confidentiality is *huge* for us. A lotta places haveta sink millions into cybersecurity protection against getting hacked, all that. But for us, the numero uno issue is the privacy of our clients. So we can't just open up the kimono anytime someone claims to have a legal issue."

"So you don't think *any* of the claims are legit? Not one?"

DeGrado's mouth twitched. He let his sneakers pull off the desk and tug him forward. Behind him, the pink neon #PROUDSLUT sign gave off a faint buzzing. "Not sure I like this line of questioning, brother."

His hand wandered over to the phone on his desk and surreptitiously touched a button, though "surreptitiously" for DeGrado was anything but. "Like I said, Frankie's getting here soon. I have some prep to do for the meeting. So: Thank you for your time. And again, let me know if you want me to get you some photos."

"Pretty simple question, isn't it?" Evan said. *"Brother."*

DeGrado blinked a few times rapidly. "I don't like your tone, man. I don't like the tenor of this interview."

"I thought you're pro giving people what they secretly want. This is what I want. An answer."

The door opened briskly and the security guard bulled through into the office, a weighty thunk reverberating as the room resealed itself. He stood awkwardly, arms crossed. He looked like he had a great affinity for squats. "Everything copacetic, Mr. DeGrado?"

Evan was pleased they were finally dispensing with first-name chumminess and the we're-all-a-big-family charade.

DeGrado stood up, hands on hips, standing at the edge of the dais elevating his desk. Now that the guard was here, he was safe to strike an alpha pose, though it was undercut by the kilt and the floral blouse. "No, it's not. Get this piece of shit outta here."

From the brass-studded armchair, Evan looked calmly at the guard. "If you touch me, I will hurt you. Badly."

The guard didn't quite sneer, but his upper lip peeled back a bit. Evan was generally underestimated, perhaps his greatest advantage.

The guard unholstered the Taser. "C'mon, buddy, let's not make a scene."

Evan watched him grow tense, amp himself up.

Two thundering steps shuddered the carpet, and the guard grabbed for Evan's shoulder, aiming with the Taser with the other hand.

Popping up from the chair, Evan took the wrist, twisted the arm, stripped the Taser, and neatly reversed the joint.

The guard sat heavily on the carpet, stared down at his arm flopping unnaturally at the elbow hinge, and vomited into his lap. DeGrado let out a squeal and darted past Evan.

Evan tripped him. He would have liked to call it a double ankle sweep, but it was just an old-fashioned schoolyard trip.

The guard hadn't spoken, hadn't made a noise. A cord of drool dangled off his chin. He was still studying his arm, the way it doubled back across his lap.

DeGrado lay sprawled on his back next to the guard, kilt askew, hands lifted defensively. "Look, man, we have serious fucking legal firepower. And I know who you are."

Evan tapped the Taser against the outside of his thigh, aiming it down at the floor. The tungsten darts had considerable girth and barbed tips. "No," he said, "you don't."

He enjoyed watching the terror work its way across DeGrado's face. Considered walking out and leaving him in his fear and the puddle of puke.

Then he thought of the scarlet speckling the mattress in that subterranean Harlem apartment, lurched the stun gun north, and tased him in the scrotum.

The pitch and duration of the scream made Evan grateful for the soundproofed door. He waited patiently for the pause of an inhalation, then dropped the Taser and walked out.

Retracing his route through the corridor, he scattered the remaining flash drives in various offices and conference rooms, sliding them unseen through open doorways or leaving them atop empty desks.

When he reached the lobby, Gracie the receptionist hopped to her feet, and he tensed, expecting an altercation. But she'd risen to greet someone coming through the door. "How was your flight, Frankie?"

"*Long.*" The slender woman tore off an enormous pair of tortoise sunglasses, revealing a face smoothed with injections and makeup. The skin at her neck and her hands betrayed her age, late sixties or early seventies. She wore a sleek designer pantsuit, pinstriped gray, and shiny black crocodile-embossed boots. Short hair expensively cut, spiky bangs teased artfully across her forehead.

Evan stared at RedLite's CEO.

She stared back at him.

He said, "*Really?*"

She nodded, seeming to get it. "Really," she said, with something like pride.

He shook his head and brushed by her on the way out.

He hadn't even cleared the lobby when Joey called.

He picked up. "Go."

"I'm already in," she said.

All it took was for one curious worker to spot a stray flash drive and plug it into a computer on the internal network to check what it held.

"The worm is roaring through the databases, nullifying their bytes. First thing it rooted out and zeroed was any stored video of Anca. Now it's making its way through the rest of the data warehouse. It's gonna take them days just to comprehend how fucked they are."

It would probably take DeGrado as long to extract the probes from his nutsack.

"How about running down Anca's attackers?"

"Biometrics are tricky given the ski masks—"

"Every hour we wait could mean another Anca. Figure something out."

"Okay, okay. I am."

Climbing in his truck, he said, "Good," and hung up.

Driving for home, he thought about the vow he'd made to use nonlethal force, to ensure that the punishment fit the trespass. He pictured DeGrado rolling on his office rug, darts sunk deep beneath his designer kilt. Those sad-sack eyes had betrayed him, his hollowed-out core, the little-boy impotence hiding beneath the strained coolness. Then there was that facial tic, the not-quite-extinguished lisp, the desperation to keep one step ahead of the other bullies.

Evan caught himself.

Nah, he decided.

In light of DeGrado's choices? The scrotum was fair game.

47

Celebration

No one was home at 12B.

Of course not. Evan had come downstairs during working hours and no one worked harder than Mia Hall.

He'd washed the Columbia Law sweatshirt, hung it dry, and then stitched up the boxer rip at the throat with a short length of paracord.

It was folded in a neat rectangle, corners military tight, like a steel plate stamped out of an industrial press.

He left it on her front mat.

Adjusting his rucksack on his shoulder, he started for the elevator. Time to head to the airport, back to New York to run down the men who had terrorized Anca Dumitrescu. Last night, Candy had passed on the news that Anca had agreed to issue a statement to Deputy Assistant Director Templeton, and Evan had texted Naomi to arrange a meet ASAP and to fill in the particulars.

Nearing the elevator, he hesitated.

Then he went back and stood before Mia's door.

Removing a pen and pad from his rucksack, he wrote out a note.

Thank you.

It seemed insufficient.

But what was he supposed to write?

He got onto the elevator, rode down to the lobby.

The doors opened. He stayed inside. Joaquin stared at him from behind the security desk, eyebrows raised. The doors closed again.

Evan rode back up to the twelfth floor.

He walked back to Mia's condo. Crouched to pick up the note.

He read it again. Then added: *For your help.*

Then he left for real.

Dog the dog keyed to Evan as he approached at the park, erect posture, high stiff tail. Assessing the threat.

Then the wind shifted, Evan's scent reaching him, and he ducked his head and his tail dropped to give a low, quick wag of submission.

Evan said, "Good boy," and Dog's head popped up, tail rising out and away from his body, describing big rough arcs of delight in the air. He pranced in place, shifting his weight from front paw to front paw as Evan neared.

Then Dog looked imploringly up at the sitter holding his leash, a young athletic woman with a round face, dimples, and a Pepperdine sweatshirt. She unclipped him and said, "Go on."

Dog launched into Evan, shoving his snout between his thighs, sniffing and schnuffling at his boots, smelling where Evan had been, reconstructing his movements, reading the passage of time in the concentration of scents. Whinnying, he wriggled between Evan's legs, his rear swaying back and forth as Evan scratched his ribs.

Finally Dog backed up and made to jump up and put his paws against Evan's chest, but Evan commanded him down with a flattened hand and crouched for the face-to-face greeting. Dog lavished him with kisses, Evan tightening his mouth against the assault.

Puppies of wild dogs lick their mother's muzzle when she returns to the den after a hunt to cue her to regurgitate food for them. The underlying drive for the genetically coded instinct had been extinguished in Dog, the behavior transformed into the messy greeting ritual that Evan endured.

Plus he had antiseptic wipes in the first-aid kit in the truck.

Dog snouted into the grass and then let his body follow with a serpentine flop, rolling onto his back to grant Evan access to his belly. His paws swatted Evan's shirt, leaving smudges on the facial-recognition-thwarting pattern. It bothered Evan but he let it go, not wanting to abbreviate the celebration.

He gave Dog long smooth rubs up along the curve of his belly and barrel chest.

"He really likes you," the dog sitter said.

Evan stood. "Thanks for meeting me out, Natalie."

"Joey insisted," Natalie said. "She can be quite adamant."

"That is one word for her."

Natalie wore a trucker cap with a Flathead Lake insignia on it, wisps of brownish-blond hair framing her cheeks. "She said you're her uncle-person?"

"Sort of."

"Family's what we make, right?"

"I suppose that is right." Standing back, he snapped a picture of Dog with the RoamZone.

"Not like *that,*" Natalie laughed. "You need his face in it. Come here. Up boy, up. Now sit. Okay. Wait, what filter are you using?"

"It's just a picture."

"C'mere. Gimme your phone. Wait— What kind of phone is this?"

"A super-secret phone."

She laughed. "Maybe you're not such a boomer after all." Poking at his screen, she brought up portrait mode. "Okay, now kneel by Dog."

Evan obeyed and she snapped his picture. She glanced at the result. "That's weird. Your face is all fuzzed out."

"That's okay," he said, taking the phone back. "No one needs to see my face."

She played with a yin-yang medallion around her neck. "Well, we got your picture. Now Joey'll get off both our backs."

"I doubt that very much."

The smell of wet grass carried on the breeze. People were out speed-walking or picnicking or playing pickleball in the courts in the distance, the *thonk thonk thonk* of the rackets scoring the overcast afternoon. Squatting, Evan scritched behind Dog's ears and Dog leaned into his touch, closing his eyes and crinkling his mouth drunkenly on one side.

Then he rose to go.

"Take care, Natalie."

"You, too."

She reclipped the leash and Dog strained after him as he walked away.

Sitting in his truck, Evan texted the picture to Joey. Immediately a flood of stupid emojis came back. Crying faces and heart-spackled smiles and brown thank-you hands.

She sent a selfie back—her in Devine's scarlet room, mouth ajar with joy.

He recalled Joey's breakdown of dopamine release in the brain's pleasure centers. He stared at the picture of her.

Girl.

Girl he already recognized looking like what she looked like.

What a dumb exercise.

Then he noticed the faintest lift of his heart.

He shut off the phone and drove to the airport.

48

Dick Games

Kesh and Rawlings flanked Evan as he ascended the antebellum staircase, which now decidedly swept to the left. He noted the direction, ensuring no confusion on his next go-around at Devine's compound. The susurration of tumbling liquid from the massive waterfall feature accompanied them up.

Rawlings had met him at the door, relinquishing Devine's black box with its solitary button. "Our credible sources on the oil-gouging scheme turned out to be not so credible," he said now. "So it's good we didn't involve Mr. Devine or move on it."

"How's he doing?" Evan asked.

"Oddly tranquil," Kesh said.

"Luke Devine? Tranquil?"

"He's been sleeping a ton, coming down finally. You said you needed to see him when you're done with Joey? He'll be in the spa on the third basement level."

They kept on up the stairs, which seemed to telescope before them, the effect like walking in place the wrong way on an escalator. The carved monkeys peered down at them ominously from their wooden perch, teeth bared, paws clamped over eyes, ears, mouth.

"What's on the first two basement levels?" Evan asked.

Rawlings: "Squash courts, basketball, gym, hair salon, ballroom."

"I've only seen the old boiler room through the trick door in the marble powder room."

"What were you doing down there?" Kesh asked.

Evan said, "Killing the last set of security guards."

She didn't ask any more questions.

They delivered Evan to the scarlet door, and he entered alone.

The inside paneling was padded, the door sucking closed behind him. Joey sat inside the Faraday cage atop the desk, legs crossed, keyboard in her lap. The Brain's massive screen loomed before her like a billboard, populated with more windows than he could count. Analytics ran. Progress bars progressed. Terminal log statements fell like snow.

The plush carpet had plenty of give beneath his boots. The baroque gilded chaise longues were upholstered in scarlet, the walls in flocked fleur-de-lis wallpaper of the same shade, the entire room suffused with a naughty red.

Joey held a bowl in one hand, chopsticks in another, conveying what looked like squiggly worms to her mouth with machinelike rapidity.

"What are you eating?"

"Hunh? These?" She circled a pinched delicacy in the air as he entered the cage. "Flamin' Hot Cheetos."

"With chopsticks?"

"To avoid the age-old Cheeto-fingertip-dust conundrum."

"I see." He chinned at the massive screen. "This part of the RedLite takedown?"

"The RedLite takedown," she said grandly, "doesn't need my assistance right now. The self-replicating worm's doing just fine on its own. The problem's gonna be dealing with them once they've recovered from the initial blow."

"Then what are you doing?"

"You don't want to know."

"Joey."

"Seriously. Save yourself."

"Joey."

"Running biometrics."

"On what?"

"Don't ask."

"Josephine."

"Fine!" The bowl clanked down along with the chopsticks. "You know how the rapist asshole fuckheads wore masks?"

"Yes."

"So I'm running biometrics on, erh, visible body parts."

"Meaning?"

"Penis-recognition technology."

He blinked at her.

"I told you you didn't want to know."

"Is that a thing?"

"Penis prints? Evidently. It's not a perfect science. But there are enough identifiers, like coloration, size, curvature, vein profusion—"

"Okay." He waved her off. "Enough."

"Oh, *you've* had enough? I'm gonna haveta boil my brain in a vat of rubbing alcohol."

In a window mostly buried by others, a flurry of images rotated speedily. It was not a carousel of imagery he needed to see any more of.

"How are you going to search for ID matches?" he asked. "I assume there isn't a national penis-print database."

"There are *so* many jokes I could make right now, but I'd like the record to show that as a trained professional on a mission, I am the picture of restraint."

"Joey."

"I mean, the 'Your Momma' repertoire alone could land me a Netflix comedy special."

"Josephine."

"No, X. There is not a penis-print database." She struggled to suppress a smile, failed. "But every asswipe like these rapists has surely sent out a bevy of dick pics in their day. Said texts can be intercepted under FISA or the Patriot Act, or by NSA operating under Executive Order 12333. Once that door's open, it's open. That's the whole point. To be able to spy on everyone all the time. And Devine granting me temporary Devine status with the Brain means that I have illegal access to everything. Like: seriously, *everything*. It would be terrifying if I wasn't using it for good."

"By doing dick searches."

"That's the least flattering manner of phrasing, but yes."

"How long for results?"

She shrugged, got back to munching. "It's slow going. I mean, there are, like, more dick pics than atoms in the known universe. But you know what they say."

"I do not."

"You just need one dick to lead you to the other dicks."

"Who says that, Joey?"

She mused. "No one, I suppose. But I'm looking to get you one ID. You can take it from there."

The black box squawked in Evan's hand, Devine's voice pouring through: "If you want to see me, get down here. I'm about to head into the steam room."

Evan clicked the button. "Copy that." He pocketed the device. "Thank you, J."

On that not-quite-occluded window, endless *membra virilia* whipped by. How many mystifying selected social behaviors, moral derailments, and technological wrong turns had coaxed such a spectacle into possibility?

He backed out of the cage. "As you were."

She gave him a chopsticks salute.

Devine waited in front of the steam room, towel around his waist. Evan had stripped in a changing stall and was likewise wrapped. The spa, large enough to accommodate a platoon, was preposterously luxurious—muted earth-tone tiles, shower enclosures hemmed with walls of blue glass, jugs of mint-infused water.

Devine adjusted the humidity dial, tugged open the thick glass door, and entered. As he reached to loose the towel, Evan gritted his teeth. He was not in the mood for dick games. He'd seen them played out in countless varieties, sunbathing nudists on display atop chaise longues, spread-legged sauna hogs, no-fucks-to-give old men parading around private-club locker rooms, their balls stretched low like prison laundry bags. The *vory v zakonye* in Muscovite *banyas* were the alphas of the sport. The way they sank into marble baths of freezing water, blue veins throbbing through their pale skin. Or how they thrashed themselves raw with birchwood branches. Evan preferred either to maintain a measure of modesty or fight to the death directly instead of sublimating all over the place, but that was his training, his measure, and the exacting nature of his sometimes disorder.

But when the towel fell away, Devine was wearing a bathing suit. It was surprisingly unfashionable, falling to midthigh, beige with an elastic waistband, and in it he looked pasty and fragile.

Evan followed him into the mist. In case of emergency, he'd brought his RoamZone, swathed protectively in a dry washcloth.

They sat opposite each other on the second tier as the steam vent exhaled an extended dragon burst, clouding the air so thickly Evan couldn't see his own knees.

At last it ceased and there was no sound aside from their wet breathing and the occasional drops falling from the tiled ceiling. Devine picked up a spray bottle and shot mist liberally in all directions. As the eucalyptus essence diffused, Evan felt it open up his pores, his nasal passages, his lungs.

"Have you helped the young woman?" Devine asked.

"More to come."

"Have you found those who harmed her?"

"Not yet." Evan pointed through the ceiling to Joey countless stories above in the scarlet room. "Waiting."

"I don't envy them."

"Whatever happens," Evan said, "will not be pleasant for them."

The vent emitted another burst, and then silence reasserted itself.

"I can't slow down enough to stay sane and do everything that I'm doing," Luke said. "And no one else can do everything that I'm doing."

Evan gave that a few minutes. "Doesn't excuse it."

"Excuse what?"

Evan said, "Anything."

The dripping sound quickened with the rising humidity, plunking musically at three- and four-second intervals. Evan felt the skin of his face as a membrane aflame from the eucalyptus, alive with heat and sensation.

The steam cleared enough for him to make out the shape of Devine across from him, heat rising off his shoulders and thighs, turning him into a mirage.

"Why did you come here?" Devine said. "I assume you have better things to do than scold me in a steam room."

"Joey and I took down RedLite. For now."

"So I've gathered from the chatter between her and Rawlings. And?"

"She has them on the ropes. But I want that company destroyed. Completely. For good. That's more your bailiwick than mine."

Devine leaned forward and thought about it, the temporal vein pulsating in his forehead, so pronounced that looking at it felt like looking at his insides.

At last, he said, "Let's go to the sauna."

When they stepped out, cold braced them like aftershave tonic, Evan's skin tightening. The towel around his waist was soaked. What looked like a fat champagne stand housed a pinwheel of tightly rolled white towelettes that exuded a fragrance of fresh lavender. It had not been there forty minutes before when they'd entered the steam room.

Devine dug his hand into the ice, came up with a sloppy three or four towelettes, and Evan did the same. Cubes clung dryly to the terry cloth. Everything misted.

Their bare feet slapped the tile as they padded across the spa. The sauna was proper Finnish—toaster-intense, delicious reek of cedar, dry as British gin. Inside, Devine twirled the wheel-mounted hourglass to set the sand trickling.

Evan gauged him to see if he was playing any games in here.

They sat opposite once more on the second tier, neither choosing the lower perch. Devine wiped the wooden backing with an iced towel so it wouldn't burn his back. Evan watched his eyes. Devine did not overtly check Evan's reaction to his concession to the heat.

Evan's back was strong. It had endured parachute landings, meat-shuddering impacts, and the heels of the foremost ashiatsu practitioner in Asakusa. It could contend with a sauna. Reclining, he pressed the flesh of his shoulder blades to the toasted cedar planks, sirloin sizzling on a grill. He looked at Luke Devine. He paid attention.

Devine blinked once.

Then gave the faintest shake of the head, a microdisplay of admiration, and he said, "The burn wrecks me."

He was not, then. He was not playing games. Could a seed of trust be planted between them?

Evan studied him in his old-man swim trunks, the lifted whorl of his hair, the thinning more pronounced here in the naked lights of the sauna.

And lowered his guard by one eighth of a standard deviation.

"Well?" Evan said. "RedLite?"

"Public markets can behave irrationally," Devine said. "I don't. At least not when engaging with them. So. Here's what I would do." His features were strong, his personality baked through them, muscled into place by the repetition of a million expressions. "They're reeling right now, in a capital squeeze. My canaries tell me they're trying to raise another two hundred fifty million, a hundred through selling stock and one fifty through new debt facility. The latter I can crush with three well-placed phone calls. As for the former? Since the cyberattack, the stock is down forty-nine percent. Juicy. But there's more to go."

He pressed his palms together and stared at the seams of his pinkies. "I'd short the stock hard—through proxies, of course, to dodge an SEC prostate exam. I have unlimited money to cover a short squeeze, so we're defended there. Next move would be to make the stock tumble harder. Before the system got cheese-grated, your associate, Ms. Josephine, made sure to grab all RedLite usernames, and the password hashes, which she cracked with stunning efficiency. That means we already have the identity of every last lotion connoisseur. The Brain can cross-index which users have died—I'm guessing at least two percent. I'd leak those names immediately and widely to key movers in the mainstream media and flood every social-media channel with their user information. That a) minimizes collateral damage for the living, b) terrorizes the other ninety-eight percent, and c) sends investors, users, and stockholders blitzing for the exits. Recovery looks unlikely, the future is lost, et cetera. Which means the stock tanks further, if we're lucky by north of ninety percent."

His breathing had quickened, his words picking up the manic patter Evan was accustomed to. Devine seemed to notice it, too, allowing the briefest of pauses, but words seized him again as they did. "I'd cash out my shorts, rebuy the stock at two cents on the dollar off the plummet, stake a majority position, fire the board members, insert my lackies, pull the plug, and let the company evaporate."

In the heat, Luke's face had grown shiny red. He sat perched on planks of cedar like a roasting fish. "I'd gut the remaining assets and affiliate companies of all prurient content, part the pieces off for Chinese scrap metal. The now-unemployed board members and C-suiters will already have had their stock positions crushed, but for a chaser I'd take out billboards in their hometowns featuring their close-up photos and highlighting their role in illicit pornographic exploitation. Then spin up a C4, name it something cutely banal and alliterative, Concerned Citizens for Civility, make an ad buy on local TV stations and flood the home zip codes of top RedLite executive officers with content featuring faces and favorite fetish videos."

Devine swiped at the sweat on his brow but did not pause. "Then I'd earmark another tranche—twenty, thirty million—to fund consumer-advocacy groups to keep whoever's still standing tied up in litigation for the next half decade. We steer the narrative publicly, legally, and legislatively so the courts are forced to arrive at a make-an-example gargantuan settlement, after which we funnel the money back to the sexual-exploitation victims so they can rebuild their lives. I can set all this in motion with two cups of espresso, a phone, and a focused half hour."

At last he stopped.

The sand kept trickling through the hourglass.

A lot of it fell.

"God," Devine said, annoyed, "are you always this . . . *taciturn*?"

More sand moved through the glass pinch point.

"That," Evan said. "Do all that."

They sat together until the last of the sand trickled through and then sat for a spell after that.

49
The Whole Putrid Mess

As a Secret Service agent, Naomi Templeton had operational planning abilities that were nearly Orphan level. She'd arranged for Anca's statement to be taken in a decommissioned admin building near the junction of Floyd Bennett Field and Barren Island, where southeast Brooklyn began to fray into spits, inlets, and tidal channels as it encountered the Atlantic. The mass of marsh and wetland, nosed into Jamaica Bay like a horse's head, housed scattered federal and state facilities and airfields, more defunct than active. These included the training grounds for NYPD's Emergency Service Unit, the Service's closest collaborator for United Nations General Assembly meetings.

This federal-state cooperation made for an easy flow of off-the-books favors. In order for Orphan X to dodge checkpoints and stray excursionists, Templeton had cleared an unofficial route along the desolate western shoreline, onetime dumping grounds for manufacturers of glue, fish oil, and fertilizer.

The meeting would be conducted in private, the location shrouded in secrecy to ensure that Evan could accompany Anca.

Though the route from Anca's would take over an hour, Evan picked her up forty-five minutes early, leaving Candy to stand guard in the apartment.

Coasting along in the 450 EQS+, Evan glanced over at Anca in the passenger seat. She was sitting still, eyes dead ahead, purse at her feet, a tome clutched in her lap.

He had initiated the heated steering wheel and the wave massage, the rollers coaxing lumbar relaxation through leather upholstery. The LED strips providing interior ambient light were dialed to a cobalt blue, and his RoamZone charged wirelessly on a pad at the front of the console. The cabin felt like a cocoon—serene, cushioned, hermetically sealed. The vehicle was a preposterous item of luxury; it felt like driving a cloud. He enjoyed it more than he wished to admit.

In contrast, the route south through Queens was less than picturesque. Flushing and Jamaica scrolled by in a haze of graffitied stone, brick projects, and rusted overpasses. There were fast-food joints and liquor stores and strip malls with Mandarin signage crowded three stories high.

Anca began to shift in her seat with discomfort.

"What are you reading?" Evan finally asked, trying to get her to loosen her nervous system.

Her gaze remained forward. "*The Gulag Archipelago.*"

Of course.

He stayed on high alert, cycling his gaze between side and rearview mirrors, keeping an eye out for tails. His trust in official channels went only as far as Naomi Templeton, extending less confidently to those colleagues she'd necessarily looped in. He'd been taken down once already by a Service-orchestrated manhunt, bound, gagged, and hooded, and was not eager to repeat the experience.

Candy's possible sighting of one of Anca's attackers outside a grocery store added another reason to keep his attention at high simmer. The First Commandment: *Assume nothing.*

Anca's squirming intensified. She excavated a trio of pills from various prescription bottles in her purse and swallowed them dry. Closing her eyes, she rubbed her temples. The bruising around her left eye, though faded, had feathered down through her cheek in jaundiced streaks.

"Would you mind stopping? I have to use a restroom."

Her purse, a roomy tote, shifted between her feet. He made out a few pairs of absorbent briefs inside.

"Of course."

He eased into a gas station, parked by the air dispenser, and walked her inside the convenience store. He safed the single-occupancy bathroom before holding the door for her to enter. Then he waited by a stand of powdered mini-doughnuts, offering a nod to the clerk who glanced up at him before returning to a sudoku book.

Evan spent a minute clicking through websites for transradial prosthetics, then put the RoamZone away and watched the gas pumps and passing traffic. An East Asian woman in her sixties was struggling with the credit-card reader, poking at the tiny key-pad. A guy in the truck behind her bleated his horn at her. "C'mon, lady!" His friend in the passenger seat rolled down his window and pounded the side panel. "Fucking move it already!"

The woman grew flustered, waving an apology, jabbing hurriedly at the keypad.

The truck had license plates and a roofing-company decal on the side with the phone number blatantly presented. The men were early thirties, out of the dangerous twenties, and they looked aggravated but not menacing.

Anca emerged.

Holding her arm gently, Evan hustled her out past the pumps, heading to the Mercedes.

"Come *on,* lady! Learn to read English!"

Anca halted.

Evan said, "No."

But she pulled her arm free and walked back to the pumps, stopping before the truck's grille. Evan hustled up behind her.

"You two!" she said.

The men's eyebrows rose, their heads retracting barely but in concert, an inadvertently comedic effect. The driver lifted his trucker cap, scratched his head, put it back on.

Evan wanted them in the truck.

"Out of the truck," Anca said.

They got out of the truck.

Evan wanted them far.

"Come here," Anca said.

They came here.

"You," Anca said to the driver. "Do you have a wife?"

"Not anymore."

"A daughter?"

"Yes."

Her head swiveled to the passenger. "And you?"

"No."

"A mother?"

"Of course."

"What would they tell you? These women. Right now. About how you are acting?"

The passenger's lips bunched a few times. His mouth was screwed to one side and he had a permanent squint in his right eye that trembled, not speed-twitching but little-kid-tic twitching. He didn't say anything.

Behind them at the pump, the older woman looked at them, unsure what was transpiring. Then she went back to trying to figure out the credit-card reader.

Evan made sure to stay behind Anca, receding into the background. Though Anca had captured the men's focus, he didn't want them to think about saving face in front of another man.

Her gaze stabbed over to the driver once more. "What if someone filmed you right now acting this way? What would your daughter say if she saw you berating this woman?"

"Don't get canceled. Not worth it."

"Not just that. You're not being kind. No matter if you're mad that she is taking long or can't speak English. You're not being a gentleman. You're being a bully. Both of you. It makes you unattractive, too. It makes you look petty and weak and small. Be a gentleman. It will look better on you."

The men shifted in their boots. Their gazes had grown uncertain. The driver chewed the inside of his cheek.

"Now help her with her credit card." Anca gestured angrily at the pump. "Go on."

The driver lifted his hat once more, dug at the back of his head with his nails. Then he lowered it into place and walked over toward the woman, speaking softly.

Anca glared at the passenger. "You, too."

Sheepishly, he walked over to join his friend. At first the woman recoiled, clutching her credit card to her chest. But the driver made a calming gesture with his palm and removed his own card from his wallet as an offering.

Anca strode back to the Mercedes. Evan followed her.

As they pulled out, he saw the woman nodding her gratitude to the men. The driver pressed a palm to his chest, a show of contrition, and his friend inserted the pump into the woman's tank.

Evan drove for a few blocks and then banked onto the Long Island Expressway. They shot past crowded clusters of gray-beige buildings, and at last signs of nature broke through, oaks and red maples rising above a wainscoting of concrete sound barriers.

"Everyone is so mad these days, they cannot hear anything," Anca said.

"Yes."

"Sometimes they have to be slapped."

"Yes."

She gave him an ungentle look. "Slapped, not *shot*."

"Noted."

He switched the seat massage to hot relaxing shoulders because why the hell not. The sound barriers gave way to lush greenery fed from the recent rains, tall grassy weeds battered by wind and six lanes of assembly-line-consistent traffic.

"You don't have to talk so little, you know. It doesn't make you stronger."

He said, "Huh."

Four point three miles passed.

"What is 'huh'?"

"'Huh' is 'huh.'"

The Gulag Archipelago was back in her lap now, across her knees like a weighted lap belt. In case the airbags failed, it would protect her with its girth and moral fortitude. "No," she said. "You are precise. Everything is precise. 'Huh' is not 'huh.' "Huh' is passive-aggressive."

"You are," Evan observed, "so Eastern European."

Her eyes flared with fury.

Then a sea change came across her face.

"And you are so *American,*" she laughed. "'Copy that.' 'Affirmative.' 'Noted.'"

His lips tensed with amusement. "Strong, silent American."

"Boring, quiet American." Her features were set pleasantly with the afterglow of her smile. "I am American, too."

"Very."

"Romanian-American. And you are?"

"An orphan. So just: American."

She cocked her head the way she did. "Who taught you then?"

"Taught me what?"

"You were raised well. Somehow."

"I learned what's right," he said, "by doing what is wrong."

"That is such bullshit." The curse left her mouth and her fingers touched her lips with chagrin, a Jane Austen heroine finding out Mr. Darcy had kissed one of the Misses Hurst beneath a full moon. She seemed to be holding back a giggle. "I'm sorry. I did not mean to say this. But really. What nonsense. You don't learn good by doing evil. Evil leads to more evil unless it is interrupted by something else."

Evan said, "Huh."

It was the first time he'd heard her laugh in full. It was beautiful.

They flowed in and out of traffic, continuing a tactically circuitous route, until he exited, merging onto the Cross Island Parkway south. Her hands stayed clasped over the thick book, gripping it tightly.

"I will give this statement to your friend," she said. "For you and for the others those men might hurt. And maybe it will help. But there is no cure, you know. For the world."

"Not a cure," Evan said.

He felt those blue eyes searching the side of his face. "What then?"

He thought.

He thought of missions past.

Lidia and Santiago Martinez, the framed school portrait of eight-year-old Gabriel on the wall, and the wrapped presents waiting beneath the Christmas tree.

Jayla Hill, orphaned as surely as he was, magically speaking again through crushed vocal cords.

The Seabrooks, Ruby and her parents, Mason and Deborah, and that jigsaw puzzle of a family photo on their kitchen table, their once-intact family put back together again.

He thought about when he'd finally delivered Anjelina home, how she'd moved through the white gate to the house, Aragón and Belicia waiting behind the screen door with unspeakable relief.

He thought about how nervous his half brother Andre Duran had been to see his daughter again, how Sofia had run over to him when he'd walked in and wrapped herself around his waist.

He thought about the way Max Merriweather had smiled shyly when Evan told him to write his own story so no one else would write it for him.

He thought about sitting in Trevon Gaines's bedroom until Trevon fell asleep, how he'd clutched his stuffed frog and murmured to himself, *We don't cry and we don't feel sorry for ourself.*

And Joey. Swinging at him with a tire iron when he let her out of the trunk. Her first time in the penthouse, ogling the poured-concrete countertops, the soaring ceiling, the walls of glass—*This place. It's like something made up.* His hands on her thigh, stanching the bleeding from her femoral artery. How she'd blown out the candle he'd set atop an MRE on her seventeenth birthday, trying not to cry.

Alison Siegler walking from the shipping container to the waiting ambulance, standing tall, unbroken, after her sixteen-day ordeal.

He thought about Isa Vasquez's proud smile and stubby thumbs-up, how her Down syndrome–slanted eyes had lit up when he'd told her she was a very brave young woman.

He merged onto the Southern State Parkway east and rode it all the way to Bay Parkway, scooping down through Canarsie and toward the neck of Barren Island. The slate-gray sky gave way to rain, big, sporadic drops plopping onto the windshield.

Not a cure.

What then?

"Balance," he answered.

Anca offered her hand palm-up across the console. The gesture was tentative. Sisterly.

He took it.

She squeezed it once.

He squeezed back.

Cutting across Flatbush Avenue, he nosed off asphalt onto the rutted dirt road Templeton had specified. Head-tall elephant grass battered the side panels and then fell away to reveal flat salt marshes. Aside from a few washed-out hiking trails, there were no signs of life. The windshield wipers worked hard. Weeds and bramble twisted up from the fecund earth, clashing with mini-forests of reeds, straight and dense as cornfields.

As he curved along the inlet of Dead Horse Bay, the smell hit, an abattoir reek. Honoring the Third Commandment, he'd pored over records of the area, memorizing the topography down to each bend and turn. In the 1850s, horse-rendering plants had dumped their residual here, enough chopped-up carcasses to clog the surrounding waters. Vat-boiled fat, fertilizer and glue, millstone-ground bone. Oil had been extruded from the forage fish in the bay, too, offal dumped along the coastline where feral dogs and pigs roamed, picking at fragrant refuse heaps. Contaminants, too, chemical and radiological, explosive nitroglycerin derived from garbage trucked in from the city to be incinerated. The whole putrid mess had been layered over with mounds of landfill waste and buried ineptly beneath sixteen feet of sandy topsoil. High-tide floods had eroded and excavated this rancid history, every wash of filthy water from the bay revealing more decay and ruin, the rot of ages compounding in the primordial soup where marsh met water. Each ebb and flow vomited up horse bones, rusted shanks of killing machinery, Medusa-hair tangles of seaweed peppered with bits of trash. It was impossible to sense how far the cesspool stretched its stink into the Atlantic, the earth, rain clouds, and sink faucets.

Anca's nose wrinkled against the stench.

Evan felt it pressing into his pores, assaultive osmosis, filth entering his lungs, his bloodstream. His OCD ticked up but he breathed it away, mission-focused.

The unofficial road dipped low along Glass Bottle Beach, named with utilitarian grimness like everything else in the vicinity. For some reason, bottles disgorged from the landfill had aggregated here, shattered and intact, brown and blue and green and clear, marked with the jaunty antique lettering of their past lives, soda and shoe polish, bleach and digestive tonics. Stranded boats proliferated, hurricane casualties—rotting junk boats christened with graffiti tags, a half-buried motorboat rearing up from the sand like a breaching whale.

The Mercedes crept along through rain and muck, wipers beating away for clarity. They'd loop down, cut back across Flatbush, and forge surreptitiously toward Floyd Bennett Field from the south. He had to slow to pass an upended tree, squat and gnarled, octopoid roots twisting out like the ruffled hem of a living dress.

Even with the windows up, the reek off the water choked him. His eyes watered.

Anca's hand reached for his, tightening. Another squeeze?

No, panic.

He looked over. Her mouth pulsed, lips sealed.

Moving robotically, she reached in her purse, flipped her cell phone onto the dash, digging for something. She came up with her seizure plan, hands fumbling automatically to get it around her neck.

"No," he said, slowing the car. "It's okay. I'm here. I'm here and will not leave."

Her hands released. Her tongue squirmed in her closed mouth. "Emerald," she said faintly. "Jade and fir."

On the dashboard, her phone showed no signal. The fallen tree partially hemmed them in from behind, a choke point. To their right, the refuse-strewn coastline gave onto choppy water. To the left a wall of reeds, vertically barred with shadow and impenetrable to the eye. Perfect ambush point.

Her eyes fluttered. "Bright. It's so bright."

But there was barely any light. The wipers thrashed against

the rain, the air heavied with gray, the sun a mere thumb smudge within the leaden overcast.

He nudged the Mercedes away from the reeds to the far side of the narrow dirt road, clear for rapid acceleration. Anca covered her eyes, a low mewling noise escaping her throat. He reached across her to the controls, lowering her seat back. A fork of lightning touched down to the water, close enough to make him blink. He couldn't face her and the curtain of reeds at the same time.

Thunder rumbled through the chassis, his bones. Rain sheeted down. He shot a glance over his shoulder. Even at a few feet, the reeds were barely visible. He unholstered his ARES, set it beneath his thigh, then turned back to Anca.

She seized.

50
The Goliath

Their position was open to attack. And Anca was worse than defenseless in this state, a full operational liability. Evan leaned over her, tilting her chin back, keeping the airway open.

Her cheeks were smooth, flushed in ragged circles. Her eyes rolled back, crescent cups of sclera. She rattled against the seat and rattled some more. Twisting on her hip, one heel jabbing her tote. Evan couldn't look away, behind him, but the 1911 was pinned between the back of his thigh and the seat, pressed reassuringly into his flesh.

Her head snapped to the side but he got his palm between her temple and the passenger window to muffle the impact. Her lower throat was visible, her blouse pulled sideways, one button popped. She was utterly, utterly vulnerable and he thought about her on the subway, drag-carried through the streets of Harlem, flopped onto that bed in the walk-down apartment. He expected rage, but all that came was a hollowed-out ache of disbelief that in encountering her like this, a pack of men had seen opportunity. Despite an imagination unbounded by convention, despite experience that had acquainted him with the abhorrent, he was core-struck by the unthinkability of taking advantage of her in this state.

His stomach roiled from the notion, the maybe threat lurking at his back in the reeds, the fetid air creeping through the vents.

At last she stilled.

Her blinks, long and languid.

He'd grown used to it a bit, the process of her emergence.

Her voice, hoarse: "There was a girl in fifth grade . . ."

Twisting awkwardly, he looked behind him. Rain pounded his window. The reeds thrashed tropically. But no one flew out from cover.

Back to her. "What?"

"A mixer. But I couldn't dance." The words, slurred but discernible. "I sat alone by . . . refreshments table. And she was good at it. Dancing. She wore . . . kelly-green sweater, had her hair pinned up in a butterfly clasp. I was . . . so envious. When she came to get water, I told her she looked fat and clumsy. I remember . . . I remember how her face just . . . *broke*."

Anca's seat was still lowered. Her light blue eyes gazed up, the pupils dilated, open to everything. He was leaning over the console, over her, looking down at her. In another context, it would have been romantic, but it was not, not at all.

"I made fun of her for being good at something I was too cowardly to do," she said, her words coming in a bit stronger. "And I had too much pride to apologize."

Evan said, "We need to get moving."

"I just lived it. I lived it again just now as if I was there. It's a part of me, do you see? And a part of her. Right now. Still."

"Yes."

"All our damage. Our sin, our virtue. It's not the past. It's the present. Everything is present . . . all the time."

Somehow the sky had cleared up. Patches of winter blue spread among the clouds and the sun had broken through, causing the endless skein of broken glass to glitter on the beach. The reeds behind Evan, now unshaken by rain, stood stiff and distinct, offering transparency through the interstitial gaps. As they waved, they cast saintly fingers of light across the car. For an instant Evan was transported to stained-glass windows and resonant voices, but he forced himself back to gaze alertly through the reed bed. No glinting eyes, no muzzle flash, just nature taking hold even here, rising from putrescence as she did. Even the stench had receded, or he'd acclimated to it.

Reaching past Anca, he brought her seat up, her face rising close to his.

She looked into him. "*Everything* matters."

"Yes," he said.

"I am ready now. I am ready to talk to your friend. For myself."

Settling back into his seat, Evan tapped the gas. The tires spun for a moment and then caught, lurching them forward out of the muddy ruts.

In the rearview, he watched the swamp tree recede.

He said, "Good."

In a word, Naomi Templeton was cool. She was cool like black-and-white photographs, like Ray-Bans, a '59 Cadillac, leather-jacket cool, nails-tough cool, tomboy-cool. As Evan and Anca pulled up, Templeton was waiting alone on the porch, leaning against the decommissioned building with her arms crossed and one tactical boot set with its sole flat against the white clapboard panel behind her. She had a strong, stubborn Irish jaw, her hair cut however, no makeup ever. Her hips were not va-va-voom wide like Candy's but sturdy, athletic.

She was on the job. Always.

Like her, the building was from another era. A Second World War wood-frame structure with a gable roof and narrow windows.

It was set apart from the training grounds and the hangars to the north, nestled cozily into a stand of black cherry trees stripped naked by winter. Branches clawed skeletally outward, red-tinged black, bark scaly and unforgiving.

Evan parked, got out, walked around, and opened the door for Anca. She emerged, the wet breeze lifting her hair. Templeton waited on the porch, unmoving.

As they approached, Evan braced himself for a thunder of Black Hawks, a storm of Counter-Assault Team members swathed in black BDUs, an incoming volley of less-lethal projectiles. But the world did not crash in on him. There was just Naomi Templeton on the porch, keeping her word.

Once they'd mounted the steps, Templeton peeled herself off the wall and offered her hand to Anca. "Ms. Dumitrescu, I'm Naomi. Thank you for meeting us here."

Evan appreciated Templeton introducing herself by first name.

"It takes courage and grit and you have the respect of all of us here," she said. "We have some folks ready to talk with you. The federal prosecutor, Gretchen Barton, is a longtime friend. You'll have support in there, too, an interviewer specializing in trauma, a victim advocate—"

"I am not a victim," Anca said. "I was victimized."

Naomi took a moment to reset, admiration clear on her face. "I understand," she said. And then, again: "I understand."

"Thank you, Naomi. I am ready."

Anca walked past her through the doorway, paused in the front room with its cozy assemblage of armchairs. Her head oriented toward the neighboring room, and then she strode in.

Evan entered in time to catch a glimpse of a conference room and several folks rising to greet Anca as the door swung shut behind her. He stood looking at the closed door.

Naomi's footsteps creaked up behind him. "It's a great team. She'll be okay."

Evan stared at the raised square panels of the door. "If she gets stuck or scared, they need to ask her to describe what happened in the third person."

"We got it."

"She has seizures, too. Can't control them—"

"You said."

"If it happens when she's in there, someone let me know."

"X."

She touched his arm, barely. He turned around.

"It's okay. We got it. We can wait right here."

Two armchairs by a fireplace, a small table between them.

Evan sat. Naomi sat.

They studied each other.

"So this is what you look like when you're not in restraints," she said.

"Easier to see without a spit hood over my head."

"Oh, come on, princess. I took the spit hood off."

The fire leapt behind a wrought-iron screen. It smelled good, birchwood exhaling wintergreen and a trace of mint.

"She's a tough broad," Naomi said.

"You have no idea."

He'd clasped his hands on his knees, worrying one thumb with the other. He stilled. He hated giving up nonverbal tells. He did not like Anca in the other room behind a closed door. He did not want to look at Naomi. He felt wildly out of control.

He wondered why.

Naomi stayed in her armchair, legs arranged in an ankle-on-thigh position, hands motionless on the armrest. Patient.

He appreciated that.

He cleared his throat. Started to speak. Stopped.

Finally he said, "She asked for help. She was in public. On a subway full of people. And no one cared. Not one person."

Naomi said, "I know."

"She had a fucking *sign* around her neck asking for help."

Naomi said, "I know."

"They dragged her through city streets past hundreds of people."

Naomi said, "I know."

He was flicking at his thumbnail with the middle finger of the same hand. He stopped.

"They shot her with fentanyl to keep her down longer."

"I know."

"After, she walked from Harlem to the Bronx."

"I know."

"That's over four miles."

"I know."

"They took her wallet. No subway card. She didn't have money for a cab. So she walked. Four miles. Know what she told me?" Beside them the fire popped pleasingly. At last, he lifted his gaze to meet Naomi's. "'No one would help.'"

Naomi leaned forward. Set a hand on his knee.

She said, "I know."

"What does that say about them? *Us.* What does that say about us?"

Templeton rolled her pale lips, contemplated. "That we have a lot of work to do. But look at us here, making it right. Look at us. Here."

They sat in silence, their thoughts punctuated by the crackle of logs.

Naomi walked them back out to the Mercedes, thanked Anca, and closed the door behind her. Then she came around to face Evan by the hood.

"She did great," Naomi said. "We'll track them down."

"I'll get there first," Evan said.

Naomi studied him. "And you'll leave them for us?"

"Yes."

"Not dead?"

"Yes."

"Unharmed?"

Evan kicked the hard earth. "Looks like rain."

Templeton tightened her face against the cold, looked up at the dreary sky. Sighed. "Want me to open your door, too?"

"I'll manage."

"Oh, before I forget." She dug in her pocket, tugged out a pack of Reese's Peanut Butter Cups. "To reciprocate. Y'know. Our ongoing courtship."

She flipped him the pack.

He caught it against his chest. Looked down at the bright orange packaging. "Hey. One of these has been eaten."

She shrugged. "Got hungry."

"You suck at this, Templeton."

She smiled, tucked a hank of bluntly cut hair behind an ear. "So they tell me."

Evan retraced the off-road route, a long slow loop along the muddy path cut through the marshland to the south. It was hurricane weather, the air balky and constipated, a wet wind buffeting the luxury car, rocking it on its chassis. He'd rolled back the shade to the moon roof, keeping an eye on the sky in case Templeton's superiors decided to reverse course and send a fleet of assault helicopters after him.

Anca clutched her book in her lap, her tote bag between her ankles. She hadn't said much. Evan figured she was talked out.

Her eyes darted back and forth, and her hands made fluttering motions at her sides.

"How it feels," she said. "I can't shake it."

"You don't shake hypervigilance," Evan said. "You use it."

"Then what? You stop seeing threats lurking everywhere?"

"You still see them," he said. "Clearly enough to meet them properly."

Wind sucked beneath the undercarriage, a bestial howl.

She glanced nervously out her window. "This weather. What time will we get back?"

Evan checked the GPS. "Around three. Why?"

"I have my rapid HIV scheduled. So I have to go back to the hospital, Our Lady of the Holy Spirit and the Rending of Garments and the Gnashing of Teeth."

Evan looked over at her. Her pug nose gave her a puckish quality.

"Is that a joke, Ms. Dumitrescu?"

She nodded pertly. "Yes. I love Catholics. They are so . . . charismatic."

On either side of them, elephant grass thrashed ecstatically, and then the rutted road tailed west toward the boiling, infected bay. They carved between the wall of reeds and the noxious beach, that upended tree coming into view, its snarled roots blocking two-thirds of the road.

A flash of color on the ground before it caught his eye.

A man in a yellow raincoat, sprawled facedown. To his side, a felled mountain bike.

Everything slowed down.

The road wasn't wide enough for a banked turn or a three-point; he'd have to reverse rapidly if an ambush sprang.

"He fell," Anca said. "He needs help."

"No," Evan said. "Do not get out."

He couldn't brake too hard without skidding. Even so, he felt the tires churning up fins of mud. The slide put them closer to the man, maybe ten meters out. Against the muddy earth shades and the dark slate waters, the yellow raincoat stood out vibrantly.

The man rolled over, features coming clear, and Evan saw it wasn't a man at all but a large boy. Broad nose flecked with pustular acne, cheeks padded with baby fat, soft jawline. Maybe twelve years old and nearly six feet tall.

The boy reached out a hand toward them for help. His face was wet either from tears or the rain.

"A boy," Anca said. "He's just a boy."

Evan said, "Don't—"

But she was out of the car.

He jabbed the end of the gear-shift lever—*park*—and shot out after her, his boots mashing divots through the mud. He scanned the ground by the boy, the ruts dappled with rainfall, hard to read. A recent-looking double swoop of tires led around the fallen tree. And the reeds at his side looked beaten back, a few of the stalks snapped low by the base, tilting irregularly.

"Help!" the kid cried. "My leg, I think I broke it."

Anca was a few strides ahead but Evan caught her easily, arm around her waist. "Back in the car. *Now.*"

"But the boy, he's—"

"Go."

He flung her back, using the momentum to propel himself the other way, checking the reeds—still clear—as he spun toward the kid sprawled at his feet.

The boy rolled over.

And slammed a hypodermic needle through Evan's cargo pants, right into the center of his thigh.

He jerked back before the plunger could fully depress, the syringe dangling loosely, needle still jabbed deep. Evan ripped it free, thoughts spinning—*fentanyl*—as awareness spiked.

In a single snapshot, his mind grabbed the calculation. The plunger had sunk about eighty percent. Eight milliliters of a ten-mil syringe would be around four hundred micrograms. An intramuscular jab gave him slightly longer onset time than intravenous, which meant he had four minutes, four and a half tops, before going out. He set his internal metronome ticking, slid it to a back burner of his mind. Intramuscular was slower to come on but slower to fade, too. At a minimum he'd be unconscious twenty minutes, and that was only if adrenaline burned it through his system at two-thirds speed. Already he felt the heat in his veins, fuzz edging into his peripheral vision.

The boy scrambled to get up but Evan kicked out his arm and he plopped face-first in the mud. Evan ripped out a ring of flex-cuffs he kept curled in the secondary pouch inside the left top thigh pocket of his cargo pants. They sprang loose, scattering in the mud, but one spun just in front of his hand and he snatched it, dropped to a knee, cinched it tight around the boy's ankles. He plucked up a handful, got a second one secured around the boy's wrists.

The fuzziness tickled at his skin now, and he drew from his appendix holster as he rose, checking Anca's unsteady progress back to the car. Wheeling to the reeds, he lifted the gun just as an enormous man bulled through the thicket, beard sprouting densely from the massive shelf of his mandible, a berserking lumberjack.

The grove shuddered at either side of him, yielding two more men, mere giants dwarfed by the colossus.

Evan had time to register a single instant of suspended terror before the Goliath lunged onto the road at him, roaring, his lessers exploding from the reeds in his wake.

51
He Kept Coming

Standing his ground, Evan sighted on the hollow of the Goliath's throat, remembered his pledge to Anca, jerked the pistol down, and shot him in the meat of the thigh.

He did not slow.

Evan clipped his left hip.

He did not slow.

But he staggered.

As he bulldozed in, Evan sidestepped him, limboing beneath a roundhouse from one of the other men—white guy, teardrop tattoos, dreads tight enough to pull his hairline back from traction alopecia. Falling backward, one palm hitting mud, the other clenching the gun, Evan shoved himself back up onto his legs. The third man came in hard, whipping something overhead—a club, no—was that a gym sock with a lock inside it?—and he ducked that, too, rolling through the mud.

He shot a quick glance over at Anca. She'd backed to the car, leaning against the hood, arms bent vertically before her like a shield, fists beneath her chin.

The three men wheeled in the aftermath of their swings, staggering to hold balance, mired in the mud. The Goliath's shot leg slipped out and he went down, a slow-motion tumble like the sluggish kickoff of an avalanche.

Over by the felled tree, the boy bucked like a stunned fish. *"Dad!"*

Evan took an eighth of a second to set his bearings. A low-grade deception ambush. He'd been caught out because the ruse was so brazenly stupid, plopped before him while he'd been monitoring the sky for incoming Black Hawks. These men were way too large to have been Anca's abusers, which meant rented muscle, probably prison boys given the teardrop tats and the lock-in-a-sock. No cell-phone range, just three ogres and Evan and Anca in a storm, with the seconds ticking down on his ability to stay upright.

He had to make serious headway before Goliath found his feet. Sweeping up the syringe, he jabbed it in Teardrop's shoulder blade, juiced him with the remaining two mils, and shot him through a knee from behind. The guy grunted as he tumbled, screaming, "Fuck, Jimmy, get him—"

Before he struck the ground, Evan kicked him forward at his partner, who was closing in, the sock stretched long as it whipped toward Evan's face. The impact shifted the trajectory, the lock snapping over Teardrop's back and bouncing off his kidney, a piss-blood-tomorrow shot. Off the snapback, Evan caught the sock in the flaccid middle, the lock tetherball-winding around his fist until he ripped the weapon free.

Nunchaku whirls of his hands cracked Jimmy in the temple, throat, elbow, the latter giving off a pleasing crackle of shattered bone. Eyes fluttering, Jimmy fell sideways and then rolled onto his stomach. At the side of the road, Goliath was up on a knee, his hulking form striated from the dumping rain.

He rose and rose and rose.

Warmth was spreading through Evan's veins, his senses blurring into one another. Exertion would make the fentanyl spread quicker through his veins, but he had no choice but to exert, a race against himself. He had to inflict sufficient damage in the next three minutes and forty-five seconds or else Anca and his inanimate body would be at the full disposal of these barbarians.

Teardrop grabbed Evan's boot but Evan yanked his leg free, firing down at him, transforming the hand into an explosion of crimson. The man wailed, clutching the wreckage. Two and a half fingers lay in the mud, one twitching at the top knuckle. His eyes were rimmed red, the first charge of fentanyl. Evan had taken in four times as much. His own eyes must have looked like the devil's. The opioid had red-lined his senses, the rancid breeze off Bottle Beach filling his nasal cavities. It felt like breathing fire. His attention warbled, came back into focus.

Jimmy coughed and stirred, the sclera of his right eye turned wine red from the blow to his temple. Over on the verge to the beach, Goliath had found his feet. A crimson rose bloomed on the front of his thigh. From the hip shot, blood dribbled down the side of his left leg. Alarmingly, he did not look unsteady.

Evan stood stooped, trying to draw a full breath. The brawl had carried him closer to the car, where Anca remained frozen against the hood.

"Get in . . . car," he managed. "Lock doors."

She broke from paralysis, feet slapping wetly as she ran to cover.

Evan's ears were buzzing now.

He was down to three minutes fifteen seconds.

He raised the ARES, trying to pick a nonlethal spot on Goliath. None of the previous had worked. He'd just sighted on the right kneecap when he was struck from behind. His pistol flew away. A cushion of mud caught him, his shoulder plowing a furrow. Impossibly, Teardrop was back on his feet, prison tough and still coming on.

Evan swung around, scissor-kicked to sweep the legs. Teardrop hit the mud next to him. For a moment, they lay flat on their backs side by side. They stared at each other. Teardrop had shockingly clear green eyes. Static cramped Evan's peripheral vision even more but he sensed Goliath reorienting toward the fight. A few feet to his side, Anca reached the door, slipped, pulled herself up by the protruding handle, her feet sliding out beneath her in the slick.

Evan punched Teardrop in the face, shattering the nose. He hauled himself up, clawing through mud, the foulness off the bay lodging in his lungs. Moving toward Anca.

A flash of movement—Jimmy up again, flying toward him for a tackle.

Evan banged into Anca, knocking her clear, grabbed the handle, and flung the car door open to meet Jimmy's head. He'd seen it in movies but it proved effective enough in reality, the smack compounded by a crash of buckling metal.

Jimmy lay crumpled beneath the dented panel. Evan hauled the door open once more, grabbed Anca from the slime in the road, yanked her across Jimmy's motionless form, and hurled her into the passenger seat.

He turned.

The concussions and fentanyl had overtaken Teardrop. He lay facedown, mud rising halfway up his cheeks toward the ears. The boy had given up bucking, watching instead with shiny eyes, the dead tree flared at his back, a ghastly peacock plumage.

Across the road, Goliath readied, breathing hard, mist pluming bull-like from his nostrils. His nose, a bulbous protrusion of scar tissue, had been broken and rebroken enough times that it was shaped like a blackjack. Before him, Evan felt like a specimen from an inferior species.

Two minutes fifty seconds, give or take.

Synesthesia mashed up his senses. He could see the fumes now as colors, could breathe in the sounds of the bay. The trash on the beach threw psychedelic streaks. Heaviness tugged at his muscles; he felt them weighing down his bones. He wondered if this was what it was like for Anca one to two times a day.

Rain spilled down his face, drenched his shoulders. He blinked hard, squeezing his eyes, opening them, fighting the haze. He couldn't allow himself to go out until he'd rendered everyone unconscious or incapacitated. If he went first, he would not have a chance to wake up.

His pistol was in the mud to his side, far enough that he couldn't reach it before Goliath reached him.

He was in trouble.

This might be it. The end of Orphan X on a shit-stained Brooklyn coastline.

He turned to face Anca through the windshield. Ridiculously, the wipers were still squeaking back and forth. He waved a hand. "Go. Leave."

She shook her head.

He said, *"Drive!"*

The ground trembled beneath his boots.

With dread, he turned.

Goliath was charging.

Jack came to him as a whisper, quoting the Greek poet: *We don't rise to the level of our aspirations. We fall to the level of our training.*

That's what Evan had right now. It was all he had.

He held ground, hips pointing forward. Front foot angled straight to blunt incoming low kicks, weight set on his back foot to free his lead to check or *teep.* Hands raised high, palms turned in, unclenched, floating to guard his face. Chin tucked to protect his windpipe. He calculated an ankle-breaking kick, a muay thai strike with his shin since his foot would likely shatter against the Goliath's bone on impact. He charted the precise angle to the inside base of the calf to break the ankle.

None of it mattered.

Goliath plowed into him, grabbed him by the shirt and belt, picked him up, slammed him into the road, picked him up, and slammed him into the road again.

Then he hoisted him once more and hurled him across the road onto the beach.

Evan rolled and rolled some more.

There was no air to be had.

A high sharp pain in his left lung, likely muted by fentanyl. He writhed in the sand-gritty trash, mouth gaping, searching for oxygen. The visual landscape swam distortedly. There were ceramic shards, perfume bottles wrapped in hides of mud, an arm of a porcelain doll, rust-eaten dog tags, a moss-coated astronaut action figure, intact jars, old engine parts, husks of horseshoe crabs, barnacle-crusted tires, a mound of leather shoe soles that brought to mind cattle cars and black smoke. That half-buried motorboat reared up from the sand menacingly. Water dribbled onto shore, thick like oil, sucking parasitically.

Breath came, relief overpowering that stabbing at the top of his lung. He wobbled in and out of clarity, drenched in opioid warmth, blanketed in drugged exhaustion. A vision came on, the beach as a sewage hellscape, the worst of everything heaved up from the bottom of humanity.

He could scarcely believe he was on the same spot of earth where Anca had blinked up at him from the passenger seat, the air suffused with a beatific light.

From the road, Goliath stared at him, unhurried.

The car was still there, just to his side. Anca had not driven off.

The giant turned to stare at her through the windshield.

Even from this distance, even through the rain, Evan saw her recoil.

He checked his metronome.

A minute and a half left if he was lucky.

"Hey!" he shouted, his voice warped, tongue sluggish. He groped the earth around him, hands fumbling across bottles and shards, somehow managing to pull himself upright. "Come on."

That boulder head tilted. Massive eyes locked on him, so dark they looked pupilless.

Leisurely, Goliath ambled across the road toward the beach, massive arms penduluming at his sides. His leg buckled slightly, the only concession to the two heat-treated copper rounds he'd absorbed. He was deliberate, his movements unwieldly, which would have been a fighting advantage for Evan were fentanyl not leaching through his central nervous system.

Goliath's enormous shoes crunched forward, popping doll heads and bottles. Nearing, he lunged. Evan managed to jerk to the side, barely dodging the freight-train bulk and jabbing a heel to tangle up the big man's treads.

Goliath tumbled, the ship prow of his chest harrowing the earth, shoving up ridges on either side. With his full weight, Evan drove his knee down onto the spot between his shoulder blades, hoping to knock him windless. When Goliath bucked, it felt like riding a rhinoceros. He spun and Evan spun with him, nearly crushed beneath the steamroller drum of his torso. Evan managed to skirt free. They wound up feet to head, though Evan's span reached neither the man's feet nor his head. Goliath seized his ankles, jerking him along the sand, gathering him up toward his chest, sausage fingers groping. Evan grabbed him through the crotch, trying to hold position, pounding away with a hammer fist to the gunshot wound on the hip. The Goliath grunted, losing his grip.

Evan squirmed free. Goliath clawed after him, and they scrabbled through the wasteland sludge. Goliath kept coming and Evan's palms scraped through the muck and the trash and Goliath kept coming, he kept coming.

Fuzziness all through Evan now, his tongue pins and needles. He was barely holding off his panic, mounting with each tick of the metronome. A massive hand clamped around his foot, engulfing the entire end of his boot. It felt like getting clinched by the claw of a crane.

Yanked backward, Evan went weightless. He snatched at the sand, came up with an intact medicinal bottle with embossed lettering—Dr. Kilmer's Swamp Root!

He felt himself gathered into Goliath, a fish furled toward a squid beak. Swinging around, he saw the looming head, the gritted teeth in that wool-mesh beard.

He swung the bottle as hard as he could, aiming for the paper-thin orbital rim at the side of the eye.

Yielding contact. Bone and glass shattered.

The Goliath emitted a protracted groan, a howl that never reached howling. Releasing Evan, he clawed at his face. Evan still had the bottle by the neck, the broken bottom an oval of fangs. His vision warbled, rot scorching the back of his tongue, the slurp of water against shore exploding kaleidoscopically in his head.

Minute and a half.

He jagged the ring of shards into the gunshot wound on Goliath's thigh and screwed hard.

Now came a proper howl.

Evan fell back, banging his shoulders against the hull of the motorboat.

Goliath thrashed and screamed.

It would not be enough.

Evan grabbed the man's hefty ankle, lifted the tree-trunk leg, and tugged as hard as he could. No movement. Dropping his center of gravity, he jerked, throwing his weight back in thrusts.

Bellowing, Goliath lurched, skidding across the broken bottles. When he twisted to reach Evan, his stomach bulged into view, slashed through with cuts.

Evan's strength was fading. His sentience, too.

Another jerk across the saw-toothed ground brought the Goliath's leg within reach of the half-buried motorboat. Evan grabbed a muddy flex-cuff from the bunch he'd stuffed back into his pocket. He hoisted Goliath's massive ankle up toward one of the boat's cleats, still bolted to the gunwale, and readied the strip of nylon.

It wouldn't fit around the girth of the ankle and the cleat.

Goliath lurched up, swinging at him, and Evan jabbed the heel of his hand into the shattered maw of his eye. The big man slapped back onto the sand.

Hands shaking, strength fading, Evan managed to get another flex-cuff looped through the first, daisy-chaining ankle to cleat.

Goliath yowled and ripped his leg back, tearing the entire cleat free of the gunwale.

Evan half collapsed against the side of the boat, tried and failed to draw a full breath.

He said, "Damn it."

Fifty seconds, maybe forty-five.

His head got swimmy and he slid off the hull, barely missing a pronged spade of metal thrust up from the sandy mire.

An anchor fluke.

He laughed like a crazy man.

The rain hammered him.

Digging frantically, sand rammed beneath his fingernails, unearthing a length of the shank, the bulb of the stock, and there—at last—the ring.

He sensed a barometric shift in the air. Goliath had pulled himself up, sit-up-style, arms within clamping distance. He grabbed Evan at either shoulder, crushing his rib cage inward.

Evan slammed forward in a head butt, aiming the thick curve of his frontal bone at the cheek below the vanquished eye.

A crack and a crumble.

Goliath flopped down onto his back again, gnarled hands shuddering over his ruined face.

Yanking the leg, Evan squirmed another flex-cuff through the loop around the bobbing cleat, cinched it around the anchor ring, ratcheted it tight.

Goliath heaved his leg once more, the anchor actually shifting in the sand. One flex-cuff wouldn't be enough.

Heaviness suffused Evan, concreting his eyelids, slowing his breaths, pulling him into sleep. He fought it, hands working furiously.

Another zip tie.

Another.

Another.

Sliding and tightening, sliding and tightening until a web of high-tensile nylon 6/6 ensnared the mammoth ankle.

Evan crawled toward Goliath's face, pinning the near arm with his knee.

"Who hired you?"

Goliath smiled through blood-matted beard. When Evan's chest hitched, that dagger of pain stabbed his left lung.

He punched Goliath on the caved cheek. *"Who sent you?"*

Goliath's head rolled back in the sand, came forward again. "You can beat me till yer tiny little fist shatters, but I ain't telling you shit."

Evan believed him.

The rain had slowed but the air still felt electric, violent.

He waded out of reach on his knees, found the strength to rise again, and staggered toward the road. He was breathing sounds and smelling colors and the world around him was moving drunkenly of its own accord.

Though bound at the wrists and ankles, the boy had squirmed

his way over toward Evan's gun. Evan stooped as he passed, picking it up.

Teardrop lay motionless a few feet away, face buried in mud. He was going to suffocate in full view of Anca in the car.

Evan kicked him in the ribs. Groaning, he flipped over.

Zzt. Zzt. Two more zip ties rendered him inert.

Nineteen seconds.

Evan heard a scrabbling noise.

Jimmy was bent over the side of the car, hands zombie-clawing at the passenger door. The handle had retracted, so there was nothing to grab, but Anca's terrified face was right there on the other side of the window.

When Evan blinked, his eyes threatened to stay closed. His knees unlocked and he almost toppled. Pulling his legs forward, he neared Jimmy.

Jimmy took no notice, kept at his half-conscious efforts.

Evan made a fist around his pistol, used it as a makeshift brass knuckles, and hammered him on the side of the head.

He fell stiffly.

Evan collapsed next to him. Patted his cargo pocket.

No zip ties left.

Wait—he felt one hard edge.

Worming the zip tie from his pocket took enormous effort. Back and forth, back and forth until he fought it free.

Jimmy had fallen with his torso lopped across his hip, his right hand nearly touching his left shoe. Evan joined wrist to ankle in the unforgiving embrace of the zip tie and then jab-kicked him with both heels to roll him away from the car.

Buzzing filled his ears now, his mouth, his head, the dermis beneath his skin. The air tasted of dumpster. Warmth tugged him down, down, down.

Five seconds, maybe six.

He rolled onto his back. Utterly spent.

The sky was nothing but overlapping swirls of dreariness.

A silhouette broke it, staring down at him.

He could not muster the energy to be scared.

Shoving his elbows into the mud, he tried to push himself up, got only as far as a slight tilt of his torso.

It was done then. He was done.

He blinked against the rain. The silhouette was slender, feminine.

It crouched.

As he collapsed, Anca caught him. He looked up at her, sprawled in her lap with his head lolling à la *pietà*—heh, funny—but there was no time for symbolism. It came on then, the fall of the samurai blade, slicing the curtain between him and the abyss. No more seconds. No more planning. No more control. Just abject terror at what was to come when he would not be there to meet it.

"Listen." Around his torpid tongue, it came out *lessun.* "'M gonna go out . . . not safe . . . can't let them . . . in car . . . just haveta . . ."

She gazed down. Behind her the sun glowed through the blanketing gloom, suffusing her backlit head with a nimbus glow. Her mouth seemed to move. The afterimpression of her words lingered, the last thing he had to carry with him into the waiting nothingness.

"Don't worry," she said. "I won't leave you."

52

Scrape, Rattle, Scrape

Scrape, rattle, scrape.

Scrape, rattle, scrape.

Anca held Evan in her lap.

She lacked the strength to pull him into the car, so she sat with him in the rain. She was drenched through as if she'd jumped into the ocean. The rain had washed them both clean before stopping as abruptly as it had arrived.

Two of the men lay unconscious and the boy was spent, crying into the earth, face crusted with mud. That was fine by her.

Scrape, rattle, scrape.

Scrape, rattle, scrape.

Exhausted, she leaned to peer around the front of the Mercedes.

The giant man was belly-crawling toward her, forearm over forearm, hauling himself from the beach onto the road. Behind him he was dragging—could it be? was that possibly?—an anchor.

She felt shockingly calm.

Setting Evan down gently, she rose.

Scrape, rattle, scrape.

Scrape, rattle, scrape.

She walked toward him. She had never seen a face as damaged as his, not even her own after the assault.

His teeth were bared, mouth stretched wide, an hourglass set on its side. Strands of gummy blood spiderwebbed the tangle of beard and lacerated flesh that was his mouth.

He kept on.

Dragging an anchor.

A leviathan freed from the deep.

As she neared, he torqued his head, that Cyclops eye staring up at her. "Fucking cunt. You'd better cut this anchor off my leg. Or you have no idea what kind of holes we'll tear into you so we can f—"

She kicked him just beneath the hinge of his jaw. Hard.

He spasmed once in the mud, legs contorted, a dead beetle.

Out cold.

Turning her back, she walked over to Evan once more to sit with him until he awakened.

She knew all too well what it felt like to come to alone.

"The prosecution team is pleased with the statement." Naomi Templeton's voice came clearly through the Mercedes's elaborate infotainment system.

Gripping the steering wheel, Evan did his best to draw full breaths, but the pain in his upper left lung refused to diminish, tightening its claws across his rib cage. Everything hurt. The arches of his feet hurt and his hamstrings hurt and his right patella hurt and both elbows hurt and his trapezius hurt and his hip flexors hurt and his forehead hurt and of course his left groin muscle hurt too because it was the weakest link in his body. The hours he spent every week—and usually every day—to hold his pain at bay and his bones in proper alignment had saved him now from being entirely debilitated.

He'd woken up in Anca's arms, the three Vikings sprawled unconscious across the road. The kid had pissed himself. As they'd pulled out, he'd cursed a blue streak at them. Anca had referred to him as a foulmouthed little creature, which had coaxed the first pained smile from Evan's bruised face.

"If we can get IDs, we have the four dead to rights," Naomi continued. "Kidnapping, aggravated sexual abuse, assault with a dangerous weapon, possession of a controlled substance, unlawful administration of a controlled substance, and a host of Wiretap Act stuff. We'll liaise with state on nonconsensual pornography, image-based abuse, unauthorized dissemination." She paused to draw a breath. "From the video you sent we can match tattoos and pull biometrics—gait, iris prints, hand geometry, voice recognition, even dental through the ski mask slits. We can bury them." A tapping sound—a pen striking a pad. "We just have to know who they are."

They zipped along the Long Island Expressway, the Mercedes shedding mud in the light rain. Evan and Anca were drenched but surprisingly clean. The downpour had bathed them.

"Working on it," Evan said. "In the meantime, I left you three more."

"What? How? Where?"

He told her. It took some time. The shortness of breath intensified and he had to take frequent pauses.

"You can charge the little delinquent, too," he said. "He stabbed me with a hypo needle brimming with fentanyl."

"Stabbed *who*?"

"Good point. Never mind."

Opioid warmth was still leaching from his system, his head starting to throb. His stomach was a pot of acid. He dug in the console, came up with the Reese's Peanut Butter Cup Templeton had thrown at him. He rarely ate dessert, but when he did, he preferred 80 percent cocoa with almonds, maybe a sprinkle of sea salt.

He extracted the cup from its foil, chewed. It was disgusting. It was delicious.

"There's a van parked right behind the upended tree." The pain in his left lung amped up with every inhalation. Even to his own ears, his voice sounded wheezy. "There're two more syringes in the console, probably fentanyl, driver's license beneath the visor, and a .357 in the glove box. Driver's license identifies the big one as Peter Macmanus. Gum 'em up on charges. Can you keep them from making any calls?"

"We can temporarily restrict access if there's an ongoing investigation that could be compromised by immediate communication. Let me talk to Barton, make sure we're squeaky clean on it so we don't jam up the case."

"Copy that." He disconnected the call.

His clutch around the steering wheel had tightened, his knuckles bloodless. Each breath tightened the left side of his torso, pressure mounting, a particular kind of claustrophobic pain he wished he was not familiar with.

For the first time, he acknowledged he had a problem. Feeling beneath his clavicle, he pressed the top rib, biting back a bark of pain.

Tension pneumothorax.

When the Goliath had slammed him onto the road, the impact must've torn a hole in the lung. The opioid muffled the pain, made it hard to gauge, but the slow onset of pressure meant the tear was tiny. Tiny was still a problem since it created a one-way valve that pumped air into the pleural cavity between his lung and the chest wall. The air was trapped there, expanding with every breath. It would continue to compress the lung until it collapsed and he suffocated.

Fingers to his neck, he gauged his heart rate. Already increased, north of eighty.

"What is it?" Anca asked. "Are you okay?"

His breathing had quickened. His blood vessels would be compressing now under the pressure. Dots of static invaded his visual field. He exited the expressway, coasting through a few green lights. The wheezing intensified, the lung leaking air. It felt like there was a balloon inflating behind his chest plate.

He did not have much time.

Anca was leaning over the console now. "We have to get you to a hospital."

". . . can't go . . . hospital . . ."

"You were just at a hospital."

". . . for . . . you . . ."

"This is ridiculous. You can't—"

"Anca." He managed to say it hard enough that she stopped.

". . . no time . . . discuss." Screeching off the road, he pulled into the gas station they'd stopped at on their way to the meeting. The Mercedes skidded artfully, missing the pumps and slotting neatly into a parking spot to the side of the convenience store. ". . . not an option . . ."

"Okay," she said. "I get it. What then?"

He unbuckled the seat belt, drew in a shuddering breath. "Help me . . . inside."

53
Let the Countdown Begin

They were sitting on benches in one of the city's pocket parks but Taz couldn't remember where exactly they were. His head itched. Under B-Roll's supervision, he'd spent the morning setting up their White On Posse vendor account at RedLite so they could run their own show.

Things were fucked up, though. The platform had gone down hard, some kind of massive cyberattack. As a new vendor, Taz had gotten corporate emails saying that a buncha their old content and backups got wiped and folks everywhere were freaking out since the vids were seriously gunked with viruses so if you downloaded or watched anything it'd Swiss-cheese your hard drive. He stared at the latest email, claiming that RedLite was rebuilding from bare metal.

"Dunno," Taz said. "Mebbe we shouldn't . . ."

"Shouldn't what?" B-Roll said.

"Dunno," Taz said. "Dunno." He drew in a breath, added meekly, "Mebbe we should, like, just chill for a while, let all this shit blow over."

B-Roll grabbed the phone out of his hand, scrolled a bit with his thumb. "No, man. No. The upshot is RedLite needs a ton of new content and fast. Says so right here. And I got that Blanca chick scheduled for Friday so that means cha-*ching*."

Mikey said, "Me and Finn-Finn got two more on the hook, lining 'em up for next week."

Taz held out his hand for his phone and B-Roll pretended to give it to him, pulled it back. Did it again. The third time, Taz managed to snatch it.

B-Roll turned his focus to Mikey. "What's with Dirty Pete?"

Mikey said, "Can't reach him."

"What's that mean?"

"Dirty Pete runs on Dirty Pete time," Mikey said, with that evil Big Mikey grin. "He'll call when it's done."

Taz's phone chimed. Now a text from RedLite. He read it, that sick feeling crawling back into his stomach.

"What's it say?" B-Roll asked.

Taz shrugged.

Before he could hide the screen, Finn-Finn leaned over his shoulder, breathing baloney fumes. "Dude, dude! Says they'll pay double royalties for live-stream content before the weekend!"

"Why live-stream?" Mikey asked.

B-Roll said, "Prob'ly uses different servers and content-delivery networks and shit. So those ones didn't get virus-fucked like the uploaded content did."

"Double royalties," Finn-Finn said. "Double royalties."

B-Roll said, "Glad my dick's finally getting paid what it's worth," and the guys cracked up.

Taz tried to keep the worry from his voice: "What day'z it today?"

Big Mikey said, "February, I think."

"Day of the week, dumb shit."

"Dunno. Check your phone."

Taz tapped his phone. *Wednesday, Feb 11.*

"Let's move Blanca up," B-Roll said. "Do her tomorrow, upload Friday in time to qualify for the bonus."

"'Kay, 'kay," Finn-Finn said.

"Where we gonna do it?" Mikey said. "I mean, no Manny. There's no Manny, which means no crash pads."

"Mebbe we should put it off," Taz said weakly. "Till we can lock down something secure."

"Double royalties, bitch," B-Roll said. "I'm not putting off shit. We can do it at my place."

"Won't she know your address then?" Taz said.

"Ain't *my* address," B-Roll said. "Month to month, paid in cash money. 'S not even in my name. Any heat and I can bounce. But I ain't worried. I got this one wrapped tight. I know the type. She won't do shit about anything. We can tell her that if she talks, we'll do her little sister next."

"Heh," Finn-Finn said. "Heh."

"Cool, cool," B-Roll said. "I can set up cams for live stream. And I still got some of the props there from last time. Was gonna bring 'em back to Manny but whoops, he's in jail."

Mikey said, "'T's why we're doing it our own fuckin' selves."

"Good props," B-Roll said as he dialed. "It'll be a good show." He held up a wait-a-sec finger, put his phone to his ear. Then: "Hey, Beauty. Friday won't work no more." A beat. "I'm bummed, too. But Luce's gotta be with her birth dad now for the weekend." He listened, rolling his eyes. "I know, I know, I really want her to meet you, too. Now we're watching *The Little Mermaid* tomorrow . . ."

Mikey said, "Isn't there a Gray's Papaya around here?"

Finn-Finn shushed him hard.

B-Roll: "Really? Thursday's a half day for you? Okay. Sure. We can meet after school, pretend it's a trig study group." He made the universal jerk-off signal to Taz and Finn-Finn. Big Mikey was too busy Googling hot-dog places to see.

Taz's temples were throbbing, his head humming loud enough that B-Roll's words sounded fuzzy. He wanted to throw up or run into traffic. He realized he was biting down hard on the inside of his cheek.

"I mean, I didn't want to push you," B-Roll went on, still air jacking off. "Want to respect boundaries, you know. But if you could? Luce'd be so happy." A beat. "Maybe me, too," he answered, putting a smile into his voice. "Okay. Fine. A little. I'd be a little happy, too." He hung up. "Got her for tomorrow."

Mikey belly laughed, raised a high-five hand to Taz, said, "Let the countdown begin!"

Taz swallowed blood, unclenched his jaw, mustered an unsteady grin.

And returned the high five.

54

Last Man Standing

Evan was in trouble.

The gas-station convenience store had slim pickings.

Four aisles, two of them dedicated to junk food. The medical section had Band-Aids, gauze, pills of various over-the-counter stripes, and an inexplicably wide array of ankle braces. No syringe. No rubbing alcohol.

He grabbed a roll of white athletic tape and moved on, frantically searching the shelves while Anca checked the neighboring aisle.

His breath grew more ragged. Oxygen was getting low, his vision cramping.

Aside from beer, the only alcohol was nip bottles behind the counter. He pointed. "Vodka." The word came out in a breathy wheeze. "Two . . . bottles."

The clerk glanced up from his sudoku book, looking end-of-shift weary. "What kind?"

"Don't care."

The clerk leaned behind him, grabbed two of the tiny bottles, set them on the counter.

Pinnacle Whipped Cream Vodka.

"No." Evan was injured, not dead. Plus whatever sugary crap they used to flavor it would not be sterilizing. "Not . . . those."

"What then?"

He pointed. Tito's would do.

"Anything else?"

Evan stepped back, scanning the rack for anything sharp enough. A pen tube, maybe. His inhalation hitched, and he had to fight to suck in a sip of air, a pain hiccup that furled his throat in its fist. Anca came around, shaking her head. "Nothing."

He staggered a bit, and she braced him with her arm around his waist.

The clerk said, "Everything okay?"

"This is why I'm keeping him on the mini-bottles now," Anca said.

Evan stepped around to the next aisle, searching frantically. Plastic lighters, condoms, tampons—and there. A pack of ball-pump needles.

The sight made him shudder. He'd used one for this once in Ankara behind a mechanic shop. It had not been pleasant.

He searched for anything else.

There was nothing else.

Beggars and choosers and all that.

Snatching the pack, he turned back to the counter, peeling a hundred-dollar bill from the wad in his pocket.

"I'm sorry, sir." The clerk pointed to the sign. WE DO NOT ACCEPT BILLS LARGER THAN $20.

Evan turned to Anca. ". . . change?"

"My purse is in the car. I can run and—"

"Do you have Apple Pay?" the clerk asked.

"I don't . . ." A full wheeze now, the lung compression intensifying, blood vessels squishing, organs getting rocked in their beds. Fire slithered down his shoulder and armpit, flicking its tail all the way down to the tenth rib. His breathing had turned shallow, quick cramped jerks that brought little relief.

"You could sign up for our credit-card line," the clerk said, sliding a pamphlet at Evan. "You get three percent back on gas purchases—"

". . . sorry . . . just keep . . ." Evan left two hundreds on the counter and staggered out.

Anca followed him and helped lower him into the passenger seat. He unbuttoned his shirt, poured vodka over his chest, took out the inflating needle and dunked it in vodka.

"Are you sure about this?" Anca asked.

He fingered across the top of his chest, finding the spot on the high rib again. He set the needle just at the top edge to make sure he missed the artery. Since it was blunt-tipped he'd have to smash it in hard enough to pierce skin, muscle, and the pleural membrane surrounding the chest cavity to get to the trapped pocket of air. A wrong guess would create another pneumothorax instead of relieving this one.

Anca had closed his door and come around to the driver's seat. "How will you push it in?"

He pointed at her tote bag at his feet. Sticking out was the thick Solzhenitsyn tome. She grabbed it, held it carefully across the base of the needle as he pinched the slender shaft.

Static sparkled across the book, his fist, the windshield. He readied his right fist to pound the book inward and punch the needle through. A rare hesitation.

It was gonna suck, plain and simple.

The hardcover was nearly flat to his chest, close enough that he could see over it and read the title: *THE GULAG ARCHIPELAGO*

A blunt, unsubtle instrument for the task. It would have been amusing were he not in the process of suffocating inside his own body.

He took a moment to relax everything within his power to relax, a total release of muscle and sclera, of the skin itself. The more open he was, the less damage the stainless-steel shaft would cause ripping through.

He smashed his fist against the book as if beating his chest.

The shaft went in smoothly, he knew it right away in the split second of relief before the pain came. And then it arrived, husky and hard-edged, looking to trample him. It did.

His throat had seized up and he focused first on unseizing it, relaxing the knot from the outside in, onion-peeling it to the core. It gave and he gasped in a clump of air.

A faint hissing reached his ears—thank God—and he counted the seconds, rewinding to account for the one and a half when he'd been frozen up breathless. The rush of air through the threaded end of the pump needle lasted another six seconds and then wisped off into a pleasing silence.

All was peaceful. Evan breathed in, breathed out. He stripped a neat square of athletic tape off the roll and stuck it over the threaded base of the needle, sealing it off.

He breathed some more.

He was sweating. All the way down and all the way through, his clothes double soaked from the rain and from perspiration that the pain had roasted out of him.

The buildup started again, a twinge in his upper left lung, the tendrils reigniting across his chest with the memory of what was coming.

He peeled the tape back, counted the hiss of relief. Just four and a half seconds now.

That was good. That was very good.

The hole in his lung was small. If it was small enough, it would heal itself over.

Slow inhalation. Slow exhalation.

Anca was perched on her knees in the driver's seat, legs folded under her so she was sitting on her calves, wide-eyed with some secret confidence.

"You're very brave," she said.

"No."

"What, then?"

He didn't know. He'd never put words to it. Never even thought it all the way through. But he took a moment to do so now.

What, then? A nightmare, a hope, a premonition? That the world might tear itself down to the last man standing.

"Ready," he said. "I'm ready."

"I understand," she said. "I understand you now."

He eased back the tape once more, and the makeshift valve hissed. Three seconds this time. Improvement.

"We can go now." His voice still rasped, but the wheezing was over.

"I will drive." She punched the ignition button and pulled out of the gas station. "You can rest at my place. Where I can look after you."

"You don't need that."

"Don't you learn anything? It is *precisely* what I need."

Exhaustion swamped him. Slumping back in the seat, he sent out a quick text update to Joey and Candy. For the rest of the ride, he dozed on and off, awakening at intervals to relieve the pressure in his lung. By the time they reached the Bronx, no more air let out when he untaped the makeshift valve. Wincing, he pulled the shaft free. Then he doused the hole with vodka, sealed it with gauze, and taped it off. He measured his breaths. The wall of the lung held, the tiny perf closing over.

Anca lucked into a parking space right in front of her building. He got upstairs with minimal pain.

Candy answered the door. His shirt was still unbuttoned, the dressing clear against his sweat-shiny skin.

She noted the position of the bandage. "Tension pneumo?"

"Minor."

She stepped back, letting them in.

Anca guided Evan to her father's room. The door was closed. Anca hesitated at the threshold. They stood there a moment. Her head was lowered, eyes closed.

Then she pushed inside. She helped him ease down to sit on the perfectly made bed, the movement lifting a swirl of motes. Leaning back on the pillows, he took in the room, that bowl of painted eggs, the toothpick flags, the poster of the circle dance. Everything perfectly preserved. Behind the door hung that cowboy hat over the jean jacket, the slippers beneath filling out the invisible man. Her father. What would he think about what had happened to his daughter? What would he *feel*?

"You sure you want me in here?" he asked. "Couch is fine."

"I am glad for an excuse to use Tată's room. He'd be glad for it, too."

"Just need a shower," Evan said.

Candy leaned in the doorway. "Want me to wash your back?"

Anca actually gasped and then laughed at herself. "Not under my roof."

Evan said, "I'll manage on my own."

"I'll take her to the hospital for her test," Candy said. "We have to assume she's being followed now."

"We can't leave him here alone like this," Anca said.

"He'll be fine." Candy's arms were crossed, her manicured nails impatiently drumming her biceps. "Come on."

Anca glanced from Candy to Evan. Then from Evan to Candy.

Giving a pert nod, she rose to leave.

He was asleep before the door closed behind her.

In the middle of the night, a movement at the doorway stirred Evan from sleep. He tried to focus, but his head was groggy from injury, exertion, and the afterwash of opioids. Someone drifted toward him.

He breathed plumeria, relaxed.

Candy sat on the edge of the bed. Her hands came into sleep-blurry view, a catheter in one hand, IV bag in the other. He tensed.

She ran her fingers through his hair. He couldn't remember ever being this tired. Maybe he was still asleep.

A dab of an alcohol pad licked the crook of his arm. With a single fluid motion, she slid the catheter into his median cubital vein. Given all his field doctoring on this mission, it was a welcome role reversal.

"Ketorolac for pain and swelling, broad-spectrum antibiotic, saline to hydrate."

"Copy that," he murmured.

"You're gonna wake up like you ate your Wheaties."

Pressure in his arm but no pain. Candy squeezed the bag, bolusing the liquid into his body. His blinks grew heavier.

At some point, the pressure lifted from his arm and he felt the softness of her lips on his forehead. When he managed to open his eyes, he was alone in the darkness.

His eyes did not stay open long.

55
Dickfest

The RoamZone's distinctive ring jerked Evan from sleep.

He felt bizarrely refreshed, his veins plumped from the rapid bolus. It was light outside, morning bright.

He blinked himself the rest of the way awake, checked his Vertex fob watch. Ten o'clock. In the A.M. He couldn't remember the last time he'd slept for seventeen hours.

The aches had receded but still made themselves known when he rolled over to grab the RoamZone. Caller ID showed Joey.

When he picked up, she said, "I got two dicks."

The flesh over his left high rib was puffy and tender but it did not look infected. Beneath the skin, blood had drifted across his pectoral, bruising the color of Syrah.

He said, "Come again?"

"Not, like, anatomically. I mean I identified the owners of two of the dicks. I'm sending their dossiers now." *Bink. Bink.* "Guess how many videos said dicks have appeared in?"

"Do I want to—"

"Eighty-seven." A pause to let the number sink in. "They always appear with the same two other dicks but I can't tie those to the humans they belong to so for now they remain just: dicks."

Sitting up, Evan flicked through the files she'd sent.

Finley Jacowski and Michael Macmanus.

They'd had enough arrests and petty convictions to have aliases listed in their jackets: Finn-Finn and Big Mikey. Michael shared a last name with the Goliath Evan had anchored to the earth at Glass Bottle Beach. Brother, perhaps, or cousin.

"Anywho," Joey said, "they left location services on because they're clearly idiots and they're in the same place. Right now."

He shot to his feet. "You have them pinned?"

"Sending link." *Bink.* "If you get there fast, you might get lucky and find out that the two unidentified dicks are also there with the identified dicks, having a, dunno, dickfest."

He thumbed open the GPS.

There they were, two blinking dots nearly on top of each other. He zoomed in until he could see the building, a diner in Turtle Bay near the East River.

"They've only been there, like, two minutes so if you move it, you can catch up to them."

Rushing, he slung on a shirt, his chest aching with the effort, and then his cargo pants, dried stiffly from the rain. As he tugged on socks and laced up his boots, his hip flexors complained. And his intercostals. And left triceps brachii tendon.

But the pain was manageable.

"And also?" Joey said. "RedLite? They're wiped out for now, X. Nothing loading, multiple sites down. They're gonna haveta toss every piece of equipment they've got and rebuild from bare metal. Their stock is in free fall and Devine is about to make his move."

"Are they shut down completely?"

"Their home page is closed for repairs. But there's a notice that they'll have live streams up by tomorrow. I'll put on my black hat and get after it but they'll have a window of operation before Devine takes control of the joystick."

His holster was empty. He looked for his gun. Couldn't find it.

His heart rate spiked.

Hanging up, he moved to the door, flinging it open.

Candy was waiting, ARES resting on the flat of her palm. Shiny and polished.

"Cleaned it," she said. "Given the mud and all. Debris in the barrel, and the extractor channel needed a scrubbing—a pipe cleaner and three Q-tips."

He took the pistol, locked back the slide, removed the magazine, eyed the chamber, and performed a function check. Everything felt like precision ceramic ball bearings running on lightweight silicone oil. Then he reloaded the ARES and spun it through the magnet buttons of his shirt straight into his appendix holster.

Candy would have performed the exact same function checks had their roles been reversed. The act of professional courtesy combined with trust was not lost on either of them.

Giving her a nod, he charged into the bathroom, brushed teeth, threw water over his face, pissed out about a liter of fluid.

As he emerged, Anca came around from the kitchen, drying her hands on her apron. "Oh. You're up! Can I make you something to eat?"

"No time." He hustled to the door. "I got a bead on the location of two of the men."

Anca looked stricken, the reality dawning. "Two of the men who did that? To me?"

He hadn't considered the impact the news might have on her. He spun to look at her. Despite the rush, she deserved eye contact. "Yes."

Anca said, "What will happen to them now?"

"Now?" Candy said. "They are fucked."

Anca fluttered her hand as if the expletive were still floating in front of her and she had to shoo it away. "So they will be effed," she said. "But not dead."

"Not dead," he said.

"Backup mags?" Candy asked.

He tapped his cargo pants over the discreet pockets, fingertips plinking against steel.

Candy nudged him toward the door. "EDC?"

With a knuckle, he knocked the Strider, his everyday carry, in the left front pocket of his cargo pants.

"Flex-cuffs?"

No.

He held out his hand. She set a tight roll of them in his palm. He reloaded the secondary pouch inside his top thigh pocket.

Nearing the door, he remembered. Bracing himself, he turned back to face Anca. "Your test."

She grinned. "Negative."

His exhalation was longer than usual.

Anca held up her hand and Candy skipped back to high-five her. The casual exchange elicited a twist of emotion in him. They were such different women and yet something had grown between them, binding them together.

He took them in, these two women standing in the calm of the apartment. The heater blew warm air with a not-too-strong mustiness that felt vaguely homey. The frayed kilim rug, the wiped-clean dark furniture, the sun-faded floral still life. And that secretary desk tilted on its venerable legs, laden with candles and pictures of Anca's parents.

Anca would be safe here with Candy. Of course—anyone would be safe with Candy. But it was more than just that. They were together and that meant something more than safe.

Anca would be okay here.

She would be okay.

He let go. A conscious effort to release, to drop into operational mode, to allow his blood to run cold.

Anca was looking at him, puzzled. "What?" she asked.

But he was gone.

Evan stood outside the diner, hands in his pockets, a point of stillness among the rush of pedestrians. It was the kind of archetypal diner found only in New York City and small American towns.

Behind a massive plate-glass window, Finn-Finn and Big Mikey sat in a booth, torpidly thumbing at their phones. Mikey slurped at the last of a strawberry milkshake.

If they looked up, they would see Evan standing right there at the window.

But they did not look up.

He'd scouted the area physically and virtually, knew which of the neighboring stores had rear exits, the blueprints of the floors above, the sprint time to the closest subway stops in case he didn't have the luxury of returning to his car. The diner was packed.

Evan entered to a jingle from the belled front door. An old-fashioned jukebox glowed red and gold, humming with doo-wop harmonization. Meat sizzled on an unseen grill. The place smelled deliciously of root beer and burger grease.

"Help you?" The hostess wore a jaunty paper diner hat that looked like a battleship turned upside down.

"My party is already here," Evan said.

He threaded through the tables and sat down next to Big Mikey, scooting him in so he was trapped against the window. The booth was padded vinyl, cherry red, the cracks spot-patched with duct tape.

"Hey, man. What the fuck?"

Big Mikey looked like the genetic runoff from Goliath, huge but not colossal, ugly but not troll-like, menacing but not intimidating. He was brutish, big features, girthy at the chest, stomach, and thighs. At first Evan thought there was crusted blood in his scraggly facial hair, but a closer look showed it to be a port-wine stain that he'd tried to hide with his beard.

Across the table, chewed grilled-cheese crusts remained on Finn-Finn's plate, and his lips were greasy like a little kid's. The men were younger than Evan had anticipated. They looked like boys still catching up to adult bodies.

He recognized their carriage and bearing from the video, images strobing in his mind. A goat-skull tattoo on sweaty flesh. Drawn-out moans. Anca's sluggish body adjusted this way and that, her limbs flung aside to grant access.

The two young men looked disappointingly ordinary here in the midday light of a bustling diner, a world apart from that subterranean apartment where they'd done things that men in ski masks did.

In person they looked like nothing at all. Even if he hadn't made a promise to Anca, Evan wondered if he would have had the heart to kill them. Sitting with them now looking into their faces was anticlimactic. His fury wasn't lost—it was still in the bucking chute waiting for the gate to lift—but in this moment he felt nothing so much as worn out.

"Finley Jacowski," Evan said. "Michael Macmanus."

"Are you a cop?" Finn-Finn said. "Because you haveta tell us if you're a cop. You haveta."

That voice. It summoned a haunted echo from the footage: *My turn! My turn!*

Evan said, "No."

Big Mikey said, "The fuck you want then?"

Evan pivoted his head. Looked at him.

"Oh," Big Mikey said. "Oh, *shit*. You're him. The scary fucking friend."

"Yes," Evan said.

"You don't *look* scary."

Finn-Finn glanced over his shoulder, gauging a route to the door. Evan watched to see if he'd make a run for it. Evan was looking for an excuse, just like when he'd baited Tyler Russell into taking a swing at him with the baseball bat so he could kick him through his house and a chicken coop to shove his face into the aboveground pool.

Big Mikey leaned back and spread his arms across the padded back of the booth. "What are you gonna do? Here? There're, like, witnesses everywhere."

The starting gate rattled, holding Evan's rage in check. He kept his voice calm. "Witnesses don't concern me."

"You related to her, or something?" Finn-Finn asked. "You related?"

"No."

"And you're not a cop. What then?"

"I don't like what you did to her," Evan said. "And I'm going to make sure you never do it again."

"Look." Finn-Finn laced his fingers together on the table to form a curved wall, his thumb pads tapping each other. He was going for a we're-all-adults-here pose but instead looked as if he was preparing to have a thumb war with himself. "I get it. I get it. You're some kinda white knight or whatever. And you think we're the problem. But we're not. We're not. You just haveta look at it different and you'll see the hypocrisy."

"Yeah," Big Mikey said. "The hypocrisy."

"You all made porn legal. You all put it everywhere. And you know how many people get human-trafficked for sex? Like: a lot. A *lot.* I mean, it's your world. We just grew up inside it. It's a dog-eat-dog world, man. Dog-eat-dog. We're animals, basically. It's the only way to work the system you all built. The only way to survive. So you made us. You made us animals. You can't expect us to give a shit about this or that."

Evan said, "She was unconscious."

Finn-Finn shrugged. "So we bang a girl who's outta it now and then. Everyone parties, drugs, whatever. But we didn't keep her, did we? We didn't keep her."

Evan said, "You held her for five hours."

The words had already left his mouth when he realized what the kid actually meant: that they deserved praise for not keeping Anca for *good.*

A part of Evan broke off inside him like a snapped match head. A tumbling flare that died in the darkness. The threat here, now, from them wasn't physical. It was worse.

"And?" Big Mikey said. "We didn't snuff her. And it's not like we couldn't'uv."

If you put Finn-Finn and Big Mikey together, you might make one human being. Equally wretched, but at least one miserable thing instead of two. But there they sat, defiantly distinct and half-formed.

"I'm gonna have to warn you," Big Mikey said. "You don't get who you're dealing with."

Evan said, "Like Pete?"

Mikey's mouth gaped in something like a smile. A breath washed out of him. It did not smell pleasant. His tongue poked at the corner of his mouth. "Don't know any Petes."

"Even the one who shares your last name?"

"Dunno. Why? What's he got to do with this? Where is he?"

"Prison medical bay."

"Oh," Finn-Finn said. And then, "*Oh.*"

"Bullshit," Mikey said. "Bull*shit* this guy takes out Dirty Pete."

The waitress came by, wielding a pot of coffee. "Get you something, hon?"

"No," Evan said. "Thank you. We're doing great."

Her gaze lingered on the tense scene but she kept moving.

Evan said, "I want the names of the other two men who raped Anca Dumitrescu."

Finn-Finn giggled, high and jittery. "Mr. Demands-Man making demands."

Mikey gathered himself up at Evan's side. He had Evan by four inches and at least sixty pounds. "You sure as shit can't prove you beat Pete up 'cuz there's no way. There is. No. Way." He poked Evan's shoulder with a wide digit. "You couldn't even go a round with me."

"No?"

"When I go off, I keep going. Nothing stops me. I saw a decapitated rattlesnake once. My buddy'd took its head off with a shovel blade. Its body was still squirming around, writhing like they do. And the head? The cut-off head? Bit the body. It bit its *own fucking body.* That's me, motherfucker. Nothing can stop me once I—"

Evan palmed the back of Mikey's head, slammed his face down into the tabletop, the Velvet Kitty move redux. The plates and milkshake glass jumped but didn't break. When he drew Mikey's head back by a fistful of hair, his nose was shattered nearly flat, smeared along his right cheekbone. Moisture had exploded from his eyes, the tear ducts running freely. Half conscious, he drooled out a long vowel sound reminiscent of the extended moans he'd made on the video. Evan tilted him against the window, his dead weight shifting, cheek smashed to the pane. He slumped there. Irregular breaths fogged the glass.

Over the din of the restaurant, no one had noticed.

Finn-Finn remained perfectly frozen, hands laced together on the table, thumbs sticking up like rabbit ears.

"How about you?" Evan asked. "You got a little speech, too?"

Finn-Finn shook his head.

"Names."

Finn-Finn shook his head again.

Reaching across the table, Evan grabbed the bowl of his clasped fingers, seized the thumbs with his other hand, and ripped them back, tearing them right out of their sockets. They dangled in the wrong place, way up by the juncture of hand and wrist.

Finn-Finn stared down at the wreckage, disbelieving. A soft wail barely made it out of his mouth. He couldn't remember to breathe.

"You say you're an animal," Evan said. "Animals don't need opposable thumbs."

Finn-Finn was going into shock now, trembling, lips quivering. He held his hands up before him, thumbs drooping grotesquely. That was good. Both of them would require ER visits. When Evan left, he would text Templeton their GPS locations and she could mop them up there.

He swept their phones off the table into his pocket. He didn't want them calling ahead to warn the others.

He snapped his fingers in front of Finn-Finn's face. "Names. First and last. Or else we move to your wrists."

"T-Taz." Finn-Finn's teeth chattered, the name shoved through pale lips. "Taswell Kinley." He pushed the words out one at a time. "He's . . . in charge of tech. And B-Roll . . . Brandon Burke."

"What's *he* in charge of?"

Finn-Finn's eyes juddered in their sockets. They stared at Evan, unseeing. "He's in charge of fucking."

"All set here, guys?" The waitress stood over them, coffeepot slung low at her hip. Then she took notice of the tableau in the booth, her jaw going slack, a dot of bright pink bubble gum visible back by her molars.

"Yes, ma'am," Evan said, sliding out. "I believe they're ready for the check."

56
Gentleman

Like the gentleman he was, B-Roll met Blanca downstairs. His pad was on the third floor, walk-up, and he wanted to make sure she didn't lose her nerve on the way. She was done up real cute, hair pulled back, shiny makeup, loose-collared crop sweater so a strip of that flat brown stomach showed. She had a little belly-button ring in, too, a hoop with a star. She wore PJ bottoms, thick flannel ones that she'd cuffed twice at the waist to keep the bottoms from dragging in the street. Perfume, too, one of those ones named Rain or Sky or whatever, that smelled all clean and natural, like you just snorted it off the back of a unicorn.

When he came out to the street, she kicked one foot behind her, tapping the toe of her lavender-check Vans high-top on the sidewalk. She had something in her hands, a little gift bag with purple tissue paper fluffed up out of it.

"Hey, Beauty."

She gave him that big smile. "Hey, Beast."

B-Roll jerked his chin at the bag. "What's that?"

"Oh, this? Just a little gift. For Luce."

"Really," B-Roll said, bored. "That's sweet."

"It's a Polly Pocket koala family. You said she had the purse playset so . . . I know, lame, right?"

"No," B-Roll said, ushering her in. "No. She'll dig it."

He took her by the shoulders, stood her against the wall, and raised his burner phone to snap a picture of her. She blushed, fixing her hair. "What's this for?"

"'Cuz I want to," he said, thumbing her photo off to the boys with a text: Get reddy to partay!! It didn't send right away. Reception was ass here in his building, especially in the lobby, but he hoped the phone'd grab signal when they got to his room so the boys could see what they had to look forward to.

Blanca handed him the gift bag, which he snatched, heading upstairs.

"It's just a dumb thing," she said, gesturing at the bag. "I thought, you know, you said there's family stuff going on and sometimes it's good to have a family you can, like, be in charge of yourself, you know? I mean, play with and feel safe and stuff. Even a koala family. Stoopid though, prolly."

Most of the light bulbs in the stairwell were out. The asshole on the second floor left his takeout boxes right on the landing, mounded like a pile of leaves, and there'd been flies and cockroaches but the dickhead landlord never did shit. It smelled like Chinese food and rot.

B-Roll said, "Just walk around it."

She did her best, high-stepping in her shiny Vans. She looked so clean, a girl like her way off her turf in a place like this. Next floor up, at his door, he fumbled with the keys, got it open.

The dude he sublet from called it a one-bedroom but it was really a studio, a three-hundred-square-foot rectangle. He held the door for her.

She went in.

He saw her shoulders deflate a few inches.

The place was a shithole, sure. Thirdhand furniture, rusty appliances, gross brown carpet, grease stain up one wall, his unpacked stuff spilling out of moving boxes. Battered window shades cast a nicotine-yellow glow across the jumble of dirty clothes and mismatched dumbbells. A freeway ramp rose just outside his window, and the traffic noise and headlights could be a lot if you weren't used to them.

But that's not why her shoulders dropped.

It was because there was no Luce in here. A younger sister wouldn't last five minutes in a place like this.

Oh. And there were the cameras, too. Set up on tripods around the main prop he still had from Manny. The prop was covered in a white sheet. Saving the surprise for later.

B-Roll closed the door behind him. Threw the dead bolt. It gave a good thunk.

Blanca spun to him, clutching the gift bag to her stomach. Her voice came out like a squeak: "Where's Luce?"

"Right, I forgot to mention. Turns out? She can't make it now. But that's okay. I have some buddies coming over."

Her eyes darted nervously to the cameras. "What're those for?"

"I shoot some art photography now and then."

"Yeah?"

"Yeah. Girls trying to break into *Broad*-way."

He threw an arm wide, palm out, the whole your-name-in-lights thing, trying to lighten the mood. But she didn't laugh.

New approach: "The woman I shot last week was super-hot. Like *model*-hot. Better looking than anyone I've seen in person."

To make them shrivel, all you had to do was sprinkle the right words, salt on a snail. Sure enough, Blanca shrank into herself. She looked small. Small and unsure of herself.

"Oh, hey," he said, adding a honeyed note of comfort, *"you're* good-looking too."

"Thanks. I mean, not like *model*-hot . . ."

"Well, not everyone is."

Just a tiny sting, keep her off-balance.

"I'm sorry, but I just . . ." Her narrow chest heaved beneath that sweater. "I think maybe I should get back home. I mean, I *do* have trig homework, and since Luce isn't here—"

"Since Luce isn't here, we can party." He sidled up, ran a finger along the line of her jaw. Stopped beneath her chin, tipped her face up to his. Her eyes were scared but her mouth wanted him to kiss her. Those glossy lips parted, her breath tasting of mint. "*Grown-up* fun."

It could've gone either direction but it went the wrong way, Blanca gently tugging his hand from her face and stepping away. "I'm not sure I'm ready for this. To meet your friends and all that. I'm sorry. I mean, it's cool, but I thought it was just us hanging out with your sister. I think I should get going."

He eased toward her again, not wanting her to scare. "But my friends are on their way. Right now. They *really* wanted to meet you. You don't want to disappoint them, do you?"

"I'm sorry. I'm sure they're, like, supercool, but—"

"We got the whole evening planned. You really want to ruin it? For all of us?"

She set the gift bag down on the desk. The computer monitor was set up there. She looked at the screen. It said, CLICK TO START LIVESTREAMING.

He watched her read the screen. Her jaw shifted forward.

When her head snapped up, her eyes were different. "I don't . . . I'm sorry, I don't get it."

He loved how they apologized all the time whether it made sense or not, whether they did anything wrong or not.

"Oh that." He waved it off. "That's just if we want to play around later."

She was standing there stiff and frozen the way they got. Sometimes you could just move them right to the futon like a broken-down robot, a life-size doll, and they didn't say anything at all. Her throat was jumping around like she was trying to breathe or talk but couldn't get her body to obey.

"You're old enough to play big-kid games, aren't you, li'l girl? You're definitely sexy enough."

Now a hushed whisper: "I think I should go."

"You're all the way here already. And you'll dig my friends. Promise."

He reached for her and she jerked back a step. Her heel pinched the white sheet where it draped to the floor, pulling it free.

Her eyes went wide. Wide and scared and quite pretty. She stared at what had been hiding beneath the sheet.

A wooden pillory with holes for the head and wrists. The top was lifted slightly on its hinge like the stick of a movie clapper board. The post had been shortened, though, so even a smaller girl like Blanca would have to bend over to get put into it. That way even once they were locked in, you had easy access to them from behind.

She turned those wide, wild eyes to him.

He smiled, traced the strips of his chinstrap beard with a thumb and fingertip, pinched it off at the bottom. "Don't worry about it. That's not something we *have* to do. That's just for show."

"I'm sorry, but I'm gonna go."

"I don't think that's a good idea."

She was breathing deeply. Her nostrils widened. Lips swollen with emotion, face flushed, perspiration sparkling at her temple. She looked so hot. It was amazing how some chicks looked turned on when they were scared. Maybe it was the same thing for them.

Some fire came up in her, a faint accent creeping in: "You know what? Fuck this. I don't want this. I didn't ask for this. Let me go."

He pretended to contemplate, tapping a finger on his chin.

Then said, "No."

She deked and then broke left, darting around him. She made it to the door, throwing the bolt, yanking it open. It didn't swing more than a few inches before it met his palm backed by his full weight, slamming shut once more.

He was standing over her now, breathing down, her face by his armpit. She was so much smaller. She turned her gaze up and he saw the depth of fear in her brown eyes. Docile at last. They both knew now that she had to do whatever he wanted.

He gave her his best smile.

"No means no," he said, and shot the dead bolt home.

57

The X Always Held

Walking his third surveillance route past the burrito joint, Evan stared again at Taswell Kinley at a high-top table inside. It was a busy street, pedestrians herd-deep on the sidewalk, the kid coming visible only in the gaps between them.

Taz. He's in charge of tech.

From the nerve center of Luke Devine's scarlet room, Joey had gotten Evan the location for Taswell Kinley. Now it was a matter of taking him down and leaving him for Templeton. Brandon Burke was trickier—no registered phone, no place of residence. Joey was still working through his last-knowns. Between her and the Brain, she'd get him soon enough.

Evan took roll call of the punctures, cuts, and bruises from his battle with Goliath. Then he turned down the volume on them. He could resume registering pain when the mission was complete. Already it was roaring inside him, not hypervigilance, not OCD, but the harmonized hum of his proper operational filters, all aligned, all in their proper place.

Armed with floor plans and blueprints, he'd nailed the Third Commandment. Moving briskly along the sidewalk, he held the space around him as a sphere—surrounding streets, subway lines, higher floors, tunnels beneath the earth. Within that outermost peel of the fixed environment, he maintained another layer of cognizance—cars, windows, traffic, humidity, crowd flow, individuals, props, weapons, and anything else distinct, changing, not bolted down. The route to the target resided here, and various paths of egress. Nesting within those, in the core, was Taswell Kinley. All his bones and muscle and tendon and pliable cartilage, and every possible movement they might make.

At the center of the core was an X.

Above and around it, the other layers gyroscoped madly. But the X always held.

The dead center of Evan was the dead center of everything else. And as long as he didn't waver or misstep, he could hold that awareness, could register all the layers synchronously.

The nearest police station was 5.7 miles away, the response time for calls this distance shockingly consistent at four and a half minutes. They had six units out patrolling. Midday traffic patterns would slow the arrival of backup, but once it started arriving it would shore up fast.

The burrito joint had a single-stall bathroom with no exterior window, a janitor's closet off the kitchen, and one back route through a twelve-foot run of corridor and a rear door. Visible in one of four store surveillance cameras Evan had hijacked and accessed on his RoamZone was a thick smear of ketchup on the floor by the trash bins, enough to send a heel out from under you. Opportunity was everywhere—varied knives in the kitchen, steaming grills ready for business, mop and bucket in the southwest corner deployed in the dining area every hour on the hour. There was a girl in a wheelchair in the booth nearest the bathroom, a mother with two boys at a four-top, and an elderly couple at the register who could need minding if—hat tip once more to Tommy—things got sporty.

The amendment to his code had been hammered into him at

the kitchen table with Anca: *Promise me. Promise me you will not kill anyone.* She'd knocked the table, her chest, grabbed the hem of her dress. *This? This is real.*

Mercy.

It was real to her.

She had been made real to him.

So it was real to him now as well.

His code weighed more now. It had more to carry.

Taz gummed at his food, burrito juice dribbling across his thigh. A blank face lowered to a phone screen, a face that might've looked intelligent in another light, with its tall proud forehead. A pair of glasses and a side part and you could almost see him as a functional member of society. But no. Instead he gave off a non-aura, a pervasive nothingness. Everything about him was languid except his jittering eyes. Those eyes, bearing the reflection of the screen, betrayed the rabbit-fast insanity jangling within, choked down behind that dumbed-out, lukewarm psychopath exterior.

Swept along at crowd-speed, Evan managed a last glimpse through the window.

Taz looked pathetic. He wore old-man khakis, a starched-to-hell pair from forever ago. His build was scrawny, his hair ugly stiff, mud-colored with a reddish tint, dandruff spots visible at distance. And his forehead, that proud forehead, had lines in it already, squiggly middle-aged lines.

His lips were parted and not slightly and he was breathing through his mouth and tapping away at the screen, gazing into it as intently as if it were the Oracle at Delphi. He appeared to be deep in thought.

Evan couldn't help but wonder what a creature like him could possibly be thinking about.

Memes against this one gray suit (a side-part politician who, Taz figured, was a cuck libtard or incel fascist) were exploding. Most of them outta Bulgarian troll farms, judging by the grammar and style. Taz gleaned the dude took some bribes or something but *he* said it was fake news, but anyways and regardless, the memes had him, like *tiny* him, in this one stupid-looking pose Photoshopped into all these weird places like on Taylor Swift's nose or on top of the French tower or whatever, and then someone started a hashtag to make the memes, like, *pornier,* and so alluva sudden there's this gray suit's face appearing in, like, *holes* everywhere and there's no way he wouldn't be forever associated with *holes*—ha, pretty funny.

Taz was having trouble focusing and he remembered he took Adderall this morning but figured another might help so he palmed that and washed it down with a sip of Coke. A few blocks over, B-Roll was already lining up Blanca at his pad and the posse was due to head over any sec once they got the go text and he didn't know what to think and feel about that so he tried to think and feel nothing. At least he had practice at that.

His stomach hurt again and he was having trouble chewing the burrito 'cuz his mouth was super dry, prolly the Seroquel and clonidine.

A couple tables over a mom was sitting with two boys in Little League uniforms. When Taz's dad had been around those few weeks of his fifth-grade summer, he'd signed Taz up for Little League. Taz had sucked at it, afraid of the ball, only made it to two practices. The boys' uniform looked familiar—maybe the same team?—but he couldn't make out the team name across the chest. His hand was up and he was reverse-pinching the air to zoom in on the lettering so he could apply the filter but he was doing it IRL! Brain glitch.

He heard a strange bark of a laugh—his own, how strange—and went back to the phone to use the actual camera zoom but he'd leaned on the screen by accident so all the apps were dancing like to move or delete them and he stared down at them all pinned and wriggling for his attention. So many shiny, shiny buttons, portals to all the friends and famous people and girls who lived inside them, each app its own world, its own mood, uppers or bennies or quick little hits of heroin. Like a fucking buffet and he could just graze and partake, could have whatever he wanted. Wait—why had he gone on the phone again? Couldn't remember.

He had a mouthful of sodden something, like a cud, a worked-over burrito bite. He'd forgotten to keep chewing.

He was weary from gorging. He had everything he wanted but he couldn't get full. He just. Couldn't. Get. Full.

He had sour cream on his chin and no napkin so he wiped with his hand and then wiped it off on his pants. It was kind of deadening to have everything he wanted inside his phone all the time. His palms were sweaty and he thought about what that one school shrink had told him one time, that sometimes your body tells you stuff you might not know in your head yet, and he realized he was bracing himself for the text from B-Roll.

His fingers felt tingly. They got that way sometimes when he smoked too much sativa in the morning, made him all spinny. He could bring it down with those indica gummies Finn-Finn stole from the dispensary, or else more clonidine.

Another fantasy about Blanca rolled through his head but it wasn't like his usual fantasies, it was G-rated. In this fantasy she was like Other Blanca but older obviously, someone he could just hang with and laugh and they could be friends, like, real friends, too, and he could see them chilling on a couch watching a movie with his arm across her shoulders.

He anxious-checked his phone for B-Roll's text—still nothing. When he looked up, he saw a guy walking past on the sidewalk. Their eyes met for a second. Taz could've sworn he'd seen him walk by before. He looked like nothing much, just a man-man.

Checked his phone again. He was breathing hard. His palms were sweaty. The burrito sat like a blob in his gut.

Who was he kidding? His G-rated fantasy of some Hallmark life with Any Blanca was out of reach. He knew himself, knew what he looked like, what his insides were like, a fucking useless loser the world just extracted from—his money, his time, his attention. They all just wanted to suck him dry.

Felt like there was a black hole in his sunken chest. He stared at the screen of his phone, waiting for a text he hoped would never come.

He didn't notice the man-man enter the restaurant.

Cutting through the bustle, Evan took a high stool next to Taswell. The kid didn't take note. He was fixated on his phone, thumbing through YouTube shorts. His other hand rested on his belly, fingers waggling in a wave pattern, and he was rocking slightly. Stimming.

Evan cleared his throat.

The kid didn't notice.

Evan said, "Taswell Kinley."

The kid pulled his gaze up molasses slow. Evan expected to read something of his internal life behind the dull gray eyes, but there was no light in there. Nothing but a mechanical flickering, speed-skittery beneath the surface. He was bird-boned, almost frail.

Taz said, "Huhn?"

"Anca Dumitrescu," Evan said.

"Huhn?"

"The young woman you took from the subway. You and your friends."

"Di'n't happen." He went back to his phone. "Whudev."

Taz's thumb hesitated, and beneath it Evan could see notifications riddling the top of the screen, piling up atop one another. Taz's eyes looked shallow, dimensionless. The pupils jittered some more. The only light they held was the reflection of the screen.

Even after giving the names, Evan could not hold his attention. It was like the kid couldn't bridge the gulf between whatever was happening behind those gray eyes and the reality out in front of him—the plate, the gnawed burrito end wrapped in foil, a drugged, unconscious twenty-five-year-old Romanian-American with her panties ripped down to her ankles.

Evan said, "Taswell."

The gaze did not lift. "Hmmph?"

Evan slid the phone from Taz's hands, dropped it flat on the table before them.

"Huh? What the hell, man? What the *hell*. You can't just grab my phone."

"Anca Dumitrescu," Evan said.

"Huhn?"

"The young woman from the subway."

"Wut? Dude. My phone. You grabbed my phone."

"You raped her. With three of your friends. Finley Jacowski and Michael Macmanus are already in custody at the emergency room. You are going to join them there. Brandon Burke will be along shortly."

"We di'int do shit. You can't prove shit."

"There's video. You and your chest tattoo."

"Huhn? I don't . . ." Taswell put his hand over his mouth and dry heaved. "Don't 'member."

A well-placed flick of Evan's knuckles would collapse Taz's windpipe.

"You're going to prison, Taswell."

"Prison? Nah." Taz gave an odd stutter of a laugh. He had bits of pinto bean in his teeth. "No way, man. No way."

Evan stared at him.

"Wait. Wut? *Prison?* For real? 'R you fer real?"

"I want you to look at me. Look at me closely. And ask yourself: Should you be scared?"

Taz's eyes skittered across Evan's chest. Eye contact seemed to pain him.

Evan stayed still. Waited. Waited some more.

Finally Taz lifted his gaze and looked at him.

His pupils constricted sharply, as if he'd glanced at the sun.

"Nuh," he said. "No way."

He had earned nothing in his life and yet he could not—could *not*—believe that his will could be thwarted.

"You kidnapped her," Evan said. "Assaulted her. Violated her."

Taswell reached for his phone on the table but Evan blocked him.

"My phone, bruh. Need my phone."

"Do you *feel* anything, Taz?"

"Huhn?"

"In there. Do you *feel* things?"

Taz gave a one-shoulder shrug. "Dunno."

Evan said, "You'll have plenty of time to figure it out."

"Wudduya mean?" Taz's face barely moved, and yet it changed drastically with the realization. A widening of his features, hairline settling back, skin gone lax. Abject terror. Evan had never seen anything like it.

"Nuh," Taz cried out. "What if they *do things* to me there?"

Evan swept his shirt open, the magnetized buttons parting to reveal a glimpse of the ARES 1911 sitting ready in the appendix holster. Taz gasped and then the shirt front swung back into place, magnets clapping together once more like a stage curtain, sealing off the pistol from view.

"Uh-uh," Taz said. "Uh-uh."

Evan considered where he'd like to shoot the boy.

Few people understand how resilient the pelvic bone is.

Two precisely placed shots would be ideal, one to the front and one just above would blow bone and shrapnel through most of the essential working parts of his lower anatomy. The damage to his pelvic region would mean agony with every step, every time he sat, every time he moved.

For what he'd done to Anca, it was not enough.

But Evan didn't want to do that here, not in public, not with children around, not against the spirit of Anca's directives. Maybe not even for himself.

He'd put Taswell to sleep quietly, call Naomi to get him to the cops and the courts, leave the kid's phone for additional evidence.

There was nothing more to say, nothing to get out of the kid, so Evan put his arm around his neck, starting to crimp the vagus nerve.

Taz said, *"Ow."*

Evan drew him tight, the boy's head cramped between his biceps and chest, his mouth against his hair, close to his ear, as if to deliver a kiss. He felt . . . he felt sad.

Evan whispered, "Feel this."

Bling!

A texted photo came up on Taz's phone, resting there on the table by their elbows. A pretty young girl against a wall, bleached in the light of an unflattering flash. She wore a caught-in-headlights expression—feigned smile, concerned eyes, forehead crinkled with alarm.

"Wait," Taz blurted, pointing with his free hand at the screen.

The message, also from B-Roll, announced: Get reddy to partay!!

Evan released him. "Where is this? Where's B-Roll? Where does he have her?"

Taz was breathing hard, almost panting. He rubbed his head, making his hair stand up in the front. When he looked at Evan, his eyes were dead. It was like looking into nothing.

And then. A spark.

A human spark.

"We hafta . . ." Shoulders hunched, Taz shoved his flattened hands between his knees, squeezed them. "We hafta hurry. 'S close."

Evan grabbed him by the back of his collar and yanked him off the stool. Taz managed to snatch his phone—his lifeline. As Evan propelled him toward the door, he stumbled but kept his feet.

They slammed out into the street, Taz starting to jog to the north, Evan hustling him along. They didn't get in a half dozen strides before Taz stopped, leaning against a news rack stacked with adult classifieds. He clutched his chest, leaning over, wheezing asthmatically.

"Can't . . . keep up."

"What's the address?"

Still hunched, Taz had his phone out, resting it against his thigh, thumbing at it. "Here, man. 'S the address . . . here. Take it. Take my phone."

Evan grabbed at it. A tug as Taz held on, muscle memory not allowing him to let go. It was like prying the black box from Devine's hands.

Taz's grip tightened around his phone. He stared up at Evan with pleading eyes.

Evan ripped it free.

And he ran.

58
What Comes Next

Blanca glowered at him.

B-Roll was lingering by the dead-bolted front door, not really guarding it but not *not* guarding it either. He was still trying to play it casual 'cuz it was more fun when they went along with it. Plus he didn't like forcing them, like *really* forcing them, and Mikey had run outta fentanyl from Dirty Pete so their options were limited.

She was sitting on the floor way across the room from him, back to the wall, arms crossed. Some of her makeup had smeared but that was okay. They could have her touch it up before they started filming.

Her chin quivered. Her eyes were glazed.

"You don't have to be all mopey," B-Roll told her. "We can still just chill, have a good time."

He was sweating so he took his shirt off. Maybe she'd like what she saw and that would loosen things up some. Didn't seem to. He remembered reading somewhere that chicks were less visual, maybe that was it.

He paced some there in front of the locked front door. He didn't like being stuck here with her just waiting while she stared at him.

"It's just fooling around some," he told her. "That's all. No biggie."

She kept on with that blank stare. She'd pulled her sweater over her knees, stretching it thin since it was a crop-top cut.

"You don't have to be such a bitch about it." He was getting aggravated, wasn't sure why. Maybe how she was just looking at him. At least when they fought back you were fighting and you didn't have to pay attention to them guilting you.

"You can just relax and enjoy it," he said. "It's not like you've never done it before."

Where the fuck were the boys? What was taking so long? He'd done his part. He'd reeled her in and set up the cameras and the pillory. Foreplay was over. It was time to go. Not to sit around staring at each other. It was so uncomfortable.

"Don't act like you didn't know," he said, getting angrier. "You flirted right back with me. You knew. You knew what it meant to come over and hang out."

She just glared at him. Man, did she look angry.

At last there came a knock at the door.

"About fucking time," B-Roll called out, backing up, groping behind him for the dead bolt. He didn't trust her enough to take his eyes off her.

He fumbled and turned the doorknob, heard the creak of hinges as it swung in behind him.

Something rippled across Blanca's face. Surprise? Relief?

When he turned there weren't three forms standing in the doorway.

There was one.

The man stepped inside. He wasn't particularly big but he was coiled tight, menacing and calm, and his presence was unsettling as fuck.

"I'm here to help you," the man said to Blanca. "Are you okay?"

She shook her head.

He said, "Perhaps you'd like to wait for me outside?"

She nodded.

The man stepped aside, made a slight gesture toward the door with his hand, inviting her to leave. "I'll just be a moment."

B-Roll was between them. He felt frozen, helpless to respond. He couldn't catch up to what was happening.

Blanca walked right past him. He let her.

He didn't know what the man would do.

He didn't know how to react.

She walked past the man and out into the hall.

The man closed the door behind her.

He threw the dead bolt.

B-Roll felt the thud deep in his chest.

He tried to speak, to reason, to talk his way out of things, but he couldn't find words. He *never* couldn't find words. But his throat was knotted up and he was having trouble breathing.

The man stepped forward. Shark eyes.

B-Roll took a step back.

The guy stepped toward him again. Cold and steady, nearly void of life.

B-Roll eased back.

He bumped into something, gave a little yelp.

The pillory.

Nowhere left to go.

The man stopped.

They were about three feet apart.

The man did not seem to blink. He did not seem to breathe. He did not seem real.

"Brandon Burke," he said. "Are you ready for your close-up?"

One wrist had snapped in the process, but that happened. Wrists could be fragile.

The jaw had broken, too, because, let's face it, it was hard to get the locking bar down when the subject was still trying to fight. It had taken a few whacks to hammer everything into place.

Now B-Roll was ensconced in the pillory, wrists and neck secured.

The camera was to the side so it could capture his face.

Evan stood behind him, texting Templeton the address and sharing Taswell's last location as well.

B-Roll struggled violently but there wasn't anger in it, not anymore. Now it was just desperation. He'd been fuming and screaming himself hoarse but no one really cared about screaming in a place like this. Cottony saliva had gummed in the corners of his mouth. Panic tended to dehydrate. He hung there, wilted.

The apartment wasn't so much an apartment as a den. Mattress on the floor, sloughed-off socks scattered like snake skins, a funk of pot and cigarette smoke and unwashed sheets. Parchment-colored blinds thickened the light.

The endless overpass outside rumbled, headlights and horns blaring through the battered blinds. Three stories up, they were still sunken, vehicles swooping overhead. The city sounds were abrasive, set the teeth on edge. It was hard to think in here.

B-Roll lurched and bellowed, but there was very little give in the stock. It was well designed. He could see nothing behind him. "Where are you?" he scream-cried, his words blurred through his unhinged jaw. "What're you *doing*?"

His manicured beard, his manscaped chest hair, his gym-toned eight-pack, they all seemed so silly. A puddle of blood-laced drool on the floor beneath his face dilated, shimmery like mercury.

"You may have heard," Evan said, "that RedLite experienced an unfortunate disruption. But that's okay. They are going up again tonight. Right now, in fact. Live streams only."

"You can't, man. You can't do this."

"But I am," Evan said.

"Wait! Wait, *okay*? You can't leave me here like this. How's anyone gonna find me? I'll be here forever!"

"Don't worry," Evan said. "The cops will get here. Eventually."

"Hang on. Just—"

"Live in three . . . two . . . one." Evan clicked to start the live feed.

Brandon bellowed and squirmed in the pillory. Staying out of the field of view, Evan walked around the makeshift stage, moving toward the door.

"Wait! Just— Wait! I'm sorry, okay? Don't leave me! Please! Please, don't leave me like this!"

Evan stepped out.

The closing door muffled B-Roll's complaints. A few steps down the stairs and Evan couldn't even hear him over the roar of traffic.

Despite a decent afternoon sun, Blanca shuddered as Evan walked with her along the sidewalk. She'd refused his jacket.

He'd just finished explaining to her how she could repay him. He needed someone to carry on the unbroken tradition and that person would not be Kenzie, whom he'd freed from extortion over the nude selfie she'd sent. Nor would it be Anca, who looked to a higher judgment.

"So just find someone else who needs help?" Blanca said. "Anyone in bad trouble? And give them your number? 1-855-2-NOWHERE?"

"Are you willing to do that?"

She scrunched up her face, lips pooched, brow furrowing. "Hell *yeah,* I will."

As she walked, she hugged herself at the stomach. Her sweater was stretched out, billowing low, and she'd tugged the sleeves down over her hands. A pretty girl, still a kid.

For a time, they walked in silence, navigating the flow of pedestrians.

"It was so scary," she said. "I was so scared."

"I know," Evan said.

"That guy? He just didn't care. Didn't care about *anything.*"

Evan said, "I know."

"I hope he rots in prison."

"He will," Evan said.

She nodded and then nodded again, as if reassuring herself. "Well, that's something."

"Yes," Evan said. "It's something."

They'd reached the mouth of the subway stop. Blanca hesitated, peering at the stairs falling away into shadow. For a moment, Evan saw it as a gaping maw, vomiting people up from the underworld and sucking them down.

She started to cry.

He stood with his hands loose at his sides, unsure what to do.

"What's the point?" she said. "The world is so mean. It's so *mean*." She swiped her eyes. She was still crying. "My parents suck, and school sucks, and there's never enough money, and I haveta take care of my sister, and what's the point? What's the point? What am I looking forward to? *This?*" She waved her hand around, indicating B-Roll, the building, the city. "What am I supposed to do? With people like him out here? What do I do when you're not around next time?"

"It's not just me," Evan said.

"What?"

"There were so many people before you. Who looked out for the next person who needed help. And the next person. And the next. All of them led to you."

Her lips were trembling, her mascara smeared. "I'm not anything."

"You're sharp. And tough."

"You have to say shit like that. You're an old-fashioned adult. You don't know anything. You don't know what it's like to be me right now."

"I have a . . . niece kind of."

"A niece kind of. Okay."

"A bit older than you."

"Okay. So?"

"You remind me of her."

"Hope that's a compliment."

"The biggest," he said. "I see what's inside you. And who you find next? Who you reach out to help? They're gonna see it, too. It's what's gonna let them know that it might be okay. That they can make it. You're it now. You're what comes next."

Her chin dipped and she took a tentative step forward and then she hugged him. A clumsy embrace around his arms, pinning them to his sides so he couldn't hug her back. In a way it was a relief; he'd been caught off guard and wouldn't have known what to do.

Letting go, she turned without looking back and moved down the stairs into the belly of the city. Standing at the top step, framed by a circle of sky, he watched her until she disappeared.

59
Gargoyles

By the time Evan caught up to Candy outside the church, Vespers was being conducted inside. The voices of the choir reached them sporadically over the city noise, the harmony like a vibration.

As he mounted the wide stairs, Candy waited with her hands on her cocked hips, a fall of bangs down across one eye.

"It's done?"

He said, "It's done."

She was dressed conservatively, long skirt, high-necked blouse with ruffle trim, pink satchel purse that matched her block heels and lipstick. Makeup invisibly contoured her face, altering her appearance slightly but effectively. Her skin was ivory today, her loosed hair sleek and shiny.

The chilled afternoon breeze smelled of roasting chestnuts from the street vendor on the corner. One hymn ended and another began, also in Romanian, this one a bit louder. He could make out a few words, all those rich vowels. They studied the homely façade of the white stucco building, with its barred windows and electrical lines.

"Didn't want to go in?" Evan asked.

"Not for me," she said. "I do better out here."

"Guarding the perimeter."

"That's me," she said. "That's us."

"Gargoyles."

She laughed. Her teeth were perfect, white and straight, like in a toothpaste commercial. He thought about the damage of her back, how she'd let him stroke the gnarls and whorls of scar tissue, as intimate a touch as he'd ever known.

Leaves fluttered on the trees below. A few people had carved love hearts into the whitewashed trunks. Traffic was constipated, cabbies shouting out windows. People scurried along, plugged into Bluetooth earpieces or talking into phones. A homeless man slumbered on a bus-stop bench, hugging himself, hands stuffed into his armpits for warmth.

A tinny song played, breaking through the city sounds.

Oh, she's sweet but a psycho!

Evan looked at Candy, one eyebrow arched inquisitively.

Candy unsnapped the top of her purse, withdrew a phone. The ringtone continued.

She answered: "Do you need my help?"

Evan blinked at her.

She listened for a moment. "How did you get this number?"

She appeared to be serious.

"Stay where you are," she said. "I'll contact you within the hour."

The phone disappeared into her purse. Balancing on one foot, she tugged off one shoe and wacked it against a concrete planter. The block heel broke off and she reseated her foot in the low shoe. Switching stork legs, she knocked off the other heel. Then she wound her long blond hair up into a tucked ponytail.

Evan watched her, poleaxed.

"I have my own missions, you know," Candy said.

"Like what?"

"A woman's secrets are her own."

Leaning in, she kissed him on the cheek. He could smell her hair, plumeria lotion, the scent of her. Behind them the plain wooden door cracked open, the service letting out, churchgoers flocking onto the plaza. Evan turned to look for Anca and when he pivoted back, Candy was gone.

He touched his cheek and his fingertips came away tacky, rouged with pink.

The exodus of congregants continued, more of them, it seemed, than the church could hold. He stood firm, the herd parting around him, and then Anca bobbed into view, conveyed toward him. She wore her rose-patterned shawl draped across her shoulders. The bruise around her eye was nearly gone and she walked fluidly, without discomfort.

She arrived before him. The crowd kept streaming out, enveloping them.

"It's over," he said. "They're in the hands of the law now. You are, too."

"No," she said. "Better hands."

The crowd kept coming, streaming by, everything feeling suddenly rushed.

"Where do you go now?" she asked. "What do you do next?"

"This again, I suppose."

"You're like a Western cowboy. Shane."

"Strong, silent American."

Her smile glowed. "Boring, quiet American."

People kept moving around them, jostling them slightly. After all they'd been through together, it was an awkward place to say good-bye. They stood there, a cocoon of stillness within the flowing crowd.

Down on the street, a cabbie laid on the horn, leaning out the window to scream at a bike messenger who'd tangled up with pedestrians at the curb. Above, an electronic billboard cycled to a new image, a close-up of a phallic lipstick core rising to meet a woman's O-shaped mouth.

"The city," he said, "keeps citying."

"And people keep people'ing." She twisted one of the shawl's tassels between her thumb and forefinger. "Everyone is just trying their best."

"Except everyone who's not."

"I know," she said. "I know."

"How much grace should they get? We. Should *we* get?"

"Some," she said.

"But not much."

Another smile. "Good-bye, Evan."

A strange impulse seized him. To hug her. But he had never initiated a hug. Not once. He didn't know how. He nodded instead.

She lingered, too.

Her eyes welled. "*This,*" she said. "This is everything." She made a fist, tapped it gently against his chest. "So know what you are. To me." Her face trembled. "I'll pray for you." The throng tugged at her and she gave him a last look and let it sweep her away.

He remained. He could feel the sun on his shoulders. For the first time in a long time, he had nowhere to go.

After a while, the plaza cleared.

His shadow lay out clear on the ground before him. Above rose that hexagonal cupola, the intersecting slashes of the cross.

An X stood on end.

When at last he turned to go, a sight at the bus stop brought him up short. The homeless man was still on the bench, curled into himself for warmth. But draped over him was a fringed shawl, dark green patterned with roses.

Evan wasn't thrilled about it but here he was, back in the speakeasy lounge with sultry scarlet lighting, sunk into the plush maroon booth with button tufting, sitting across from Joey. Mercifully it was earlier in the evening than the last time they'd met here, which meant no Betty Boop onstage and no drunken carousers from the finance sector.

Joey had decided to stay in Manhattan for a few nights to do young-person-in-the-city things with some hacker friends she'd met on a HexChat hacker IRC server. She'd asked Evan to meet her here to say good-bye. He had one stop after this, Devine's, before Aragón's plane would convey him home. He was ready to get back to the soothing quiet of his penthouse, with its shiny clean surfaces and polished windows.

Joey flipped the menu over. "We should have a celebratory drink," she said. "Like a 'mission complete' cocktail."

The last beverage here had not worked out. "No."

"No? Why?"

"The vodka selection," Evan said, "is lacking."

"Well, sorry they're not up to your standards. Next time I'll pick somewhere that has vodka derived from, like, unicorn milk."

"Unicorns are genderless," Evan said. "Thus, no unicorn milk."

"Unicorns don't exist. Like your sense of humor." Joey thumped down the menu. She was dressed for going out, dark eyeliner and a scoop-neck sweater, nothing too risqué. "You said we'd talk in person after the mission. So here we are. In person. After the mission. So?"

He was unsure how to start.

Fortunately, Joey wasn't one to let a silence linger. "Last time we were here, you looked at me like I'd barfed chunks of dead gigolo all over the table."

"Vivid image," he said. "But 'dead' is a bit redundant."

"Fair. 'Cuz the gigolo has already been rendered down to chunks."

"Yes."

"Okay." Leaning back, she crossed her arms and waited. The wait did not last long. "Well? Why'd you get so mad? What was it?"

He watched his blink rate. Had to resist rubbing his face. Vodka snobbery aside, he was having second thoughts about turning down a drink.

"X, you don't get to just *not answer*."

"Why not?"

"Because. I don't know. *Because*."

He drew in a deep breath, held it for a moment. "When I saw the video of Anca . . ." He paused. "It was bad. Really bad."

He stopped again.

"X," Joey said, softly prompting.

"Then when I was with you, I couldn't help but think about what would happen if it was . . . if *you* . . ." His voice caught a wobble.

It was just a split second but Joey missed nothing and her brown eyes filled instantly. She reached across the table, put her hand on his forearm. "You can feel that," she said. "It's okay for you to feel that."

Four-second inhalation. Four-second hold. Four-second exhale.

"If you feel more," he said, "you have to feel more."

There it was.

A new Commandment. His own.

He said, "How am I supposed to let you go into the field and trust that you won't get hurt?"

"The closer I am to you, the stronger I am," she said. "And the stronger I am, the more I can handle."

"I can't protect you, Josephine."

"I'm not asking you to. Anymore."

"That's not . . ."

"What?" she said. "'A mission that ends'?"

"No," he lied.

She smiled. It was great. "Maybe this is what it feels like to be someone's kid."

"Same," he said. "But reverse."

"Weird."

"Yes," he said. "Weird."

He really could have used that vodka right about now.

"So *this* is, like, what real people feel like," Joey said. "All emotional and shit."

"There are no real people."

"Or we're all real people," Joey said. "We're all just the same."

Evan thought. "Except the really bad ones."

"I know. I fucking *hate* the really bad ones."

They smirked a little and then sat there looking at each other, suddenly awkward.

Joey checked her watch. "Welp, my friends are here any sec. So you'd better blow. Remember"—she did Dumb Evan voice: "'Your job is to remain unnoticed, inconspicuous. Not to present ostentatiously and elicit shitty cocktails from people at the bar.'"

"The voice," he said. "You're getting better."

"Been practicing." She was beaming. Even her eyes smiled at him.

He did not want to leave.

He did not want her meeting up with hacker friends from online.

He did not want her out in the world unchaperoned.

He considered what to say. No idea. He thought about what someone wiser than him might say. He summoned a smile or at least a more neutral shape for his mouth.

"Have fun," he said.

He slid out, stood.

Joey looked up at him. Her eyes were brimming again and he felt something deep in his chest, something like anguish. If he allowed himself to have this, to have Joey, then he would have something to lose that could end him.

It was not a risk worth taking.

But he no longer had a choice.

She hesitated and he saw her trying for it, trying for it more. But she couldn't quite get there.

"You're the worst," she said.

Evan dipped his chin. "Me, too, Josephine."

60

Roundup Complete

A brisk wind off Shinnecock Bay peppered Evan's cheeks. The towering door parted, the face of the mansion opening in a slit just slender enough to admit him. He stepped in from the nighttime cold.

Keshishian stood in front of a phalanx of guards, uniform pressed, name tag straight, her abundant hair clasped in the back. "Welcome back, Mr. Nowhere."

"How's it been?"

"Alarmingly quiet."

"I take it that's rare?"

She smirked. "Last week, I would have put the odds around: When flying pigs freeze over."

Rawlings emerged from one of myriad doors letting into the foyer, his footsteps clacking across the vast space. He looked clean and compact, as if he'd been poured into his suit, a perfect mold of a man. He shook Evan's hand firmly but not as though he had something to prove.

"Glad you're here." Rawlings's hand dipped into the side pocket of his jacket and came out with the little black box and its solitary button. He relinquished it to Evan with a ceremonious flare of his hand. "Devine asked to receive you in the drawing room."

Pocketing the device, Evan followed him. Across the huge foyer, past the three-story waterfall, up the staircase sweeping to the right, across the landing, down a corridor, and into the empty drawing room.

Rawlings withdrew with a nod, leaving Evan alone before the curved bar with its dozen stools. The bookcases seemed to stretch higher than before. Kahlil Gibran gazed down morosely from his portrait, taking Evan's measure.

He pulled up a stool at the bar. It felt like tucking into a boat hull.

The selection was immense, at least five hundred bottles.

Folding his hands on the polished mahogany, he waited. Pain throbbed meekly where he'd hammered a pump needle above his high rib.

Five minutes passed. Ten.

His RoamZone dinged.

A text from Naomi Templeton: Roundup complete. Four for four. They've been treated, arraigned, charged, and are being held without bail.

She'd promised to fast-track the proceedings, and fast-tracking them she was.

He texted back: I owe you a solitary peanut butter cup.

The door opened with a whoosh of air and Devine entered. He had returned to his particular way of walking that seemed more like coasting. He looked healthy, well rested, alabaster skin glowing.

He was dressed keenly—white button-up shirt with gartered sleeves, pleatless wide-leg trousers that looked to be cashmere. Approaching, he greeted Evan with a tilt of his head and, for once, no words. Without slowing, he hopped lithely over the bar and stood facing Evan from the other side.

His hands dipped beneath the bar and there came a clanging of metal. He came up with a stainless-steel cocktail shaker, tossed in five ice cubes, and poured in two fingers of Kauffman Vintage.

Since the war, the vodka was harder to find, the price spiking into the thousands per bottle. For Devine, that was belly-button change.

"RedLite's head has been cut off," Devine said. "They just don't know it yet. They'll hold their feet another seventy-two hours, ninety-six tops. Then they'll collapse and I'll scatter their ashes to the wind."

Evan said, "Good."

"Anything else you require?"

Evan considered. "There's a young man who lives in East Los Angeles, name's Lesandro Candella. He'd just lost an arm in an attack when I . . . ran into him. I've been looking into getting him a customized prosthetic—the Hero Arm from Open Bionics—but they're backlogged at the moment. Can you pull a few strings?"

"Consider them pulled."

"I'll get you his information."

Devine pressed his hands to the polished mahogany bar on either side of the resting shaker. He jerked his head to one side, cracking his neck. "I've noticed lately that my aches, my dysregulation, they feel more pronounced. Muscles, joints. Up here." With one hand, he tapped his forehead. "I can see now a time when my usefulness will be diminished. And I am *so useful.*" He said it without arrogance. It was merely a fact. "There is so much more work to be done."

"Always," Evan said.

"I can't afford to burn out."

"No."

"You helped me see that. You were . . ." Devine's eyes searched the soaring ceiling. "Well, I don't know what to say."

"*That,*" Evan said, "is the greatest accomplishment of my life."

Devine laughed. "I don't know how you did it. How you got me to . . . I don't know."

"I thought about everything I would do to damage you," Evan said, "and then I did the opposite."

Devine's mouth puckered downward, a thoughtful frown. Then he fitted the top to the tumbler and hoisted it beside his ear. He shook and shook and shook and then shook some more. From a freezer drawer, he removed a stainless-steel martini glass. The vodka poured syrupy, cloudy from the workout. Ice crystals pocked the surface, unique as snowflakes, augmenting the subtle froth.

With a gleaming silver cocktail pick, Devine skewered a single Spanish Queen olive, dunked it once into the vodka, and set it on a tiny square plate. He slid glass and plate to Evan.

Evan's favorite drink. Distilled fourteen times, filtered through birch coal and then quartz, Kauffman's was the world's first vintage vodka, made from the wheat harvest of a single year.

He sipped.

It was perfection.

His eyes were closed. He kept them closed. He could still sense it, the single sip, the heat on his palate, the glow down his throat, in his stomach, that pure-as-the-driven-snow finish.

He set the drink down. One sip was all he required.

He offered his hand across the bar.

"I'm Evan," he said.

Luke took it. "Pleasure."

They shook.

Evan inched the barstool out and stood. He had a long flight ahead of him yet.

He withdrew the black box from his pocket, set it on the bar before Devine, and walked out.

Devine stood for a moment, the once-sipped martini before him. He stared at the calligraphy on the giant piece of art on the facing wall: YOUR PAIN IS THE BREAKING OF THE SHELL THAT ENCLOSES YOUR UNDERSTANDING. There was a faint smudge mark on the lip of the martini glass where the Nowhere Man had sipped.

He watched it evaporate.

For a moment, he wondered if Mr. Nowhere had ever been here at all.

The black box chimed and then spoke in Rawlings's voice: "Mr. Nowhere?"

"No," Luke said, "me again."

A half second of surprise, but Rawlings was one to recover his composure quickly. "Sorry to bother you, sir, but there's a problem that has come to a head. North Korea."

Devine looked at the little black box. He did not touch the button to reply.

"I don't want it," he said, to the empty barstools, to the rows of bottles, to the watercolored poet looking down from the enormous framed painting. "I don't. Want it."

He closed his eyes.

There was light there behind the lids, a tiny spot in the darkness.

Drawing a deep breath, he opened his eyes once more.

He clicked the button.

And said, "I'll be right down."

61

Pushing the Boulder Up to the Light

The contoured seats of the Embraer Lineage 1000 were even more comfortable than those in the Mercedes 450 EQS+. Aragón Urrea's plane also sported a full-length couch, a queen-size bed, and a shower. A global clock mounted on the wall showed off a dozen time zones.

Evan was getting accustomed to luxury.

He was winging across the cloud-choked night somewhere above New Jersey. The red-eye flight would land him in Los Angeles Saturday morning.

The in-flight phone rang.

Aragón, of course: "Is everything to your liking?"

"Indeed."

"Did you save the damsel in distress?"

"She saved herself. I just helped."

"Did you kill the motherfucker?"

"Not this time."

"Bah," Aragón said. "Well, I suppose you can't win them all."

"Not even close."

But Aragón had already hung up.

Evan settled back into the seat, let the foam receive him.

A thought wiggled its way into awareness.

He took out his RoamZone.

Stared at the blank screen for a moment.

Then he pulled up a picture of Joey.

He looked at it. Considered the faint movement occurring within his chest.

He called up another picture: Candy McClure, a surveillance shot he'd saved to her dossier.

The next one: Mia Hall.

And then Melinda Truong.

And then Naomi Templeton.

Quite a roguettes' gallery.

He scrolled through them once more, faces shuffling by.

His heart rate was steady. Blood pressure low. Breathing even.

And yet.

His mouth had curled up ever so slightly at the edges.

Interesting data point.

Putting the phone away, he leaned back to sleep. Then he felt it, that twinge of the quadratus lumborum muscle in his left hip.

That's what life was now. Pushing the boulder up to the light. And readying himself to do it again.

He unclipped the seat belt. Got down on the silk-cut pile carpet.

Private jets could be surprisingly roomy.

He did his asanas, working through the forms, loosening his body. He ended up in good-morning stretch, toes pointing down, hands reaching the other way. Then he cast his arms and legs jumping-jack wide and relaxed like that, belly breathing, pulling oxygen up into his lungs, filling his chest, a final resting pose.

Joints popped. Muscle released. Fascia stretched.

The power of the engines rumbled through the fuselage and into his bones.

The clock on the wall ticked to midnight.

February 14.

Not the first Valentine's Day he'd spend alone. Wouldn't be the last, either.

He was unsure where he was now, somewhere in the clouds above Pennsylvania, untethered from earth and whatever was above. Soon he would be home, at least as close to home as he ever got. Soon there would be another mission and then another and so it would go until he could not roll that boulder up the hill anymore.

Soaring along at forty thousand feet, each limb stretched toward a cardinal point, he held the resting pose.

A map and a bearing.

A signature and a destination.

In this suspended moment, a perfect X.

Acknowledgments

Orphan X would like to thank:

CORE OPERATIONAL TEAM

Kurata Tadashi (lead and steel)

Michael "Borski" Borohovski (1s and 0s)

Dr. Melissa Hurwitz and Dr. Bret Nelson (precision injury advisors)

Kevin Compton (financial wrecking ball)

Luis Urrea (innovative cursing)

Philip Eisner (creative savagery)

PSYOPS CREW

Minotaur: Andrew Martin, Sally Richardson, Jennifer Enderlin, Martin Quinn, Hector DeJean, Paul Hochman, Grace Gay, with a special hat tip to Keith Kahla and Kelley Ragland

ACKNOWLEDGMENTS

Michael Joseph/Penguin Group UK: Louise Moore, Mubarak Elmubarak, Jennifer Harlow, Ciara Berry, Christina Ellicott, Anna Curvis, and the irrepressible Rowland White

Lisa Erbach Vance of the Aaron Priest Agency

Stephen F. Breimer of Brecheen Feldman Breimer Silver & Thompson

Angela Cheng Caplan of Cheng Caplan Company

Caspian Dennis of Abner Stein

Terry McGarry

LOGISTICS AND SUPPORT

Delinah Raya (light)

Natalie Corinne (wit)

Alfred and Marjorie (steadfastness)

Micah Schiff (cheer)

Zuma, Nala, Lili, and Buster (*Jurassic Park*–level shenanigans)

About the Author

Melissa Hurwitz

Gregg Hurwitz is the author of the *New York Times*–bestselling Orphan X novels. Critically acclaimed, his novels have been international bestsellers, have graced top ten lists, won numerous awards, and have been published in thirty-three languages. Additionally, he's sold scripts to many of the major studios and written, developed, and produced television for various networks. Hurwitz lives in Los Angeles with his three Rhodesian ridgebacks and a scrappy mutt who believes she is the fourth ridgeback.